INTRODUCING SAVIORS

Darian Ross is an unlicensed PI struggling against his family legacy (father in prison, brother a crook at large) in the independent kingdom of Scotland. In earlier centuries, when the Scottish empire stretched all the way to Central America, Challaid was one of the country's busiest trading ports. But Scotland is not what it was, and the only remains of its illustrious past are the networks of power and corruption that keep the country running.

A LINE OF FORGOTTEN BLOOD

These investigators aren't his first choice, but they are his best hope.

Police constable Vinny Reno is both a friend and a valuable contact for Douglas Independent Research, Darian Ross's shadowy employer. And PC Reno is desperate for help: his ex-wife is missing, and he's the main suspect. The finest thread of a clue points to one of the city's oldest, wealthiest banking families. But pulling on one thread can unravel a whole tapestry... until events are moving too fast for even the most powerful people to control.

MALCOLM MACKAY is the author of *The Necessary Death of Lewis Winter, How a Gunman Says Goodbye,* and *The Sudden Arrival of Violence* (known collectively as the Glasgow Trilogy) as well as *The Night the Rich Men Burned* and *For Those Who Know the Ending*. Malcolm Mackay's novels have won the Deanston Scottish Crime Book of the Year Award and have been nominated for the Edgar Award for Best Paperback Original, the CWA John Creasey (New Blood) Dagger, and the Theakston's Old Peculier Crime Novel of the Year. Mackay was born in Stornoway on Scotland's Isle of Lewis, where he still lives.

FLIP THIS BOOK OVER FOR ANOTHER THRILLING SAVIORS CASE!

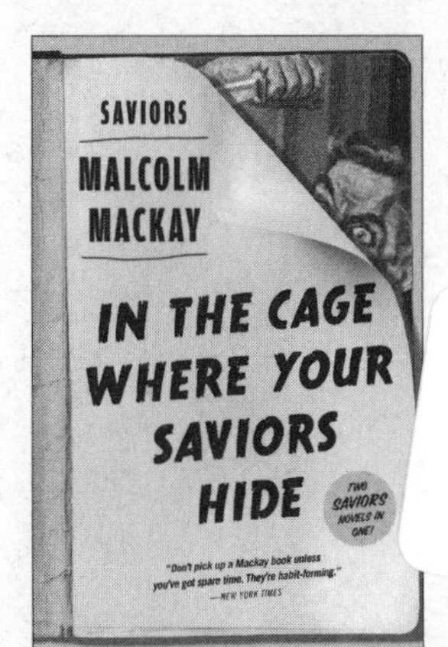
SAVIORS
MALCOLM
MACKAY
IN THE CAGE WHERE YOUR SAVIORS HIDE
TWO SAVIORS NOVELS IN ONE!
"Don't pick up a Mackay book unless you've got spare time. They're habit-forming."
—NEW YORK TIMES

D0951675

Books by Malcolm Mackay

The Necessary Death of Lewis Winter

The Sudden Arrival of Violence

How a Gunman Says Goodbye

The Night the Rich Men Burned

Every Night I Dream of Hell

For Those Who Know the Ending

SAVIORS

A LINE OF FORGOTTEN BLOOD

MALCOLM MACKAY

MULHOLLAND BOOKS

Little, Brown and Company
New York Boston London

The characters and events in this book are fictitious. Any similarity to real persons, living or dead, is coincidental and not intended by the author.

Cover design by Allison J. Warner
Cover art by CSA Images / Getty Images

Mulholland Books / Little, Brown and Company
Hachette Book Group
1290 Avenue of the Americas, New York, NY 10104
mulhollandbooks.com
Twitter @mulhollandbooks
Facebook.com/mulhollandbooks

First United States omnibus edition: August 2019
Originally published in Great Britain by Head of Zeus, London, as *A Line of Forgotten Blood,* June 2019

Mulholland Books is an imprint of Little, Brown and Company, a division of Hachette Book Group, Inc. The Mulholland Books name and logo are trademarks of Hachette Book Group, Inc.

Also available as an ebook.

ISBN 978-0-316-48250-9
Cataloging-in-publication data is available at the Library of Congress.

10 9 8 7 6 5 4 3 2 1

LSC-C

Printed in the United States of America

A LINE OF FORGOTTEN BLOOD

PROLOGUE

THERE WAS a bang and her head jerked forward. The world fell into a blur, a feeling of movement and noise but nothing making sense, her brain swamped with shock. The world was slowing but vaguely she knew nothing was slowing fast enough. That was when she snapped back into real time, when her instincts scoffed at her sluggish brain and took back control.

Freya Dempsey slammed her foot on the brake pedal and the car screeched to a stop. She took a few seconds to breathe deeply and consider where she was, what had happened and where she should direct her rising anger. She had pulled out on the corner of Siar Road and Kidd Street and some eyeless half-wit had gone straight into the side of her car. It had to be their fault because the shock commanding her system wasn't willing to move over and make room for guilt. Some idiot had crashed into her and if they weren't already in great pain she intended to do something about that. Traffic was stopping around her and somewhere in the background a committed moron was leaning on his horn as though it might help.

Freya began to swear loudly and prodigiously in the car, as a woman from Whisper Hill would, and she toned it down to a feral hiss as she stepped out into public, as a woman living in Cnocaid should. Nothing felt painful as she stood up, although she was pretty sure she could whip it up into something chronic should the need to lay it on thick arise. She grimaced at the damage to her car and repeated the look when she spotted what had hit her. Now she could see how expensive it was she decided it was definitely their fault.

A man in a dark blue suit and white shirt was getting out of a black car that would have been gliding luxuriously through the streets of Challaid until it crossed her path. Now the front right was tangled up in itself, the bumper pushed into the wheel arch, and the well-dressed driver was looking at her with the sort of anger that promised trouble before he opened his mouth.

He shouted, "What the hell were you doing? Don't you even look where you're going, or are we all just supposed to play dodgems with you?"

It occurred to her that she hadn't looked carefully because a van had blocked her view, but she shouted back, "Of course I looked. You must have been rocketing up that road like you owned it, thinking you can drive however you want. You're going to have to pay for the damage you've done."

His mouth hung open for a few seconds before he said, "Have you been on the glue or something? That was your fault, you'll pay for that."

Before either of them could spin the argument round in another circle the back door of the heinously expensive saloon car opened and a man got out. He wore a dark gray suit and white shirt with a yellow tie and a long black coat that was open. He had a trim goatee beard and was bald on top, hair shaved short at the sides and wearing gold-rimmed glasses. He couldn't have been much past forty, Freya guessed, and from the second he stepped out of the car it was clear that he not only owned it, he also owned anything else that caught his fancy.

He didn't look angry as he walked over to the woman and young man, instead rather amused. Freya Dempsey was thirty-one and boldly attractive in a way that warned you in advance she was more than two handfuls, so whatever trouble you got into with her was your own fault. The owner of the car seemed to have worked all that out by the time he reached her, and he was still smiling.

He said, "I am sorry about that, a terrible accident, no one's fault."

Freya said, "Not mine anyway."

He laughed again, turned to his driver and said, "Will, see if you can get the cars off the road so we don't block the traffic, and deal with the police when they finally bother to show up, their station's only up the road. Oh, and if you see who's been blowing their horn for the last few minutes see if you can stick their steering wheel up their backside and make them spin on it."

The driver was used to doing what he was told and scurried off, leaving Freya alone with his boss. They stepped onto the busy pavement, ignoring the pedestrians who had stopped to watch the pleasurable spectacle of a minor accident that inconvenienced others but not them.

The smiling man said, "My name's Harold Sutherland."

"Oh, wow, so you can afford the repairs."

The Sutherland family ran the Sutherland Bank, and it wouldn't be a skip into hyperbole to say the Sutherland Bank had a controlling interest in the city of Challaid, and undue influence over the country of Scotland. The bank often seemed to have its hand on the tiller of the entire economy, and the family who founded it still very carefully controlled it. If you lived in Challaid and your name was Sutherland you had no excuse for not being wealthy, and if you sat on the board of the bank you were probably rich to the extent that counting the zeros on your bank account became a long snooze.

Harold laughed at her bad manners and said, "I suppose so. Can I ask your name?"

"Freya Dempsey."

"Were you going somewhere important? Perhaps we could call a taxi for you."

"Nowhere important enough to make me leave my car. You?"

"A meeting, but they'll wait for me."

The driver had by now moved both cars to the side of the road so the traffic was moving again, crunching slowly over broken glass. He was tall and broad, still in his twenties but with the sort of downturned mouth that suggested he had a lot to frown about and lines on his forehead that gave an equally negative second opinion. He had a narrow face and thin eyebrows, all a little too angular to be attractive. He glared at Harold as he stalked across to Freya and handed her car keys to her without a word.

He turned to Harold and said, “I’ve called another car; they’ll be here in a minute or two.”

Before another word was said the police arrived and started asking questions of them all, looking to apply blame as quickly as possible. When they heard the Sutherland name the blame rushed with open arms toward Freya, and when an even more extravagant car arrived to help him complete his journey it was all they could do not to take off their jackets to cover the puddle Harold stepped over as he made his way to it. Freya stood on the pavement, abandoned by everyone, including the police who had independently decided not to care about her a millisecond after Harold Sutherland suggested she had done nothing wrong and they should leave her be. All she could do was stand on Kidd Street, shops and shoppers on either side of the road, and wait by her battered car for the tow truck to arrive.

1

IT STARTED, as other worthwhile stories have, with a phone call. Darian Ross was sitting at his desk by the window of the Douglas Independent Research office on the second floor of a building on Cage Street when his mobile rang. His boss, Sholto Douglas, was downstairs at The Northern Song, the Chinese restaurant on the ground floor, where he was buying them lunch, so Darian was alone. Leaning back with an elbow on the windowsill, looking down into the narrow pedestrianized lane, he picked the vibrating phone from his desk and saw the name on the screen: *Vinny*. PC Vincent Reno, a friend and police contact in the Whisper Hill district to the north-east of Challaid. They did each other favors, Vinny the cop on the toughest beat in the city and Darian the unregistered private detective pretending he was a humble researcher.

He answered the phone and said, "Vinny, what flavor of favor are you after?"

"A bitter one, Darian. I have this missing person thing, I think she's missing anyway, and I was hoping you might be able to help me out with it."

The gregarious, barrel-chested copper sounded more somber than usual, so Darian said, "Who's the missing person?"

"Yeah, that's the bitter pill, it's Freya."

"As in your ex-wife Freya?"

"There can be only one."

"Freya, the woman you've been hoping would go missing for the last five years?"

"Well, we only split up five years ago, so I've been hoping she would go missing for a little longer than that, if we're counting. Now she's gone and I'm buzzing around all over the city like a blue-arsed fly trying to find her, this is just way out of her brutal character. Wee Finn is missing his mother something chronic and my weekends just aren't the same without her verbal abuse to bookend them. Listen, can we talk about this, just the two of us to start with? I've got nothing against Sholto, but I'd rather start with your advice before you bring in the old man for wit and wisdom."

"Sure. Where and when?"

"How about Misgearan, six tonight, when I knock off. We'll get a room and have a drink and I'll tell you what I know, which will take about half a glass."

Darian said he'd see him there and hung up, wondering if he'd ever been to Misgearan and not woken up the following morning with a jackhammer dismantling the inside of his skull. It was a tough little drinking den up on Long Walk Lane in Whisper Hill, a place that should and would have been shut down long ago if the local police didn't also use it as their own little alcohol-sodden hideaway. It had long been a favorite of Vinny's.

Sholto Douglas returned with their lunch and they ate at their desks. Darian didn't mention the call to the former detective because there was much they didn't tell each other until circumstances prised their mouths open. That makes it sound like they didn't get along, but they did, very well in fact; it was just that each respected the other enough to see his limitations.

Sholto was a man hitting fifty who had been ecstatic to free himself from the Challaid Police Force and seek employment that better suited his stress-free aspirations. In the one-room office on the second floor of a modern gray building in the Bank district, right in the center of Challaid, he had set up his private detective business and called it a research company so he wouldn't be held to the legal restrictions of a proper agency. He hired the young son of his former colleague on the force and tried to teach Darian everything he knew about keeping your head down and staying out of trouble.

Darian, a handsome twenty-three-year-old with soft features and intense large brown eyes, looked across the room at his boss, short and chubby, bald on top and with hair at the sides that had won whatever battle they had recently fought with a comb. His white shirt was a size too small for him and the top button was open under his tie, his desk so shrouded in papers that the folders his phone, laptop and foil lunch tray rested on might have reached to the floor for all anyone knew. Sholto played the figure of bumbling innocence well, but he was fiercely loyal and there were sharp edges to his placid mind that cut through his well-constructed image from time to time. Darian wasn't going to bring trouble to Sholto's door; he had done so before and owed his employer better this time around.

They spent the next couple of hours filing separate reports on a man they had been hired to find, a pension fund manager who had apparently fled Challaid with £45,000 of other people's hard-earned cash. They worked out he had only made it as far as his teenage lover's flat in Whisper Hill before she relieved him of the money and made it all the way to Costa Rica with it, one of the Caledonian countries. The only thing she'd left behind was the pension fund manager, and his employers weren't paying to get him back.

They did what they always did: wrote separate reports, one for the insurance company that had hired them which was full of what the customer wanted to hear, and one for their own files containing all the gory little truths and judgments that might prove useful in the future. Sholto always wrote for the client because he had the reserve and diplomacy of a man who wanted repeat clients, and Darian always wrote for their records because he had the bluntness of youth.

At ten past five Sholto said, "Well, doesn't look like the phone will ring with a lucrative job to rain riches upon us. I might as well go home and mourn the remains of the day with Mrs. Douglas."

Sholto spent roughly forty-six percent of his working life

complaining about a lack of money and clients but the truth was they were doing okay, well-paid, petty jobs that kept them bumping along in the potholes of society. Their work for big companies wasn't often dignified, and as the rich couldn't stomach parting with money those paydays were infrequent, but their heads, necks and shoulders were above water.

Darian said, "I'm nearly done as well. I'll be off in ten minutes."

"Okay, lock up behind you, we wouldn't want anyone coming in and stealing…well…"

Sholto had his laptop and phone in his bag; all they left behind in the office overnight was paperwork they weren't scared of others seeing. The good stuff was well hidden now and there was enough on those files to keep gossipmongers and curious coppers up reading all night. The security of those files was absolute and no one other than the two members of Douglas Independent Research staff got unfettered access to them.

He waited in the office for twenty minutes, knowing Sholto wouldn't go straight home; he'd be downstairs in The Northern Song, chatting to Mr. Yang and collecting his dinner. All of Sholto's three square meals a day came from there, and they were responsible for his changing shape. Darian waited a few minutes after seeing his boss walk along Cage Street, laptop bag in one hand and white plastic bag with food in the other.

With the door locked behind him as promised, he made his way down the stairs and out through the side door. The Chinese restaurant took up the entire ground floor, the Yang family flat and a talent agency office on the first and Douglas Independent Research, Challaid Data Services and an empty office on the top floor. Growing up, Darian had wanted to be a detective like his father, with all the bustle of a big station, but this was the next best thing. From Cage Street it was a well-worn twelve-minute walk to Glendan Station, he had no car of his own, and then the train up to Whisper Hill to meet Vinny.

REPORT INTO FINANCIAL AFFAIRS OF WALTER REILLY

BY SHOLTO DOUGLAS, DOUGLAS INDEPENDENT RESEARCH—

FOR ROXANA GILBERT, PORT ISOBEL NEW EDINBURGH INSURANCE

This page contains a breakdown of our investigation, and how we were able to find Mr. Reilly. Our investigation began by locating Mr. Reilly's whereabouts from the moment he was last seen at your office.

- My colleague, Darian Ross, was able to ascertain that Walter Reilly, after leaving your office on Sheshader Street at his usual time of five thirty, had traveled by train from Bank Station to Three O'clock Station in Whisper Hill.
- After extensive inquiries we were able to identify the taxi driver who collected Mr. Reilly from outside Three O'clock Station and he was able to tell us the street where he had dropped off Mr. Reilly.
- We were able to learn from one of the neighbors which address on Woodbury Drive Mr. Reilly had been frequenting in the two months before his disappearance. He had been visiting flat number 3-9, which is owned by Harbour Housing and was rented to a Miss Filis Marrufo, a nineteen-year-old woman from Costa Rica who had been resident in Challaid for seven months.
- Having received no answer from the flat we were able to obtain the help of the owners to gain access where we found Mr. Reilly, injured but not seriously, where he had been for two days, now alone.

At this point it became clear the nature of the criminal acts committed but as you have urged us not to contact Challaid Police, as did Mr. Reilly, we have not yet done so. Despite finding Mr. Reilly we have since continued to investigate the case and have discovered that Miss Marrufo was assisted by a Mr. Arturo Salamanca, a twenty-two-year-old Costa Rican national who had earned residency through twelve months' work in Challaid several months ago.

As you know the money was transferred to a small bank in San José where it was collected in cash on Saturday evening. Miss Marrufo and Mr. Salamanca traveled on a direct flight from Challaid International Airport the morning after the theft (Saturday) and so would have collected the cash themselves, us not finding Mr. Reilly until Sunday evening. While the money has not been recovered we do not consider the case closed, and can work with colleagues in San José to recover it should you so instruct us.

REPORT INTO FINANCIAL AFFAIRS OF WALTER REILLY

BY DARIAN ROSS, DOUGLAS INDEPENDENT RESEARCH—

FOR COMPANY USE ONLY, STRICTLY CONFIDENTIAL.

We were called in on Sunday morning, nearly 40 hours after Walter Reilly walked out of PINE Insurance on Sheshader Road with £45k from the pension pot. They hadn't realized it was gone until it was withdrawn from a bank in San José on Saturday and wasted the next 12 hours with their own security trying to recover the money in the hope the news would never leak out. This made it much more difficult for us and we assumed Reilly and the money would be out of the country already, in San José, something we made clear to PINE executive director Roxana Gilbert when we met in her office. She made it clear that the priority was finding Reilly; she didn't seem to believe he would have stolen from them. Mrs. Gilbert believed finding Reilly would find the money, and she obviously hoped to avoid the reputational damage they would receive if they had to report the missing cash in their accounts. The company has had bad PR lately, told off by a parliamentary report, and secrecy mattered more than the cash, although she didn't say so.

The first step was working out where Reilly had gone with the money because even he wasn't stupid enough to return to his own home with it. He was, fortunately, stupid enough to use his railcard, which took him from Bank Station to Three O'clock Station on the 17:52 train on disappearance day, Friday. We were able to find this out after Sholto made contact with source #S-61 who used access to the database showing every journey using a registered card.

A man fleeing the country with his bags packed was unlikely to walk the streets of Whisper Hill so we assumed he had either been collected at the station or had taken a taxi. As usual the taxi drivers were a total nightmare and had to be bribed excessively to open their usually flappy mouths, the only time they ever do shut up is when you need info from them. We paid £100 to recipient #362 to find out who had been working on the evening in question and another £200 to recipient #363 to tell us where he had dropped Walter Reilly. He informed us he was certain he had dropped the man in our picture on Woodbury Drive and that he remembered him because he was a "twitchy bugger."

We were skeptical but it only took a short time of checking with people living on the street to find someone willing to tell us that Reilly had been a regular visitor to flat #3-9, and that he wasn't the only man who was. The neighbor, who made no attempt to hide the grudge she harbored against the resident, informed us that a young man stayed in the flat with the young woman who was the only listed occupant but he always left before Reilly arrived and returned only when he had left. The neighbor named the occupant as Filis Marrufo, a Costa Rican national who has not yet completed her 12-month employment period that would enable her to claim citizenship. From the research into her we've done it doesn't seem as though she works at all, and may have a "paper job," a fake job created by criminal gangs to trick immigration officials into thinking she's earning citizenship here.

We attempted to gain access to the flat but there was no response so we called the owners, Harbour Housing, who sent a member of the staff round with a key. She let us in and we found Walter Reilly sitting in the living room, the curtains drawn, cut and bruised and drinking from a bottle of vodka. He was the only person in the flat and a quick search revealed no sign of the money, just his packed bags.

When the Harbour Housing employee left the room to inform her employers their flat had been abandoned and to check if any rent was owed, Walter Reilly told his story to Sholto and me in the living room. He informed us he had met Filis Marrufo at a nightclub some three months previously and that despite the 24-year age gap he had thought she loved him. She appeared to know no one else and was lonely and unhappy in Challaid, wanting to return home to look after her sick mother (he actually somehow believed this) but needing to earn money first. He claimed that stealing the money from PINE Insurance was his idea and that he had planned it all alone. When he arrived at the flat with the cash he found she was not alone, and that she had another long-term lover. Marrufo and Reilly had booked seats on a flight to San José the following morning, the 07:15 flight, and he had already sent the money ahead and could collect it when they arrived. Marrufo's lover is Arturo Salamanca, a 22-year-old Costa Rican national with a joint Scottish passport, and he too had bought a ticket on the same flight, unbeknown to Reilly. Marrufo and Salamanca beat Reilly and held him in the flat at knifepoint through the night, flaunting their own sexual relationship in front of him, making him watch them as they had sex and mocking his stupidity. He claims that in the morning they drugged him and left for the airport as he passed out.

While he was clearly drunk, full of self-pity and conflicted about how much he wanted to blame Marrufo, it is our belief that he was mostly telling the truth. Most likely Marrufo picked up a dunce like Reilly who would buy her gifts and help her with cash when needed, and would have looked for ways to exploit him further. When she expressed a desire to find money to return to Caledonia she was probably hoping for him to come up with cash to help her, and likely pushed him toward the plan to steal the money, although he carried out the actual theft all on his own. Marrufo and Salamanca saw their chance and took it.

There is no doubt the money is now in San José, along with Marrufo and Salamanca. We have alerted Corvus Security, the detective agency we cooperate with in the city, and are ready to take the next step in the job of recovering the stolen money. We now await a response from PINE Insurance.

2

TAXI DRIVERS in Challaid would all be millionaires if there weren't so damn many of them and they didn't keep picking fights with each other. Our city is built in a U shape around the bottom end of Loch Eriboll, a sea loch on the north coast of Scotland. There's a single rail line that runs through the six major districts, but if your destination isn't close to the line you either need cash for a taxi or a comfy pair of shoes because there's only one branching line which goes to the airport, no underground and an infuriatingly unreliable bus service made worse by the recent collapse of one of the local operators. The taxi ranks outside the stations were always frantic, but this time Darian decided to join the battle of elbows at the roadside. The journey to Long Walk Lane lived up to its nickname and he didn't want to be late for the meeting with Vinny.

The driver who took him from Mormaer Station dropped him on Fair Road near the entrance to the lane because you couldn't get close to Misgearan without running over six drunks and a cop and there was nowhere to turn at the end of the cul-de-sac. Darian paid the man and strolled through the smattering of people already milling around the narrow space between the ugly, flat, single-story buildings on either side of the road. On the left were the backs of the buildings that faced Fair Road and so were at least pretending to be respectable, but on the other side the buildings fronted the lane and backed against a large metal fence that blocked access to the railway line. Darian had spotted the rear of Misgearan as he whizzed past on the train many times and the only difference between that pitiful blur and the front of the building was the smell of booze, piss and vomit. At any hour you chose to visit, the picture of humanity splashed across that place suggested that if the end wasn't nigh then it should be.

The front door led to the bar and the bar was no place to have a conversation, so Darian went to the side door and knocked. It took seconds for Caillic Docherty, the sixty-something manager of Misgearan who saw all and knew all, to open the door. No one had managed to persuade her to tell the stories of all that had passed there, the criminal chronicles of Misgearan, but there would be a lot of people lining up to hear if she did. She let Darian in without asking him what he was there for.

"I'm here to see..."

She was already walking along the corridor, ignoring him, opening the door to a small private room where Vinny was sitting. Darian went in and Caillic closed the door behind him, leaving them alone in a windowless room lit by a bare bulb with a small round table, two chairs and no room for a third.

Darian sat opposite Vinny and picked up one of the two whisky glasses filled from the half-bottle of cheap Uisge an Tuath in the middle of the table. He said, "This is romantic."

"Isn't it? You could lose your virginity in here and not be sure it happened, rubbed up against each other like this."

Every room Vinny entered seemed to shrink around his booming presence, over six feet tall and with the barrel-chested build of a circus strongman. He had a large, wide face with an easy smile and twinkling eyes, pale skin that blushed red with the effort of his ebullient storytelling. He was loud and cheery and a bloody good cop and loyal friend. Among his greatest skills as a police officer was that he didn't take the challenge of life too seriously, but as he took a San Jose cigarette from the pack on the table and lit it, to hell with the smoking ban, he looked unusually serious.

Vinny said, "You working on anything fun?"

"You call a middle-aged moron running off with other people's pension money only to be shafted by his gymslip lover fun?"

"Round here? I'd call that an average day."

Darian said, "So, Freya."

"Aye, Freya. Saying her name still sends a shudder through me, but it's a different sort now. She's just disappeared and left Finn behind and he's upset about his mother not being around and that's upsetting me. He's with my mother while I'm working; she picks him up from school, which she isn't really fit for, her hip's in bits and she won't go to a doctor. The only thing I've got in common with Sherlock Holmes is that I once fell down a waterfall but even I can deduce the trouble in this. Freya's never gone missing before, never left Finn. She was an unmanageable wife, but I would never knock her ability as a mother, not even behind her back. There's no explaining it, Darian, and it needs explaining."

"What's the search party so far?"

"I reported her missing to Cnocaid station, that's where her and Finn have been living. They'll keep an eye out for her, up above and out beyond normal because she's connected to me. We look after our own."

Vinny had said it without thinking and didn't notice Darian's grimace. His experience of Challaid Police was not as optimistic as his friend's, as the son of a detective framed for murder and currently serving a life sentence in The Ganntair, the prison in the city. The year before Darian had also become entangled in a case that centered on a bent cop and his corrupted acolytes, a man now out of the force.

"You want me and Sholto to join the hunt?"

"I do, yeah. The reason I didn't go to the office with this is because I don't have a lot of dough, Darian, so whatever I pay you will be half a peanut at best. Sholto's always been a decent old duffer but he might be able to pluck up the courage to point out that what I'm asking for is charity and what he's running is a business. I know you need to earn."

Darian took another sip of the rough whisky and said, "I can keep an ear to the ground free of charge, I've got one to spare. I can ask a few questions for very little, so can Sholto. We're mercenaries, we're not bastards. Tell me what you know."

"She dropped Finn off at my place on Friday evening, as usual, and she seemed the same as she always did, insufferable. She didn't mention any trouble, but she wouldn't anyway because only my failures get the spotlight. No hint that she wouldn't be back on Sunday afternoon for Finn, that was the routine. She just didn't show, and when I phoned to mock her timing the line was dead, not even voicemail. We went round to her house and couldn't find her. Called her friends and her work but there's been no sign of her. That was four days ago and there's been nothing. Her keeping her mouth shut for four days? No bloody way. It's something bad and every cop that can spare the time is looking and finding nothing. Right now no one has seen her since she left my place on Friday, which makes her miserable ex-husband the last person to see her. It's not good, Darian. 'I want her back' might be the last words I ever thought I'd utter but that's Freya, always taking me by surprise."

They emptied the half-bottle as they talked about Freya and Vinny's marriage. It had been a whirlwind at the start and a natural disaster by the end. As soon as it slowed down they realized they'd been spinning with the wrong person, but by then there was a child involved and that tied them together. They disliked each other with cheerful purpose, each committed to genially attacking the other without ever landing verbal blows Finn could see or hear.

It was after eight when Darian took the long walk to Mormaer Station, the cold night air helping to sober him halfway up and the journey a good opportunity to think of what he was going to say to Sholto. As with all the neatest equations, this one was pretty simple. Vinny couldn't pay them much to help, but there was much goodwill to be won from Challaid Police by helping one of their most popular members. When you're running a private detective agency under the false banner of a research company it pays to have the favor of the local law enforcers. Darian took the train down to Bank

Station and walked up to his flat on the corner of Fàrdach Road and Havurn Road.

It was a small, one-bedroom place that easily contained the few fragments of Darian's life that existed outside of work. It was in a good area, though, and from the living-room window he had a view of the loch and the lights crying into the darkness around it. He sat at the table there and thought of Freya Dempsey and the couple of times he had met her. She was unfriendly but interesting, harsh but smart, tough but not wild. People like her didn't just wander off.

3

IT WAS uncomfortable for Darian to be in the Cnocaid police station, the place his father had worked, and where the anti-corruption unit Darian had broken apart was still based. Wasn't the same ACU anymore. Most, but not all, of the former officers had been pushed out and its remit severely narrowed, but the memories were the same.

Wasn't much more fun for Sholto who had worked there for years and hated every brick of the building, but it was his idea to go there as a first step in finding Freya Dempsey. Darian had told him everything Vinny knew and Sholto decided the police officially leading the search for her would probably know more, which meant Cnocaid station.

It had been an easier conversation than he'd expected that morning when Darian pitched the case to Sholto, spelling it all out, including the fact that Vinny's trousers weren't falling down because of the weight of the wallet in his pocket.

Sholto had nodded and said, "He's quite popular, your pal Vinny, among the rest of the force, I mean."

"He is, yeah."

"I do enjoy getting paid for my work, but I also like being able to do it without fear of the police shutting us down. We can help him out, but I'm not making it my life's work."

He had found out the detective with responsibility for the Freya Dempsey search was DS Irene MacNeith, and that pleased him because he had never heard of her. Cops who had worked with Sholto tended not to take him too seriously. They had introduced themselves at the front desk of the building on the corner of Kidd

Street and Meteti Road and were waiting for DS MacNeith to come to them.

She was in her mid-thirties, a short woman with dark skin and shoulder-length black hair, large eyes and a squint front tooth. Her expression suggested she was going against her better instincts by talking to them. Those brown eyes were flooded with showers of contempt for the two private investigators she had been saddled with, and that annoyed Darian. In his noble opinion a person serious about achieving their aim didn't turn down help, whoever it came from, but perhaps knowing where it came from was the source of the scorn. She led them into what the plate on the door called a "family room" where vulnerable witnesses or victims were usually questioned. The only differences between it and a typical interview room were that the table and chairs appeared to have been stolen from someone's kitchen and there was a window from which you had a charming view of the side of the building next door.

As she sat she said, "I'll be honest with you both, if you hadn't been sent by PC Reno I wouldn't be talking to you. You're friends of his and everyone here seems to be friends of his, too, so we'll talk."

The blunt tone with which she attacked her mention of Vinny made clear his popularity meant less to her than him being the last person to see Freya.

Darian said, "Whatever you might think of us we're not bumbling amateurs and anything we do will be done carefully. We're all trying to find Freya Dempsey."

"Some of the stories I've heard about you, Mr. Ross, suggest bumbling would be a generous term, but you are trying to find her and that could be useful to me. I'll give you a few pointers then. There was no sign of her from the moment we're told she left her ex-husband's home on MacWilliam Drive, although the CCTV coverage in Whisper Hill is about as useful as a two-inch stepladder. It's like the Forth Rail Bridge. By the time you're done fixing one vandalized camera the last two repairs have been broken again.

Someone's targeting them, probably the Creag gang, and the force have practically stopped funding replacements."

"So you have nothing to say if she was being followed."

"No. What we can say is that her car has also gone missing and it didn't leave the city. The Southern Road, Heilam Road and Portnancon Road are all covered by working cameras and the ferry terminal is, too. We can't find her car at all, a two-year-old light-blue Volkswagen Passat, so if you want to help the investigation you can focus on that and let me know how it goes. The registration is CX41 VMT."

"How many people do you have working on this?"

"Officially? It's one of four missing persons cases that I and two other colleagues are working on."

"Unofficially?"

"PC Reno has a lot of friends on the force. There are plenty of people in this station with an eye open, hoping Freya Dempsey will come into view, and I'm sure the same is true of officers in other stations. He's a boisterous and talkative person, PC Reno, the fact he's friends with you both is probably further proof of that."

"You don't sound like you've fallen under his spell."

DS MacNeith looked at him and said, "When a woman goes missing do you know what the statistics are on a partner or ex-partner being involved?"

Darian said, "In this case, misleading."

"You told me you wouldn't bumble, Mr. Ross, but you're already bumbling."

She walked them back to the front desk and left them without a goodbye. As they headed back to where Sholto had parked his Fiat he said to Darian, "Well, we found one woman immune to Vinny's lovable roguishness."

"She seems to hate him. I hope it's not clouding her conduct of the search."

"Darian, listen. I know it's hard to think about a friend like this, but you have to realize that right now Vinny ticks a lot of boxes he wouldn't want to get trapped in. He's her ex and they got along like a bull and a china shop after they split up. He was the last person who saw her, and the alibi his young son gives him is gossamer-thin. An alibi from an infant offspring isn't exactly the Rolex of cover stories. Right now he's the person at the top of DS MacNeith's list, and he's the only name on ours, even if he did hire us."

"He's not on my list at all."

"Then you don't have a list, you have a blank sheet of paper and a lack of imagination. If it wasn't Vinny then we have to come up with someone else who had motive and opportunity."

"We'll start with the car. If that hasn't left the city then we can find it. We do that and it gives us a thread to pull at."

As he opened the driver's door Sholto said, "It does, but until then we have a case where the person who hired us is the front-running suspect. Don't know about you but that's eerily familiar and I don't like it."

Darian tutted at more memories he wished hadn't been reawakened and got into the car.

4

THE FIRST step to uncovering what had happened to the missing car was to go and speak to someone with an extensive knowledge of under-the-radar vehicles. In the spirit of using a thief to catch a thief they drove over to Bakers Moor and onto Tuit Road, an ugly reminder that not all squalor in the city lived in Earmam and Whisper Hill. These were industrial buildings where the industry was mostly carried out at night when the police were less likely to have their eyes open. It was tucked back against Bakers Hill on the east side, buried in shadows and as cold as the welcome most occupants would give a stranger. It might seem like an odd place for a car hire firm to base itself, but JJ's car hire was a specialist lender to the underfunded, the secretly industrious and the legally unfussy.

As they turned onto the patch of waste ground where the cars were parked they both spotted JJ talking to a rightly nervous young customer. Sholto parked beside a small office building in such disrepair that a solid head-butt could have sent the whole thing tumbling. It was short and flat and as they got out Sholto thought he could see a gap between the window frame and the wall.

Darian said, "We'd better wait for him. He won't be happy if we interrupt his swindling."

Sholto took a wander over to the nearest cars, those parked closest to the gate because they looked the most roadworthy. He ran his hand along the top of one and, as he looked at the cardboard sign on the windscreen, said, "This one looks okay, how do you suppose it's only eight hundred quid?"

Darian shrugged and said, "Probably various bits of different cars welded together. A lot of them are."

It was at this moment that JJ arrived, round-faced, jaundiced, like someone had stuffed too much mince into a yellow stocking, with a long scraggly goatee beard that looked like a kid had pinned the tail on entirely the wrong donkey. Every time he spoke he sounded as though he was halfway through swallowing his teeth and determined to finish. He had an optimistic look in his beady eyes as he saw Sholto touch up a banger and said, "You interested in that one?"

Sholto said, "Do you have an actual whole car, like the manufacturers and safety testers intended?"

JJ looked hurt as he wiped his oil-stained hands on his oil-stained blue overalls and said, "I'm sorry, we're just not that sort of company."

Before they lost him to unethical outrage Darian stepped in and said, "We need a bit of help from you, mate, some information about a car we can't find. It hasn't left the city, but it isn't on the road and we've got some money that says you can't find it."

JJ, like many avowedly dishonest people, didn't like helping those who were almost police, but a bet with some roguish private detective was just a bit of harmless fun he could profit from. "I've got two hundred that says I can."

Sholto grimaced at having to pay two hundred for the information but he stayed miserably silent as Darian said, "You're on. A light blue VW Passat, twenty fifteen, number CX41 VMT. How long do you think you'll take?"

"Give me a day or two. I'll call you."

They drove back to the office unsure of their progress. Sholto parked on Dlùth Street at the bottom of Cage Street and they went in through the side door and up the stairs to the office. They sat at their respective desks and tried to find some work to kill the day with. There were often empty periods with little to do and they tried to fill them by doing the things they assumed professionals did.

Darian said, "Even if we find the car there's a good chance we don't find Freya with it."

"Or who's behind her disappearance. There are a hundred ways of getting rid of a car in this city that don't leave a spot behind. It'll be the next step on the path and we have to walk it."

"There is a chance the journey ends with us finding out Freya did a runner because she was sick of this place. We hear she was a great mother and would never leave the boy, but we don't know what was inside her head. She might be shacked up with some lover boy as we speak."

Sholto nodded. "Could be, but you heard what DS MacNeith said about women going missing. I've seen cases of men going walkabout because they thought they'd found a better option than carrying on with the life they had here, but women often take a more sensible approach. We should all be braced for bad news here."

"The odds of her being picked off the street by a total stranger after leaving Vinny's place?"

"Similar to my odds of waking up tomorrow with Miss Challaid next to me and a winning lottery ticket clutched in my sweaty hand."

"You don't play the lottery."

"Exactly right. If Freya was picked off a public street then it was almost certainly by someone who had been following her and targeted her specifically, almost certainly someone she knew."

There was a warning in his tone and Darian thought again about Vinny. He was a mate and had been for a couple of years, one of the most helpful cops he had ever met. Somewhere deep inside Darian's head there remained the vision of the police force he had carried as a child, the tough group of men and women motivated by a desire to make hard lives better in the unfair city of Challaid. A lot had happened in his life to chip away at that belief in the force, but nothing had been able to destroy it yet and that was because of people like Vinny. He represented all that was good about the local police, the ideals a young Darian had aspired to, and he couldn't be guilty of this. Another thing the passing of time had taught Darian was that Challaid had a smaller percentage of good and honest citizens than he had originally thought, and more who were potential targets for their investigative work.

LIBERAL PARTY WEBSITE

LIBERALPARTY.SCO

COUNCIL LEADER MORAG BLAKE GIVES SPEECH ON CHALLAID'S ECONOMIC FUTURE

Challaid city council convener Morag Blake today gave a speech to the Morgan Institute, the group representing business leaders in the city, in which she outlined the progress Challaid has made since the Liberal Party took control of the council in the 2015 elections. Speaking after the latest economic figures showed the Challaid economy back in growth, albeit at a slower than predicted rate, she made it clear that not only has the city changed, but the expectations for the city have too. Below is council leader Blake's speech.

"First of all, ladies and gentlemen, I want to thank you for having me here today to address the Morgan Institute, a group whose tireless work to promote and develop business opportunities, and with it employment, in Challaid I have always had the utmost respect for. I'm sure you will all want to join me in thanking Lamya Khan for her running of the institute and all the staff here at Morgan Hall, a most wonderful setting for this event.

When I was invited to speak to you on the theme of Challaid's economic journey my mind raced back to Barton Secondary and Mr. Smith's history class. I thought of Captain MacDougall being put in a rowboat in the North Atlantic by the crew of his ship after trying to swindle them, and I thought of Jack MacCoy, hanged on Stac Voror for his theft of the city's money, or Joseph Gunn being sent to Panama for his. Our city has a history of holding to account those in control of the finances, and I find it serves me well to remember it all.

All joking aside, there are indeed valuable lessons for us to learn from our economic history, where we have come from informing where we are going. When we talk about Challaid's culture we frequently talk about our language, our great writers, our role in the world, love of the sea and our sport. What we rarely talk about is what allowed all those things to flourish and that helps us to be the success we are today, our sense of entrepreneurship.

Our history is littered with great business leaders, like the Sutherlands, the Duffs and the Forsyths, but that sense of creating wealth from humble beginnings permeates every level, with ingenuity the engine of our economy. Small businesses spring up when they spot the opportunity because they know it is the very spirit of this city to have a go. It's important that we're never afraid to try, so the atmosphere encourages the sort of decision-making that necessitates an organization like the Morgan Institute. For all our other cultural strengths it is this that provides the foundations every other part of Challaid's identity is built upon.

I want, today, to talk a little about how that spirit of endeavor and creativity has been viewed by people outside Challaid in the past and how it's viewed now. For many centuries we were seen as isolationists, a city on the edge of the map that only interacted with the rest of the world to take money from it and interfere occasionally in the Scottish political process. We were the outsiders. This, I have always felt, was something of a misleading view of a port city, but it stuck. From the Caledonian expedition to the Spanish conflict to the trade wars to the two world wars, Challaid has always done its bit, its men sacrificing all to serve the greater good for Scotland. Indeed, if you even look at the evolution of our city's name to its current, simpler spelling and pronunciation, that was due to our connections with the outside world and our desire to interact more easily. But it was something else said about us that really rankled with me and many others.

People in other parts of Scotland, perhaps other parts of the world, viewed Challaid as a city hard to trust. There was a belief that the very entrepreneurial spirit we celebrate today was something untrustworthy, a mark against us. Many read the poem 'Black Challaid' and saw it as a fair reflection of us, and in a world then so disconnected it was hard for us to argue back. Challaid was seen as a place where business was done in a way the rest of Scotland disdained, and we have long been tarred by that brush.

So what has changed? Not us. We should be proud of the companies that have such a long history here in Challaid, we should be celebrating the work they have done over the centuries to help create an environment where now companies can spring up, employ people and create wealth in our society. What has changed is how we are seen, because we are no longer isolated. In Challaid we have worked harder than any other city in Scotland to make sure all our citizens have access to superfast broadband, to make sure we are front and center of the technological advancements that are making the world smaller every single day. It is because of that that no one can be misled and we can be seen only as we should be seen, as a bold city that encourages and supports enterprise, which relishes the opportunity to create jobs and prosperity for all of its people.

We don't want Challaid to be an urban museum like Edinburgh, and at the same time we don't want to be always chasing modernity because we've lost the identity we had, like Glasgow. Challaid must be a city that with one hand grips its past and with the other, the future. Ladies and gentlemen, our economic story has been a long one, and much has changed since that first day, when Challaid began as a place to trade, a place to do business, but some things remain the same. Our reputation, ill-deserved, for criminality and duplicity, is gone among all but the most doggedly ignorant, Challaid now recognized as a fine hub for all manner of local, national and international industries. It is together we have achieved this, and together we will achieve much more. Our past is one of bold, enthusiastic entrepreneurship, and our future is too. Thank you."

5

THE FOLLOWING morning was spent hunting down as much information about Freya Dempsey as possible, which was not an awful lot. Darian had met with Vinny to get some more details about who her friends and family were and then made his way back to Cage Street, bumping into Sholto coming out of The Northern Song with their lunch.

As they walked up the stairs to the office together Sholto said, "The problem with Freya Dempsey is that she is terribly normal."

Darian already knew what his boss meant, but this was Sholto venturing to spread some of his many years of gathered knowledge around and Darian knew it was best to let him get it out lest the weight of it crush him. "Vinny would say she was normally terrible."

"That may also be true, but there was nothing remarkable about her. We're used to chasing after criminals, Darian, people who have gone missing because they have something to run away from. This is different. A woman like Dempsey, the hard part is working out where the start line is, not the finish."

Sholto stopped to unlock the office door, putting the bag of food down and glancing along the corridor as he did. He was looking at the door of Challaid Data Services, the only other company on the top floor, and he had just opened his mouth to say something about them when he heard the phone ringing in the office. Sholto didn't enjoy hurrying and held pressure in great distaste so the need to rush caused the key to wriggle out of his fingers and drop into the carrier bag of Chinese food.

As he fumbled in the bag the phone stopped ringing and he said, "If it was important they'll ring back."

"Or ring Raven."

Sholto pushed open the door at last and said, "Now, Darian, you might think that sort of thing is funny but if you can't hear anyone else laughing you've botched the joke and I'm not hearing so much as a chuckle right now."

Raven Investigators was a company in the south end of Bank who actually admitted to being a private detective agency. They were the biggest in Challaid and the bane of Sholto's life. A company headquartered in Edinburgh with a big budget, lots of employees, many ex-cops, and who had a reputation for playing by the rules and so got a lot of juicy contracts Sholto would have easily fallen in love with. Joking about them was considered to be in very poor taste. No message had been left on the office phone; few ever were because people didn't want to leave recordings of their business with Douglas Independent Research lying around.

"This number is on the private contact list."

Darian went across and looked at it, not recognizing the number. He returned to his desk and switched on his laptop, finding the number on his private file as he tucked into the first of his two hoisin wraps. The phone number belonged to contact #D-09, better known to the rest of the world as JJ. They each had their own contact list, secret from the other, and Sholto's all began with S and Darian's with D. He picked up the phone and, his mouth stuffed with food, called.

"Yeah?"

"JJ, it's Darian Ross, sorry I missed you just now."

"You sound like you're talking to me from under a duvet."

Ignoring the irony of JJ complaining about someone else being unintelligible Darian said, "I wish. Sorry, let me just swallow this. Right, what's your news?"

"You still ready to pay for that bet on the Passat?"

"Of course. You found it?"

"Bits of it. The thing was broken up for parts a few days ago, some of it was sent for scrap. Wasn't an old car, so the people breaking it knew something was going on but they were far too smart to ask questions. It was MacAskill's garage up in Earmam that handled the dismantling, sent parts to a few places. Only thing he could tell me was that it was a man who brought it in to be broken, late twenties, early thirties."

"No description?"

"He was being paid to look the other way. He probably took that literally."

Sholto had stopped eating to listen to Darian's half of the conversation, and Darian knew he needed a bit more detail. He said, "There couldn't be any clean reason they wanted the car broken apart, could there, JJ?"

"Clean? Well, there's impress-your-minister clean and there's Challaid clean, if you know what I mean. There's no honest to God reason for it, not a car that new. There are reasons that aren't virgin pure but round here are common enough, this is Challaid we're talking about. Someone gets in a crash and decides to take the insurance company for a ride, getting some extra dough and a nice new car, pretend the old one was wrecked. That happens plenty. A lot of garages play along, diddle the insurers because they've got it coming to them for having such high prices. That's the Challaid way, dozens of scams like that. Don't listen to the politicians, Darian; we're the same city we always were."

"Okay, thanks, JJ. I'll be round in the next few days for a cup of tea."

That cup of tea would cost Darian two hundred quid. He put the phone down and looked across at Sholto, who said, "The car was broken up?"

"Taken to MacAskill's in Earmam by a man in his late twenties or early thirties."

"No sighting of Freya?"

"No."

Sholto chewed furiously on a prawn and said, "If she was picked up outside or near Vinny's flat then let's assume that was someone who got into her car. They wouldn't leave the car behind and take her on their own, that would be too much of a risk for a sensible psycho. Are we really saying that someone carjacked her in Challaid? Got into her own car and did her harm there, meaning they had to get rid of the motor?"

Darian didn't like the direction this was racing in when he said, "What else are we saying?"

"The police will say, because they prefer to start with the obvious and climb down the ladder from there, it would make a lot more sense to say she didn't disappear outside Vinny's flat but inside it, which meant he could swipe the keys from her pocket and get rid of the car so he could pretend she had left the place. Their second suggestion would be that she was working with some lover boy on an insurance scam gone too far, but they'll start with Vinny."

While Sholto dipped another prawn in sauce and shoveled the whole thing into his face Darian turned in his chair and looked out of the window, not hungry anymore. Knowing what had happened to the missing car was a step forward, but they were still walking in mud.

6

MACASKILL'S GARAGE was, as you would probably expect a wrecking yard to be, tucked away in a dreary part of Earmam. Sholto drove along Purcell Road, narrow with high fences on either side of it that blocked access to a bunch of warehouses and industrial units that didn't want people wandering in off the street and seeing what they were up to. MacAskill's had a large gate for cars, vans and trucks to get through, which was closed and locked, and a smaller one for people, which wasn't.

Sholto parked out on the street and said, "Looks like we're getting some unwanted exercise."

They walked in through the gate and found themselves in a valley of car parts, the empty shells of vehicles piled up on either side of them. The innards had been picked clean by the vulture that ran the place and the frames stacked and left to rust in the hard rain falling over Challaid. They were way up over head height so neither Darian nor Sholto could see past them and they led in a straight line to a sharp corner, forcing anyone who entered to walk along the muddy ground for a few valuable seconds before they had the chance to turn and see the building. It felt like the defense mechanism of a paranoid owner so it wasn't a surprise when a dog came hurtling round the corner to check on them. Rather than a snarling security beast, however, it was a border collie with a shiny coat and its tongue lolling out of the side of its mouth. It looked delighted by its newfound company.

Sholto didn't share the joy, stepping back behind Darian and saying, "Bloody hell, a junkyard dog. That's just what I need, to get torn to pieces in a car graveyard."

The dog had reached Darian and turned sideways to walk with him, pressing itself against his leg so he would reach down and stroke it behind the ear. As he did Darian said, "Well, he might be crazy because I think he just wants to be your friend, don't you, boy?"

"It's not his taste I'm worried about, it's his teeth."

They turned the corner to see MacAskill's Garage ahead on their right, a single-story brown brick building with a flat roof and two large garage doors that you could squeeze a small truck into if you really needed to. Both doors were open and there were no cars out in the open square in front of the building. There was a large yellow machine opposite the garage that looked like a small crane and a fat green box the size of a shipping container that Darian assumed was the crusher. A man in his sixties with silver hair and blue overalls sauntered out of the garage with a cigarette in his mouth to see what his adorable alarm had gone running to greet.

Darian said, "Joe MacAskill?"

"Yeah. You the pair JJ was on about?"

"How did you guess?"

He nodded and said, "You look like the pair he was talking about. Come in."

Neither of them knew whether to take that as an insult or not so followed MacAskill in without reply. The look he gave them and then the dog as he patted it told them what little cheer he had was reserved for his canine pal, so there was no need to aspire to good manners.

Darian asked, "Did JJ tell you what we're looking for?"

MacAskill had deep lines on his face, a weathered charm to him. "Told me you were wanting detail on the cove that brought the Passat for removal, didn't say much else. Said you would pay."

"Yeah, I thought he'd remember to mention that. We will, if you can help us."

MacAskill watched Sholto who was nervously eyeing the dog. Every time the animal made eye contact with him it thought it was going to get a scratch so shuffled a little closer, which caused Sholto to move back a half-step and confuse the dog.

MacAskill said, "She won't bite you. Might lick you to death, but that's about it."

"Aye, well, I'll be dead either way so I'd rather avoid it."

MacAskill shook his head. "Come through to the office, I'll show you what you're looking for."

On the desk in his office he opened a laptop and switched on a media player, selecting the file dated the day the car was destroyed. He pressed play and they watched in silence as the footage showed the car coming in the front gate first thing in the morning. He opened another file that showed footage from a camera just inside the garage, the man getting out of the car and talking to MacAskill on the threshold. The new arrival was wearing a coat, a baseball cap and dark glasses. Darian paused the footage on the best angle it had of his face but the quality was too poor.

Darian said, "Can you remember anything about him?"

"He was youngish. Twenties, maybe thirty. He was in a hurry, but that isn't unusual. Local, I think."

Sholto said, "A man comes in dressed to conceal and you do business with him, no questions?"

"A man comes in with cash in his hand and he can have on a fat suit, a plastic mustache and a plasticine nose for all I care. I trained as a mechanic, not a minister of the kirk."

"Would you recognize him if you saw him again?"

"Couldn't say that I would, no. You two can look over that, I'll be outside waiting for you to pay me for my help."

MacAskill and the dog went out of the office and left them alone to look at the paused footage.

Darian said, "Could be anyone."

"Could be Vinny."

Darian groaned, thought about saying it was too small to be

him but stopped, the coat and the angle making it hard to rule anyone out.

Sholto said, “Doesn’t help us a great deal then.”

“I don’t think that’s likely to be Vinny, too narrow.”

“I’m afraid think and likely aren’t going to cut it in court, kid, we need actual proof. I’m going to go out and see how little I can persuade Cerberus’s master this is worth. You watch it again and see if your younger eyes can make anything of it. Oh, and save it onto something for goodness’ sake. Make sure we have a copy before the dog pees on the laptop or something.”

Darian watched both videos again on his own, trying to persuade himself it couldn’t possibly be Vinny and not quite managing.

7

THE MOST important thing about working *with* the police is to act like you're working *for* them. Know your place. Sholto had always intended to ram that lesson home but didn't get round to it in time, instead having to watch as he and Darian were dragged into battle with Challaid Police's rotten anti-corruption unit and sort of won. Since then Sholto had been careful to make sure he mentioned the value of deference toward the good people of Challaid Police at least once a day, twice if the opportunity came along.

As they drove toward Meteti Road and Cnocaid police station Sholto said to Darian, "Just you remember not to get chippy with her, no matter what she says about Vinny."

Sholto did what he always did when he was trying to talk and drive at the same time, which was to slow down, and he wasn't winning any time trials to begin with.

Darian said, "You concentrate on the road now and I promise I'll concentrate on keeping my mouth shut at the station if we make it there alive."

"I don't know why you always criticize my driving, it teaches you patience."

As if to dispute the point an irate driver, which could describe most motorists in Challaid, who was stuck behind them, sounded his horn and Sholto was spurred to put his foot down. The drive to the station still took longer than necessary and the adventure of a flustered Sholto trying to reverse the Fiat into a narrow parking space in the station car park could rival any theme park for intensity.

Darian said, "That wouldn't make a good impression, reversing right into some detective's car. Might even be DS MacNeith's."

"You know, I'm becoming convinced that there are times when you're not even trying to help."

They went in through the back of the station and waited while a sulky desk sergeant called DS MacNeith to come down and retrieve her guests. When she did she looked about as thrilled as her colleague by their arrival, but showed them into a cold interview room where they sat across the desk from her like a couple of obviously guilty suspects.

She said, "So what have you found out about the car?"

Sholto said, "We found out that it isn't a car anymore, it's a pile of scrap metal and some reused parts. A man took it to a garage and had it broken up on Saturday, less than twenty-four hours after she went missing."

"Do you have a description of this man?"

"Tall, white, late twenties, early thirties, probably local accent. That's about it I'm afraid, not exactly pinpointing the target."

She looked at Darian and said, "Do you think PC Reno could pass for early thirties?"

"He could, but so could tens of thousands of others in this city. There's a chance it wasn't the person who took her, if she's been taken. It might be a third party the car was passed on to afterward. Some insurance setup, perhaps."

At the mention of an insurance scam DS MacNeith gave a little twitch. Darian spotted it and said, "Are you looking at an insurance angle? Was there something to do with the insurance on that car we should know?"

"Not that you should know, but I'll tell you. It was involved in a minor accident out on Kidd Street a couple of months ago, no one hurt, no great damage done. We didn't connect the two events."

"So she claimed insurance on the car?"

"Not on her own policy, that was the thing. The owner of the other car picked up the tab on his, or theirs, to be more exact. The car was owned by the Sutherland Bank, used exclusively by Harold Sutherland, one of the vice-chairmen, although our record of the crash shows one of his staff was driving it and he was in the back at the time. We've checked all her financial records and she made no personal claim on the car, although there was a receipt for the repairs the bank's insurers paid for."

"But that doesn't mean there wasn't a scam here."

"It also doesn't mean there was."

"Let's say Harold Sutherland offered to pay all the expenses because his driver was at fault and she thought it would be a breeze to swindle him out of some money, pretend the car had been much more badly damaged than it seemed. Maybe she claims a fortune, he smells a decomposing rat and gets the bank security people to investigate so she does a runner. They can be scary bastards, those security people."

"So who dumped the car for her?"

"A friend. A lover. Could have been anyone that was in on it with her."

"I know what you're thinking, Mr. Ross, you're thinking that if she was trying to hoover the wallet of a Sutherland family member and ran away to hide of her own accord then the next person you want to speak to is a member of the Sutherland family. I know PC Reno hired you and he's your friend, but take my advice as someone smarter than both of you. Don't interfere any further in a police investigation. Some of us in this station have goodwill for Douglas Independent Research for forcing rehabilitation of the anti-corruption unit, but don't assume it will stretch to the end of my tether."

Sholto jumped in and said, "Oh, you don't have to worry about that, we're not going to chase Harold Sutherland, not at all. We'll stay well out of the way of smarter people than us, won't we, Darian?"

The kick under the table Sholto gave him was neither subtle nor necessary, and Darian said, "I won't do anything to get in the police investigation's way. You have my word."

They left the station having delivered their update to DS MacNeith. Sholto led the way and neither of them said a word until they were back in the car and had driven along the side of the building and back out onto Meteti Road.

Sholto said, "I wish you wouldn't lie to the police like that."

"I wish you wouldn't make me. And I wish you wouldn't kick me."

"Too good an opportunity to miss. So what are you already plotting?"

"I'm going to talk to Vinny and he's going to help me talk to a Sutherland."

COLLECTED PROPHECIES OF SEER ANNASACH

CHAPTER 16—THE CITY OF CHALLAID

Such a place, born in the darkness of a frozen winter morn, and to return unsought, punished for a spirit of wantonness undimmed by the touch of places beyond. On the stone where the first man stood so shall stand another to herald the slip of the sun to ever darkness.

This hill will be riven asunder and men will step inside and such men will disappear from this place.

In this place a prince will be loved by all men, his destiny to sit upon the stone. In the street where I lay in arms a man of peace will strike this prince down with a blade, and mourning will follow.

The last stone of Dubhan Abbey to fall will be the last stone of Challaid to fall, and will be the end of this place.

On the day that greed so holds the rulers of Challaid that true friends are dismissed and distant needs ignored then the punishment shall see the mouth of the loch dry to nothing and this place will have no route to the world, to be forgotten.

A man shall see the edge of the world, and from this evil place bring home with him the devil's laugh, and it shall fill the mouths of the young and the old and will leave no house silent of its horror.

The wealth of kings shall reside in Challaid, but the blood of any that sits upon it shall turn to poison.

The blood of Challaid's brother will poison the world, bringing man from millions to thousands and hastening the dark end.

That the city of Challaid shall stretch beyond the mountains and reach to the lowlanders, and that all men from all the world shall seek it.

Buildings of the city shall rise above the hills and look out to the sea.

Ten score of ships will pour into the loch, thick that the water will be covered and the waves pushed down, the loch made wooded land, and on these ships will be the warriors of three nations, and with coldness to their bones will attack Challaid and its people with axes.

The hero of this place will ensure the glory of the king and country with the blood of people unseen, in lands of power and wealth.

When men of the north hold Challaid to their order winter shall last four years and no crops will grow.

The last man of Challaid will stand on the bank, alone in the place he loves most as the cold water rises around him and he will not move. The water will rise to cover his mouth and then his nose, as he falls below the water at the end of us.

Seer Annasach MacFie was born around 1380 and died in 1426. He was born in Challaid and spent the early part of his life there. He left around 1400, by which time he was already gaining fame for his ability to see events of the future, traveling Scotland to share his gifts with the great houses of the day, including many royals. He was considered a great showman, never revealing his true first name, his long beard and bright blue eyes striking, and his public appearances were said to always draw a crowd. Some of his predictions were characterized by self-interest, suggesting favorable treatment for those who had helped him such as the monks of Dubhan Abbey and the Lord of the Isles, and a hatred of the Scandinavians that had unknown origins. Many of his predictions were petty and inconsequential, relating to the fortunes of the great houses that were offering him shelter at the time, but of those that were genuine he was said to be a passionate guard, going as far as threatening, and perhaps even carrying out, acts of violence against those who doubted him.

8

THERE ARE only three parks worthy of the name in Challaid and two of them are barely large enough to contain an exuberant frisbee thrower. It's strange that we have so few green spaces in a city this size. It's been said the reason there's been no call for more is that if you stand on the street in the north-east of Challaid facing south you can look to your left and see Whisper Hill, Dùil Hill and Bakers Hill, look straight ahead and see Stac Voror and Gleann Fuilteach, and look to your right and see Loch Eriboll. You would have to suffer extreme long-sightedness to miss the mass of concrete and brick sprawled out between you and those landmarks, but there is a true sense that wherever you stand in the city of Challaid the wilderness is pawing at your peripheral vision.

The one park that lives up to the billing is Sutherland Park, right in the middle of the Bank district and the heart of the city. Major buildings surround it on all four sides, but within the ornate black railings that surround it there are trees and walkways, some rough heather and Loch Bheag, a small patch of water that had been the largest of five before the others were drained and concreted over, even Loch Bheag shrunk from its apparently larger original size. Nothing is allowed to inconvenience the expansion of the rich.

Darian went in through St. Andrew Gate, the large black metalwork made from the guns of the ship of the same name that had been on the original Caledonia expedition, directly opposite the Sutherland Bank headquarters on the east side of the park. He walked with the speed of a man who needed to warm up, getting to the white marble fountain dedicated to Isobel Barton where he had agreed to meet Vinny. The cop was there ahead of him, broad and bold, a man built for the rugged area he patrolled and not the genteel surrounds of the park. Here he looked like a brute just waiting for the right target to wander past so he could cheerfully mug them.

He nodded and said, "Darian, mate, what's the news saying?"

"Maybe something not terrible. We've found out a couple of things that might help us track her down. Did you know she'd been in a minor car crash a couple of months ago?"

Vinny, wrapped in a thick coat, said, "Yeah, she moaned about something, getting shunted by another driver and it being their fault. Everything is someone else's fault with Freya. She couldn't pin the blame for that shit on me so she didn't say anything else about it. Is it relevant?"

"It's worth looking at. Her car was taken to a garage and broken up for parts a day after she went missing. It might be...did she tell you who she crashed into?"

"No, just that she was definitely a safer bloody driver than them."

"Huh, that's strange. The car she hit was owned by Harold Sutherland. It was his chauffeur behind the wheel but he was in the back at the time. Maybe she didn't even see Sutherland, I don't know, but her not telling you fits with a theory I have. She has a minor bump that's Sutherland's driver's fault and realizes she can milk it. Instead of the small repairs the car needed Freya claims for a lot more and panics when they rumble her, gets rid of the car and goes into hiding. She doesn't tell you because you're a cop, and, well, she knows she won't get much but laughter from you anyway."

Throughout most of that Vinny had been shaking his head like it was caught in the wind. "No, Darian, no way. You don't know her like I'm unlucky enough to. Freya can be sneaky when it suits her but there's no way on God's blue earth she would go in for scamming people like that, not a single bloody chance. And let's say she did, which she wouldn't, but we'll play make-believe. You think she'd run away from someone challenging her on it? Come off it. You know her at least well enough to understand that if she was caught with bright red hands she would find a way of claiming they proved her innocence. That whole theory is a nonstarter."

He said the last few words with the sympathetic tone of a cop who knew the feeling of seeing a perfectly good idea being hacked to death by other people's logic. Darian shrugged and said, "That leaves us with the Sutherland connection. It might be nothing, but the car being destroyed is going to be an angle for the police, I've told DS MacNeith about it."

"Yeah, she'll dig into it, and I'd rather get my spade in the ground first because given half a chance she'll smash my skull in with hers. Good job I'm the wisdom-spewing mentor of an actual human Sutherland."

"Your twelve-year-old partner in crime prevention."

"He's not twelve, he just looks it. He's twenty... something. Come on, we'll take the train up to Whisper Hill and pay him a visit."

PC Philip Sutherland was twenty-four and a cop at Dockside station in Whisper Hill, traditionally the hardest beat to walk in Challaid. It was said his mega-rich parents had objected to him joining the police force instead of going into the family business of hoarding other people's money and had pulled strings to get him placed in the worst situation possible, thinking he would soon come running back into their welcoming arms. Most often paired with Vinny, he had turned out to be an excellent cop and embraced not only Dockside station but the whole frenetic, absurd, dangerous Whisper Hill experience.

He lived on Chester Street, a short, straight road with four-story flats on either side that looked like the ugly arse ends of more appealing buildings. It was hard to believe an architect had conceived them to look this way, but somewhere in the council building there would be 1960s designs for them that someone must have shamefacedly signed. Because the city is relatively narrow and was expanded with the sort of gleeful lack of forethought we've turned into an art form we have a lot of short streets, another issue that makes getting around quickly a near impossibility. This one felt like a street designed for bleak experiences and yet nothing was damaged or out of place. When they went into the building it was clean and the hall looked like it had been recently painted a fresh shade of beige.

Darian said, "Did we stumble through the back of a wardrobe or something because this doesn't feel like a Whisper Hill block of flats."

Vinny said, "You noticed that, huh? He doesn't talk about it, wee Phil, but I reckon the almighty family send people round to keep the place spick-and-span and free from the sort of everyday human grime that interacting with working-class bastards like me might bring. I don't think he likes them doing it, but then he hasn't moved somewhere else, has he?"

Phil was on the top floor and he was expecting them, Vinny having called from the train not to ask him if they could come but to tell him. His flat was small like all the others, two bedrooms, one bathroom and a living area, but there were little hints that this occupant was sitting atop a trust fund that would one day make him incalculably rich. Small luxuries, and the occasional style over substance choice, but nothing too obvious, and nothing worth going out of your way to rob the place for.

In the living area they sat at the small, round dining table and Philip Sutherland, skinny and baby-faced, probably fed up with being called cute, perfect teeth and carefully styled hair, said, "So what happened with my uncle Harold?"

"Right, well, you know my heartache has gone missing and I'm on the hunt for her, and it turns out she managed to drive her car into your uncle's wagon a couple of months ago. What we hear is that your uncle accepted it was his chauffeur's fault and paid out, and then the next thing that happened to Freya's car is that it was ripped to bits at a wrecker's yard the day after she disappeared. I doubt very much there's a connection because the only way there would be is if she was pulling a scam and that's beneath her highness, but, shit, I have to check everything here. DS MacNeith will go calling on your illustrious family about it so I want to go, too. Do you think they'll have any record of what your uncle paid Freya?"

"Bloody hell, yes, they have records for every penny any member of the family or the bank spends. Literally every penny. If a family member threw a coin down a well someone would abseil down with a torch to find out how much it was worth. Pretty sure they have a file somewhere listing every penny of pocket money my father gave me. My mother gave me more because she's the Sutherland."

Vinny said, "Listen to this, Darian. Your parents are still married, Phil, so how come you have her surname?"

He didn't enjoy his family traditions being prodded for Vinny's amusement but he said, "That's how we do it. My father keeps his name but the kids are always Sutherlands. If you don't carry the family name you won't get shares in the bank."

Darian said, "Well, you sure screwed up their plans for you. You ever think of switching to your father's name?"

"No, I'm a Sutherland, I'm not ashamed of that. We might be poison but we're still a family and I still get on well with most of them."

"So why become a cop?"

"I could spend years sitting in boardrooms listening to people moan about pension fund deficits and South East Asian liquidity, or I could have drunken sailors try to punch my lights out and drug dealers try to run me down with their gaudy cars. It really wasn't a difficult choice at all."

"So could you find out about any payment to Freya?"

"I can, yeah, and I can do better than that for you, Vinny. If you want I can get you a face-to-face with Uncle Harold. He's a good sort; he'll help if he can."

"Great, let's do it."

This was the first time Darian had heard Phil speak and he was surprised by how normal he was. He had expected every Sutherland to speak as if he had a bunch of grapes wedged in the back of his throat. Yeah, he had a posh accent, less phlegmy and softer on the vowels than his working-class colleague, but this offspring of the elite was likable and friendly and he was going to get them a meeting with someone from the very highest branch of the mighty family tree.

9

BEFORE EIGHT O'CLOCK the following morning a group of four men made their way up the steps and through the grand front door of the Sutherland Bank headquarters on East Sutherland Square. This was a family with a perverse obsession with projecting humility while at the same time slapping their name on every damn thing they owned, which was a lot. The group was led by someone who knew the way, PC Philip Sutherland, a man who should have spent his working life inside the building. Behind him were Darian, Vinny and Sholto, three men who lacked the confident air of their leader.

The hall of the Sutherland Bank was colossal, high and wide enough for a Harris's hawk to get lost in and, it felt like, the Isle of Harris itself to just about fit in. As they walked across to the reception desk, staffed by six people, Sholto said, "I'm sweating like a bank robber here. I should have brought a towel, or a sponge. People are going to be falling and breaking their necks on the puddles I'm leaving, and I can't afford to be sued by the sort of people who work here."

There were two things that always made Sholto sweat: rich people and dogs. He was safe from the latter here but the former were unavoidable. People tended to think of the Sutherland building as a grand sort of place because it was big and old. The front half of it, which could pass for a cathedral, was built on the site of the bank's previous headquarters in the early eighteenth century, with a huge extension going onto the back around a century later. The only part the public tended to see was that entrance hall, the towering room with balconies around the first- and second-floor levels, and the scale of it could deceive you into believing it was beautiful. The truth was that every part of it was plain. There was no hint of imagination in anything, as though the builders had finished their work and no one had thought to tell the decorators it was their turn. The hall was huge because when it was opened it was a functioning bank the public used so space was needed for them, whereas now it was the reception area for the headquarters of a corporate giant. The reception desk was dark brown and plain, the tiles beneath their feet dark gray and without design, the walls unadorned.

The other three hovered shiftily by the desk while Phil spoke to the woman behind it and told her they had an appointment with Harold Sutherland. He didn't tell her he'd been able to get an appointment at such short notice because he was the man's nephew. Darian looked to his left at the security. Two guards were sitting on chairs across the hall from them, tucked in at the side of the room. They were unobtrusive enough to make sure you didn't feel intimidated, but watching just blatantly enough to make sure you realized that one dodgy move would see you rugby tackled across the tiles, out of the door, down the steps and into the middle of the road.

The receptionist had checked and confirmed they were all entitled to head deeper into the building. As she handed him a security pass she said to Phil, "If you take the main lifts past the security door up to the third floor and when you get there go straight ahead, eventually the corridor will turn into two open-plan spaces and you want the one on your right."

Phil smiled, having been raised to be too polite to tell her he knew his way around the building because he had visited many times as a child, and said, "Thank you."

They went through security and took the lift up, packed in with four other people as the bank began to fill up with its resident desperate money grabbers. A couple of them looked at Sholto and wondered just what exactly he was so nervous about, and the more he was watched the more erratic his facial expressions became.

Phil led them with the confidence of a man who needed no directions, along the corridor, through another security door and across to the open area he knew his uncle worked from. There were about a dozen desks in the open-plan office, all of them tidy with no personal touches, no pictures on the walls and nothing to suggest this was a fun place to work. Phil led them across to a desk outside an office door where a woman in her fifties was settling in to start a day's work.

Phil said, "Good morning, Mrs. Robin, is my uncle in yet?"

She looked up at him and smiled with the warmth of someone who considered herself closer to family than staff and said, "Yes, he is, go right in."

Harold Sutherland's office kept the same glum tone as the rest of the building—no individual tokens and nothing that could be described as decorative or attractive. The closest thing to a luxury was the window with a view of the park, but that seemed accidental as one side of the bank inevitably had to face the nice scenery. Darian was surprised to note that a man who had been club chairman of Challaid FC for nearly a decade didn't have any memorabilia or photos of their triumphs at his place of work.

Harold Sutherland got up from behind his desk and reached out a hand, saying, "It's good to see you, Philip; it's been too long since you were in the bank."

"You say that every time I see you and I keep telling you it makes no sense for me to visit a place I don't work at."

Harold sighed with a smile on his face and obviously decided not to poke the touchy subject any harder. He had great affection for his nephew and no wish for an argument with him, certainly not when three strange strangers were filing into the room behind him. It took the best part of a minute for handshakes, introductions and everyone to get seated in front of the cheap-looking desk; time enough for Darian to realize that Harold sat with his back to the window so that he couldn't even have that small pleasure distract him while he worked.

"I understand this is about the car crash a couple of months ago?"

Vinny said, "Yes, the woman involved is my ex-wife, Freya, and she's gone missing since it happened. One notable thing is that her car was destroyed at a wrecker's yard the day after she was last seen, so we're working backward through its history to see if it might have something to do with all this. What do you remember about the accident?"

Harold nodded, pushed his glasses up the bridge of his nose and said, "I do remember it well. I wouldn't say it to her because she seemed, well, fiery, but I think it was probably her fault; she pulled out when she shouldn't have. She was exceedingly insistent that she wasn't to blame and I didn't want a scene. It happened on Kidd Street so there were plenty of people around and I thought agreeing to pay for it would take the sting out of the tail. It all only took three or four minutes before a replacement car picked me up."

Phil said, "And she made a claim?"

"Yes, she did. I remember signing off on it because it reminded me of the accident. It was, if I remember rightly, about six hundred pounds, but I can have someone dig out the receipt for an exact number."

That ended any speculation she was trying to rip him off. People didn't go on the run for the sake of fiddling six hundred quid, not even in Challaid.

Darian said, "Did you have any other contact with Freya?"

"No, I assume I must have given her my office contact details, or perhaps Will, my driver, did, so that she could put the claim in. But, no, that was it."

"Could your driver have had any further contact with her?"

"Will? I don't know, I don't think so. He's never mentioned her to me again although that doesn't mean a lot. I don't think he appreciated her blaming him for the accident. You could ask him. I can call across the road to Eideard's Tower where the drivers wait. We don't have room for them in here so they're next door. This place wasn't built with the modern needs of the company in mind, I'm afraid, and we have no room left to expand."

"If it's no trouble."

He looked at Vinny as he said, "No trouble at all. I know you've been looking out for Philip while he's been working with you and the family appreciates that. I'll do whatever I can to help."

A quick phone call and some hurried handshakes and they were out of the office and back in the lift, Sholto beginning to breathe properly again, Vinny and Phil looking like they both understood this was going to be a waste of time and Darian trying to take in the whole robotic, unblinking, unfriendly atmosphere of the place.

10

THEY NEEDED their security passes to get out through the guarded door at the back of the bank and onto MacAlpin Road. From there they just had to turn right and cross the road to Eideard's Tower. It was a circular building that had gone up not long after the first part of the Sutherland building in the early 1700s, and at the time it would have been a tall and majestic thing. It wasn't built by the Sutherlands; it was instead a watchtower that served to advertise the paranoia of Eideard Brann, a man strange enough to be locked up but rich enough to be dismissed as eccentric and left to his own devices. In the centuries since it had fallen into disrepair, then been bought by the Sutherlands because it was next door, with new buildings around it turning it into a place of unremarkable size and mediocre function. Modernity has a habit of trampling across the past like that.

Disappointing as it was to see a striking old building put to such poor use the simple fact was that no one else wanted to own the watchtower. It had no historical significance, being nothing more than a rich man's curious whim, and its only achievement was not falling over during one of the hundreds of winter storms it had lived through. The cost of keeping it upright was more than the council considered worthy, so the Sutherlands got to own their odd neighbor.

The tower where the drivers waited was a thirty-second walk across the road; they had to be close enough to run to the multi-story car park opposite the bank and round to pick up the executives at the front door at the drop of an expensive hat. Phil led them into a small reception area that needed its lights on all day because there were no windows, just the light coming in from the open door. As Phil stopped by the reception desk a thick wooden door at the side of the room, that looked like it might have been there since the place went up, opened slowly and a man stepped out. He was in his late twenties and had a sour expression that showed no surprise at seeing them.

He said, "I'm Will Dent. Come through here."

Dent spoke with all the joy of a man on death row whose last meal had turned up burned. The four of them followed him into a room that was supposed to be a kitchen because a sink had been added and a microwave stood on a counter, but the madness of its creator was still on display. There was one small, high window near the ceiling, grated and set in the remarkably thick wall. There was a long, sturdy, wooden dining table that filled the room, one wall curving to make it feel smaller, and they all sat at it.

Darian took the lead. "We just wanted to know what you remembered of the crash you were in with Freya Dempsey a couple of months ago on Kidd Street. All the details you can remember."

He shrugged. "It was her fault, that's about all I do remember. She pulled out and hit me, another car came from here to get us, that was it."

When he spoke it was mostly out of the left side of his mouth, the right appearing to stay half shut, and it sounded like he was picking every word reluctantly. He looked at the faces of the four men staring back at him, clearly under pressure and unsure why it took so many to ask about a minor prang.

Darian said, "You must remember more than that. I would hope it's not every day you crash into someone. Even your employers don't get to play bumper cars in the streets."

"I didn't crash into her, she crashed into me. It was only minor anyway."

Sholto, feeling more at ease with staff than the fabulously wealthy who employed them, said, "You wouldn't be much of a gentleman if you got out of the car and ignored her and I'm sure you're something of a gentleman. What did you say to her?"

Dent shrugged again, looked to the side and said, "I can't remember. Told her she shouldn't have pulled out when she did, something like that. That was it."

Sholto said, "That was it?"

"Probably, I think so."

Dent spoke like a man afraid that in every word might lurk the kernel of truth that would choke him. It may have been because he was afraid of saying something that contradicted his boss and got him the sack, or his fear might have traveled from a further, darker place.

Sholto said, "You must have given her a number, though, so that she could put a claim in."

"Uh, yeah, I suppose so. A card or something, probably."

"And you gave her the card, not Mr. Sutherland?"

"Maybe, I don't know, I can't remember. Look, that was two months ago, right, and it wasn't that big a deal. I don't know what your problem is here."

Sholto gave him a smile that was supposed to indicate he knew more than he was letting on and said, "I don't know why you're getting so worked up. I'm just asking you a few harmless questions. Have you spoken to Freya Dempsey since the crash, any time in the weeks since?"

Quietly he said, "No."

"You weren't in contact with her when she called about the claim for her car?"

"No. I'm a driver, I don't handle insurance stuff."

There was silence for a few seconds before Phil said, "Okay, thanks, Will, we'll let you go now."

They had less than they needed but all they were going to get so the four of them left the tower and walked back round to East Sutherland Square. As they marched two abreast Sholto said, "Of the two thousand or so shifty-looking buggers I've questioned in my time I think he might crack the top hundred and fifty."

Phil said, "He was certainly nervous. Might not mean much, might just be scared of losing his job. Uncle Harold likes to keep the same people around for as long as possible, and he pays them well if he likes them. It's a cushy number to lose for a man whose only skill is driving."

Vinny grunted and said, "Well, my Spidey senses are telling me he knows more than he's willing to let on, and I think he might be a lead worth following. We have to skip on up to Docklands, though; we have a shift in the pig market starting in half an hour we're already going to be late for."

He was looking at Darian when he said it, almost with an expression of pleading. Darian said, "Don't worry, we'll have an eyeball stuck to Dent for the rest of the day and night."

Vinny and Phil went north in Phil's car to start their working day at Docklands police station and Darian and Sholto got into Sholto's Fiat.

Darian said, "I'll get a motor from JJ for the day and watch Dent. I take it you're going to call DS MacNeith to let her know about our progress."

"Don't say it like I'm sticking my tongue in her ear and a knife in your back. This is a good lesson for you. We're not cops, which means we have to suck up to those who are hard enough to inhale the bastards."

Darian couldn't, and didn't want to, argue. He had more interesting things to do than debate the strategy of Douglas Independent Research with its owner.

THE CHALLAID GAZETTE AND ADVERTISER

11 MAY 2018

HAROLD SUTHERLAND UNVEILS MACBAIN PAINTING AT TALL AN RÌGH

A large crowd of dignitaries gathered at Tall an Rìgh on Macaulay Road as Harold Sutherland, chairman of Challaid Art Foundation, unveiled a recently purchased Rachel MacBain painting, *The Gaelic Queen at Camp*. The painting, bought by the charity for the gallery two months ago from a private owner in California for a sum believed to be in excess of two million pounds, was revealed in its new spot in the atrium gallery in a grand unveiling that brought many recognizable faces to the event.

In his speech Mr. Sutherland said, "It is a great honor for Challaid Art Foundation to be able to present this truly special piece of work, not just for what it brings to Tall an Rìgh but what it brings to the entire city of Challaid. Our hope is that it can prove to be another step on our great city's evolution as a place of art and culture, and bring more recognition to the great artists, writers and poets of our history, among them Rachel MacBain. Over the years Tall an Rìgh has been at the forefront of promoting Challaid as a place of real influence in the art world, and with the crowds we anticipate this painting will draw that influence should only grow further."

The painting has been described as one of the finest examples of MacBain's bleak style and ingenious use of light, a dark scene of *The Gaelic Queen* at fireside, only her face and hair clear while the remainder of the scene is partially lit by the fire and moonlight. CAF have justified their spending on the painting by saying they believe having such a piece back in the city where it was painted will draw many visitors to Tall an Rìgh and raise the standing of the city among culture tourists, making such a large outlay worthwhile.

Harold Sutherland, who is thought to have provided much of the funding, is the first member of his family to have taken a prominent role in either the cultural or charitable sector in the city. For generations the generous funding of Tall an Rìgh, and other institutions around the city, came from the Duff, Stirling and MacBeth families, jokingly referred to as the No Sutherlands Club.

"My family has always taken great pride in helping to provide the economic environment in which institutions like this can thrive," Harold Sutherland told the *Gazette*. "Our role has always been behind the scenes, and our involvement in CAF, Challaid FC and other organizations doesn't mark a change of policy, merely a moving of the spotlight toward us."

There has been some criticism of the painting's arrival in Challaid as some have argued such a sum could have been better spent, pointing out that the gallery has failed to instigate a strategy to use the painting to draw more interest to art either through a long suggested but never implemented program of free visits for schools or with a strategy to attract people from poorer backgrounds.

None of these concerns were evident in the gilded surrounds of the gallery as special guests, including Tall an Rìgh patron Prince Alastair and the arts minister, enjoyed the occasion. The event passed late into the night in high spirits as the always charming Harold Sutherland and his equally impressive staff ensured that one of the biggest cultural events in recent years in Challaid lived up to its billing.

11

WHILE SHOLTO was talking to DS MacNeith, Darian was picking up a fourteen-year-old Ford Focus from JJ's yard and paying him for the info previously provided. They stood beside the car and Darian said, "I'll need her for the night. Might be back tomorrow, or I might keep her longer."

"That's okay, Dar, there's no queue waiting to use her."

"Will she last a few days?"

JJ shrugged. "She's soldiered on this long, so she's either good for a few more months or ready to collapse in a heap underneath you. The fun is in the finding out."

It was on the third turn of the key that it started and Darian heard JJ give a small cheer that contained a hint of surprise. He pulled out of the yard and headed for Bank and MacAlpin Road where he could watch Eideard's Tower, ready to follow Will Dent into a dark Challaid night. Finding somewhere to park was as much fun as usual in the city. On the fourth time circling the block he saw someone pulling out and slipped into the vacant place by crossing a lane of traffic and nipping in front of someone coming the other way already indicating to enter the same gap.

After an hour his mobile rang, Sholto's name on the screen. "Hello."

"It's me, Sholto."

He always announced himself, seemingly unaware that his name flashed across the screen on other people's phones just as theirs did on his. "Yeah, how did your squealing to MacNeith go?"

"I got three eye rolls and a curt thank you. If we were twelve I'm pretty sure she would have given me a wedgie."

"Still time."

"Well, I found out something that might be of interest to you. Are you still watching Dent?"

"I'm watching the tower, no sign of the driver yet."

"You might be in for a long night. I just saw that Harold Sutherland has a big thing on tonight at Tall an Rìgh. He's unveiling some grim-looking painting he paid the gross domestic product of Luxembourg for. That starts at half seven, so they won't be finished until... Well, I have no idea how long it takes to unveil a painting, do you? Five seconds to lift the veil and then however long it takes rich people to get drunk and congratulate themselves. But if Dent's working it you could be in for a late one."

"If Phil's right about his uncle always using the staff he likes then he will be."

"Phil. That doesn't sound right, it should be Philip. A kid that posh needs at least two syllables. Let me know how you get on."

It was boring but that wasn't a novel experience for Darian. He had long reconciled himself to the fact that doing a good job rarely meant racing through the city at high speed or chasing thugs down alleyways and over fences. It wasn't until half past five that Dent finally left the tower and when he did it took Darian a few seconds to spot him. There was some distance between them—you don't trail someone by standing close enough to see their nasal hair—but what threw him was that Dent had changed his clothes from the morning. At the interview he had been wearing a shirt and tie, ready to look formal when called upon by his boss. Now he was in a hoodie and jeans. This was not a man on his way to the glamourous unveiling of a piece of fine art. Dent went into the building across the street from the tower where the cars were kept and emerged driving a yellow hatchback, final proof he was no longer working.

The driver went east into Bakers Moor and Darian followed. The traffic was, needless to say, appalling, so it was easy enough to crawl along behind without standing out. Eventually Darian could drop back further because he knew Dent was going home, a flat on MacLean Street. By no means the great heights of luxury his boss occupied, but a sweet spot for a young man working as a driver. Phil had said his uncle paid good people well.

The block of flats he lived in had a small car park at the side which Dent drove into and Darian drove past. He couldn't get too close here; had to make sure Dent didn't spot him given it had been only hours since they'd met. He circled the block and came back, parking in the car park of the flats across the street where he had a good view of the entrance to Dent's building.

Darian sat and listened to his stomach cry out for the meals that had skipped on by. More than two hours later a taxi pulled up outside Dent's building and the man himself strolled out wearing a blue shirt and black trousers. He got into the back of the taxi and it pulled away. Darian tried to start the Focus and it wheezed back at him as if it had a fishbone stuck in its throat. The second attempt was no better but the third brought joy and he pulled quickly out onto the road and managed to catch up with the trademark red of the Challaid Cabs taxi. He trundled along behind it for a few minutes until it stopped outside Transistor nightclub on Martin Road. This area had once been the fast-beating heart of Challaid's party district on the borderline between Bakers Moor and Bank, but as the partygoers had softened so the center of fun had gravitated over toward the more genteel Cnocaid. By this time Transistor was a still good club in a now mediocre area.

Darian made his way in and couldn't spot Dent anywhere. The place was packed, a couple of hundred people, and Darian moved through the throng, down a couple of steps toward one of two bars. The place was lit in blue and green, the music slower and a lot better at this early stage. Darian could actually hear a woman singing rather beautifully on the track playing. He spotted Dent alone at the longer of the two bars, downing a shot of a clear liquid and demanding another from a big barman who served him before others ahead of him in the queue. That wasn't because of status; it was because the barman was trained to spot trouble and Dent looked like trouble.

Darian went to the smaller bar against another wall and the barmaid nodded to him. She was a woman with a mass of unnaturally red hair and smart eyes who looked too young to be working there.

"Two orange juices."

The barmaid looked left and right for a companion who wasn't there and then went to get Darian's drinks for him. He took a stool at the end of the bar that gave him a good view of the huge room and sat there sipping steadily, aware he was likely to stand out in a place where most people were trying to have fun.

Dent was perhaps the one other person in the place who wasn't trying to tempt a smile onto his face. He was blowing off abundant steam, and after three drinks he went onto the dance floor and approached the first pretty girl he saw, a young blonde who was dancing with her arms around her boyfriend. Dent butted into the middle of them and started trying to dance with the girl. She shoved him away and her boyfriend shouted something while standing in front of Dent, a fist clenched. In Challaid it's rare to spot a nuanced response to a simple problem; sledgehammers have been used to crack many a nut. The driver laughed at the couple he had upset but Darian couldn't see any pleasure in the pain he'd caused them. He was laughing to save face and walked back to the bar for another drink. This, Darian realized as he started on his second glass, was Dent's plan. Other people were looking to decimate their stress by dancing up close with another person but Dent would get his kicks from something harder.

12

KEEPING WILL Dent in view from the small bar was a challenge, but no more difficult than making sure the girl with the red hair didn't have him thrown out.

For the third time she came across to him and said, "Can I get you anything else?"

"Another orange juice, thanks."

She frowned and said, "You've had three orange juices and you haven't gotten off that stool. You know you're in a nightclub, right?"

"I'll dance, maybe...I'm building up to it."

"God, after this kind of buildup if you don't dance like Disco Stu it's going to be a terrible disappointment for both of us."

Despite her very reasonable concern that Darian was some sort of creepy oddball, she got him another orange juice and left him alone. The music was getting faster and louder and further out of step with Darian's more acoustic tastes, but he blocked it out and focused on the reason he was there.

Will Dent was all over Transistor, at the large bar and then on the dance floor, back to the bar and off to the bathroom and back on the floor. He seemed to be making a point to be as annoying as possible to as many people as he could encounter in the crowd, bumping into some at the bar and stepping on people who were trying to dance. It was all so deliberate that even in a place so full of movement and noise it became noticeable to more than just the spy ensconced at the small bar. The barman who had been serving Dent was alert to it and Darian saw him make a call on the phone behind the bar. A minute and a half later two very large men wearing T-shirts with the Transistor logo made their way inside and took Dent by each arm, guiding him to the exit.

That was Darian's cue to leave but he had to play the role carefully. If Dent was on the hunt for a battle then spotting Darian would give him a target. He walked slowly round the edge of the room and out to the main exit, thirty seconds behind Dent and his burly escorts. Out through the double doors and into the street, colder now than when he had come in but louder, life tumbling out of the bars on surrounding streets and trying to fall into the club to round off a night of inebriated entertainment. Dent was over by the curb where a near-constant stream of taxis was picking up and dropping off, drivers beeping horns and shouting abuse at each other, their industry increasingly heated. It was easy for Darian to skip out unnoticed and move along Martin Road until he found a nook to hide in. He took up position and watched Dent make another attempt at picking a fight.

His drunken indignation was turned toward the two bouncers who had chucked him out, one a completely bald man built like the sort of rugby player who would be banned for excessive violence while the other was tall and thinner, dark and with the sort of matinee idol looks that wouldn't have lasted long on a doorman in Challaid had he ended up sticking around.

It was at that one Dent shouted, "It's people like you that they shouldn't let...people like you into this country."

If he'd known what the person he was shouting at would go on to become the abuse would only have been more unpleasant. If there's one thing drunken racists hate more than foreigners it's foreigners that become successful in their new country, and Baran Vega would go on to great success. At that point he was a twelve-monther, earning his dual passport with a year of employment in the city.

The bald man said in a thick Challaid accent, "It's arseholes like you that shouldn't be allowed in this country, but maybe we can get rid of you one building at a time because you're barred from this one."

"You can't bar me because I quit. I wouldn't come back here if you paid me."

The two bouncers glanced at each other, laughed at the stupidity of it all and went back inside. The look they gave their female colleague on the door was sympathetic.

Being thrown out and barred was a poor return for his night's aggravating work so Dent was never going to leave it at that. Darian watched from the doorway of Sharik's Pet Store two doors down while Dent looked left and right for the easiest target he could find, which happened to be a young and drunk couple who seemed to be suffering from an excess of gravity as they fought to avoid being pushed to the ground under the weight of it. They found the struggle hilarious as they swayed about, and neither of them was paying any attention to Dent when he walked up to them and punched the young man in the guts.

The girl screamed, "Hey, that's my Duncan, that's Duncan."

Dent didn't care that he was punching Duncan. It could have been Prime Minister MacDonald and he would have kept swinging those fists. He got three or four punches in before a couple of other revelers jumped in and pulled him away and the woman on the door ran across. Darian noticed her putting something back into her pocket and guessed correctly it was an alarm to inform her colleagues inside she could use backup. They would be out in a second and Dent would be monstrously outnumbered and outgunned. He was about to become the target in a game of whack the bastard, and he was smart enough to realize it, which was why he started to run.

If he had gone the other way things could have turned out very differently, but he didn't, he ran down toward the pet shop. He didn't spot the young man lurking there, so he didn't see the foot that Darian stuck out and tripped him with, standing back in Sharik's doorway and watching a ruck of people pile on top of the sprawling Dent. It didn't take a beautiful mind to deduce what was going to happen next so Darian slipped away from the rumble on the pavement and made his way back to the car.

The first person he called was Sholto.

"Darian? Tell me you're not still working. Tell me you don't expect to be paid for all these hours."

"Dent didn't go to work tonight, he went partying, which in his world means getting hammered by both alcohol and doormen. He's about to get arrested outside Transistor on Martin Road. Do you have a number for DS MacNeith? She can use this as an opportunity to question him."

Sholto sighed down the phone and said, "I'll call her, persuade her this is worth her time, I'm more charming than you. You didn't get him beaten up, did you? Because you know we're not allowed to make these things happen."

"He didn't need any help from me or anyone else."

Darian hung up and tried to start the car, getting a cough of life from the engine on the second try and enough power to trundle back to his flat. He went straight to bed, knowing he would be up early, desperate to find out if the formidable DS MacNeith had cracked open Will Dent and ripped the truth out of him.

TRANSCRIPT OF SUSPECT INTERVIEW

12 MAY 2018

CNOCAID POLICE STATION, 18–20 KIDD STREET, CNOCAID, CHALLAID, CH2 1WD

Suspect—William Dent
Lawyer—Kellina Oriol
Interviewing officers—DS Irene MacNeith, DC Cathy Draper

10:32

DS MacNeith —My name is DS Irene MacNeith, joining me is DC Cathy Draper, interviewing William Dent, also present Kellina Oriol. Just to let you know that this interview is being filmed by a camera mounted on the wall in the corner over there. Do you know why you're here, William?

10:33

William Dent —I was in a fight, I got arrested for it. I said I was sorry, but I didn't start it anyway.

DS MacNeith —That's why you were arrested last night in Bakers Moor and it's being investigated by the officers at Bakers station. What I'm asking is do you know why we asked to have you brought across to Cnocaid so we could speak to you?

William Dent —No.

DS MacNeith —Do you remember Freya Dempsey?

William Dent —Her, yeah.

DS MacNeith —Do you know that she's gone missing?

William Dent —I heard. Some people came. I think they were cops or something, they asked me about her, yesterday morning. You can talk to them about it if you don't believe me. I already spoke to you lot; I don't [unintelligible].

Kellina Oriol —As my client has said, he's spoken to Challaid Police about Miss Dempsey already, and I assume they were operating in an official capacity because it would be unacceptable if they weren't.

DS MacNeith —Sounds like you already know something of this case. So when I asked your client if he knew why he had been brought here and he said no, that wasn't entirely true.

William Dent —I didn't know.

10:34

Kellina Oriol —He didn't. I asked him when I arrived here why he might have been brought across and he couldn't think of a reason. It was his employers who informed me of the visit from the police yesterday.

DC Draper —Your employer.

Kellina Oriol —Excuse me?

DC Draper —Sutherland Bank, they're your employer, too.

Kellina Oriol —They are. Is that some sort of issue?

DC Draper —Does the bank send its lawyers to defend every member of staff arrested for brawling in the street and public drunkenness?

Kellina Oriol —Seems to me we're talking about potentially more serious allegations than that. In answer to your question, the bank sends its lawyers to support any member of staff it thinks deserves help.

DC Draper —In my experience that's not very many.

Kellina Oriol —Then your experience must err on the side of negativity, unless you're less experienced than you look.

DS MacNeith —William, tell me about the morning you met Freya Dempsey.

William Dent —I told you that already.

DS MacNeith —No, the people you told were not Challaid Police officers.

10:35

Kellina Oriol —But there were two police officers with the men who questioned my client.

DS MacNeith —They were not at that moment acting on behalf of Challaid Police.

Kellina Oriol —That doesn't sound good, detective, two officers working out of hours.

DS MacNeith —Do you wish to report them?

Kellina Oriol —I may yet.

DS MacNeith —You might want to clear it with your employer, Harold Sutherland, first.

Kellina Oriol —Oh, I know one of the officers was his nephew, and I would imagine he would be thrilled to get the young man he cares about out of the toxic culture of Challaid Police.

DS MacNeith —Would he be thrilled to have a nephew who never spoke to him again?

Kellina Oriol —We appear to be getting side-tracked by family issues that are none of our business.

DS MacNeith —Freya Dempsey. Tell me about the morning you met her.

William Dent —It was ages ago, I don't remember everything about it, not all that clear. She pulled out and hit me, down the road, corner of Kidd and Siar, just down the road from here. It wasn't anything big, just a dent for her. Front to side, though, so our bumper got pulled down into the wheel arch. I called for another car, it was all done in a few minutes and we were gone.

DS MacNeith —So it was her that hit you? Her fault?

<u>10:36</u>

William Dent —Yeah, I thought so.

DS MacNeith —But that's not what your boss thought because he paid her costs.

William Dent —Yeah, well, that's the gaffer, isn't it? He didn't want trouble, not out on the street, and he didn't want to have to spend time hanging around dealing with her. Just said he would pay for it so he could get into the new car as soon as it got there and get to his meeting. Getting to that meeting was worth a lot more to him than fixing the car. Every meeting he has would be.

DS MacNeith —And she claimed for the cost?

William Dent —I don't know, I don't handle any of that. I suppose she must have. Next time I heard anything about her was when the cops came round yesterday morning.

DS MacNeith —Could Mr. Sutherland have heard from her?

William Dent —The gaffer? The gaffer wasn't going to waste his time handling insurance claims for a person like her.

DS MacNeith —What sort of person was she?

William Dent —Ordinary.

DS MacNeith —So you know nothing about what happened to her.

William Dent —No.

DS MacNeith —Nothing about the fact that her car was destroyed after she went missing, the same one you crashed into?

William Dent —How would I?

DS MacNeith —You don't seem to like talking about her.

William Dent —I don't like talking to you.

Kellina Oriol —My client has cooperated with you, and if you don't have any more questions of worth then I'm sure he'd like very much to go home.

<u>10:37</u>

DS MacNeith —Where were you in the late afternoon and early evening of the fourth of May?

William Dent —I don't know. I don't know what day that was.

DS MacNeith —It was a Friday. Eight days ago.

William Dent —I'll have been working then.

DS MacNeith —All afternoon and evening?

William Dent —All afternoon, some of the evening, I think. Maybe all of it.

DS MacNeith —And the bank will be able to prove that?

William Dent —My work file will tell you when I signed out for the day, to the second.

DS MacNeith —Good, we'll be sure to check. You can go now, Mr. Dent.

END

13

DARIAN ARRIVED at the office on Cage Street the following morning shortly after Sholto. He knew his boss was already there because he could smell his breakfast from the top of the stairs, picked up from The Northern Song on the ground floor as he made his way into work each morning.

As Darian closed the office door behind him Sholto, with a gob full of grub, said, “I have no idea what happened last night other than the fact that every time you go to a party someone ends up getting arrested. That’s why you and me will never socialize.”

“Yeah, well, this time he actually wanted to be.”

“Takes a special sort of fool to go looking for an arrest in this city. What got into him?”

Darian sat at his desk by the window. “I don’t know, but it was in there before he reached the club, so it must have been in there before he left work. He didn’t work that swanky do his boss was throwing, so he might have been in a huff about that. Maybe he feels like Sutherland set us on him, or maybe Sutherland gave him a bollocking for the evasive way he spoke to us.”

“Or maybe he spoke to Sutherland about her in the same evasive way and the big boss man thinks the driver might be a worthy suspect.”

“Have you heard anything back from DS MacNeith?”

Sholto piled more rice onto his fork and lifted it toward his gaping mouth, grains falling onto his desk, and said, “Not yet. If he was in the state you say he was then they would have let him sleep it off in the salubrious surrounds of the drunk tank. Let's say they questioned him at Bakers Moor about the attack first thing this morning and then sent him across to Cnocaid. They might not have started talking at him yet."

"Hopefully she'll get some useful info out of him."

Sholto nodded. "She might, but it might not be the info you're looking for. How likely is it that a man who committed a perfect kidnap in near broad daylight would then go and get himself arrested for something as tedious as a drunken scrap outside Transistor?"

"You don't think he's involved?"

"If he is then he's gone from criminal genius to colossal goof in the space of a week. That's the sort of drop in standards that only a witch doctor could bring about and I don't know any living this far north. I do think he's up to something, but I'm beginning to wonder if it's something we care about."

Darian was about to say something he hoped would avoid decreasing the number of alternative suspects to just Vinny when his mobile rang. He looked at the screen and saw the code that told him it was JJ.

"JJ."

"Hello, Darian, is it good to talk?"

"It is."

"I thought I'd call you and tell you a funny wee story about what happened to me when I turned up at work this morning. I wasn't even into my boiler suit when a car comes into the yard and these two spivs in fancy suits get out and tell me they're working for an insurance company and they're looking for Freya Dempsey's Passat. I told them I didn't know anything about it because I did know more about them than they realized. One of them was Alan Dudley, and unless he's changed jobs in the last couple of months I know he works for Raven Investigators, not some insurance company. Isn't that funny? Anyway, I'll see you when you come back with the Focus, if it makes it back."

Some people, Darian thought as he hung up, were very good at being informants. Like many who worked on the fringes of criminality JJ knew who the threats were, made sure he would recognize them if they showed up in his vicinity. Douglas Independent Research he saw as a potential friend because they weren't official, but Raven were the biggest private investigators in the city, probably the country, and JJ viewed them with a level of suspicion usually reserved for the police.

Darian repeated the story to Sholto, who stopped scraping the bottom of the container with his fork to say, "Raven? Bloody Raven? Who are those pound store Pinkertons working for?"

"The obvious candidate would be Harold Sutherland. He knows about the car, realized his driver was a suspect and decided to dig a little deeper himself."

If you asked Sholto about Raven Investigators you would likely be on the receiving end of a forty-minute diatribe about them, the highlights of which would be this. The private investigations industry had a good thing going in Scotland until Raven managed to cock it up for everyone. They had, at that point, four large offices in the country, in Challaid, Aberdeen, Glasgow and Edinburgh, although they shut the one in Aberdeen a couple of years ago. They cultivated good relationships with the police and did a lot of their work for big businesses, so they were well insulated from the occasional act of stupidity they were prone to committing. They were, and these would be Sholto's words, arrogant morons, reckless half-wits and a cretinous collection of corrupt clowns. It was their Edinburgh office that ran a little too wild and free, bumping shoulders with alarmed politicians and accelerating the formation of government policy to tighten controls on private investigators across Scotland. It was a policy so quickly thrown together it almost matched one in England word for word. Even though they had shrunk since then, Raven's Challaid office remained the biggest investigator in the city, and on the list of things Sholto could bring himself to hate Raven were in with a bullet at number one.

Sholto said, "Well, if that lot are involved in this case we're not having anything more to do with it. I don't want to be anywhere near them... Or, no, wait, if they're involved then we need to get all the information we can and get this solved. That'll show them. Or...Murt mhòr, I don't know, I hate them too much to make a decision."

"If you can get in touch with MacNeith we might be able to get a small lead on them."

Sholto shook his head. "If Sutherland hired them then he'll know a lot more about what Dent said in the interviews than we will. But I'll give her a ring anyway, see what she spits out at me. If we could get this wrapped up before that lot, oh, that would be sweet as three bags of sugar."

Darian smiled and nodded. He leaned back in his chair and thought how sad it was that the investigation was a challenge to them, a process about finding a truth, while for Finn Reno it was about waiting for someone to tell him why his mother had disappeared. It wasn't that Darian and Sholto didn't care, it was just that for them Freya Dempsey was a part of their week, whereas for Finn she was a huge part of his life.

14

DARIAN SUSPECTED Sholto didn't want him to hear the phone conversation with DS MacNeith so he went downstairs to the bathroom of The Northern Song for a pee he didn't need. Darian was well used to hearing his boss being deferential toward police officers, rich people, the moderately wealthy, large people, angry people and people he thought unpredictable, a trait Sholto was no fan of. There was, however, an elite level of obsequiousness he could wallow in when someone presented a particular problem, and he preferred to do his wallowing without witnesses so he could later pretend he had maintained his polished dignity throughout. Darian gave it five minutes before wandering back upstairs.

They were busy in the restaurant on the ground floor, some passing trade in the morning but mostly preparing for the lunchtime rush. There were only two doors on the landing of the first floor as he made his way back up, the Yangs' flat and the other with a nameplate for an entertainment agency, Highland Stars. No one had ever used the office, and if any money passed through the company based there Darian assumed it was part of a scam. On the second floor there were three doors, theirs closest to the top of the stairs, Challaid Data Services at the far end of the corridor and the empty office in between. He had thought he'd heard someone going into the data services office after he arrived that morning, but their door was, as always, firmly shut. Neither Darian nor Sholto had ever been inside.

As he stepped back into the office Sholto said to him, "I've managed to sweet-talk the dragon, although it was a struggle to keep my food down at the same time. She's questioned Dent, he's going to be charged by Bakers Moor for his fight last night but he gave her nothing at all on Freya so she can't take it further. That's on the record; off the record she thought he was as honest as a Challaid councilors' manifesto, and she hinted with all the subtlety a Tyrannosaurus Rex can muster that we can keep our eyes on him if we want and she won't object because, if he's going to give anything away, now might be the time."

"A Tyrannosaurus Rex is a dinosaur, not a dragon."

"Aye, and they'd both bite your bloody head off given half a chance. Seeing as you're so good at identifying unpleasant threats you can go and watch him. He's out of the station so he'll either be at home or at work."

As he drove to MacLean Street to look for Dent's car Darian realized Sholto had sent him on another full day's work on this case despite knowing Vinny almost certainly couldn't afford to pay them. That was typical of him, complaining about the unappreciated value of his hourly rate at the start but getting so wrapped up in a case that time became a worthless commodity. Darian had often wondered why Sholto had set up a private investigations company when he left the murky environs of Challaid Police and this was the answer—he grudgingly loved the work.

The car wasn't on MacLean Street so Darian drove to MacAlpin Road and went into the multi-story car park across the street from the Sutherland Bank, circling until he spotted it. That meant Dent was in the tower, waiting for a call from the boss to say he was needed. Darian parked just close enough to watch the only door of the tower and bedded in.

Will Dent made four journeys in a company car throughout the day. The first was with Harold Sutherland, driving him to Bruaich Drive and the glass-fronted headquarters of Glendan, the massive construction company with whom the Sutherland Bank no doubt did a lot of business. Harold Sutherland was inside for forty-five minutes before he returned to the car and Dent drove him back to the bank. A little after midday Sutherland left again when Dent picked him up from the front of the building. Darian tried to follow but toward the end of MacUspaig Road he got snarled up in traffic when they turned off. He tried to catch them up, joining the daily chorus of cursing drivers, but couldn't see them after looping the area and wasting petrol, so he went back to the tower to await their return.

The third journey of the day was the one that mattered. Dent went on his own, heading west through Cnocaid and up into Barton. He stopped at a Forsyth's Supermarket and went inside. Darian waited in the car park for half an hour before Dent came out with seven or eight bags. He put them in the boot of the car and drove over to the edge of the loch.

They were on quiet roads now, and it took real effort to keep the Focus from looming big and ugly in Dent's mirrors. When the driver turned onto Geug Place, a short, single-track cul-de-sac near Ruadh Rock, Darian had to let him go. He couldn't follow and stay invisible, and this was an area where the very sight of a fourteen-year-old Focus might spook some nervy old biddy into calling the police. The few houses down the lane, a rich and tree-lined area with the mansions on one side enjoying an uninterrupted view of the loch, were all worth more millions than Darian would earn in six lifetimes. He drove around a bit and missed Dent leaving, so went back to the tower.

The last journey Dent took in a company car was driving his boss as close to home as he could. Harold Sutherland lived on Eilean Seud, the island in Loch Eriboll toward the west bank that was so teeming with money the mainland couldn't contain it. Dent dropped his boss at the pier on Cruinn Road and Harold boarded the little ferry that would carry him and his equally wealthy neighbors across to their island. You could get four cars on the boat at a time, but Harold was on foot, perhaps a car waiting for him at the island pier. Normally anything with the whiff of the working class, like public transport, would send the mega-rich of Eilean Seud into paroxysms of anguish, but the ferry was a necessity they couldn't ignore unless they were happy swimmers.

Someone once asked Magnus Duff, the young scion of the shipping family, on Twitter why his family had never lived on the island. He said it was because if they did the ghost of Morogh Duff would rise from his eighteenth-century grave in Heilam and smite them all down. When asked why the company founder would so object to the island, Magnus said it was because it was populated by people who thought being rich people made them good instead of believing that being good people would make them rich. That, to many, seemed a fine description of a community which repeatedly blocked a bridge being built to the island because it would have granted easy access to "ordinary" people. That meant the fire service had to keep a boat on Cruinn Road pier in case of an emergency on the island, and if there was a medical crisis the helicopter from King Robert VI Hospital in Cnocaid would have to zip up for them, all at the taxpayers' expense, of course.

Having dropped off his boss Dent drove back to the tower, changed, switched to his own car and went home to Bakers Moor. Darian watched the flat for a short while and then tried to start the car to go back to the office. It took five attempts to find rasping life in the engine and Darian was reminded of his older brother Sorley's entreaties that he buy a motorbike so he could get around the city at his own pace and with a helmet covering his face during dangerous jobs. When he did get back to Cage Street, Sholto had gone home so Darian quickly typed up a report, collected some food from downstairs and took it home to eat.

15

THE FOLLOWING morning Darian and Sholto met at Glendan Station and took the train together up to Three O'clock Station in Whisper Hill. Darian had called Vinny and told him they needed to force another conversation out of his ridiculously wealthy junior colleague, Vinny texting back a few minutes later to say Philip was happy to meet.

Sitting on the train Sholto said, "That wee cop loves his uncle. I could see it when we went to Castle Greyskull."

"You think he's going to talk to us and then call up his uncle to share the transcript."

"Aye, and then the uncle tells Raven and we have that army of arseholes keeping pace with us."

"Vinny trusts him."

"And with good reason, I'm sure. The boy will have his back; they have the kind of relationship forged on the wicked streets of The Hill late at night when blades flicker under lamplight. But he's still a Sutherland, and if his uncle is after info then family comes first."

"I'll mention Raven to him, see what his reaction is."

Sholto nodded and said no more, believing he had imparted enough wisdom for one train journey and keeping the rest stored away for future use rather than spoil Darian with it all at once. In their working relationship each thought he was teaching the other about how the world really worked, and to some extent they were both right.

They walked out of Three O'clock Station and made their way

to Bluefields Road, a short enough distance on foot. Bluefields was next along from Docklands Street, the road that ran around the huge industrial docks and was lined with large buildings that served shipping, among them the police station. The streets around it had the noise and smell of the shipping industry, and captured the spirit of the city's history in bottles of seafaring nostalgia. Darian always liked to visit, but it would have taken considerable danger money to persuade him to work at the police station there.

About halfway along Bluefields Road was the Silver Cinema, a cavernous place built in the thirties that had undergone more face-lifts than anyone who appeared on its screens. It had been opened with much fanfare in 1932 by some Hollywood starlet on a flying visit to the city and had been on a crawling decline ever since. Its last makeover had been about ten years before and had been a noble attempt to recapture the style of its lost youth, dressed up to look something like it had been back in those optimistic early days. But instead of looking young again it looked old and caked in enough makeup to give it an air of desperation. No matter what it wore, the building seemed to make just enough money to keep operating and one of the reasons why was the huge café that now occupied the front of the building. Vinny and Phil, in their uniforms, were sitting under a poster of Gregory Peck and a fishy friend, a nod to the whaling past of the city, over in the far corner where the sleepy young woman behind the counter wouldn't be able to hear them.

As they sat at the small table Vinny said, "I hope you've made more progress than we have because we've been a dog chasing its tail in a tumble dryer."

Darian said, "I don't know if I'd call it progress exactly, but we've got a couple of questions worth asking. DS MacNeith interviewed Dent as well and she didn't like the shape of his attitude any more than we did. I followed him yesterday, mostly just running your uncle around, Phil, but he went to one of the mansions on Geug Place with a boot full of groceries in the afternoon, I couldn't follow without being seen so I don't know who..."

Phil put up a hand to stop him. "My cousin Simon lives on Geug Place. My uncle Harold mostly looks after him, makes sure he's all right."

Sholto said, "He can't look after himself?"

Phil shook his head. "He's severely agoraphobic, never leaves the house. I heard he has severe OCD as well and I don't know what else, a shopping list of terrors. I haven't seen him for two or three years, he doesn't like visitors, but last time I went round with Uncle Harold he was, I don't know, nice but shy, nothing to say, didn't want any part of the outside world getting in."

Sholto said, "Is there nothing they can do for him?"

"Uncle Harold has tried, but apparently Simon doesn't want to be helped. He has his own world and it's very small and he has total control over it and that's all he wants. Uncle Harold gets his shopping delivered, has a housekeeper go round to cook his meals, makes sure he's looked after. Look, people think that because you're a Sutherland you've won life's lottery, but Simon got the short straw in the parent sweepstakes. There were three siblings. My mother was the youngest, Uncle Harold was the oldest and Uncle Beathan in the middle. He took after both of his parents, my grandparents, who were a pair of flakes by all accounts, and I'm not sure Simon's mother was a stabilizing influence on that shipwreck either. I was lucky with my parents, but our family has been very rich for a very long time and that's corroded the wires that attach us to reality."

Darian said, "So he doesn't like visitors, huh?"

"No, they upset him, and it would upset me if you went round there. The man doesn't leave his house; he has nothing to tell you."

"But he sees Dent regularly?"

"I don't know who delivers his food. I would assume the housekeeper. She's the only one he allows in. You guys are swinging from the wrong tree here."

Darian nodded and said, "Well, we seem to have shaken your family tree already. Raven have been on our heels for the last day or so, and I can't think of anyone other than your uncle who would have called them in."

Vinny looked sharply from Darian to Phil and said, "Why would your uncle call in Raven?"

"Shit, it's probably instinctive. They do it a lot, whenever there's any investigation going on that might affect the company in any way, cause bad PR, hurt the finances. They're obsessed with knowing what's happening and what's going to happen to them in the foreseeable future. They see it as allowing them to control the direction that future goes in. It's probably nothing, but your best bet would be to pretend you haven't realized they're there because once you acknowledge them they'll move against you. I won't mention any of this to my uncle, though; make sure he can't pass anything on to Raven."

That was said in a way that showed obvious hope that he had won a favor from Darian, like leaving his cousin alone. Vinny and Phil got up to leave, and as they were going Vinny shot Darian the sort of urging look that told him to keep on pulling the thread he had caught ahold of. Darian and Sholto left the Silver and walked back up toward Three O'clock Station.

Sholto said, "Not hard to picture a scene in which a lonely obsessive millionaire gets his creepy chauffeur pal to lift a girl off the street, is it?"

"No, it isn't."

"See, that's jumping to conclusions and a good investigator always keeps his feet on the ground. We have no idea if Simon Sutherland or Dent were even involved, and there are no estimates in this business. It's certainties or nothing."

"So what do we do?"

"We go have a peek at this hideaway on Geug Place and see if it has stories to tell."

THE BLOOD TREE

He had planned to go to the airport and get on whatever plane would take him west, or, hell, east, it didn't make much difference. He was on the wrong side of the world and both directions led home. A concierge, or whatever they called them in Tokyo, stopped him in the lobby of the hotel and told him there was a phone call for him, said it was from England, the daft bugger. Not England, Scotland. Challaid. Home.

Harold Sutherland stepped into the small office behind the front desk and closed the door on the young woman trying to follow him in. He was twenty-six and used to paying for what his charm couldn't earn. He picked up the phone on the table.

"It's Harold," he said.

A couple of seconds' delay and a voice said, "Harold? At last. I didn't think that stupid girl had understood me. Don't go to the airport yet, we're getting a plane especially for you and it'll be ready in a couple of hours. How are you?"

The voice sounded far away but it was recognizable and the lack of true concern was familiar. It was Rodrick Sutherland, a first cousin and managing executive of the bank whose primary role was to put out any fires that threatened to scorch the family business. He was forty-four, a cold and unpleasant person, but he was ruthlessly effective in a crisis.

"I'm okay," Harold said, knowing Rodrick wouldn't care about the lie. "What about Beathan?"

Another delay. "Beathan? They'll keep the body for a few days but we already have people on that. The report will say what it needs to say and we'll get the body back here for burial. Take longer to bury than is traditional but nothing we can do about that. No point you staying with it."

"Shit, the meetings with Marutake."

"Forget about that, the chairman called them an hour ago to

explain everything. What time is it where you are? They told me your plane would be ready at four o'clock."

"Ten past one."

"Get there with time to spare. It'll just be you on board."

They had left the airport two days before and been chauffeur-driven to the hotel. Harold and Beathan Sutherland, the two brightest young stars of the family bank, brothers here to do business with a long-standing financial partner. It was the first time they had been sent abroad alone, just twenty-six and twenty-five. They had both been determined to enjoy the trip. On the first night they went out into the city and got lost among neon and noise, drinking it in, walking into strange-looking bars and spending what might have been a lot or a little, they had no idea or care. They went into a place they thought was a bar and turned out to be a small seafood restaurant so they ate and had a tortuous conversation with a waiter about where to find one of the hostess clubs they'd heard so much innuendo about.

By the time they reached the place they were sure the taxi driver had ripped them off but didn't care much. They were here to have fun and had more than enough money to cover the cost of someone else's enterprise. The club turned out to be a real disappointment, ear-clawing music and flailing attempts at polite conversation with pretty girls who weren't interested in anything more. They did meet a man there who assured them he could provide what they really wanted, and an hour later they were back in the two-bedroom suite on the top floor in the center of Tokyo with a young woman each.

"Do you think this is how they all do foreign trips?" Beathan asked his older brother.

"Probably. I mean, they're almost human, most of them. Even chairman grump must want to have fun now and again."

Beathan shook his head. "Nah, fun would kill that old bastard, he's allergic."

* * *

The plane taking him home was luxury, but Harold barely glanced at it. The crew, Japanese, seemed to know enough to leave him alone, telling him only what food and drink was available and how quickly they would be taking off. If it was a commercial plane this one could have held over a hundred people, but instead had fewer than twenty seats. Harold sat and stared out of the window as he thought about the conversation they had had the previous morning. Thought about the letter in his pocket. He remained stony-faced.

After the girls had gone they had sat at the table in the kitchen of the suite having breakfast. Brothers with all of life's gifts, far from the constraints of home.

"Daisy wants to have another baby," Beathan said, speaking of his wife.

Harold felt his brother had married much too soon, rushed into something he had convinced himself couldn't wait. Daisy was a striking young woman who occasionally bordered on terrifying and she had already produced one son, Simon, to guarantee their branch of the family would carry on beyond them.

"You don't want another one?"

"I didn't really want the first one," Beathan admitted for the first time.

It wasn't a surprise to hear and Harold didn't react. "Tell her you're not ready for another one yet, put her off, not like she can get the job done without you. I mean, she can, but she gets kicked off the gravy train if she does."

"It should be a good thing, though," Beathan said with that familiar faraway look. "I should want it but I don't. That's not right."

"Jesus, Beathan, you're a young man, that's why you don't want it yet. Don't worry, you're young and she's younger so you have plenty of time to wait and pick your moment. Your moment, not hers."

Harold didn't eat until they were more than halfway home. As he did his mind went back to that morning, what he had seen. They'd had a first meeting with the people from Marutake Financial Group that day, an introductory thing that had lasted a couple of hours. Then some sightseeing for which Marutake provided a cheerful guide and an expensive dinner with a couple of executives. They were both in good spirits when they got back to the hotel and went to bed.

Harold had woken with a start at six o'clock in the morning. He knew. Some instinct deep inside him screamed that something was wrong and told him to get out of bed and check. He grabbed his glasses and went out of the room, across the corridor to Beathan's door, knocking on it. No answer. He tried the handle and the door wasn't locked, Harold realized later, because his brother wanted to make this as easy for him as possible. Beathan was lying on the bed, on his back, head propped up on the pillows. His eyes were shut and when Harold spoke his words seemed impossibly loud in the room. Beathan didn't stir. He shook him and there was no response. His brother was dead.

Harold knew what had happened before he switched the light on. Beathan must have brought the bottle of pills with him because he hadn't had the chance to go out and get them here. A look at the label confirmed they had come from a pharmacy in Cnocaid. There was a note on the table opposite the foot of the bed. Harold read it, folded it carefully and kept it on him at all times thereafter.

He had gone back to his room and dressed, putting the letter in his pocket, and everything else he did had been an automatic reaction. He knew what the family would want him to do, the protection he had to provide. They would all say it was to safeguard Beathan's name, and his wife and child, from the unpleasant headlines that the truth might provide. Harold knew the first priority of any Sutherland was to protect the bank. The family had always been careful to hide the struggles some of its members had.

At Challaid International Airport he stepped off the plane and into a car waiting on the tarmac. He knew the driver worked for the chairman, Nathair Sutherland, their great-uncle and the man who ran the bank and so ran the family. The driver said nothing as they went down around the loch and up the west side to Barton, stopping at Cruinn Pier where a boat took Harold across to Eilean Seud. He felt as though he hadn't slept for days and he was hungry again, but he had to do this. He had to show he had the mental strength to perform a horrifying task. The family would be judging.

There were fewer than he expected in the high-ceilinged drawing room of the chairman's mansion. Nathair and his wife, newly widowed Daisy, Harold's mother Marcail, and Rodrick, who had organized his return.

"Harold," the chairman said, "sit down. You look ready to drop."

That was, he knew, an invitation to talk, to tell them everything that had happened, so he did. He omitted nothing but the girls they had picked up, telling anything that might be relevant. He told of the bottle of pills, the few he had picked off the sheets and put back in the bottle, the bottle now in his bag, unseen by anyone else. Rodrick would make sure the cause of death was put down as natural causes, the family untouched by the shame of suicide. He took the note from his pocket.

"It was lying on the table in his room. There was no envelope, so I've read it," he said, passing it to the chairman.

Nathair didn't even glance at it, passing it instead to Daisy who read it quickly. She looked as if she had just stopped crying and was determined never to start again. When she was finished she passed the note back to the chairman.

I have to do this. It's not that I want to, this isn't a choice, it's something forced on me. I understand the burden this will place on the family, especially Daisy and Simon who will have to carry this for the rest of their lives, and if there was another way I would take it. I have always, deep in my heart, known that father's death was what he wanted, and I think I understand why he chose it, because there were no other options. He was right. I'm sorry.

Beathan Sutherland.

16

THERE WAS no way of getting a view of 5 Geug Place without driving up and parking outside, and there was no way an aging Fiat Punto could park on that street and not draw unwanted attention. The question was how long Darian and Sholto could sit there eyeballing the gates to Simon Sutherland's house before the presence of the working class made the locals, and their security staff, jittery.

Sholto turned onto Geug Place, its end hidden by the tall trees on either side. The foliage was intended to keep the large houses behind the tall gates hidden from the road, and they mostly served their purpose well. You had to get close to see that there were driveways behind those gates and no matter the strength of your prescription glasses you wouldn't be able to spot the houses themselves. They parked in the passing place closest to the gate of Simon Sutherland's house and sat watching it across the road.

Darian said, "I can see half a gate and nothing else."

"You're not looking close enough then. I can see half a gate and at least three security cameras, maybe four if that thing in the tree there isn't a bird... It flew away. Okay, three."

"Not a surprise, is it? All the houses round here probably have a paparazzi of cameras outside for security. And someone who doesn't want to leave the house is probably paranoid about other people getting in."

"See, for all the swings you've taken at it there you've still missed the point. Security cameras mean a security team watching the pictures, but we were told only the uncle, the driver and the housekeeper ever get into the house. If someone's seeing us and thinks we're suspicious, who comes to shoo us away?"

"They might have security staff somewhere near here, in another building."

Sholto shook his head and said, "All the other buildings on this street are other people's giant houses."

"You could squeeze a few small buildings onto Sutherland's land behind that gate. He doesn't want other people in his house but surely they're allowed into other buildings nearby if he never leaves his own."

"We'll see what shows up, but be ready to pretend you're sorry for causing alarm."

Enough time passed for a security team to arrive from streets away but no one appeared and they sat in silence watching a closed gate. It did occur to Darian that the joke was rather on them, sitting watching nothing while security guards watched them from a comfortable office somewhere nearby. He didn't mention that to Sholto because why turn boredom into depression?

After twenty minutes the gates began to open slowly and Sholto said, "Put on a hat and hang onto it, we've got action."

There were long seconds as the electric gates slid back and then nothing. No car emerged. Instead, eventually, a short woman in her fifties with the black hair and tanned skin of a Caledonian walked out and marched straight for them. She had thin lips and small eyes, a round shape to her. She stepped beside the passenger window and rapped on it with her knuckles with just enough strength to suggest she was giving real thought to putting her fist through it.

Sholto cleared his throat loudly, the internationally recognized signal that he was going to do the talking, pressed the button to drop the window and leaned across Darian to smile out of the window as he said, "Can we help you, love?"

The woman took a shocked step back from the grinning mug, scowled and said in an accent that retained only trace amounts of its original Panamanian, "Don't call me love because I have no love for you. If you want to help me you can tell what you're doing parked out on the street like this."

"We're looking for a young woman who's gone missing, name of Freya Dempsey, thirty-one, about your own height, shoulder-length blond hair, pretty, wouldn't say boo to a goose if she had time to kick it in the face first. Have you seen her at all?"

"You're police?"

Having decided to be honest about their reasons for being there Sholto was compelled to stick to the risky strategy. Besides, one thing he had told Darian repeatedly they mustn't do was pretend they were policemen. Impersonating the law was a good way to piss off the police in half a nanosecond and an ingeniously stupid way to ruin your own investigation.

"No, we're not police, we're independent researchers, but we are working in conjunction with the police on this case."

"I haven't seen this woman. Why are you looking for her here?"

"You work for Simon Sutherland, don't you? It was actually him we wanted to see, just to find out if he might have seen her, or if he might have heard anything about her."

"Heard anything about her? Don't be so stupid, he couldn't have heard anything about this woman, you're wasting your time and mine and I am not a person who has time to sit looking at a gate all afternoon."

Before the housekeeper could leave Sholto said, "William Dent had contact with Freya Dempsey, and we know William Dent comes to this house, he delivers food here."

Darian chipped in, "Quite a lot of food for one person."

The housekeeper, determined to win some part of the argument, said, "Some of that was cleaning materials for me to look after the house. It's a large house to look after."

Sholto said, "Can I ask you your name?"

"My name is Olinda Bles. I am resident here; I have had my passport for nearly thirty years so you can't threaten me with that."

"I certainly wasn't going to threaten you, Miss Bles, I wouldn't think of it. The last time I threatened a Panamanian lady I had to put my food through a blender for the next three or four days, and you don't want to know what that many Chinese takeaways look like blended."

"Huh, well, maybe you deserved it."

"Well, yeah, I probably did. Listen, Miss Bles, it's a bit silly us talking through a car window out on the street like this. Can we not come in and talk to you and Simon in the house?"

The look she gave him suggested he had just invited her to the International Space Station for a cup of tea. Before she gave what seemed like an inevitable dismissal of the idea she stopped and looked up and down the lane, thinking about things she had no intention of sharing.

"You say you're working with the police?"

Sholto nodded with the conviction of a reluctant liar and said, "In conjunction with them. We're working...in conjunction with them."

"Maybe it would be right for you to come in. Mr. Sutherland has done nothing wrong, and this will stop you coming back because you won't be welcome back, but you must respect that he has very strict rules in his house, and it's necessary that you keep to them. You will only be allowed into one room and you must leave nothing behind, you understand?"

Having not planned on parting with anything for the privilege of entry Sholto said, "Sure, yeah."

They both got out of the Fiat and followed Olinda Bles through the gates and up the curved, cobbled driveway to the house. Behind them Darian heard the electric gate begin to slide shut.

17

FROM THE outside the house didn't look like a home, rather the sort of cavernous modern steel structure a museum would build on the outskirts of town to store its less attractive artifacts out of public view. The original house was still there, a pretty mansion with a hundred years of genteel life written in every stone, but now looked like a small bird trapped in the jaws of a metal wolf, the new extensions sticking out the back and right side. They had obviously been added at different times, and although the presumably expensive architect had made every effort to design something striking, in this setting they couldn't look anything other than monstrous and threatening.

What stood out for Darian as he walked up the drive to the front door of the house, part of the original building, was how little there was to see. On either side of the driveway there were lawns and the grass was cut short but there were no flowers or shrubs whatsoever. The only trees were those ringing the garden wall and there was no evidence of garden furniture. The windows of the building were all covered by blackout blinds so there was no chance of seeing in and there was one car on the drive, a little hatchback he assumed was the housekeeper's. Darian couldn't see a garage and assumed Simon Sutherland had no car of his own.

Olinda Bles led them into a hallway that was remarkable only for its pristine state: it was clean and bare. The floor was dark wood, as was the staircase to the right, and both looked polished enough to slide along with minimal propulsion. There was no furniture and nothing on the walls. Miss Bles turned right and along a long corridor and through to a room that was, very obviously, part of the extension. The wooden floors gave way to black tiles, the walls were plain white, and there was a huge window to their right covered entirely with a white roller blind. The high-ceilinged room was totally empty, with nowhere for them to sit, but this was where Miss Bles wanted them to wait.

She said, "You will stay in this room and you will not go into any others. If you do I will call the security team and have them throw you out."

Darian said, "There's a security team?"

"There is, and if they want to keep their jobs they will do what I tell them so you will do what I tell you."

"Are they here, the security team? In the building?"

"No, but they're close."

As she turned to the door behind her, which led deeper into the extension, Sholto said, "When was the last time Simon left the house?"

It took her a few seconds to decide to answer and when she did she threw it hastily at them. "It was a few months after his mother died, so he would have been fifteen. That was nine or ten years ago. They forced him out and he didn't want to go. He didn't speak a word to anyone for months afterward, so they didn't try again."

"So they built the extensions around him?"

"Yes. He didn't enjoy it but he insisted they be built. He needed the room. But that is not why you're here. I'll get him, you'll have a few minutes and no more and if you say something I don't like it is over."

Now she went through to the extension and left them in the meeting room. Alone in each other's company in the bare room, Darian said, "What do you suppose he needs all this room for?"

Sholto shook his head. "Normally with rich young men it would be frivolous crap that my life savings wouldn't buy a fraction of, but he doesn't seem to be the frivolous crap type."

"He doesn't seem the any-crap-at-all type."

"I don't suppose there's any harm left in asking him because we're not getting a second interview no matter how we play this one. Just being here burns every bridge in Challaid that might lead us to a Sutherland, even the one across to Vinny's Dr. Watson."

There was movement behind the door Miss Bles had left through and it opened. She led in Simon Sutherland for their first look at him. He was tall and thin and pale enough to inspire Bram Stoker, and there was a clear resemblance to both Phil and Harold Sutherland, especially in the shape of the round mouth, but Darian could also see sharpness in the blue eyes that all Sutherlands near the center of the family tree seemed to share. He had a thin face and high forehead, and his long fingers were entwined as he stood in front of them.

Sholto said, "Thanks for talking to us, we appreciate this."

Simon nodded and didn't say anything, remaining just inside the door so that he wasn't close enough for them to touch. Neither Darian nor Sholto made a move to shake his hand as good manners would usually dictate because he obviously didn't want that.

Sholto, convinced he was the less threatening of the two, said, "We won't keep you long, Simon. There are just a couple of questions we wanted to ask you. Miss Bles will already have told you that we're looking for a woman called Freya Dempsey, and I wondered if that name meant anything to you."

Simon shook his head and said quietly, "No, it doesn't, sorry."

"You've never seen her, met her, heard about her?"

"No, I never have."

"You know William Dent, Simon?"

"Yes, I know Will."

"What does he do for you?"

Sholto, bored with yes or no answers, had asked him something that required more and Simon looked annoyed by it as he replied, "He's a driver for my uncle Harold, sometimes he brings my shopping here, that's about all."

He had, of course, a posh end of the Challaid accent, smoother than a cue ball and less obviously designed to speak Gaelic. Still, there was a hint of something in it that Darian didn't think was local, as if he was a young man who didn't hear a lot of other Challaid accents so was influenced by the housekeeper and what he saw on TV instead.

"And Will Dent never mentioned her? Because he has met her."

"No, not to me."

"Does anyone else come to the house, other than Miss Bles and Will?"

"My uncle Harold comes round now and then."

"That's it?"

"Yes, just those three."

"Okay, well, last question then, Simon. Why do you need so much space when you're living here on your own?"

Simon seemed shocked by the question, as though it were more intrusive than Sholto realized. He said, "I like to keep things, my own things, so I need it."

It was a halting, uncertain response, as though he felt the need to justify it, which from someone else might have seemed guilt-ridden, but from Simon Sutherland appeared no more than the words of a man not used to talking to strangers.

That was the end of the interview and Simon left through the same door he had entered from while Miss Bles led Sholto and Darian out of the house and down the driveway to the gate.

"You can see he has nothing more to say to you, he knows nothing about this woman, there's no way he could. He doesn't leave the house, he doesn't have people here and he doesn't like to touch people."

Sholto said to her, "Why did you let us in to talk to him?"

"To get rid of you."

With that, Miss Bles walked back up to the house, the gates sliding shut automatically behind her. Darian and Sholto got into the Fiat and Sholto started it with his usual entreaty, "Come on, Fiat, don't fail me now."

Darian said, "What did you think of that?"

"I think if you told me there were bodies piled up in that place I wouldn't call you a moron straightaway. And I don't believe for a second that she let us in to get rid of us."

"So why did she let us in?"

"That, my boy, is the next wee puzzle we have to crack."

DIARY

15/05/2018

Today was more difficult because there were visitors. I slept in W last night but woke earlier than usual today. Olinda came to the room and told me there was a car across the road with two men in it. I got up then. I laid out Tuesday's clothes and went to the bathroom to wash. I finished the bottle of shampoo in the shower so it will go to N now. I can see it there with the others. When I went out of the bathroom and through to 5 Olinda was waiting for me. She told me the two men were working with the Challaid police. They wanted to talk to me and so I met with them in the white room. That made the rest of the day much more complicated for me.

I did my best to work out how much time I spent in the white room. I tried to make sure I got times right for the other rooms throughout the day. Even now I'm not honestly sure I did. I spent less time in the white room later to try and make up for it.

After the men's unwelcome visit I went round W and touched each item that requires it. My mind was pushed sideways by these men being in my house. Olinda was right about having the white room set aside for this sort of thing though. The thought of strangers among my items makes me sweat and shiver. Just touching the items that needed touching made me realize how important it is men like them never get in. They would disturb every room and every item.

I tapped all the outdated remote controls and the old video players. I touched the old game controllers and ran my finger along the top of every book. The room settled down quickly when I did. All the disruption of me being late, of me being in the white room, was forgotten. It wasn't the same, not for the whole day, but it wasn't as bad as perhaps it could have been.

The whole day was now inevitably off balance. I knew N had been waiting for me. Every room had an atmosphere when

I arrived. N never takes long to settle, light billows through it in seconds. It's the room other people would understand least. That's why I care for it so much. That's why it forgives. I opened each sealed box for a few seconds to let all the wrappers and cartons know I was there.

I went up the stairs and touched every item of clothing on the rails but one. All but the bra that scares the room. N is the boldest room because everything can still serve its purpose, just not for me. I've outgrown the clothes. I can't wear them. That's what they exist for and I can't use them at all. I spent time there to let them know they won't be forgotten.

Being in 5 felt heavier than usual today. Whenever the day is damaged being among mother's things is more difficult. The pain of struggling reminds me of how strong she always was. How hard she tried. When a person dies they leave a gap, and it doesn't shrink. It's forever there, standing broad in the very center of your existence. You're always stepping carefully around it, trying hard not to fall in. Every sidestep you make provides another stinging reminder of what you've lost. There are days 5 can be a happy place but not today. Today it was hard and I felt painfully beaten by it by the time I left.

Tomorrow will be better. I will sleep the first half of the night in W and the second in N. I hope there will be no interruption tomorrow and time will be in the right place. When everything is done properly the world is a place of calm. I can live like that. Hopefully no more visitors. To think of people from outside coming and upsetting this place is too much for me. I'll struggle to sleep tonight if I think about it any more.

18

DARIAN AND Sholto sat in the office, putting reports together in lieu of anything more productive, Sholto trying to write out a suitably polite but firm reminder to PINE Insurance that they still hadn't paid for the work done. People who had never hired them before were the most likely to think they had an excuse not to pay at all. Having refused his offer to chase the money to San José, Sholto was nervous the company were now planning to pretend the whole thing had never happened. He wouldn't allow that because he knew they were under pressure from past scandals and would have to cough up for silence.

They were actually waiting for a phone call while this attempt at looking busy was going on. Not one they were looking forward to, but Sholto had his excuses ready for whichever Sutherland called up and shouted in his well-prepared ear.

He said, "It'll be Harold Sutherland first because he's the one that looks after the boy."

Darian said, "The boy is twenty-five years old and he's entitled to talk to whoever he wants. We were invited in."

"Oh, aye, by the housekeeper, and don't think for a second she won't throw us under a fleet of busses if the pressure cranks up. She knew what she was doing, all that stuff about us working with the police, that was so she can pretend she thought we were the police, accuse us of misleading her, like she wasn't sharp as a tack and with better English than the two of us."

"It was you that said we were working in conjunction with them."

"Darian, it's very rude to throw a man's words back in his face, especially when they were as carefully chosen as mine."

"Once the uncle finds out we'll have Phil Sutherland after us as well."

"Your friend Vinny can hold him back if he wants us to keep on helping."

Darian didn't ask who would hold the lawyers back. They waited all day and the two occasions on which the phone rang it was a previous client asking for another receipt after losing the last one and someone assuring them that their computer needed to be fixed. Sholto claimed that he didn't have a computer, that he'd never heard of such an invention, didn't trust modern technology and did not, in fact, own a telephone, at which point he hung up.

The clock ticked round to eight minutes to five, which Sholto decided was exactly the right time to go home.

"I've had enough of doing very little. You get in touch with Vinny and update him, and if he doesn't have anything else to offer then we pass what we know to DS MacNeith and let her take shelter from the hail of Sutherland lawyers if she goes after Simon."

Sholto put the files into the cabinet and locked it before putting his laptop into his bag. Darian left his laptop in the office but all the files that mattered were stored only on the little memory stick he put in his pocket and took home with him. Sholto locked the office behind them and they made their way downstairs together, both with the mid-investigation blues. It happened a lot in difficult cases, the sort that more often than not went unsolved, the sense that they had reached a point where the roads all around them were blocked. There were people who seemed worthy of further inspection but there was nothing approaching the sort of proof that even the worst of Challaid's collection of erratic judges would be convinced by. It was hard not to slip into a funk.

While Sholto turned right to walk down to Dlùth Street where he parked his car, Darian turned left and walked up to Glendan Station. He had two travel cards for the train line, one for work and one for personal use. He could claim the cost of traveling the city to the client when it was for work, but this was going home. He took the train through the tunnel and across to the next stop, Bank Station. From there it was a pleasant stroll to his flat.

Darian always enjoyed that walk, especially at this time of year, going up Fàrdach Road and then cutting round the back of the building, walking along the large square of grass that served the four L-shaped buildings around it. There were washing lines and when the sun made an appearance it would be filled with kids kicking balls around. They tried to play in the rain too until someone stopped them for ruining the grass, but this day was rare in its pleasantness. There were four boys booting each other more than the ball and using a stretch of wall without windows as the goal, the three outfield players pausing their mutual assault only to try and chip the keeper in a pale imitation of the goal Arthur Samba had scored for Challaid FC against Hearts in the league the previous Sunday. The largest of the boys kept claiming his chips were dropping in despite the fact that he was endangering first-floor windows and Stretch Armstrong couldn't have caught them. None of the others argued with the bigger boy as Darian walked in through the back door.

The building was better than a man on Darian's salary should have been able to afford. The three Ross siblings had gotten an even split of the proceeds from the sale of the family home after they were done living in it, their mother dead and father in prison. As Darian walked along the corridor the place smelled of the polish the janitor used on the floors. His feet tapped out an echo as he skipped up the stairs to the first floor, round the corner and then up to the second.

Someone was on the landing already. A man in his thirties with a slack gut even his nice coat couldn't hide. He had dark hair, the puffy lips of a low-quality boxer and bags under his eyes. Darian's first thought was that he was with Challaid Police. Then he realized the man's suit was too good for that and his mind leapt from police to gangster, although he couldn't work out what he might have done to upset that lot.

"Darian Ross?"

The man had the local accent of someone raised by a Caledonian parent, which told Darian exactly nothing.

"Might be."

"Alan Dudley. I'm with Raven Investigators."

Like a hitman's bullet Raven staff always came in twos and were always unwelcome. The other one was presumably out front.

"What do you want?"

"I'm here with a job offer. You're wasting your time at clown college, come work at a place where you'll actually learn how to do the job."

"I'm learning plenty."

"Bad habits don't count."

"I'll take my chances."

"You only get one chance, Darian, and you're pissing yours away working for a man that can't protect you from all the wrong enemies you're making."

Darian frowned and said, "And what enemies would those be?"

"If you don't know that much then you have got problems. This was your one chance, Darian. I'm about to walk right past you and leave you way behind. You can stop me by saying you'll come work for us."

Maybe it was all the very many times he had heard Sholto bad-mouth Raven, or the times he'd heard other more reliable witnesses disparage them just as loudly. Maybe it was because Dudley was a cretin who said work for instead of work with; even though it was factually correct it seemed like an attempt to make him feel junior. Whatever the reason, the thought of going to work at Raven ranked alongside lava-surfing on Darian's list of things to do.

He said, "Off you go then."

Dudley scoffed and stepped forward, shoving past Darian. Being young and full to the brim with vim, Darian shoved back. Dudley pushed hard, pressing him against the wall, getting right in his face and hissing through his small yellowed teeth, "I'm going to enjoy bringing you down, Ross, you and the old wanker on Cage Street. Thank fuck you turned us down."

Darian, expression unchanged, said, "Spit on your lips after one little push? I wouldn't work for you if you were holding my balls for ransom. You're the clown, Dudley, right out of a Stephen King novel."

Dudley scoffed again and went quickly down the stairs, his footsteps echoing behind him. He'd come with two destructive messages and had delivered them both. A job offer and then a threat. Darian went into the flat.

19

DARIAN GOT something to eat because that was the reason he had gone home in the first place. He would have described it as dinner but the word sandwich would also be true and his definition of what constituted a meal was not widely shared. When he had finished the feast of bread and ham he called up Vinny.

The cop said, "I'm working tonight, but it's okay, come to the Darks on Conrad Drive, meet me backstage."

So Darian was out of the flat again, walking back down to Bank Station and taking the train, this time on his work card, up to Three O'clock Station in Whisper Hill. It took five minutes just to get off the overcrowded platform and along the concourse to the door and from there another twenty to get down to Conrad Drive, a street that ran across from Docklands Street to the train tracks. Dark, Dark, Dark was a graceful music venue with a long history and strong reputation, one of few venues in The Hill that work had never taken him to but his social life had.

At the entrance Darian asked a woman working there if she had seen Vinny and she told him to go up the stairs at the side of the foyer and follow the corridor along to the back. Darian did as he was told and found himself turning onto a walkway with an open space looking down from above the stage where a man was playing guitar and singing beautiful songs to a couple of hundred quietly happy people. Vinny was standing watching.

"So why does this gig need a police goon like you to work it?"

Vinny whispered, "It doesn't. I know the owner, Lyall Maddock, a reformed cop, he's a mate. Every time there's a gig on I want to see but I'm working he calls up the station and asks for me to come along and keep the peace. They know it's a swizz but they let it slide, means I can't say no when they send me to police a venue populated by screaming nutjobs trying to bottle each other."

They had been whispering low and fell silent as they listened to the song "Stained Glass." When it was finished and the crowd below applauded Vinny turned to Darian and said, "So what's the news?"

"Speculative. Every avenue we've gone down has been a complete dead end except maybe Dent and Simon Sutherland, and they're both maybes at best. We went to Simon Sutherland's house and got in and he was as odd as every other number. That's probably an offensive way to describe someone with his issues but..."

"True?"

"Aye."

"Did he know anything about Freya?"

"He said no, but there wasn't a convincing word in him. Add to that the housekeeper letting us inside in the first place. She didn't have to but she wanted to, and I don't think it was to help us. There are secrets in that barn of a house and we'd need to have a proper sweep of the place to find them."

Vinny nodded with the expression of a man about to make a friend do something he didn't want to. He led Darian along the corridor and down the stairs, out through the front door and across the road to The Whaler's, the sort of all-night café that served you a plate of grease which, if you were one of the lucky ones, might have something solid in it. It was a good place to go if you wanted to test the mettle of your digestive system, and Phil Sutherland was already there. Vinny and Darian sat opposite him and his usually distant expression took another backward step.

Vinny said, "Darian has a wee update on the case and you're not allowed to piss your pants about it."

Darian said, "I'm sorry that I went to your cousin's house."

"You *what*? You went to Simon's house? What for?"

"You hadn't heard already?"

"No, I'm not in contact with Simon."

"But you speak to your uncle and your uncle speaks to Simon. I would have guessed he'd have called your uncle as soon as we left and your uncle would be straight onto you. We were round there this morning."

"Right after I specifically asked you not to go."

"Pretty much."

"Maybe my uncle hasn't heard yet. I don't know his exact relationship with Simon, how often they speak. I don't know what anyone's relationship with Simon is like."

"I'd be surprised if your uncle didn't know something because when I got home this afternoon there was a Raven agent at my flat flapping his dark wings, offering me a job with them that I'm sure would have involved leaving every member of your family the hell alone. When I turned it down he all but threatened to peck my eyes out."

Vinny said, "Raven, that shower of pissants. At least you and Sholto are honest in your dishonesty. I can't stand people who pretend to play fair."

Phil said, "They tried to buy you? That does sound like it might be Uncle Harold's style. He would try to put out a fire with money before he thought about water. But that's just him trying to protect the company."

"Not him trying to protect his driver, or his nephew?"

"You can't actually think Simon had anything to do with Freya going missing? The poor sod hasn't left the house in years. How could he do it?"

"With the help of a shifty driver who treats violence as casual amusement."

Phil shook his head. "I don't buy that. Simon, the way he is, he would never get involved in something as messy as this."

"Simon the way you think he is, perhaps. Maybe there's more to him than we know, like what does he need all that space for?"

"The story I heard is that he keeps everything that comes into the house and doesn't have the ability to walk back out. Every single thing he's ever owned. If Freya had gone into the house and, worst-case scenario, wasn't able to walk back out, she would still be there, which means the housekeeper would have seen some sign of her."

"The housekeeper who let us in, like she wanted us to see something?"

Phil didn't look at all ready to be convinced by that. He shook his head but said, "There's a simple enough way to solve this. I go to the house tomorrow and have a look around and if I see something I'll let you know. If something happened in that house, and I think you've wandered off the edge of the map looking for a clue there by the way, then we'll know."

Darian nodded and said, "Maybe Simon has nothing to do with it, but Dent might and he has access to that property as well. It's a huge space, and I think you, me, Vinny and Sholto should all go."

Phil said, "No, no way will he let four in and I wouldn't try to force him. You and me then. Vinny, you stay out because it's too personal; I don't want you putting heat on a fractured mind. Me and you, Darian, and any link to Freya will stand out like a sore thumb in there. We go and we put an end to this one way or the other."

"Okay, fine, just us two. I'll meet you there at nine."

Phil stayed in the café to finish sucking mouthfuls of grease off his fork and Vinny went back across the road in less of a mood for the music. His mind, Darian knew, wasn't on Freya but on their son, Finn. What was he going to tell the boy if the worst ended up being confirmed? Darian tried not to think about it on the train home.

20

THE FOLLOWING morning was a Monday and the traffic was horrendous as Sholto drove Darian back up to Geug Place. When they arrived they found Vinny and Phil already there, both in street clothes. Vinny had driven them up in his car, which looked like it had finished the Dakar Rally about ten minutes earlier and had parked in the passing place across the road that Darian and Sholto had used the day before. There wasn't room for a second vehicle so Sholto had to park in front of Simon Sutherland's gates.

Vinny and Phil walked over and Phil said, "I managed to have a difficult conversation with Simon and Olinda, the housekeeper. They've both agreed we can go in, just the two of us, but there are conditions. I'm pretty sure this has already upset him, and I think what we're doing will take him months to recover from. If it wasn't Freya we were looking for I don't think I'd let it happen."

Standing on the road beside Sholto's car Vinny said, "Yes you would. You're a cop. You have a cop's instincts, whether you want them or not. Whoever it was you would want to find her."

Before Phil could think of a humble reply the gates began to slide open. The four men stood in silence and watched as Olinda Bles came into view, walking down the driveway toward them. She stood on the threshold with her arms crossed and looked out at them as though they were barbarians she had been sent to negotiate with when she'd much rather go to war with them instead.

"If you were not police you would not even get as close as you are now to the house. And you, you should know what this will do to your own cousin."

Phil nodded slightly and said, "I do know, and I'm sorry about it, but this is very important. It'll be me and Darian coming in and we'll be as respectful as possible."

She made a wordless noise that dismissed utterly the value of their respect and turned to walk up the drive. Darian and Phil followed in her furious wake. As they walked Darian noticed her slip a hand into the pocket of her black trousers and suddenly the gate began to close, so that explained that little mystery. He glanced back over his shoulder to see Vinny standing on the road, looking nervously through the bars at them, Sholto sitting on the bonnet of his car.

They went in through the front door and turned right to reach the same bare room Darian had found himself in the day before. This time Simon was waiting for them. He looked like a man wishing the room was even emptier, crushed by the weight of the new arrivals.

Phil nodded and said, "Thanks for letting us in, Simon. How are you?"

"I have been better. How are you, Philip?"

"Sorry about all this. We'll try and make it as fast as we can, and once we've ruled out what we need to rule out this will be over and you won't see us again."

Miss Bles said, "He shouldn't have to see you now. If you're going to be here then you're going to follow house rules."

Both Darian and Phil said, "Okay."

"You will both take your shoes off and leave them in this room. Neither of you will touch anything. Nothing, okay? You don't lay a finger on anything you see in there. You will only go places I take you, so do not try to wander off on your own. If you don't like those rules you can leave now."

Darian and Phil looked at each other and nodded their agreement.

They removed their shoes and stood by the door. Miss Bles did the leading, Darian and Phil the following, while Simon Sutherland drifted around behind them looking on the verge of tears. The first room they went into was enormous, more a warehouse than a home, and all the way along the bare floor were metal shelves packed with all manner of useless items that anyone else would have thrown out long ago. Among it were three clear plastic boxes full of neatly tied up cables, another with old telephones with their cables curled up behind them. On another shelf there was an old PlayStation 1, a controller plugged into each port and neatly laid out in front of it, a memory card in its slot and a stack of old games beside it. On the next shelf along was a PlayStation 2 with a couple of controllers and a much larger collection of games. Darian leaned in close to the PS2 games, not touching them, and saw *Final Fantasy 10* and *Sly Cooper* were at the front.

He glanced across at Simon and said, "These aren't in alphabetical order?"

Simon looked insulted by the question, as though he thought Darian was making fun of him. "They're all in the order I got them."

"When was that?"

"I got those when I was about nine or ten years old."

Darian and Phil moved around the room, taking it all in, Miss Bles always hovering within striking distance should either of them raise a hand toward the belongings. Phil looked stunned by it, his cousin's entire life laid out on display like that. He had known some of Simon's health issues, but family members speaking of it meant little until the scale was visible before you. Having completed a careful circle of the room Darian turned to Miss Bles.

She said, "Upstairs."

More of the same was waiting, another long, tall room running most of the length of the extension with two smaller rooms off to the side. After a circuit of looking at what any other person would politely term unsightly garbage they were shown into a bedroom and bathroom that contained the absolute least those rooms reasonably could. Every item in every room was individually displayed so nothing could be hidden in a pile somewhere.

As they walked across a corridor to the top floor of the rear extension Darian said to Simon, "Why are all the items given so much room? Why not pile everything together?"

Simon said, "I'm not some hoarder. I give everything room."

In the upstairs room of the rear extension they found clothes that dated back to childhood. Some were well worn, none would have fitted Simon anymore, but all were either hung neatly on racks or had been folded and placed on shelves with the sort of care usually afforded to religious relics. Darian and Phil made their way down the aisles, Miss Bles close behind and Simon holding back near the door. Toward the end of the middle lane Darian came to underwear, pants and boxer shorts, socks and vests, and then the first thing that stood out. Among the scattered remains of a life it might seem hard for any item to catch the eye but there was a bra sitting alone on the top of a shelving unit.

Darian looked back over his shoulder at Miss Bles and said, "All the other clothes are his. Whose is this?"

She shook her head. "I don't know. I've never known, and I don't think he does either. It's been there for a long time, though."

Simon came round the corner at the top of the aisle and walked toward them. He stared at the plain black bra and said, "That's been there for more than a year, last January, I think. It just turned up. One day it wasn't there, next it was. I've never touched it."

"You never touched it?"

"No, it's not mine. It doesn't belong here."

"So why don't you throw it away?"

Simon looked at Darian as if he was an idiot, which, having seen the rest of the house and still asked the question, was not an unreasonable accusation. He said, "I don't throw things out, even if I don't want them here."

Darian and Phil both stared at it for a while. It was black, small and a bit grubby, like it had been put through the washing machine too many times and not been washed again for a couple of years since. Unlike Simon's own clothes it had been dumped in a heap instead of being laid out so it was harder to see all of it, but Phil noticed something.

He said, "The clasp is broken. Look, it's ripped from the edge there."

They both stared at it, thinking of a bra being forcibly removed. This one item, left to lie untouched by a man who couldn't throw it out even if he wanted to. Both Darian and Phil had heard enough stories of perpetrators keeping mementos, but Simon had known they were coming and did nothing to hide it.

Phil said, "You don't know who left it here?"

"I've asked all the people who come here. None of them know, or will admit it."

They toured the rest of the house. They saw his late mother's belongings, which gave them the chance to mentally compare her bra size with the one upstairs. Apart from the fact that not one of hers looked as if it had been bought at a supermarket they were also much too big to fit the owner of the mysterious one upstairs. They saw photos of the family through the years, including a group one showing a young Phil with his parents and a varied collection of aunts, uncles and cousins. Miss Bles led them through the rest of the original house, which felt like an empty home rather than the storage facility the rest of it did. There was nothing else to catch their beady eyes. When they were finished they returned to the bare white room and put their shoes back on.

Phil said, "Thanks for letting us in, Simon."

"Is this over now?"

"I doubt it. Don't you want to know where that bra came from?"

"Well, yes I do."

"Okay then."

They walked down the driveway and the gate slid open. A bored-looking Vinny and Sholto got out of the Fiat and stood expectantly.

Darian said, "We found a bra. He says it's been there since last January, that he doesn't know where it came from. We should call DS MacNeith."

21

I CAN feel it, you know. It's like pinpricks in my back."

Darian looked across the office at Sholto and said, "What are you talking about?"

"When a rich person is angry with me and they're hunting me down. There's going to be hell to pay and I'm all out of cash."

Vinny and Phil had gone to Cnocaid station to give details to DS MacNeith about the bra, Sholto having called already. They had known what would happen next. Simon Sutherland was arrested and taken to the station, leaving the house for the first time in a little over nine years. According to the text Vinny had sent it was the housekeeper, Miss Bles, who had put the fear of God into the arresting officers. Simon had been quiet while she had been extraordinarily loud when she found out why they were there. The police had taken the bra for tests to try and identify its owner.

Darian said, "Perhaps Harold Sutherland won't come after us. It's his nephew he'll be most annoyed with."

"Oh, Darian, no, that's not how these people work, has no one told you that already? I'll tell you how they operate. Behind closed doors he'll be fuming with Phil, sure he will, because that was a family betrayal, or that's how he'll see it. But people like the Sutherlands, very old money, very big money, their greatest skill is protecting what they have. It's probably genetic at this point, instinctive, like when the son of a great camanachd player turns out to be decent without trying. The last thing Harold Sutherland will do is allow anyone outside the family to think Phil is to blame. Protect the business, that's what they do. Someone else is going to have to become the enemy, and I'm willing to bet his impressively expensive lawyers will paint a large target on my sweaty back. Just thinking about it...I hope he phones rather than comes round. I can at least sound like my rectum isn't imploding underneath me but I can't look the part if he's in front of me."

They sat and waited for the phone to ring, wondering whether they would hear from an excited cop or a fizzing lawyer first. Instead they heard footsteps on the wooden stairs, more than one person making his way up to the second floor. Sholto closed his eyes and prayed that it was two of the three men from the data services company along the corridor. Instead there was a single knock on the door, and then, having clearly decided that knocking was a courtesy they didn't deserve, the door was flung open.

The expression on Harold Sutherland's face was one that had probably never been seen in public before. This was a man who prided himself on being friendly and charming but was now in a rage so powerful that only the presence of the lawyer beside him was holding back violence. The lawyer was a tall, skinny man in his forties with the look of a referee at a boxing match who feared both fighters were wearing knuckle dusters under their gloves. It was all he could do to stop himself from physically restraining his client.

In a near-trembling voice Harold said, "How much would it cost to purchase the use of your inconsiderable talents for this case, then? Hmm? To have you conduct a proper investigation."

Sholto chewed nervously on the question for a few seconds and said, "One billion pounds."

"Excuse me?"

"I intend either to die an honest man or a billionaire, Mr. Sutherland. One billion pounds."

"Good grief, the price of your virtue is going to cost you your business."

Darian said, "We're valuable men."

Harold Sutherland looked back and forth between Darian and

Sholto, the façade crumbling after his first, failed attempt, and said, "You bastards. You lying little bastards. You came to me for help and so I helped you, and in response you've tried to ruin the life of an innocent boy just so you can pretend you've cracked a case. Do you understand how long it's going to take Simon to recover from this? Do you care? Years. They'll question him and my lawyers, who are there now en masse, will destroy their scattergun of stupidity and lies and Simon will be home by the end of the day but the damage will have been done. You and that bloody police force. This isn't just a bad day for Simon; this is years of his life you've ruined."

Darian, assuming Sholto would be momentarily silenced by his phobia of the intimidatingly rich, said, "We certainly didn't mean to do that. We're trying to find Freya Dempsey, and I'm sure you can understand our urgency."

Harold Sutherland took a couple of steps toward Darian's desk, his teeth bared as if he was trying to decide which part of him to bite first. He said in a near hiss, "Don't you dare try to pretend that I'm the uncaring one here. I and my family have gone out of our way to help you find this woman on the basis of a tenuous connection, while you have bulldozed your way into my nephew's life and toppled over the contentment he's spent a decade trying to build. He had to try to find a balance that made life livable for him, and you've shoulder-charged it because you don't care about people, just the case in front of you."

"That's unfair. You don't know us."

"I know you're friends with PC Reno. I know he was the prime suspect before you decided to concoct this nonsense against Simon. I know you're going to suffer the heaviest blow I can throw at you, and I know I'm not going to stop swinging haymakers at you even after I've shut this place down and made you both unemployable in Challaid. I have a long memory and a long reach."

Harold turned and marched out of the office and his lawyer, seeming to think that it had gone better than expected, nodded and went after him.

Sholto breathed out heavily and grabbed the edge of his desk, or at least the folders hanging over it, and said, "Chee whizz."

Darian was looking out of the window, watching the young man walking uncertainly up toward the office. William Dent, presumably having dropped off his boss and ready to pick him up again. Harold still using his favorite driver. A loyal man, Phil had said. Harold and the lawyer emerged down below on Cage Street and walked quickly down to Dlùth Street, Dent alongside them now to show where he had parked.

Sholto said, "Oh, that was unpleasant, my guts are doing enough somersaults to win an Olympic bronze medal. Do we have any legal or semi-legal drugs that might help?"

"No. You can try downstairs. Mr. Yang will have some."

"That better not be a crack at his cooking. Even at a time like this I won't hear a word said against it."

"I mean he has a cupboard full of that sort of stuff for the family."

"Never mind, I'll ride it out. Have to keep riding for the rest of my life if he was serious about coming after us. The rich, Darian, they're nothing but trouble."

It was hard to argue and better not to, so he said nothing. Instead they waited to hear how the questioning of Simon Sutherland had gone. If he was guilty they were off Harold's hook.

BLOG POST

15/02/17

RUBY-MAE SHORT

04/08/96–12/01/17

They found my sister's body beside the train tracks in Whisper Hill a month ago and now all anyone ever talks about is her being a murder victim. There's nothing I want more than to see the police catch who killed her and I know that raising awareness of what happened to her is a part of that but someone needs to talk about who Ruby was when she was alive. She wasn't just a murder victim, she was a person.

The first flat we lived in was a small place on Mòine Road in Earmam that I mostly remember being damp and cold. I was a year and a half older than Ruby so I don't really remember her much as a baby but I do remember her as a toddler and always being on the move. Even back then she had so much energy. It's funny how the things that annoyed me most about her as kids are the things I miss the most now.

She was five when our parents divorced and a couple of years later our mum met our stepdad and we moved into a bigger, more modern flat in Bakers Moor. It was strange for us as kids, a time of upheaval, but the one constant was Ruby and her energy and happiness and loudness. She was always singing and dancing and had more space for it now. At Caisteal Secondary School she was involved in everything, dancing and acting and all sorts of clubs. She made friends easily and kept them forever. The people in her life meant everything to her, and she made time for each and every one.

As she got older she started to think about what she was going to do with her life, but she was so full of enthusiasm for so many things that she never really settled on one. I started engineering and when I got a placement with Duff she insisted we go out to celebrate. She was probably happier and more proud than I was, but that was Ruby. That was the last time we spent together and it was one of the best. Seeing her so happy, the way the energy radiated out of her and infected everyone around her, it's a memory of how special she was, how just being around her was a gift. I was on a ship that had just docked in New Edinburgh when I got the message saying she had been killed and Duff had me flown home to be with my family.

I hate having to write all that, even the good memories, because it means talking about Ruby in the past tense. Every mention of her life brings back memories of what we as a family have gone through in the last month. Hearing talk of what happened to her, newspapers and websites speculating about why a young woman was out for drinks and hinting at things I know are untrue and that I will never forgive them for suggesting. All those people want to talk about her death and the investigation into it. I want everyone to know that Ruby-Mae Short was not just a murder victim, Ruby-Mae Short lived.

Nathan Short

22

THE VISIT from Harold Sutherland had shaken the ground but they were still waiting for a phone call to say whether Simon had been charged or not. Waiting to hear what he had said under pressure.

Sholto was beginning to calm down to his usual mild discomfort when he said, "We shouldn't expect much of a result out of that interview. A good lawyer can make a decent cop's day very difficult but an entire team of very expensive and determined lawyers can run the rings of Saturn around the whole legal system."

"DS MacNeith is a good detective, she won't let this slip."

"No, not on purpose, not out of ignorance or stupidity, but she's spent her whole career learning how to dish out justice and she'll encounter an entire squad of goons who've spent their working lives helping others sidestep it. I don't like how long it's taking either. That boy, he was already cracked, so if he was going to fall apart it would have happened by now. The legal eagles must be holding him together."

"You really don't like lawyers, do you?"

Sholto shook his head. "They do important work and everyone should have one, but you can say that about bowels as well and I wouldn't want to shake hands with one of them without gloves on either."

"Would be worse without them."

"It would, yes, but when I was a cop I saw the difference between a good lawyer and a brilliant one. A good one could get you off the hook if the evidence said you deserved to go free, a brilliant one could set you free no matter what story the evidence told. I saw too many guilty people walk free from police stations because brilliant lawyers came up against mediocre police investigations."

Sholto didn't often hark back to his time as a detective at Cnocaid station, a period he hadn't much enjoyed. Darian thought it was partly because Sholto didn't like the job and partly because he didn't want to have to talk about Darian's father, his former colleague now in prison. Occasionally Darian was reminded that his boss just might have gone through a lot more in life than he cared to admit.

The problem with waiting for the phone to ring was that no one intended to call them. Instead they heard another set of feet making their way up the stairs and stopping outside the door, this time knocking and having the patience to wait to be let in. Sholto's desk was next to the door so he got up and opened it nervously. The woman on the other side of the threshold had dark hair and eyes and was wearing a red coat and black trousers. Her eyes were bright with mischievous laughter as she sauntered past Sholto and into the office, taking a good look around, a smirk on her wide mouth.

She said, "So this is the famous office of Douglas Independent Research."

Sholto closed the door before any other surprises could sneak past him and said, "We've met?"

"Oh, no, sorry. I've met your colleague before, though, not yourself. You must be the famous Mr. Douglas."

The second-to-last thing Sholto wanted to be was famous. He said, "I didn't think either me or my office were so well known. And your name is . . . ?"

"DC Angela Vicario, it was me who interviewed Ash Lucas when Darian brought him in, and I did a little work on the Folan Corey case as well."

Sholto's face lit up with joy at his memory's success as he said, "Oh, yes, that's right, I remember, we have sort of met, or were in the same place at the same time anyway, Sgàil Drive, when . . ."

The mood in the room collapsed into misery as they remembered the last and only time the three of them had been together. Darian had called Vinny for help that desperate night and some of the aid he'd brought had been in the form of the playful but razor-sharp DC Vicario. There was nothing as happy as a smiling blade.

She said, "I have come with what I think is good news, but not all good. I was called to Cnocaid station with a colleague because when they ran a check on the bra they found it matched one we were looking for. Do you remember the Ruby-Mae Short murder?"

Darian shook his head but Sholto said, "Young woman found dead on the tracks behind Misgearan. They never got anyone for that, did they?"

"No, we never got close. One thing we didn't make public was that when we found her body we didn't find a bra on her. There was a possibility that she had been wearing it and her killer had kept it as a memento. We're still waiting for DNA to confirm it but the bra is from the same store where she bought most of her underwear and I'm convinced it's Ruby's, plus Simon Sutherland says it turned up in his home last January, which is when she was killed."

Darian said, "Why would he admit that?"

She shrugged and said, "Perhaps it's a clever move; he knows we're going to identify the owner of the bra and he wants to set up his excuse as early as possible. Or it might be that someone is trying to make him look guilty. It's complicated, but I'm hoping to simplify it when we move him up to Whisper Hill and get him talking there."

"Has he said anything about Freya Dempsey?"

"Nothing. There's no sign of her, unfortunately, but if he was involved in what was done to Ruby then he's very dangerous and we can't expect to have a good outcome with Freya. Look, we all like Vinny at Dockside, he's like a cool older brother to a lot of the young officers and we want to find out what happened to Freya for his son's sake as well. Have either of you heard any mention of Ruby, or anything else about 12 January last year when she was killed? Any shred of info we can get on that might help us with Freya, too."

Both men shook their heads and Sholto said, "No, but we've

only been looking for Freya, only been asking questions about her. If her disappearance ties in with Ruby-Mae Short then we can start looking into that as well as part of the same investigation."

"Obviously nothing that might interfere with what we're doing, but if you could check what your contacts have to say that would help. I have to go; I need to sit next to my boss while he goes jousting with the sort of lawyers a rich man can buy, which should be fun. I'll keep you updated."

As he walked her the three steps to the door Sholto said, "We'll hunt around our contacts and let you know if we come up with anything."

DC Vicario stopped in the doorway and looked back into the office at Darian with a small smile before she said, "I like your famous little office, it's unassuming."

After closing the door behind her Sholto and Darian looked at each other with the shared expression of men who had just seen their case balloon out beyond their reach.

23

WITH THE phone in the office set to divert calls to Sholto's mobile they went downstairs to The Northern Song to get something to eat. The lunchtime rush had passed so they could sit at the table at the back and Mr. Yang brought their food to them, otherwise they could speak without fear of being overheard.

"You better start by telling me everything you remember about the Short case because I know nothing."

Sholto nodded. "I don't know a lot, to be honest, just what I read in the papers at the time. She was a twenty-year-old girl on a night out in Whisper Hill, nothing remarkable in that, drinking and the like, was spotted in Misgearan and a few hours later she was dead. They found her body the next morning; a train driver saw it from his cab so it can't have been hidden. It was dumped behind the fencing round the back of Misgearan so there was some attempt to keep it out of view."

"Tipped over the fence?"

Sholto shook his head as he stuffed some sweet and sour into his mouth. Darian was thinking of a person trying to lift a body over the ten-foot corrugated iron fencing behind Long Walk Lane, something that couldn't be done subtly.

Sholto, chewing rapidly, said, "No, it was over the line on the other side, I think. They didn't say that publicly, but they were looking for witnesses who might have seen anyone on Border Street, other side of the tracks, and the train driver who saw her was heading north to Three O'clock Station so I guess must have been on the left side of his cab, easier to spot her at speed. If we can get more information from the cheerful Miss Vicario we'll know for sure."

"You think Misgearan matters?"

"Maybe, maybe not. Short was drinking there on the night, and last I heard the police hadn't identified everyone she was drinking with. Given Dockside station's relationship with that place I would guess they've gotten every slice of information possible from the staff. We can also assume old lady Docherty would rather be roasted over a spit than install any cameras in the place and the boys from Dockside would probably agree with her."

"If the cases are linked then it rules out Vinny."

"That's an if. Sometimes one case leads to another, or gets tangled in another, without them being directly related. I know you want them to be linked because it would make the Sutherland boy front-runner. Before Simon leapfrogged over him Vinny was a prime suspect, and you want it to be anyone else, but Vinny is still number two on that list with the potential to reclaim top spot. I like Vinny, he's a nice guy, but never forget that nice people can do terrible things, too."

For a few seconds the only sound was that of eating until Darian said, "How do you know she's Miss?"

"Who, Short? She wasn't married, didn't have a boyfriend at the time either, they don't think."

"No, DC Vicario, you called her Miss Vicario a wee while ago."

"Did I? Well, she's not ringed, so I'm guessing. Is her marital status of any personal concern to you or was that question just professional interest in the accuracy of my statement?"

"Just curious about how well you know her."

"Less well than you and not nearly as well as I'd like, and I don't mean that in a smutty way because Mrs. Douglas is more than enough for a timid man like me. Vicario is smart and we know she's brave because she was willing to put herself in the middle of the Corey investigation. Just the sort of cop that would be a useful ally to have."

"You always said to steer clear of cops. I'm getting mixed messages here."

"Steer clear of the ones that don't like you, try and get a good relationship with the ones who do. Never personal, always professional. Simple enough."

"She seems easy to talk to."

Sholto said, "Says the man hoping to talk to her a lot more. You do like the strong and playful types, don't you, Darian? I've warned you a hundred times and a hundred times again, nothing personal with cops. Forget about anything unprofessional, okay, she has far more important people to talk to right now than you and, well, maybe even me."

"You think they'll get anything out of Sutherland?"

"They'll need to be more than smart and brave to manage. With all those lawyers around him he might be able to get out of that place in one piece, and you can be sure there's already a lot of pressure on Dockside to let the boy go. The Sutherland machine will be turning every cog at a furious pace to get the political help it needs. The bra is a heavy piece of evidence, but it might not be enough on its own to weigh down a member of that family."

Darian said, "He seemed vulnerable. Surely he'll fall apart if he's guilty."

"No, think about it, if he's guilty then he isn't really vulnerable at all. If he's guilty then all that stuff about never leaving the house was invention, and the Simon Sutherland we met is just a character he's dedicated most of his adult life to playing. Why would anyone go to such freakish lengths? Maybe to cover up the despicable things they like to do when no one's watching. That's the sort of character that belongs in a dodgy thriller movie and he'll have no problem handling the police."

Darian thought about that for a while before he said, "The story about leaving the house might still be true, and the compulsive hoarding. He didn't throw the bra away when he knew it would be seen and implicate him. He's a rich young man who could pay for help. Simon Sutherland doesn't need to go outside because Will Dent can trawl the streets for him, pick out the girls and do the dirty work of getting them back to the house. Was Ruby-Mae murdered at the track or somewhere else?"

"Well, that's another interesting question I don't know the answer to. We'll need to find that out as well. We'll also need to find out if Dent's thirst has ever brought him as far north as Misgearan on a cold January night for a dram or three. Time for us to start poking our noses around again."

Sholto paid for the meal before they left; no matter how often Mr. Yang tried to give them a discount for their loyalty Sholto always paid full price for the things he loved.

24

AS THEY were sitting in the traffic near The Helm roundabout in Bakers Moor, Darian got a message from Vinny. While Sholto tapped the car's steering wheel Darian read it to him.

"It's from Vinny. He's asking if we've heard anything?"

"Nothing he won't have heard already."

A car behind them beeped its horn and Sholto nearly jumped through the roof at the sheer bad manners of it.

Darian was considering not telling Vinny they were focusing on the Ruby case right now. He had hired them, albeit with no intention of paying them, to look for Freya and this might seem like a deviation from the job description, maybe even an acceptance that if she hadn't run of her own free will then she was probably dead. In the end Darian decided his reply should embrace the naive concept of honesty being the best policy.

"I'll tell him we're going to Misgearan, that there might be a connection to Ruby. He might know a lot more about it, it's his station."

The car inched forward until they were at the roundabout, which meant a long wait until Sholto saw a gap he considered big enough for his little car. Impatient people do not get into a car that Sholto Douglas is driving, and after more than a minute a gap appeared so large that even he was willing to drive into it. As he did Darian's phone buzzed again, another message from Vinny.

"He says he'll meet us there."

It took longer than it should have, and Darian wished his boss had listened to his suggestion to take the train instead, but they got to Fair Road and found somewhere to park. Long Walk Lane was quiet by its standards, not the drunkening hour yet, but there were always a few people hanging around outside Misgearan. There was no sign of Vinny so Darian led Sholto to the private side entrance because it was unlikely the cop would be waiting in the main bar, not if he was there to speak to the staff. A single knock and Caillic Docherty opened it in seconds, letting them in, closing it and leading them down the corridor, round a corner and along another corridor to a room Darian had never seen before, her office.

Vinny was there, sitting large on a small couch with a bright floral pattern, Phil Sutherland alongside him. The office was small but felt like it belonged in a different building, full of very green and quite ugly plants, in tubs on the floor and pots on an old, rickety-looking desk, with faded paintings of rugged landscapes on the walls. It was a room of brightness in a building where most people preferred the dark. It was a room that didn't fit with Darian's gloomy preconception of Caillic Docherty.

He said to her, "I didn't know you were a horticulturalist."

In her grumpy rasp she said, "There are eight hundred and twenty-seven interesting facts about me and I doubt you know more than two of them. Three now, if you count the plants."

As she closed the office door Vinny said to her, "So, Ruby-Mae Short, what can you tell us about her, Caillic?"

The look she gave him was damn near violent and would have set a herd of buffalo scurrying. Misgearan had an understanding with the cops from Dockside station and here was Vinny stomping all over it by dragging awkward questions about a serious case into her office. It was a minor and not unexpected betrayal.

She lifted the glasses that were on a string round her neck and put them on, saying, "There's always a consequence to talking. What is it here?"

Vinny said, "The man we're asking about works for a Sutherland. You're either pissing off me or a very rich man."

"I bank with them."

"Aye, but there are other banks, Caillic. We're the only police force in town."

"You'd be a better force if you had some competition. Let me have a look at him then."

Vinny took his phone from his pocket and got a picture of Will Dent up on it. She studied it carefully and shook her head.

"I don't know. I can't be sure. Not exactly a memorable-looking face, is he? It was January last year and it was busy the night the Short girl was in. I don't recognize him so he's not a regular, if he's been here at all. I remember telling the detective investigating it that the night she was in there were other new faces, one-off visitors. Thrill-seeking students and tourists looking for an authentic experience, a few lads off a boat I think, Caledonians. There was no trouble, though, and she wasn't draped all over anyone. The things they said about her in the papers, that's the bastards you want to be going after as well, the ones lying about some poor dead girl who can't argue back. She was no good-time girl, just a lassie on a night out."

Vinny said, "We'll focus on trying to catch the person who killed her first, maybe go for the ones who insulted her afterward. There's nothing else you remember?"

"Nothing I haven't told your better dressed colleagues and I didn't hold back a word, not for something like this, a girl getting murdered like that."

Caillic left them to use her office for a few moments and Vinny leaned forward on the couch to tell Darian and Sholto, standing by the door, what he knew of Ruby's case.

"I remember being called to it, myself and another cop, Seamus MacRae, first on scene. She had been dumped on the far side of the tracks, top of that wee hill over there, but she wasn't killed there. She'd been lying a few hours in the wet and cold, all we could do was secure the scene and hand it over to the suits. She had been placed there carefully, flat on her back, hands at her sides, not dumped.

No sign of disturbance in the area so she was killed somewhere else and taken there afterward, probably because that's around where she was picked up from. There were signs of sexual activity but that might have been after she was killed. She was conscious when she was strangled, apparently. There was alcohol in her system but less than I would have on a quiet night out, and there were no drugs. The missing bra was the big point of interest, either taken as a memento or ripped off during the attack and left behind by accident when the body was returned. I never heard of anyone becoming a meaningful suspect, certainly no mention of any Sutherland, or Dent for that matter."

Phil said, "I just don't believe Simon could have been involved, he's not capable."

Darian said, "They're certain the bra is Ruby's and not Freya's."

Vinny said, "It's not Freya's, it's not her size, it's for someone smaller like Short. I know Freya's size for a fact because every Valentine's Day she would send me to buy her lingerie out of spite because she knew asking the salesgirl for help made me cringe myself inside out. I wouldn't have minded if she'd ever worn what I bought."

"So it's Ruby's and it's probably been there since last January. Maybe someone put it there to set him up, but how many people ever get into that house?"

Sholto said, "If someone did go in with it would the security cameras have picked it up? I spotted a battery of them."

Phil said, "I know the team questioning him have already gotten access to the security footage. If there's a story to tell from it they'll find it."

"If someone else put it there then they'd know about the cameras, do something to stop them. But you should prepare yourself for your cousin knowing more than he's told us."

"You know how sometimes you just know someone isn't capable of doing something?"

Sholto smiled sourly and said, "I do, but sometimes you don't really know a person at all."

All four of them left Misgearan that evening without having touched a drop of alcohol, a rare enough event to be worthy of mention. Sholto drove Darian home and he went up to his little flat and sat at the living-room window looking out toward Loch Eriboll and the lights of a large boat that must have just left the Whisper Hill docks and was heading out to the mouth and into the North Atlantic. Ruby-Mae Short had been a young woman looking to have a night out and enjoy herself. When she had died she was the same age Darian's sister Catriona was when he was investigating the case. That night he messaged her to ask if she was okay. She was fine.

TRANSCRIPT OF SUSPECT INTERVIEW

16 MAY 2018

40 DOCKLANDS STREET, WHISPER HILL, CHALLAID, CH9 4SS

Suspect—Simon Sutherland

Lawyer—Kellina Oriol

Interviewing officers—DI Ralph Grant, DC Angela Vicario

18:53

DI Grant —I'm DI Ralph Grant, with me is DC Angela Vicario, interviewing Simon Sutherland, also present is Kellina Oriol, Mr. Sutherland's lawyer. Do you know why you're here, Simon?

Simon Sutherland —Because of the bra.

DI Grant —Because of the bra, the one we found in your house. Can you tell me who the bra belongs to?

Simon Sutherland —I don't know who the bra belongs to. It was left there.

DI Grant —In your house?

Simon Sutherland —Sometime last January. The exact date will be in my diary. One evening it wasn't there, the next day when I went through the house it was.

DI Grant —It's a big house, easy to miss it for a few days. Could you be wrong about the day it turned up?

Simon Sutherland —I know the exact date it turned up. I go round the house every single day. If there's change I see it straightaway.

DI Grant —And is there often a change?

18:54

Simon Sutherland —Never, except the bra.

DC Vicario —Did it upset you, Simon, having that bra there when you didn't put it there?

Simon Sutherland —Yes, it really did.

DI Grant —So why not get rid of it?

Simon Sutherland —I can't, I don't get rid of things.

DI Grant —You keep everything?

Simon Sutherland —Everything I can keep.

DI Grant —Mementos of your entire life, every moment collected in items and preserved in pristine condition in the safety of your house.

Simon Sutherland —I suppose so, yes.

DI Grant —So if you had a girl in the house so you could have fun with her you would want some memento of that, something to remind you of the good time you'd had together.

Simon Sutherland —That's not what happened. And it wouldn't be, because that's not how it works at all. I don't want to keep any of it, the things I keep. It's not because I want to have it, it's because I have to keep it all. I don't want anything added, any new things. They make it harder. I don't want that.

<u>18:55</u>

DI Grant —But you must have urges, Simon, every man does.

Kellina Oriol —Be careful, DI Grant.

DI Grant —I'm being exactly as careful as I need to be when investigating a murder, don't you worry about me. I'm right, though, aren't I, Simon? You must have some sort of sexual feelings, there are very few people that don't. You say you don't leave the house, so what happens to those feelings?

Kellina Oriol —You don't have to answer that, it's puerile. He's trying to embarrass you.

Simon Sutherland —That's okay, I'll answer. I don't go out and I don't like other people coming in. I've learned to accept the many things I can't have in life.

DI Grant —That must have been a very difficult thing to accept.

Simon Sutherland —It actually wasn't very. I don't miss things that haven't been a part of my life.

DC Vicario —So few people come into your home that you must have some idea of who could have been in last January and left the bra.

Simon Sutherland —I really don't know who brought it in. I don't know why anyone would do it.

<u>18:56</u>

Kellina Oriol —It should also be stated that Simon has willingly made all of his security information and footage, as well as his private diary, available to you in an attempt to help in any way possible.

DI Grant —Yes, he's been very helpful, up to a point. Tell me about Ruby-Mae Short.

Simon Sutherland —I don't know who that is, I'm sorry.

DI Grant —Ruby-Mae Short.

Simon Sutherland —I've never heard that name before, I'm sorry.

DI Grant —It was her bra we found in your house, torn and dirty.

Simon Sutherland —I don't know her.

DI Grant —We found her body by the railway tracks not too far from here, in the south of Whisper Hill, behind Long Walk Lane. Behind Misgearan, in fact, the bar she had been drinking in on the night she was murdered last January. Then her missing bra shows up in your house and now you claim you've never heard of her.

Simon Sutherland —That's because I haven't.

DI Grant —But her bra turned up in your house, quite possibly on the night she was killed, your diary and security footage might tell us for sure.

Simon Sutherland —I've already told you that I don't know how it got there.

DI Grant —You need to get real with me, Simon. All those security features in your house and you can't even take a guess about how the bra got in there?

18:57

Kellina Oriol —My client has already told you that he doesn't know, DI Grant, he's not going to magically learn it because you're sitting there verbally abusing him.

DI Grant —You'd be amazed how many people do.

DC Vicario —William Dent is one of the people who visits you regularly, isn't he?

Simon Sutherland —He sometimes brings the shopping, sometimes Olinda does.

DC Vicario —And do you talk with him much, discuss things?

Simon Sutherland —Not a lot, really. We talk, but not in any personal detail.

DC Vicario —When he delivers the shopping he has access to the house, though.

Simon Sutherland —Yes, he gets in.

DC Vicario —Who else has that sort of access?

Simon Sutherland —Olinda and Uncle Harold.

DC Vicario —Has William ever spoken to you about women, maybe bragged about girlfriends or offered to set you up with someone?

Simon Sutherland —He's offered to take me out to parties. He does that often. I think Uncle Harold encourages him to try to help me out. He does it to be polite and he knows I'll say no.

DC Vicario —You don't want to go out with him, party a bit?

18:58

Simon Sutherland —I do want to. I'm not able to.

DC Vicario —It must be very hard for you to be here now.

Simon Sutherland —Yes, it is, but I want to help.

DI Grant —Let me ask you something, Simon. A bra shows up in your house, dirty and ripped and even with your lack of experience you know that isn't how a bra should look, but you still don't report it to us, or to anyone else as I understand it. You just accepted it being there. If something else was dumped in your house, something that was vital to a murder investigation, would you tell us?

Simon Sutherland —Of course I would. It was just a bra, I thought someone had left it there to tease me with. I thought they were trying to force me to throw it out. My family used to do things like that. They pushed me because they thought it helped. I was just embarrassed by it being there. I really didn't see any reason to report it to the police.

Kellina Oriol —I take it from this little period of silence that you have nothing left to ask Simon. I'd say you've probably tortured him enough already.

END

25

DARIAN HAD a simple routine every morning, getting out of bed around eight, showering and then going through to the kitchen where he would look in the fridge and swear he would do some shopping really soon. For several years there may not have been a single day when that flat contained enough to feed a grown man. Faced with the desolation of a fridge that held a nearly empty tub of butter, an out-of-date carton of milk, some green and beige cheese that had started out oddly orange and a lightbulb Darian had just realized didn't light, he decided to pay for breakfast at The Northern Song instead. It was an unhealthy but convenient option that both he and Sholto leaned on far too often.

He walked in the cold down to Bank Station, content with his decision to put the hire car back to JJ. Walking and taking the train to work was enjoyable for Darian and perhaps him alone in this narrow city with its clogged roads and absurd public transport. He liked the walk and making his way through the packed station, getting onto the train for the short trip through the tunnel to Glendan Station. It was the people-watching he found the pleasure in, the population of Challaid being a channel that never ran repeats and refused to commission a single dull day. He left Glendan Station and walked down to Cage Street and in through the front door of The Northern Song.

Two people were standing at the counter, waiting for an order that had already been placed. Mr. Yang was there and saw Darian.

He said, "Breakfast special, Darian?"

"Yes please, Mr. Yang."

The owner went through to the back and returned three minutes later with a warm foil tray and passed it to Darian, taking the money to pay for it with the feigned reluctance of a businessman dealing with a friend. Darian took his breakfast upstairs.

Sholto was already at his desk and when he saw the food he said, "I can't stop myself turning into a fat old man on greasy breakfasts but it's not too late for you to save yourself."

"Is that you trying to persuade me to give you my breakfast?"

"It would be an honorable solution to a real problem."

"My problem is hunger and I'm holding the solution and not letting it go. Have you heard anything from Dockside?"

"No, and I can't help thinking that's probably not a good sign. They're catching up with the twenty-four-hour mark since they took him in and I don't see them going for an extension if they've made no progress, not with his lawyers waiting to pounce and claim victory if a judge refuses them more time. Better to keep their powder dry."

"Surely the bra is enough for something."

Darian sat and gulped down his food with the haste of a man determined to find better things to do with his time. They had no other active cases, just one that was now gripped by the police, and they needed to drum up a little business. That's what Sholto was doing with his spare time because Darian was so damn bad at it, unenthusiastic about corporate work and no good at hiding the fact.

The breakfast carton was in the bin and Sholto had the phone in his hand, about to call Glendan, the construction giants they did regular work for, when he heard footsteps on the stairs and a knock at the door. When he opened it DC Vicario walked in, looking more tired than she had the day before, many long hours in the station ago.

When the door was closed she said, "I'm on my way to flop into bed but I thought I'd take a detour south and tell you we're releasing Simon Sutherland. Right now all we could throw at him is withholding evidence and even that would be shaky because he didn't know it was evidence."

Darian said, "He didn't crack?"

"We couldn't make a scratch on him. Now they'll be complaining about us mistreating a man with mental health problems, so this isn't going to get any easier."

Sholto said, "It was good of you to come and let us know."

"There is a selfish motive. We're still going to pursue this, for Ruby. Simon Sutherland is at least a link to whoever killed her so we're not going to step away from him just because his lawyer's watch cost more than my monthly salary. Oh, you should see the watch, the sort of gaudy you could easily get hooked on. Anyway, we'll keep on it but we'll be under pressure, watched all the time by seniority that could hold us back."

"And we'll have a little more freedom."

She smiled at Darian and said, "Exactly. You dogs of war are off the chain."

Sholto said, "Hang on, hang on, us mutts are all tied up in the kennels. We're a research company, and the Sutherland lawyers that can inconvenience you will shut us down before we can so much as peek in Simon's letterbox."

"You're helping to try and find Ruby's killer and helping Cnocaid try to find Vinny's ex-wife, although I fear what you'll find by now. I can assure you, no station in the city will pursue a case against you."

"Using private companies to chase police cases is not how it's supposed to work."

She said, "Maybe we won't have to, maybe we'll get Ruby's killer without your help, but I'd rather know you two were in my corner. You have a good reputation, Mr. Douglas, and I'd want your skills on my side."

Despite the transparency of the buttering-up Sholto couldn't stop himself beaming like Heilam lighthouse. He said, "Well, of course we're in your corner, DC Vicario, that goes without saying. We'll keep looking into the Ruby killing as well as Freya's disappearance. We won't be reckless about it, no, but we will be professional."

"That's more than enough for me. I'd better go home before I fall asleep on your floor and get rice in my hair. I'll be in touch again soon."

As she left, Darian, embarrassed at the mess, kneeled down and picked the rice off the floor that one of them had dropped in the last few days.

Sholto said, "We're in deep enough now to feel the heat of the earth's core."

"You do always say you want the police on our side."

"Aye, but if they're the only ones who are on our side, who the hell is going to pay us?"

26

SHOLTO WAS about to give Darian a warning about the googly eyes he was giving DC Vicario, had it all planned out in his mind, spelling out how dangerous a beautiful cop could be to a private detective, when he heard more footsteps on the stairs outside.

Sholto looked at the ceiling and, instead of his worldly warnings, said, "Oh, bloody hell, give me strength, it's busier than Ciad Station in here today."

It was only their second visitor of the day, but Darian didn't point that out. He was thinking instead that the new arrival must have been watching Angela Vicario, waiting for her to leave before they called in. He could only think of a short list of people who would wait for her to go before they thought it safe to enter.

The knock came on the door, an elaborate rat-a-tat. Sholto got up from his desk and opened it, looking at the new arrival. His face fell.

"Noonan. DS Noonan, I mean."

"Sholto, you old bugger, how the hell are you? Aren't you going to invite me in?"

DS Dennis Noonan. Darian had heard the name before, heard Sholto talking about him in terms that would make an honest man's skin crawl. Noonan was, according to Sholto, corrupt to his core. He was the very worst of the bad news that floated around in Challaid Police Force. Avoid at all costs, that was the easy-to-follow advice. Couldn't avoid a man who had just walked into your office, though.

Noonan was in his late forties, stocky and with a gut, graying hair that looked like it needed a visit to the barber, blotchy skin and a fat, red boozer's nose. He had a mocking smile on his face as he sat down in the chair on the other side of Sholto's desk, glancing across at Darian.

Noonan looked at him and said, in his thick, working-class Challaid accent, "You must be the Ross boy, eh?"

"Darian Ross."

"Aye, aye. I remember your father, you know. Didn't work with him, probably a good thing, isn't it, given what happened to him. Not a man to be associated with."

He was chuckling as he said it, and Sholto, who had worked closely and extensively with Darian's father, sat heavily opposite him. "What do you want, Noonan?"

"Noonan? Dennis, it's Dennis, call me Dennis, Sholto. I wanted to come and see this place, see how you work. Oh, I fancy this, I do, I really do, you know, when I pack in the proper job. A wee office like this, nice and easy cases, none of the shite we get in the force, get a nice wee assistant. Wouldn't have one like yours, a lad like that, oh no. I'd have a wee dolly bird with tits out to here, have her answer the phone in a short skirt, just sit here watching her. Och, it's a good wee gig you have here, Sholto, eh."

Sholto didn't smile, didn't nod along, didn't react at all. It was unlike him, Darian was so used to seeing him try to ingratiate himself with whoever was sitting opposite him, always trying to be pally with the old cops. Not Noonan, though. Not this time.

Sholto said, "It's no picnic. We have tough cases, and we have a lot more restrictions in how we handle them than you do. A lot more. We're working very hard here, Dennis, so don't go thinking it's an easy retirement plan."

Noonan smiled, looking round and grinning at Darian with yellow teeth, then back at Sholto. "Well, it's good to see you still care, eh, got some of the old passion for this job. No, I still think I'd like to do it. Getting toward the end of my run with the force, they're always dropping hints about my age, makes a man feel unloved, you know. I think something like this could be for me. And there'll be a gap in the market, won't there, eh, Sholto, because you're not going to be doing this for very long."

"Is that right?"

"Oh, aye, aye, you'll be evacuating the office. Hey, you know, I might even rent this very office for my own, eh, if I decide to follow in your footsteps. That would be a laugh, wouldn't it, Sholto? I'll sit where you are and get my glamourous assistant sat over there by the window where the boy is, get her in a tight top with a breeze coming in the window. You'll be... Well, I don't know where you'll be. Might be in The Ganntair, but probably not. You'll get convicted, I mean, that's guaranteed, you know that, but I don't suppose they'll waste a cell on either of you two. You'll be pottering about your garden, if you have one."

Sholto was still expressionless when he said, "That a threat, Dennis?"

"Not a threat, oh no, come on now, I would never threaten a friend, a former copper. No, no, I'm trying to help you out here, Sholto. The force, it's watching you and it doesn't like what it sees. Let you get away with a lot of nonsense in the past, all that palaver with Corey and his mob, and now you're at it again. They're coming for you, Sholto. Coming for Douglas Independent Research. Running an unregistered private detective agency, oh, Sholto, tut, tut, they're not going to let that go on."

Sholto glanced past Noonan to Darian, then said, "We didn't fold when Raven tried to lean on us, tried to lure Darian away. We didn't crumble when Harold Sutherland came in here shouting his mouth off, and we won't be intimidated now."

Noonan smiled and said with mock shock, "Harold Sutherland? You've been making an enemy of Harold Sutherland? Oh, Sholto, I had no idea, things must be even worse than I realized. I came here to try and warn you, help you, but I can see now it's too late. You're finished, the pair of you."

Noonan got up and walked to the door as he was speaking, that last sentence delivered sternly enough to be a threat, whatever the cop wanted to call it. He let himself out, left Sholto and Darian sitting in the office. Darian leaned back in his chair and looked out of the window, watching Noonan stroll off down Cage Street, making sure he was gone before they spoke.

"A cop."

Sholto nodded. "A dirty cop. And he wasn't here representing the force, he was here on behalf of his other employers. He was here for Harold Sutherland."

"He could shut us down, though. You've always said it, cops are the ones we have to fear the most."

Sholto was looking unusually thoughtful, staring down at his desk. "They are, but Noonan is a bad choice for Sutherland. He works out of Bakers station, not Bank, so this isn't his patch, and he's not loved. Other cops hate Dennis Noonan. Other *humans* hate Dennis Noonan."

"So…?"

"So we still have a job to do and we're still going to do it. We'll, uh, keep an eye out for Noonan and his colleagues, though, maybe try and shore up a few friendly cops of our own. The police can destroy us, but they can rescue us, too."

27

THEY WERE dividing up responsibilities for the rest of the day when Darian got another message from Vinny asking if he'd heard that Simon was about to be released. When Darian gave him all the details Vinny suggested meeting up at Dio's, the arcade on Last Street. It wasn't an obvious location, but that just added to the intrigue. Sholto was hitting the phone. He wanted to try and get hold of a contact that might be able to show him Freya and Ruby's mobile phone logs for the week or so before each went missing.

He said, "The police will already have seen them I suppose, but Challaid Police are quite capable of missing things that are obvious even to me."

It took Darian twenty-five minutes to get down to Last Street, not that close to a railway station and he'd put the car back, which he now regretted. It took him another five minutes to find Dio's because the big sign that had been above the door had either fallen off or been sold for scrap, likely the latter. The place was still open, the machines hooked up and flashing, the building almost empty on a Tuesday morning. There were a couple of kids who should have been in school and were dressed in their uniforms to prove it, a couple of alcoholics who were sheltering from the cold and had no intention of parting with a single coin in machines that wouldn't give them a drink in exchange, and Vinny. He was at a cabinet near the door playing *Streets of Rage* with a level of concentration unbecoming in the circumstances. The arcade was long, narrow, low-ceilinged and had an outdated and dark decor that smothered the room in gloom, punctured only by the too-bright machinery.

Darian stood next to Vinny and said sarcastically, "Gee, they must be making a killing in here."

Vinny smiled. "I used to come here all the time when I was a kid. Heard the place was shutting down so I thought I'd come for one last visit. Dio hasn't owned this place in twenty-five years, you know. Used to belong to the Creags, and I heard the Scalpers, the Caledonian gang the Creags are pally with, had the place last, pretended people they were hiding in the city worked here legitimately. White Hawk Drive is just round the corner. I thought we could go and interview a few of Freya's friendly neighbors."

"You haven't spoken to them yet?"

"I was told to keep my nose out of it when Cnocaid station started their investigation so I did. I let them get on with it but they haven't gotten very far."

"You think your nose has any place on her street now?"

Vinny groaned as Axel Stone died another death and he stepped away from the cabinet. "I gave them plenty of time and they gave me nothing for it. Now they're getting all pumped up on Simon Sutherland and Ruby-Mae Short and there's no word of Freya, like they've given up on her when she's running out of time here."

Darian was shocked and didn't hide it. "Vinny, mate, she's been missing eleven days, you know what that probably means, you don't think she's still alive, do you?"

"I know the chances are skinny. Shit, I knew that from the start, there was no way she would run away from Finn and not get in touch if she could, but if there's a tiny chance we can bring her back then I'm going to push for it, and it would help to have your weight behind the effort."

They walked round to White Hawk Drive, Vinny lighting a cigarette and vowing he would quit once the packet was finished, just like the last few hundred. Freya lived on a pleasant street, a much more suburban feel than you would expect in that area, trees lining one side, most of the houses with drives and manicured front gardens, semi-detached houses on both sides. It was the sort of place where residents would secretly compete to have the nicest garden and bitch about any that bettered theirs.

Darian said, "She somehow managed to live well for a woman who let your good self slip through her fingers."

"Aye, a miracle that. Her job, she's an account manager at Caledonia Advertisers, pays pretty well. She's smart, that one, knows how to get the most out of herself."

"So how do we do this?"

"There were a couple of neighbors she absolutely hated. Actually, she didn't have much time for any of them, I think, but there were a couple in particular she talked about, one next door and the other across the road. She said one of them was always peeking out of the curtains when she was in the garden, spying on her, and the one across the road was an interfering busybody, so if anyone knows anything it'll be one of them."

"Spying on her?"

"She said he was a dirty old man. You know what she's like; if you look at her sideways she thinks you're sizing her up for a wedding dress."

They started with the old lady across the street who had once made the mistake of giving Freya advice on how to discipline her child. That had made her an enemy for life. They knocked on the front door and got no answer, but they both saw a curtain twitching and knew she was home. There were plenty of good reasons for an old lady to refuse to answer the door to two young men and forcing the issue could have resulted in an awkward appearance from Vinny's colleagues.

Vinny knocked on the front door of the house next to Freya's and it was opened with the undue haste of a man desperate for any conversation he could get his teeth into. He was short and had a mop of white hair and glasses so thick Darian thought he could probably see into the far reaches of space with them. He must have been watching them across the road which meant he had seen Vinny stub his cigarette out against the man's wall and flick it into the bushes.

Vinny said, "Hello, I'm Vinny Reno, this is Darian Ross from Douglas Independent Research, we're trying to find out what happened to Miss Dempsey from next door. I know you'll have spoken to the police already, but I wondered if you could tell us anything you saw in the days or weeks before her disappearance?"

The man nodded fast and said, "Oh, yes, yes. I told the police and I don't know what they did about it. I told them she was getting parcels nearly every day. And, as well, there was the car."

"The crash she had?"

"No, no, not that, a new car. It was left for her in the driveway and when she came back that afternoon with the boy, Finn his name is, F I N N, she just looked at it and took him inside. Wasn't long after that someone came and took it away, a young lad he was, looked sheepish about it, too. It was a fancy car, one of them Mercedes, I looked it up, very, very expensive."

This was information they didn't already have, gleaned from an old man who seemed to spend most of his day looking out of his windows for Freya. They thanked him and walked back out to the street.

Darian said, "There are explanations. A mix-up with insurers sending her a loan car when she already had her own back, giving her an expensive one because it was tied to the Sutherland account."

"Maybe, but the sort of insurers who handle the Sutherland account wouldn't make that sort of sloppy mistake. Easy to find out if they did as well."

"The parcels could be from work. I guess she handles a lot of different companies."

"She does, and they send anything she needs to see to the office. Why the hell didn't Cnocaid station tell me about this?"

"You know why. You're still a suspect, Vinny, whatever they might say to your ugly face. If they were presents then maybe they thought it was a motive for you, jealousy, her moving on from the marriage while you're still single."

Vinny stopped in the middle of the street and gave him the look of a man who'd just discovered a new limb he never knew he had. "Me? Jealous? As in, wanted her back jealous? Are you completely loopy permanently or is this just a phase you're going through?"

"I know it's daft but as long as you're a suspect you're going to have to put up with it. If it wasn't the insurers then who could have given her the car? Not William Dent, he couldn't afford a classy piece of metal like that."

"Simon Sutherland could."

Darian nodded and said, "Yeah, but he's not the gift-buying sort, is he? If she sent it back he would have to put it on a shelf in his house."

"Unless he's faking it."

"There is that, but if he's faking it why not ditch the bra? There's also the uncle, Harold. There's a suave piece of meat that banged into her on the road, met her in person, gave her his work contact details and could afford all the show-off gestures of love, lust and casual interest you could wish for. Maybe they had a thing going."

Vinny puffed out his cheeks and said, "Hitting a man with her car until he went out with her, that's her style all right. But she sent the motor back, so if it was a gift then she was about as receptive to it as she was to most attempts to be in any way impressive toward her."

"Unwanted attention? The sort that might make a man used to hearing yes angry?"

Vinny grimaced as they got into his car back on Last Street. "I suppose, but how does that tie in with the Short girl's bra being in Simon Sutherland's house? It has to be the boy in the billionaire's bubble, doesn't make sense otherwise."

"It's your partner's family."

"I don't like leaning on the boy so much, but we'll have another chat with him about his weird bloodline, see what he has to say. We'll go together."

THE CHALLAID GAZETTE AND ADVERTISER

07 FEBRUARY 2018

BRIDGE PROPOSAL DROPPED

Plans for a bridge from the Barton district of the city to Eilean Seud, resubmitted in a council meeting in late October, have again been shelved after significant objections from islanders. Put forward this time by Labor Party councilor Aila Donald, the idea was for a bridge from Cruinn Pier to the southwest edge of the island with the belief it would make Eilean Seud more accessible for the rest of Challaid and emergency services, as well as making the mainland easier to reach for the citizens living on the island.

"The idea for the bridge is an old one," Councilor Donald said, "it's been around for more than a century and remains as relevant now as it was then. This is an opportunity to join the one detached part of Challaid with the rest of the city and make it a safer place."

Residents on the island disagreed, with Lyle MacBeth, a representative of Eilean Protection, a campaign group set up to oppose the bridge, calling Councilor Donald's proposal "mischief making." Mr. MacBeth told the *Gazette*, "Ms. Donald well knows that islanders don't want this and that the rest of the city won't benefit a jot from it. This new submission never had a chance of success, and Ms. Donald only brought it forward to try and create divisions between people on the island and those on the mainland."

Councilor Donald has disputed this, stating that there is a strong economic and safety argument for the bridge, but she did repeat her accusation that the people of Eilean Seud have consistently opposed the bridge on the grounds of snobbery. The value of an average house on the island, none of which have come on the open market in over twenty years, is estimated at somewhere around two and a half million pounds, with the population dominated by a select number of families considered unwelcoming of outsiders.

Eilean Protection have dismissed all of those allegations, with Mr. MacBeth saying, "This has nothing to do with property prices or stopping people from the mainland coming across to visit the island. If we wanted to keep people off Eilean Seud we would hardly be funding the regular ferry service from Cruinn Pier from our own pockets, a service which has made the island more accessible now than at any point in Challaid's long history. What we oppose is millions of pounds being spent on a needless eyesore that will increase pollution and disturb a unique way of life on the island."

When asked if she intended to put her proposal forward again Councilor Donald was noncommittal, saying only that "No good idea should be entirely off the table." Challaid council leader Morag Blake and her Liberal Party have previously stated their opposition to a bridge, but gave no statement when asked by the *Gazette* about this new submission.

NBOS RAID HUNT MOTHBALLED

Police at Dockside station in Whisper Hill and the anti-organized crime unit at Bakers Moor station last night confirmed that the investigation into the notorious theft of over six million pounds from a National Bank of Scotland security van at Challaid International Airport in 2013 is no longer classed as active, although both have stressed the investigation remains open. No one has ever been arrested in relation to the case, and what started out as a large joint investigation has gradually dwindled to now have no dedicated officers working on it, with a spokesperson for—p8

28

GETTING TO Phil proved more difficult than expected. Having called Freya's insurers and found they had no record of delivering the wrong car, and then her employers who said work parcels were never sent to her house, Vinny then phoned his colleague and had a brief conversation which he recounted to Darian in the car as they made their way north.

Vinny said, "He's at Loch Chalum, behind Dùil Hill."

"What the hell's he doing there?"

"Fishing. It's one of his things. He's well into what he considers working-class pursuits. Fishing is one, playing darts is another. He's in a darts team in some pub league. I've heard he's pretty good."

"A man who stands to inherit millions playing in a pub league in The Hill? Have you thought to warn him of the potential dangers of being around sharp objects in nasty hands given his wealth?"

Vinny chuckled. "He's a cop going round pubs in Whisper Hill, doesn't matter if you're piss poor, that's a dangerous game and he knows it. I think that's part of what he enjoys. His family collects paintings and yachts and private jets so he does fishing and darts."

The drive from Cnocaid to the closest road to the loch was a long one, with eighty percent of the time taken up by the first forty percent of road. From Cnocaid they had to go east through Bank into Bakers Moor and then north through Earmam and Whisper Hill. They left the city, through the narrow gap up to Heilam, going past the graveyard, the council estate and the old lighthouse. From there Vinny could put his foot down and drive with the sort of abandon that only a man who's friends with every cop that might possibly pull him over could possess. They followed the road that looped round the back of Dùil Hill and saw Phil's car parked at a passing place on their right.

Vinny looked at it and said with a sigh, "We're going to have to plod it the rest of the way to the loch. You bring your hiking boots?"

"No. You?"

"I'm in my trainers. I don't really do countryside, too many things that can bite you in ways I wouldn't pay for."

"You sound like Sholto, he's terrified of dogs."

"I was thinking more of midges, ticks and gamekeepers."

A fifteen-minute walk uphill to the dip where the small loch was hidden from the world turned into a twenty-five-minute walk on account of their footwear, both of them hopping around to try and avoid the boggy parts of the moor, which was most of it. One twisted ankle and a near-record-breaking amount of swearing later, they crested the ridge and saw Phil, a five-minute walk away at the lochside. They stumbled down to find him sitting on a large rock, a plastic tub of worms to the side and a bottle of water in his hand, watching the float from his rod lie still on the calm surface. He knew the terrain and his well-scuffed wellies proved it.

Vinny stood next to him and said, "Why the hell can't you just take up alcoholism as a hobby like everyone else in The Hill, least then we could meet you in a pub? Even camanachd, which tends to lead to the bottle anyway."

Phil looked out at the loch, surrounded by hills and birdsong, no sign of Challaid or any other smear of modernity, and said, "Don't tell me this isn't beautiful."

"It sure is beautiful, and I would have mildly enjoyed looking at a photo of it back in Challaid."

"You need the exercise, a man your age and your size. Doesn't take much to go from barrel-chested to barrel-bellied, you know. So what dark theory about my family have you brought to my bright hideaway?"

Vinny sat on the rock beside Phil and Darian stood in front of them both. This was going to be an awkward conversation so Vinny decided he might as well be sitting awkwardly for it.

He said, "We've been talking to some snoopers, one of them a very possible pervert, and found out that Freya was getting presents sent to the house before she went missing, including a car that a Sutherland and not many others could afford. Looks like someone sent it and she sent it right back. Freya wasn't the sort to spit out a free lunch if she liked the food, so she really didn't want whoever was throwing luxury motors at her."

"I don't know, Vinny. My family might be famous for having money but we're not famous for throwing it around. Besides, as a theory, that the person who ki-kidnapped her sent her the gifts, it doesn't add up. Who would risk sending presents like that?"

Darian said, "What about your uncle Harold?"

"What about him?"

"He met Freya; they talked, might he have gotten back in touch with her? Is he the sort to fall hard and make big romantic gestures?"

Phil shook his head as he thought about it and said, "He's had a few girlfriends over the years that I know of, got engaged once but it didn't pan out. They were all just playthings for him."

"I thought your family was supposed to take a terribly religious view of these things, the high moral standards of a churchy family."

"That's what you're supposed to think. The business comes first. Always does with that surname. I don't know how romantic his gestures have ever been, but I do know it's not the family way. The fact we have the money to spend if we wanted to is enough. You don't have to actually go ahead with the grand gesture to get attention."

"Is there a way of finding out what he's been sending people?"

"Well, they're obsessive about accounting for every single penny that goes in and out of the bank but he would never put it through the company accounts. It would be unforgivable for a personal item to intrude on profit. Anything like that would be at his house on Eilean Seud."

Vinny tutted and said, "He's one of that lot is he, wanting to float off into the North Atlantic instead of sharing the same land mass as us scum? Probably takes a helicopter to work."

"He doesn't. You're not allowed anything as noisy as a helicopter on the island and you couldn't land them anywhere near the bank for security reasons anyway. Listen, I want to help, and I can probably get you into his house, but I don't think it's a clever idea."

Vinny said, "I laugh in the face of clever ideas. What have you got?"

"He's having one of his parties at the house, he has them every month. He does it to try and improve the bank's image among other rich people. You'd be amazed how many of them hate our family."

"I wouldn't. Rich people love their money and hate the people who control it, which is you lot."

"Well, for a few hundred years we didn't give two craps what people thought of us but now Uncle Harold has a penchant for PR. He's good at it, nice and subtle. I remember him telling my mother that PR at its best persuades people to believe in you, to support what you're doing and even want to be a part of it. At its worst PR is a loudmouthed half-wit screeching wildly at the converted. You have to be friendly and reach out. It wouldn't be hard to get a couple of extra people in, it's pretty much an open house, but you'll be in a crowded place with a lot of security and he's hardly going to have left something incriminating lying around."

Darian looked at Vinny and said, "It might still be worth it, get a closer look at his life and lifestyle, see if there's anything that can educate us about him."

Vinny nodded thoughtfully. "True, but I can't go. I'm a suspect and a serving police officer, so if I get spotted it botches the whole investigation."

Phil said, "Same here, and it's not like half the guests wouldn't recognize me straightaway. Uncle Harold always invites me to these things and I always say no so it would raise an eyebrow through his scalp if I turned up now. You and your boss could go, dress up in a couple of fake names and make sure you're not seen by anyone who might recognize you."

Darian nodded slowly. Sholto would go through the roof and into the upper atmosphere but if it gave them a snapshot of Harold Sutherland at play it would be worth the horror.

29

DARIAN WAS standing in the office with Sholto, who was hovering somewhere between fury and giddy panic. It wasn't the prospect of sniffing around a suspect that had him turning puce; it was the thought of being at a party filled with the rich and powerful.

"Not just a room full, not just a house full but a whole bloody island of them. How are we supposed to fit in there?"

Darian said, "I don't know about you, but I plan to lie through my teeth."

"I used to be a detective in the Challaid Police Force, Darian, I know how to keep a lie running, but how does anyone fit in among that lot? I don't know what to wear, not a clue."

Darian had called and told him about the party they were going to, so they had met at the office in the early evening, Sholto dressed in a suit that was a little tight but smarter than usual after Darian told him to tuck his shirt in at the back. Darian had on his one good suit with a blue shirt and no tie.

He said, "The dress code is smart casual."

"What does that mean, Darian? Those two words cancel each other out and any sensible person knows it. I have a tie in one pocket and a bow tie in the other. Do I wear one or the other or neither or both?"

"Neither, and if we get there and everyone's in ties you can slip it on."

"It's brown and yellow."

"*Brown and yellow?* Why the hell do you have a brown and yellow tie?"

"It's the only one I've got. Well, I have a black tie as well, for funerals, obviously, but this is the only one I've got for the living. If I wear the black one they'll think I'm a waiter and I won't have the confidence to correct them. I don't want to be serving drinks all night."

"What happened to all the ties you had when you were a cop?"

"Burned them in a wee metal bin in the back garden the day I retired, my way of celebrating. In hindsight it was a rash move, but the thing about hindsight is that you can only have it after the event."

They left the office and drove up to Cruinn Pier in Sholto's Fiat. The small car park on the pier was almost full with cars whose heated seats were worth more than Sholto's entire vehicle. They parked at the back and walked toward the dock where the ferry would arrive in a few minutes. There were a handful of people waiting with them, most going to the party and all in good spirits. Someone made a joke about financial speculations and Sholto laughed much too hard, the way people do when they really wish they'd understood the punch line. Nobody asked who they were or what they did for a living so the lies they'd prepared could stay in their thin wrappers a little longer.

A loud man was defending the honor of the Sutherland Bank to a bored-looking woman. "I know a lot of people view us as some cynical company that seeks to hold back the progress of others but that isn't at all the case. We're as committed to social progress and equality as anyone, but we've always insisted that these things have to be sustainable, that we spend only what we have and go at a pace that ensures nothing is rushed and the foundations are well set. I would argue that this is the very opposite of the anti-progress attitude you're accusing us of, wouldn't you? We don't just want progress, we want it to last. Isn't that what you want, too?"

From where they stood they could see with relief the ferry pull away from the pier on the southern point of Eilean Seud and make the five-minute run across to join them. It was small and white but the deck they stood on was well covered and had hot air blasting from one end. It was well scrubbed and any seagull that even thought of taking a shit on it would probably have been blasted out of the sky before it could take aim. The ferry brought them quickly across the cold water and the island came more starkly into view, lit up and laden with hundred-and-fifty-year-old mansions of understated elegance and trees older still. Darian and Sholto hung back and made sure they were the last off the boat so they could walk to Harold's house alone.

There was one narrow, cobbled road on Eilean Seud that ran from the pier in the south and curved up to the north of the long and thin island, each step carrying them further back in time to a fantasy land of old money. The Challaid rich had built mansions from banking money and merchant money and pirate money and slave ship money and whaling money, in a time when the city belonged to them and the outside world didn't get a say, a time they wished had never passed and one they were trying to re-create in miniature.

There were houses on either side, thirty-two on the island, and each was pristine. Living on the island brought with it a responsibility to maintain aesthetic standards. Even the lampposts along the street looked like they would be powered by gas and lit every evening by a man with a thick mustache and wearing a hat. Alders stretched across from both sides of the tree-lined lane to touch in the middle in places, providing a picturesque canopy for the sunlight to filter through on good days and on bad ones a flimsy cover from the worst of the rain, which, when it did get through, fell in large, heavy blobs of collected water. It would have been fairy-tale pretty in the fading light of a Challaid night if it hadn't been trying so desperately hard.

As they walked along the road Sholto said, "And to think, I used to be jealous of people who lived in Barton. I thought that was the pinnacle. How naive I was."

"I don't know, has a whiff of the gilded cage about it."

"No, Simon Sutherland's house reeked of it, but this is just gilded. Not everything attractive is a trap, Darian."

At the gates to Harold Sutherland's mansion a couple of smiling young women were asking people for their names and checking them against their list. Darian noticed that a pair who had been on the boat with them, who must have been regulars at these shindigs, had been allowed straight through without a check. Now it was time to test the false IDs in the face of a brief check.

Sholto smiled and said, "I'm Corvun Reed, this is Gito Conin."

The young woman, dressed in a trouser suit and with her dark hair tied back, looked at the list on her tablet. "Yes, McCourt Securities. Go straight in, the house is just ahead at the end of the drive. Drinks and food are in the main study and also the garden at the back. Enjoy the evening."

"Thank you."

It was always a strange thing to watch, the casual lies Sholto could tell when he was getting into a performance and his nerves settled. It was as fragile as a butterfly's wings. One gust could blow him miles off course, but his acting was still, at its best, pretty good.

The drive was cobbled like the road and the long front garden was a colorful beauty parade that looked as if it had been lifted from a painting. The house was, as expected, large and imposing, and the main study the woman had mentioned was staring straight at them. It was two stories high and had large French doors and cathedral windows which flooded it with light. Even before they stepped inside they could see it stretched back to the rear of the building, with the same design to give a spectacular view of the loch at the end of the back garden. The room had plenty of couches and chairs and sitting in them were people well used to the luxury around them. The view didn't awe them, nor did the paintings on the wall or the cost of the wine they were gulping down and would be pissing away in a few hours.

As they stood at the open French doors Sholto said, "We'll sniff around but not too loudly. If you see the man himself, duck behind a millionaire, we don't want to get kicked out. Even a classy pair like ourselves might struggle to restore our standing in elite society if we get rumbled here."

Sholto hiked over to the side of the room where several waiters were milling around with trays, food always a relaxant for him. Darian walked slowly through the scenery, picking up snatches of conversations that sounded as though they were competing with each other in the world championship of sleep inducement. Politics and business were the prime subjects and the subtext of both was money. As Darian reached the end of the room he turned back and saw that Sholto was deep in conversation with a smiling woman who appeared to be trying to explain what all the available nibbles were.

Darian, with hands in pockets, stepped out into the back garden, stopped, and took a step back inside, out of view. Harold Sutherland was just outside, holding court before a gaggle of sycophants.

"Don't get me wrong, I love Challaid FC, but only for what it can do for the city. There's a poisonous pall over the sport in this country, so bitter and parochial, and the people underneath it are so busy looking down on others all the time that they haven't noticed it up there. I was at the Motherwell game a few Fridays ago and the crowd loved Friday night football, but because it inconvenienced a small traveling support from the central belt it's being shelved. No mention of what's better for our fans, or that we had a Champions League match on the Tuesday, representing our country. People are more interested in establishing moral superiority than improving the actual football. Honestly, the only thing more tedious than actual politics is football politics. That's why I'd like to do something in camanachd as well, if I could find a club in this city that knew how to listen to reason. Such a great sport and yet they're proud of their amateurism. It's absurd. I may have to set up a club of my own and get them into the league; if I do they'll show the rest just what professionalism looks like."

When he had finished his spiel there was some muttering of agreement from men pretending to be interested and some flirtatious cooing from the one woman whose husband was standing with his arm round her. Harold Sutherland was a charismatic man who found controlling a conversation easy and it was the simplest thing in the world to make a powerfully good impression on people. That, Darian thought bitterly, was something that could easily be abused and perhaps its rare failures could provoke a stern response. At the same time, though, this did not seem like a man who would need to throw a car at a woman in a crass attempt to win her over.

When Sutherland moved away from the patio outside the door and across to the side of the garden to speak to people there Darian stepped outside. He took a glass of wine from a passing waitress just so that he wouldn't stand out so much and headed toward the end of the garden to check the view.

"Quite something, isn't it?"

Darian turned to find a woman in her thirties with short hair, high cheekbones and skin dark enough to shine under the lights in the trees.

"It's extraordinary, yes."

"I'm Asteria Hobnil, everyone calls me Asti. I work for Duff Shipping. I handle our Asian accounts. I don't think I've seen you here before."

"Gito Conin, McCourt Securities, first-time visitor, long-time wisher I could afford to live here. I thought the Sutherlands and the Duffs didn't get along."

"Hate each other with a passion. If they didn't love being rich so much they would have burned the city to the ground fighting one another centuries ago. The Sutherlands still think all the Duffs are boorish and the Duffs still think all the Sutherlands are stuck up and they might both be right, but at least the Duffs have fun and do some good. Harold keeps inviting people from the company because he's trying to build bridges, metaphorically speaking of course, and Duff keeps sending us along to pretend we're all pals now but really to spy on him."

Darian chuckled unconvincingly at the mention of spying and said, "So what's he like, Harold Sutherland? I've only met him once through work."

"He's determinedly likable, which is impressive at first, but I have a deep distrust of people who only behave one way, only have one setting. He never switches off."

"Oh, I've seen him angry."

"Really? The one time you met him and you managed to make him crack. You'll have to tell me your secret. Every Duff in the city would love to know...Is that man looking for you?"

Darian turned to follow Asti's gaze and saw Sholto, sweat glistening on his face under fairy lights, walking through the garden, staring to left and right. It looked very much like time to leave.

THE DESCENT OF POISON

A man lay between white sheets, the full-length window open and the wind blowing salt air into the room. Beside him lay a woman of twenty-six, as beautiful as any he had ever met, naked, the mother of his children. Life was the idyll he had been told throughout his youth it would become.

Out on the air he heard the low drone, moving closer and flitting in and out of view, the small white plane sweeping across Loch Eriboll and over the hills to the east, beyond the horizon. He smiled to see it and think of the endless sky, the truest freedom he had ever known, the only one that brought him joy.

Joseph Sutherland leaned across and kissed the perfect bare shoulder of his wife Marcail, listening to the sweet sound of her sleeping mumble as he slipped out from under the sheet. He put on the trousers and blue T-shirt lying on the wicker chair in the corner, the clothes he had worn the day before, his shoes at the foot of the bed. He made his way down to the garage in silence.

It was early morning, the staff awake and working but the three children still asleep. He slid open the garage door, pulled on his helmet and started one of his classics, the Matchless Silver Hawk, riding it along the single street of Eilean Seud to the pier. The boatman was already in place and smiled a good morning as he always did when Joseph rode the motorcycle up the ramp and onto the small deck. Without instruction they sailed across to Cruinn Pier and the boatman let the ramp down.

The ride north along the lochside was at first slow but then, beyond the edge of the city where the road was always empty, gloriously fast, revitalizing. The ride to Portnancon Airfield offered a taste of freedom, dressed in its speed and danger but limited by the road below him.

At the Second World War airfield he stopped at the gate at the end of the narrow road and opened it with his personal key, riding up to the three green hangars with curved roofs and the one at the end that belonged to his family. His twin-engine plane was ready for him, as always, kept so for the whims Joseph's staff were paid to serve. That was his good fortune.

It took minutes to start and get the plane out of the hangar and then he took off, roaring fast from the strip, one of his favorite places and almost abandoned now because of the monstrosity on Whisper Hill. He would never follow the others to the other side of the loch.

Challaid was below and from the sky it seemed so small, a narrow horseshoe of gray looping round cold dark blue, not the suffocating mass of people and expectation that it seemed on the ground but a toy he could fit in his hand and crush when it bored or frustrated him. The buildings were specks and the hills at its back no longer a cage, but a bump easily scaled, far away and irrelevant as he soared above.

He had spoken many times with Marcail about how pointless it was, how all of his achievements could never add up to more than a sentence in the book of his family's existence. He was twenty-eight and all his life had understood that the only journey he could make was in other people's footsteps. It was a path rich and beautiful and perfect and empty.

Marcail would be down there, probably with the children, Harold, Beathan and Nina, perhaps eating breakfast out on the lawn by the loch as she liked to do on warm mornings. There were so few of those in a city built on coldness, but this summer had been more generous than most and children could believe that made up for past failures. One day they would understand.

Joseph flew over Stac Voror and north toward Whisper Hill, the sight of the scar on its top he wasn't allowed to fly over souring the view. Much of Challaid was ugly from on high, gray and brown stone and concrete, cars and lorries and dirt, while a glimpse beyond the hills showed the unspoiled, the world before people chose to ruin it.

He brought the plane left and pointed it toward Eilean Seud, the slip of land that had always been home. He had never had an excuse to be unhappy with the life it gave. He thought of his family and he smiled. A glimpse of the horizon, of what might be and what he knew would be, his mind finding rest.

Far below they would be watching him, enjoying breakfast and laughing at the obsession that sent him into the sky. They would watch the white bird-like speck, turning back to face them. They would see it dive suddenly and hit the water, and they would know that he was dead.

30

SHOLTO SPOTTED Darian at the end of the garden and came toward him at a sort of trot, a man trying not to run because that would draw unwanted attention but unable to walk because urgency shoved him forward. He paused when he saw Asti, unsure of her before he decided that caution had to be thrown into the storm that was brewing.

"I just saw Bran Kennedy, the head of Raven, and I think he saw me."

Darian frowned. "You think?"

"He gave that little shudder he always gives when he sees me. Even from across the long room I'm sure of it. He'll be coming after us and he won't be alone."

They both looked up toward the French doors and it wasn't the head of Raven Investigators in Challaid they saw but Alan Dudley, his thuggish junior, doing a terrible job of standing in the doorway and searching the garden while trying to look like he wasn't. That told them Kennedy wasn't at the party to enjoy himself. He was providing security and had help with him.

Sholto said, "How do we get out of here without them seeing us?"

Darian looked over his shoulder at the loch and said, "How's your swimming?"

Asti Hobnil, who had been listening, said, "I don't think you need to get your nice threads wet. See those bushes over there? Go round behind them in the gap at the bottom and you'll end up on a path that runs along the side of the house, keeps you as far from the party room as possible. If they haven't alerted the front gate you can make a run for the ferry. If they come down this way I'll stall them. Shouldn't be hard, last thing Harold Sutherland would want is a scene."

Darian and Sholto both stared at her and Darian said, "Uh... thank you."

She smiled. "I told you, I'm a spy, it's my duty to help fellow rogues, Mr. Incognito."

Dudley had left the doorway and was walking slowly through the garden, which meant there was no time left for conversation. They turned and walked with conspicuous speed across to their left and behind a tall hedge that ran up toward the house and hid the large greenhouse and toolshed from view of the main lawn. They moved quick, Darian striding and Sholto shuffling, until they found themselves on the narrow path Asti had promised would appear.

At the front corner of the house they stopped and peered round, checking for Ravens. All they could see was the idle rich making their way in and out of the doors to the party room on the other side of the building so they stepped out. There was a long, curving path that led to the drive and then the gate. From now on it was walking only because innocent men didn't run. The innocent probably didn't walk as quickly as Darian and Sholto did either, but they were trying their best. There was no way to look anything other than odd as they strolled past the two girls at the gate on their way out just twenty minutes after going in. One of them gave Darian a curious look as he passed them and he tried to respond with the most adorably innocent smile he could muster, not breaking stride in the process.

On the walk along the lane to the pier they were the only people leaving and passed a few stragglers heading the other way. They both looked back over their shoulders and saw no one pursuing them. The only people at the boat were the two sailors working it and timing was perfect because they were just about to leave. Darian and Sholto stood nervously under the canopy on deck as they inched away from the pier and into the dark water between the island and the mainland.

The older of the two sailors, a man in his forties with the sort of beard and thick jumper combination that seemed designed to announce his occupation to the world, joined them at the railing. "Nothing wrong is there, lads, leaving so soon?"

Even though the man was smiling Sholto shook his head vigorously and said, "No, not at all, not at all, absolutely not."

The sailor laughed, and leaning back on his heels he said, "Would I lose my shirt if I put a bet on you two being nervous about security waiting for you at Cruinn Pier?"

Darian judged the man perfectly when he said, "You can probably hang on to your clothing."

"Thought so. Come into the cabin so they don't see you. If they're there we can hide you below until they bugger off. You wouldn't be the first."

They went inside where it was a little warmer and a little quieter and where they could see anyone on the pier before anyone on the pier saw them.

Sholto said, "How did you know?"

The sailor said, "The only people at these parties who get their suits at Polla Clothing are either working the event or not supposed to be there and the waiters don't get to leave this early. I managed to live forty-three years without being able to tell the difference between something off the rack and a tailored suit. It's only in the last three since I started working this route that I've seen enough of the latter to get it."

"You haven't fallen in love with the posh hard enough to turn us in?"

"Ha, some of them are all right, but I'm a man of the sea, not a man of the bank. So what did you lads nick?"

"Nothing, we just didn't have an invite."

"Ah, okay. We see that often enough, people running from the security, most of them manage to grab a keepsake on the way out, a candlestick that turns out to be worth six hundred quid, something like that."

"You can get candlesticks worth six hundred quid?"

"Oh, aye, a lot of these rich folk, they're full of..."

Sholto said, "Shit?"

"I was going to say creativity, but I suppose that, too."

As the boat edged toward Cruinn Pier a radio crackled and a garbled message came through that the sailor leaned in to listen to. He turned to Darian and Sholto. "That's them telling us to look out for you. Of course, we haven't seen you."

As his crewmate steered the boat into dock the older man went out and stepped onto the pier to secure the vessel. From the cabin Darian and Sholto could see a handful of people waiting for the ramp to be let down for them, but they all looked dressed to thrill, not kill.

The sailor came back inside and said, "No one dressed cheaply enough to be security; you two can make a run for it."

They thanked him, even though he seemed to consider helping people get one over Harold Sutherland's security team a privilege, and got off the ferry. They practically sprinted to the Fiat at the far corner of the small car park. Sholto mumbled under his breath as the car started and they pulled away. They both remained silent, scanning the mirrors, until they were out of Barton and down into Cnocaid, which felt just far enough to relax. Now that Sholto was heading steadily east toward Bank and Darian's flat they could talk.

He said to Darian, "So what did we learn tonight, apart from the fact that I was right about rich people being more trouble than even they are worth, that we should wear trainers to their parties and that this city would be nothing without its sailors?"

Darian said, "I learned that on the evening Freya went missing Harold Sutherland was at Challaid's match with Motherwell, so all the way across the city from where she was last seen."

"Okay, but you would expect him to have concocted a neat wee alibi for the time it happened, because he was hardly going to do it himself, was he?"

"No, I suppose not, but the more I see him the less I can picture him showering Freya with expensive gifts. It would be far too desperate for someone like him, women cooing in his ear at the party the whole time we were there. He would see buying her a car as crass. A man like that would be smart enough to know what a woman like Freya would want from him. He'd know her pride wouldn't let her be bought."

"Or maybe the charm is all part of the act and when it failed with Freya he lost the plot. Maybe it failed with Ruby as well and that's why he targeted her."

"We seem to be accusing a lot of Sutherlands of acting. Do you believe Harold is performing?"

"Not really. He doesn't strike me as the sort, but you'd be amazed how often I've said that before and very quickly been proven wrong."

Darian said, "I still think tonight was worth the effort, just to learn a little more about that family."

Sholto muttered noncommittally and then pointed out they were on Havurn Road and coming up to Darian's flat on the corner. He found a spot and parked.

31

DARIAN WAS about to say goodnight to Sholto, who we'll be honest and say wasn't the last face he wanted to see before he went to sleep—that honor belonged to Angela Vicario—when Sholto's phone rang. It took an almost indecent struggle with his hand reaching into his pocket before he pulled the phone out, leaning back and wrestling with his seat belt as he did. God knows what anyone walking past outside would have thought was going on.

Sholto frowned at the number and answered. "Hello, Sholto Douglas."

Darian sat and listened but only because he knew from Sholto's formal response that it was work and might have been about the party. If he had thought it was Mrs. Douglas he would have given his boss some privacy. This was someone Sholto wasn't sure of and the pacey mumbling on the other end told Darian the subject was something someone found exciting.

Sholto said, "I'm in the car with Darian, we'll come straight round."

He hung up and Darian said, "What's this?"

"That was Warren Corvo."

"Who or what the hell is a Warren Corvo?"

"You know him, one of the three lads from Challaid Data Services along the corridor, I can't remember which one of them, they're all the same to me. He called to say that someone's breaking into our office and that we need to get round there sharpish if we want to stop them."

As he was talking Sholto was putting the car into gear and pulling out from the side of Havurn Road, heading east to try and get to the office on Cage Street. Darian was thinking about the phone call and sticking his brain in the holes he found.

"If they know we're being broken into why aren't they stopping the burglar? They're twenty feet along the corridor."

"They're not at their office. He was calling from home."

"Then how the hell does he know we're being broken into? Does he sleep under his desk?"

"I didn't exactly have time to interrogate him, Darian, I was a little too concerned about getting off the phone and onto the road. Now stop talking to me, you know I can't drive quickly when I'm distracted."

The problem with that statement was the crucial point it left out. Indeed Sholto couldn't drive quickly when he was distracted, but that was principally because he couldn't drive quickly at all. This was the painfully annoying part for Darian, having to sit in the passenger seat knowing that if they stopped and switched places they would spend thirty seconds stationary but get there minutes quicker. He couldn't suggest it because Sholto would call that a distraction and his pride would never accept it anyway. If he was going faster than usual then to him it meant they were already going remarkably fast.

Darian knew all these streets, could recognize them even in the false light of urban nighttime when the city was clothed so differently and the familiar tried to look strange. They were on Raghnall Road, or Rag Road to locals who mostly don't remember the sketchy story of the eleventh-century hero it's named after. There were the two sets of gates to the dock on the south bank of the loch on their left, once the entrances for working men who powered the city and now a monument to the gentrification that had slain the soul but kept the wallet of the area. That meant they were about five minutes of Sholto's driving away from Cage Street, three if Darian had been behind the wheel.

Stuck at traffic lights, watching two cars go past and knowing that neither could possibly be in as much of a hurry as they were, then they were pulling away again, minus the screech of tires Darian would have aimed for and going past the Glendan HQ building on Bruaich Drive with its glass frontage, and Darian knew they were two minutes from Cage Street, a minute and a half of his driving, so beyond the point where switching roles would help.

He had been thinking on the journey that this couldn't be a coincidence. They were on Eilean Seud when someone decided now was a good time to try and break into their office. Oddly perfect timing. So who would know? Raven Investigators because their boss Bran Kennedy had eyeballed Sholto at the party? One call to an underling and they could have had someone forcing the door, believing that Sholto and Darian were hiding on the island and bound to be caught there. They were the most likely candidates but that brought questions.

Darian said, "How are you going to handle this?"

"We're going to go in and try to stop our place from being turned over."

"But how do we stop them? There might be three or four of them and they might be armed. Do we attack? Do we hold back and box them in?"

"Oh, chee whizz, I didn't think of that. Maybe we should hold back. I do like my office, but not enough to give it my last breath."

"We'll get closer and play it by ear."

"I do wish my hearing was better."

Sholto found a spot on a double yellow on Greenshank Drive and they got out, heading round the corner and onto Cage Street.

32

THEY RAN down Cage Street with no view of the office from that direction. What they saw as they got closer was Mr. Yang, Mrs. Yang and the three junior Yangs standing out on the street looking back at the building.

As they stopped beside them Sholto said, "Mr. Yang, what's driven you out of your bed?"

"We got a call, one of the Data people. There's someone in there, breaking in. I don't want my girls in there with someone breaking in, they could be dangerous."

His son Michael, the eldest child and probably big enough to look after himself at that point anyway, gave his father a sulky look but said nothing. Mrs. Yang looked much more annoyed than frightened, a woman usually full of fire and mischief that their two daughters had inherited.

Darian said, "Has anyone called the police?"

Mr. Yang said, "Of course we did, someone is breaking into the building where we live. The man called and said you were coming but we called the police, too, as many as possible."

Sholto said, "Any sign of them?"

"The police? The Challaid Police? Even if the man had thrown me out of the window and my blood ran down to the corner they wouldn't be here until three weeks next Tuesday. I would be better calling my school friend who's a policeman in China. He would be here faster."

His wife whispered something in Chinese and Mr. Yang grabbed her hand, holding it firmly. Darian and Sholto, on this occasion, considered the reliably lackadaisical police response to be no bad thing. They wanted to know who was breaking into their office before the cops turned up and spoiled the surprise.

They looked at each other and nodded, Darian assuming his boss was thinking the same as him. So he was, but with a lot less enthusiasm. They knew they were going to have to go in and at least try to identify the intruder and their intentions, because waiting out on Cage Street with the Yang family was only offering the person an easy escape. Sholto grimaced, sighed once, then a second time and nodded again at Darian.

Darian said to Mr. Yang, "We're going in. Get yourselves off the street and away from the doors in case he comes out this way. He might be armed."

Mr. Yang said, "I'll wait, and if he comes out this way I'll tackle him."

"No, seriously, he could be very dangerous; we don't know what we're dealing with here."

"I'll get one of my cleavers, one that can stop any animal smaller than a cow and slower than a rabbit."

Sholto said, "No, Mr. Yang, really, that lad in there could be any sort of dangerous if he's daft enough to spend this long robbing the place. Never hit a crazy person with anything smaller than a bus, not even a cleaver. You get the family somewhere safe. I couldn't stand the thought of you getting hurt and me not getting fed because of it."

The nod Mr. Yang gave was stiff enough to pass for a short headbutt but it was agreement and that was enough for now. They had wasted too much time getting to Cage Street and speaking out on the street in hissed urgency. Whatever the intruder was looking for he was bound to have found it in the one-room office by now. Unless, Darian realized, he wasn't very good at this. That shifted suspicion away from a well-prepared Raven employee and onto someone else. Darian just didn't know who that someone else would be.

They went in through the side door, the one they always took. It gave them access to the stairs that would take them straight up to the office. Even opening the side door was a risk; if the intruder had an unseen accomplice that's where they were likely to be. If there was a backup then he wasn't lurking in the stairwell, which was empty when they went in. They closed the door behind them, Sholto holding the handle and pushing it softly to avoid any noise.

This was all about stealth now, not a strong suit of either man. They walked up the wooden stairs, looking up into the darkness as they went and neither spotting danger. They could have been walking into a trap, bubbling with treacherous danger, and they wouldn't have had a clue. It only occurred to them later how this break-in had exposed their inability to properly handle this kind of threat. Two men walking into an unknown but probably dangerous situation by going up two flights of stairs in the dark toward a threat that may have been waiting for them, watching their every movement. Not for the first time, Darian would later wonder how he ever managed to make it from one end of the day to the other unscathed.

On the first floor they could see the closed doors of the Yangs' flat and the Highland Stars Entertainment Agency. There was no sign of disturbance. They turned the corner and sneaked slowly up to the second floor. Two steps from the top and leading the way Darian stopped. He could see their office door ajar, and he waited for Sholto to get alongside and see for himself. Through the slit they could see feeble light moving, someone with a dim torch. Before Sholto could think of a convincing way to articulate retreat Darian moved forward.

They stood on either side of the door and gave each other the sort of look that vaguely competent gunslingers in movies give each other because they didn't know what else was expected of them in the circumstances. They were working this out on the hoof.

Darian pushed the door open and called out, "Okay, you're blocked, so stay right there."

He ducked his head round the door to look inside and saw the mess, paper from Sholto's desk all over the floor, and a single person by the filing cabinet at the back of the room. He was trying to force the locked drawer and struggling pathetically because he hadn't brought the right equipment. With the torch in his hand he spun round to face the door and Darian recognized Will Dent.

"Come on, Will, what the hell are you doing?"

The Sutherland driver stared at the doorway and made a calculation. He could only see Darian and Sholto which meant it was two against one and he wasn't scared of either of them. Suddenly he made a sprint for the door, head down and shoulder-charging into both men. All three fell out into the corridor, Will crashing into the banister. Sholto rolled over and swore vividly while Darian tried to grab Will by the ankle and got a kick in the neck instead. Will was the first to his feet and bolted down the stairs.

ON RAILS

Every evening, at eight o'clock, Mungo Alason would get out of bed in his flat in Whisper Hill and have a shower. He would then walk through to the kitchen and from the yellow cabinet take a bowl and a packet of cornflakes and sit down to eat. It was silent, but for the rumble of his fridge that he had long intended to replace. He was forty-one and some variation of this had been his life for twenty years. It never occurred to Mungo that he deserved better or that he could have more. This was so normal to him and any change in routine would have been frightening. Having finished eating, he washed the bowl and spoon and returned them to their places before he left the flat and went down the stairs to Garbh Street. It wasn't an attractive place, the tall and ugly flats on either side of the narrow road, and it wasn't a fun four-minute walk to Three O'clock Station, but he was so used to it in the dark and rain that he barely looked up as he went, automatically sidestepping people on the crowded streets around the station building. They were all coming in and out of the main doors, the large front all lit up, but Mungo was going in a different way, as ever. He hardly needed to break stride, taking his security card from his pocket and swiping it into the slot on the door and quickly punching in his passcode as he put the card back in his pocket with his free hand. The red light on the panel turned green and he pulled the door open and entered. He was in the back corridor and made his way along to the changing room, opening his locker and putting on his overalls with the Duff Shipping Company logo on the breast like a football shirt. A second man walked into the room, older and smaller than Mungo. "All right, Mungo?" he said as he began to open his own locker and pull on the overall that exactly matched Mungo's in everything but size. That was the other driver, there were always two of them for security reasons, and they would exchange no more than a handful of words in the next eight and a half hours, provided nothing went wrong. Mungo went out of the changing room and along a corridor, using his card again to get out onto the platform and along to the train. It was platform number seven, right at the back and only ever used for the freight trains that Mungo drove. The company manager was already walking along the platform with clipboard in hand, marking something on every page of the wad he had, each page representing the cargo of each car. There were eight and Mungo could see that two were the red tanks that meant chemicals; they would have been collected at the docks and taken here. The manager met him by the engine and flipped to the last page for Mungo to sign, which he did. "Good night and good luck," the manager said as he always did, probably thinking it was clever, and walked away. Mungo went up into the cab and made a few checks before he stepped back onto the platform. "Here," a voice said quietly behind him, and Mungo turned expecting to find the other driver. Instead there was a man in his thirties, dressed like a station cleaner but with the look of someone who had never suffered manual labor in his life. He was holding out a small but thick envelope for Mungo to take. "What?" Mungo said. "Take it," the man told him, "give it to their guy at the other end, he'll be in the staff toilet, he'll give you your five grand. Take it." He pressed the envelope into Mungo's hand and made off down the platform. Mungo stood and looked down at what he'd been given. The man had spoken as though Mungo was supposed to expect this, but it had never happened before, there had been no warning. It felt light and insubstantial. It wasn't drugs because surely an envelope full wasn't worth this much effort or five thousand pounds of anyone's money, and it was too flat to be the precious stones they said passed through the docks routinely. It was something someone wanted to sneak out of Challaid by unpredictable means, and he couldn't imagine what that might be. He heard the thick security door to the platform open and, without thinking, stuffed the envelope inside his overalls and began to climb back into the cabin as the other driver emerged to join him. Could it have been for the other driver the man had the envelope? As he stepped into the cabin beside Mungo his companion looked his usual self, not like someone expecting a delivery that hadn't arrived.

"Right, we got clearance, call it in and let's go. Sooner we go the sooner we get back," the man said, all the conversation they would have in the loud cab. The other driver started them up while Mungo radioed in to get final permission to depart, and they pulled slowly away from the freight platform, past the passenger platforms and out from under the protection of Three O'clock Station, the lights of the built-up area around the station puncturing the view ahead. Mungo sat on his too-narrow seat with the envelope pressed against his chest, feeling it when he moved, wondering what he had done. He should have refused to take it and then he should have reported it to someone. Having failed to do those things he should have thrown it out of the window when they got clear of the city so he couldn't be caught with it at the other end. It could have been a trap, a test he had already failed. They took security seriously, the company, their ships bringing cargo in from all over the world as they had done for hundreds of years and shifting them by rail to the central belt, and that included many sensitive items. They moved slowly through Bank and up to Ciad Station, slowing to a halt as they were switched onto the tracks heading south through Gleann Fuilteach and into the mountains. As they crawled forward Mungo leaned a little more on his seat than usual, looking out for anyone in a policeman's uniform, or the Duff Shipping security officer. No one tried to stop them. The journey was the same as all the others, as it had been since the national rail line came through the mountains to connect with the city in 1907, leaving the lights of Challaid behind and swooping into the dark beauty of the empty Highlands, few named places, nothing touched by man's spoiling hand for so many miles but the line beneath them. It was four hours and twenty minutes south through the blackest hours of the night and there was nothing but the noise of the train and very occasional radio messages. They reached Glasgow and slowed again, rattling into Queen Street Station and stopping at the given platform, both getting out. Few people were there in the dead hours, and some wore security uniforms, but it was the same collection of sleepy faces that always met them. Mungo signed for them as he always did, confirming the delivery and time, and then told them he needed the toilet. He was pouring with sweat when he went in. There was a man in a suit with stylish hair and a gold watch standing by the sinks, dark eyes and a dimpled chin, showing his too-white teeth when he smiled at Mungo. "You have it?" he asked in what sounded like an English accent. Mungo reached into his overalls and took out the envelope, passing it to the man and looking sideways to the cubicles to make sure no one was there. "Good work, I appreciate it," the man said, taking another envelope from his pocket and passing it to Mungo. "I'll see you next month," the man in the suit said and walked out of the bathroom. Mungo took the new envelope and unzipped his overalls, reaching down to put it into the pocket of his trousers and zipping back up again. He walked back out to join the other driver, nervous again, and they walked together across the station to get into a different cab. There were three cars attached to it and he signed for them. The train they had delivered would be moved out of this station by a driver already getting into it, taken to be unloaded elsewhere. They would return this one in the night with whatever small cargo it carried and be finished with their shift as the sun came back around. They were given clearance to leave, slowly and quietly at this hour as they moved through the edges of the southern city, and it felt excruciating to Mungo. The long journey north in silence, moonlight rolling silver down the sides of the mountains and showing snow on the peaks, sometimes smothered in the clouds and nothing but the blackness, then into Gleann Fuilteach and the lights of Challaid. They switched tracks again at Ciad Station, moving through Cnocaid, Bank, Bakers Moor and Earmam before reaching Whisper Hill, the long straight run north in the dip with the backs of the buildings on either side looking so tall. Back where they had started as they rolled slowly into Three O'clock Station. Mungo signed the return slip and went into the changing room, taking off his overalls and hanging them in his locker. "See you tomorrow," the other driver said as Mungo left. He used his security card at the door and stepped outside. No alarms went off and no one was waiting to grab him. He walked through the cold hours of early morning, his breath jumping out ahead of him, trying to get away, and he reached Garbh Street and home. His checked shirt was sticking to him and he could smell the sweat as he sat at the kitchen table and carefully cut open the envelope with a knife. There was exactly five thousand pounds inside in fifty crisp one-hundred-pound notes, the roguish face of King Alex looking back at him from every green one. Mungo didn't know what he'd done and didn't know what to do with what he'd been given for it, but he knew he'd do it again. A month later the same man handed him another envelope, this time in the corridor just inside the security door. It was the same size and feel as the first, the same reward given by the same man in Glasgow. It happened again the following month, and again after that, and after the eighth month Mungo was no longer nervous about it. He never looked in the envelopes. He was getting sixty thousand pounds a year for almost no extra work, and as long as there were no disasters no one would ever find out.

33

DARIAN WAS on his feet before Sholto, and after a glance confirmed his boss was okay he was off down the stairs after Dent. He could hear footsteps ahead of him, hitting each step at pace. This was where Darian could catch up because even in the dark the stairs were familiar to him but not to Dent. Darian could use instinct to move faster than his quarry. He felt he was getting closer and Dent felt it too because he started to gamble on the first-floor stairs, going down two at a time and risking breaking the only neck he had. Dent jumped the last five steps and landed hard. It must have jarred his ankles, but desperation can persuade you to ignore any pain that might try to slow you, so he bounded to the side door and out into the night, ahead of Darian.

As he came down the last of the steps Darian heard a noise outside, the sound of a person who had been hit by something they wished they had avoided, a wobbly shout smothered by the noise of the door banging shut. Darian pushed it open and ran out into Cage Street, nearly tripping over Mr. Yang. The restaurant owner was sprawled on his back like an upended turtle, waving his hands around as he tried to remember how to get up.

Darian shouted, "Are you okay?"

As Mr. Yang rolled over and raised himself onto his knees Darian saw the glint of a meat cleaver big enough to halve a horse lying in the street. Mr. Yang, in a tone of self-disgust, said, "I missed him. I swung and I missed him."

Darian, who had stopped the chase to check on his friend, asked, "Did he hit you, are you hurt?"

"Shouldered me, that's all, I'm fine. Go after him, Darian, go after him. He went up to Greenshank Drive, go."

Before Darian could start to run the door behind him burst open and a red-faced Sholto wheezed out onto Cage Street. Under the streetlights he saw Mr. Yang on his knees, gasped and said, "Mr. Yang, he got you too, are you okay?"

"I'm fine. Don't waste time with me, get after him."

They began to run up the street, Sholto struggling to keep up. At the corner with Greenshank Drive Darian stopped to look for Dent and Sholto caught up with him, saying, "That Mr. Yang is a hardy old bugger, shame he won't do what he's told."

Darian was ignoring him, looking up and down the road and catching a glimpse of a man who might have been Dent going round the corner with Morhen Road, the route you would take if you were aiming for Glendan Station and a train that could put meaningful distance between you and your crime.

Darian said, "There, Morhen Road. I'll chase, you take the car. If he gets on a train I'll call you and tell you where to go. If you corner him…"

"Don't worry, I don't corner bigger people than me without shouting for help first."

Darian set off at a sprint toward the corner with Morhen Road, hoping to close the gap. By the time he reached it, Dent was nearly up at the opposite corner with Gallows View, the street on which the railway station stood. Darian wasn't the natural athlete of the Ross siblings; that honor went to his older brother Sorley, an exceedingly good camanachd player who wouldn't only have caught Dent by now, he would have battered every ounce of useful information out of him. Darian's reaction to falling behind was to run with longer strides, right on the edge of his balance, which felt faster but perhaps only because of how close he was to falling over.

Up to the corner and onto Gallows View, the long curving road with the station to his right and more people around. He couldn't see Dent, but that was because he was looking in the wrong place. When he looked away from the station entrance he saw a man running down a gap between two buildings, a travel agency on the ground floor on one side and an estate agent's on the other. Behind the buildings was a large corrugated fence to block access to the railway lines, and Dent was going for it.

Getting across the busy road took thirty seconds, too many taxis threatening to run him over, and then he had to get down the alley and over the high fence. He quickly reached the conclusion that Dent had toes more pointed than his because Darian struggled to get a foothold, pulling himself up and feeling the metal at the top dig into his fingers. It hurt, but not as much as Dent getting away would, and he forced himself up and over, trying to lower himself carefully on the other side but eventually having to let go and drop into the long grass, the fence higher on the rail side.

The grass was tall and the embankment before him was a steep drop into darkness, a wide valley with the twin tracks leading into the tunnel on one side and the station lit bright on the other, the backs of buildings opposite visible as silhouettes. Darian moved to the edge of the drop, almost falling as his dress shoes had no grip. The only pair of nice black shoes he owned, cheap but presentable, were no better for stalking through wet grass than they were for sprinting, but he had to do all this in an outfit designed for a rich man's party.

There was something there, a shadow that didn't quite fit with its surroundings, and Darian crept closer. It was toward the tunnel mouth: Dent crouching in the grass at the top of the hill, hoping Darian would go the other way. Stealth suited Dent because he had darkness behind him but Darian was framed by the lights of the station and as soon as he started to walk toward him the driver made his move. He began sliding down the embankment on his backside, looking for more distance and taking risks to get it.

Darian shouted, "Come on, Will, we know it's you, you can't outrun this."

Darian was about to slide down after him when he saw movement on the other side: Sholto at the top of the embankment opposite.

Sholto called out, "You're surrounded, Will, just climb up and give up."

Dent was down on the line now, standing in the middle of the westbound tracks, and a sense of terrifying inevitability grabbed Darian's stomach and squeezed it hard. He shouted, "Come on, Will, come back up, we can help you. Come up."

Dent was a shadow, standing looking back and forth between Darian and Sholto, and then his face became clear. Someone had shone a light on him and Darian could see the fury and desperation in his face. It wasn't the light but the sound that made Darian turn and look, seeing the large freight train clear of the station and moving toward them, a blocky cabin and bright yellow front to make it unmissable. Dent saw it and stared, jerking as though he was about to take a step but then not moving.

Sholto screamed, "Will, please. Will."

Darian screamed too but when he thought about it later he couldn't remember what he had said and it was unlikely to have been anything more than a terrified shout. The train was close. There was a wail of brakes and a deep horn but it was too late to stop. Darian and Will Dent were looking each other in the eye, the driver not moving. The tension went out of him and his shoulders dropped. Darian forced himself not to turn away when the train hit him.

34

THE WORLD stopped for what seemed like hours but was only seconds. Darian stood on the top of the embankment and looked down at the train, now still on the tracks, no sign of Will Dent. The two men in the cab of the train sat where they were and didn't move, stunned by what had happened. Sholto was across on the other side, and although Darian didn't notice it at the time he too was rooted to the spot. In the seconds after another man's death a moment of respectful silence was forced upon them by shock. Dent was under the train. Darian couldn't see him because the massive metal beast had moved forward another seventy or eighty feet before stopping at the mouth of the tunnel.

Everyone seemed to move at the same time. Darian tried to run, skidding down the slope as Dent had done, trying to kneel and slide on his feet but slipping and going on his backside instead. By the time he was at the bottom two men in overalls were getting down out of the cab of the train, a man in his forties and a smaller, older one. The three of them stumbled toward the section of track where Dent had last been seen. Darian caught movement from the corner of his eye as he passed the link between two carriages and turned his head sharply to see Sholto struggling to make his way down to them.

The taller of the two drivers got down on his belly and looked under. He said, "Oh Jesus."

Darian looked to see for himself the grim scene below. A description isn't necessary because no one needs or deserves to have the details darken their mind. No one's family should have to read about what became of their loved one in a book like this. They knew at a glance that Will Dent was dead.

The older train driver said, "I'll call it in."

He climbed back into the cab as Sholto finally reached them. He looked at Darian and said, "He's dead."

"Yeah, he's dead. Don't look."

It took only a couple of minutes from that point for the police to arrive. The first on the scene were a couple of constables who had been at the station and came running down the track with torches. The line had been shut, bringing an unsympathetic city even closer to a grinding halt than usual. They checked the body and asked a few basic questions, not getting too far above their pay grade. A still-breathless Sholto handled the talking.

He said to them, "There was a break-in at our office, Douglas Independent Research on Cage Street. It was William Dent, that's the deceased. We chased him and he climbed the fence on this side. My colleague, Darian Ross here, he went on foot, I took the car because we thought he was going for the station. As I drove past I saw Darian climb the fence on Gallows View so I went round to Cladach Road thinking I could intercept him, cut off his escape. He stood on the train tracks in between us. He just stood there and let the train hit him."

One of the officers said, "He must have done more than break into an office to take that way out."

Whatever that may have been they never found out because the officer chose not to follow up his speculation. A couple of minutes later more cops arrived, and then a couple of ambulances. Within five minutes the area between the station and the mouth of the tunnel was crawling with people and shifting light. One of the train drivers was with them and Darian asked if he was okay.

The man touched the place on his chest where his shirt pocket would be, a nervous twitch Darian had seen him do a few times, and said, "Yes, aye, I'm okay. I'm...okay."

He sounded like he was trying to convince himself, but at that point they all were. There was no way to be okay in the wake of what they had seen, what they had been a part of. It was horrifying and they were all shattered by it, but the need to focus on what Dent had been doing forced Darian and Sholto to turn their minds away from the death and back to the break-in, and that helped.

A detective from Bank Station appeared beside them. "Sholto, fucking hell, I thought this sort of thing was behind you, bodies and mayhem."

"I hoped they were, but it seems where there's life there's death, Conall."

"Very profound, Sholto, very profound. So what's the God's honest reason for this life turning to death? More to it than a burglary gone wrong?"

This was when they had to share everything they knew. Darian had hoped they might get away from the scene without spilling it all, give them time to talk to Vinny and DC Vicario before the nasty truth shocked everyone. Once Dent's motives were out in the open word would filter instantly back to Harold Sutherland, and on to his nephew, and that was going to give them time to distance themselves from their employee, set up defenses. Darian's first instinct was that Dent was obviously involved in Ruby-Mae Short's killing and Freya's disappearance, but his second thought told him it didn't mean he was working alone. He had known they were at Harold's party, that's why he had attacked the office that night. Someone had told him. Raven or Harold or perhaps even the Sutherland who had gotten them on the guest list, Philip.

Sholto said to DS Conall Archer, "When you dig around you're going to find out that William Dent was working for Harold Sutherland as his personal driver, and you're going to find out that he's being investigated both for the murder of Ruby-Mae Short from last January that Dockside are looking at and the disappearance of Freya Dempsey that Cnocaid are handling."

"Sutherland? Wait, Freya Dempsey? Is that Vinny Reno's missing ex? Oh, shite."

He moved away quickly to make what looked, under the arc lights now set up alongside the train, like a series of frantic phone calls. DS MacNeith arrived and addressed Darian and Sholto only to tell them she would speak to them properly the following day, and it didn't seem like she was planning on offering any good wishes. DC Vicario showed up with a colleague a few minutes later.

She told them, "I'll make my pitch for information, but we'll be at the back of the queue. Bank will handle the scene and Cnocaid are working an active search for a missing person so that'll get priority. You really should have called us about the burglary instead of handling it yourself."

Sholto said, "The police were called, they just weren't arriving. We went to our office and found he was still there. There wasn't much else we could do."

Vicario nodded and said, "That might be enough to keep you out of trouble if it's accepted he was going to flee before the police got there. I know you've given your witness statements twice already, so you should go home. There'll be a lot of people wanting to talk to you tomorrow. If I can hold back some of the wolves I will."

Darian said, "Thanks, Angela."

He didn't notice her smile at the mention of her first name; he had been familiar without thinking. If he had thought about it, he would have realized he hadn't earned that yet. Angela patted Darian gently on the shoulder as he and Sholto turned away from the train and the lights and the teams of people in white forensic suits and made their way through the long grass and up to the fence on the far side. A panel had been cut away from it, the whole section would have to be replaced, and people were coming in and out. They got into the Fiat and Sholto picked an exceedingly careful path out between police cars, an ambulance, a large black van and, just coming up the street, what looked like a large crane on the back of a lorry.

35

THE FIAT pulled into the parking place on Dlùth Street at the bottom of Cage Street that Sholto always used when at the office. Neither of them had said a word on the short drive from the station. Tiredness had hit them both in a heavy wave and was making smart choices difficult. They should have gone straight to their beds, but the night wasn't done with them yet. They had to check on the office and they had to check on Mr. Yang. As they turned the corner they could see the whole Yang family out on the street, talking to cops. Challaid Police had finally turned up, but only because someone getting hit by a train had forced them to accelerate a process that typically moved at the speed of coastal erosion.

Sholto walked up to Mr. Yang and said, "You okay, pal?"

"I am, yes, we all are. We heard what happened; the police are here because of it. Are you okay too?"

"We're all right. Saw some things our eyeballs would rather have avoided, but these pictures get placed in front of you in life now and then."

A young detective from Bank Station came over and introduced herself as DC Sarah Lowell. She said, "I know we already have statements from you, but it would help us if you could check your office to see if anything was taken."

They walked past the spot where Mr. Yang had been knocked over and Darian noted there was no sign of the meat cleaver now. Had the police seen it they would no doubt have wanted to talk sternly about Mr. Yang's intentions, so Darian guessed that either he or his eminently more sensible wife had returned it to the kitchen where it belonged. No need to make the Yangs' night any more awkward than it had already been.

As they were walking up the stairs to the second floor an only slightly familiar face appeared above them, waiting. He nodded when he saw them and said, "Mr. Douglas, Mr. Ross, I'm Warren from Challaid Data Services. I called you earlier on."

He was a dashing man in his late thirties, sweeping black hair and large eyes, an expensive black coat and silver wedding ring. His local accent tilted toward the posh side of the loch, which typically meant it sounded a little more Anglo and a little less Gaelic, not so much spit in the pronunciation.

Sholto said, "We appreciated that, thank you, Warren."

Warren ran his hand through his hair nervously and said, "What a night. I was talking to one of the cops when I got here, they told me what happened with the guy and the train. A hellish thing to be a part of, but I'm glad you're both okay."

He sounded like he meant it too, this man they hardly knew, which was unexpectedly nice of him. People were treating them as though they had been the ones hit by the train, and nobody seemed to have a lot of pity for Will Dent.

Warren continued, "I told the cop I wanted to come up and make sure our office was safe, but I figured it would be, it was yours he was targeting. I'm glad I bumped into you. We'll need to talk about security for the building at some point, maybe try and get a meeting with the owner about it if we can find the guy."

Darian nodded and said, "I didn't know we had any security as it was."

Standing in the dim light of the landing Warren said, "We put some in a few months ago. We got a contract with the council, handling some data for them, and part of the agreement was that we had to make sure everything was extremely secure because they're paranoid about information being stolen or leaked, so we upped the security from nonexistent to minor. There's a camera up there so we've got the landing covered and it sends alerts to my phone if there's movement registered outside of working hours. I checked the feed and here was some guy making a hard job out of forcing your door."

Darian and Sholto both looked up at the white plastic circle on the ceiling that he had pointed to as a camera. Sholto said, "I thought that was a smoke alarm."

"No, no, that's a camera."

"So we still don't have a smoke alarm."

"I put a letter into your mailbox telling you about it when it was being put in, I thought you knew it was there. I got in touch with the owner, eventually. He said he was on holiday in Mexico, so I emailed him the details and he agreed to it. No one else in the building objected, although I never managed to make contact with the talent agency downstairs, if there's anyone there to make contact with. I should have made the effort to come along the corridor and talk to you about it."

"I don't remember seeing that letter."

Darian glanced through the open office door. The light was on now and he could see the piles of paper that had smothered Sholto's desk now carpeting the floor. There could have been a letter from the king in there and it would have had a fifty-fifty chance of ever being read. Darian had always suspected that a lot of worthwhile offers and information got lost in those piles.

Darian said, "Well, thanks for the call."

The two of them went into the office. It wasn't hard to work out that Dent hadn't taken anything with him because the only things of importance or value were still locked up in the now slightly damaged filing cabinet. They stood in the middle of a room that had never looked or felt smaller and scanned the damage he'd done trying to find something that in the end would have done him no good.

Sholto said, "What the hell did he think he was going to find in here?"

"I don't know. He must have known where we were so he took his chance, but for what?"

"Unless he thought we were sitting on the evidence that proved his guilt and didn't realize it."

"Then how would he know we had it?"

"That I can't tell you."

They left the office in the hands of the police, no point giving them a key because the lock was broken on the door. Sholto drove Darian home for the second time that long night.

BAKERS MOOR STATION—SEARCH REPORT

16/05/18

Name of suspect: William Dent
Case No.: BM06-160518
Address searched:
40 MacLean Street,
Bakers Moor,
Challaid, CH5 1NI

Search of domestic premises

Catalog of items of interest found—

Samsung tablet—Found on tablet were deleted searches relating to murder investigation of Ruby-Mae Short (Case no. WH22-120117)

Searches dated: Jan 13th 2017, Jan 14th 2017, Jan 19th 2017, Feb 16th 2017, May 11th 2018, May 14th 2018

Terms searched—

Jan 13th 2017—

- Ruby Short
- Ruby-May Short
- Ruby-Mae Short
- Ruby-Mae Short murder
- Ruby-Mae Short Misgearan

Jan 14th 2017—

- Ruby-Mae Short murder investigation
- DI Ralph Grant

- Detective Inspector Ralph Grant
- DC Angela Vicario

Jan 19th 2017—

- Ruby-Mae Short
- Ruby-Mae Short witness's
- Ruby-Mae Short witnesses
- Ruby-Mae Short Misgearan

Feb 16th 2017—

- Nathan Short
- Ruby-Mae Short family
- Ruby-Mae Short pictures
- Ruby-Mae Short murder investigation
- Dockside police station Challaid

May 11th 2018—

- Ruby-Mae Short murder investigation
- Douglas Independent Research
- Ruby-Mae Short Douglas Independent Research
- Sholto Douglas
- Darian Ross
- Ruby-Mae Short Sholto Douglas
- Freya Dempsey

May 14th 2018—

- Ruby-Mae Short William Dent
- Ruby-Mae Short Sutherland
- Ruby-Mae Short murder
- Freya Dempsey

Single page with Raven Investigators logo relating to ongoing investigation. Page listed as page 2 of 2, not clear who it was addressed to, page 1 not found.

Quote:... *Ross and Philip Sutherland gained access to the house and searched the property. The evidence they found was presented to the police and our belief is that they are convinced of the involvement of William Dent. It's likely they've gained additional evidence from following Mr. Dent, and that evidence would be held securely at their office, 21 Cage Street, Bank. We will continue our investigations, as instructed.*

Sincerely,

Bran Kennedy

Cash totalling £2,560 was found in a plastic bag hidden in a basket of potatoes in the kitchen cupboard. Request has been made to access details of Mr. Dent's account with Sutherland Bank. No bank slips found on premises.

Holdall in wardrobe containing several changes of clothing and Mr. Dent's passport in a side pocket. Possibly left from previous holiday but clothes unworn and possible exit bag.

All relevant information passed on to Dockside station in relation to Ruby-Mae Short murder investigation (case no. WH22-120117) and Cnocaid station in relation to Freya Dempsey missing person investigation (case no. CN35-070517).

Deep search of premises to be carried out afternoon of 16/05/18, will be attached to this file.

36

DARIAN WOKE with the sort of sore muscles and dull headache that overexertion caused. Sleep had been fitful and he was up early, the scenes behind his eyelids grimmer than anything he was likely to see in daylight. He shaved and forced himself to eat a bowl of cereal with milk as suspicious as anyone he had met in the last few days. Normally he would have ditched it and gotten his breakfast from The Northern Song, but he wasn't sure Mr. Yang would be open this morning.

The trip to Cage Street was bleaker than before, Darian looking at the floor of the train instead of at the people, not interested in how the good and more often bad of Challaid were conducting themselves that morning. The line was open again, the disruption now behind everyone else. As he walked through Glendan Station he looked around for any sign that something tragic had happened, that a man had lost his life just a few hundred yards down the track, but there was none. The death of Will Dent had caused only temporary inconvenience.

Walking down Cage Street he could see a strand of blue and white police tape tied to a drainpipe on the Superdrug store opposite that had presumably stretched across to the other side of the street but had been ripped away hours ago. That was the only admission this had been a crime scene. How quickly a place moved on from the events that occurred there. To his surprise, The Northern Song was open as usual and people were going in to collect their food. Darian went in the side door and up to the office, surprised to find Sholto ahead of him.

Sholto said, "You sleep as badly as I did?"

"Yeah, sleep didn't want me to begin with and when it came around I didn't much like the look of it."

"Bad pictures playing?"

"The same one, over and over. I just don't understand why he didn't step out of the way."

"We'll never know. Maybe a person gets to the point that they realize the game is up, that their guilt is about to be proven, and the choice between a lifetime in prison and a quick death is a decision we wouldn't all agree on. People like to say the survival instinct keeps them fighting, but that's not always true."

Sholto was trying to convince them both that Will Dent was guilty of killing Ruby-Mae Short and possibly Freya Dempsey as well, because believing he had been evil was the one thing that extracted some of the poison from the trauma that surrounded them. He had to be guilty.

Neither of them got any work done. They sat at their desks and stared into space, unsure what they were supposed to do now anyway. They were looking for Freya but if Dent was guilty then the police were likely to find some trace of her before they could. Darian kept checking his phone to see if there had been a message he had missed, but no one was calling. It was a strange relief to hear footsteps on the stairs and a knock on the door because it meant something was about to happen to break the chilly grip of nothingness.

Sholto let DC Vicario in and she looked at them both sympathetically. "Well, you two have a habit of keeping me up all night with nothing happy to show for it."

Sholto said, "Nothing to show? What did you find out about Dent?"

"A few things, but not enough. We know he showed a lot of interest in Ruby's murder right after it happened, but we haven't found anything that clearly says he was involved and nothing to say he had ever heard of her before her death was reported in the media. We still have to check his phone, it was in his pocket and it's... broken. That might have more on it, more web searches; we're hoping it'll help."

Darian said, "It says something that he had any interest in it."

"It says he had an interest, it doesn't say why and we can't just guess."

"What about Freya?"

"Nothing. The only indication he had ever heard of her came from searches made after you questioned him the first time, which is a reasonable time for him to get interested in her case. There were other things, though. He had cash and a bag packed to run with, so there was either guilt or fear there. There was one particularly interesting thing. When Bakers Moor raided his flat they found the second page of a two-page note from Raven Investigators that mentioned you and your work, suggested that you thought Dent was involved in Freya's case and might have evidence to prove it. It had your address on it. We've talked to Raven and they say it was days old and part of a security update to the Sutherland Bank, not even to Harold Sutherland specifically, just the security department."

Darian looked at her and said, "Do you believe that?"

"I don't know, it looked like it was written to point someone in your direction. I hear Bran Kennedy is a good liar. We couldn't get any more out of him but maybe someone else could. Would help to know how Dent got his hands on a letter sent to the security department of the bank. If he stole it then he looks like a desperate man trying to cover his tracks. If someone gave it to him..."

Having rolled her grenade into their morning DC Vicario announced she was going home to get some sleep and left the office. Darian and Sholto both grabbed their coats and left the office just a minute behind her, down to Dlùth Street and the Fiat. They drove straight to Alexander Street in the south of Bank and the Challaid office of Raven Investigators.

The building, on a pleasant curved street, was four stories of brick with plenty of tall windows to let in the little light that beat its way through the clouds and the shadow of Stac Voror. They had to park a way down the road and walk back up. In the reception area inside the front door they saw that Raven had the top floor, so they trudged up the stairs and found themselves in a hallway where a secretary behind her desk was the only person in view. To get to the Raven offices they had to get through the double doors beyond the smiling woman looking up at them.

She said, "Hello, welcome to Raven Investigators, how can I help?"

Sholto said, "We'd like to speak with Bran Kennedy."

"Do you have an appointment?"

"We've got something better than that. We've got a boiling hot pan of trouble to throw over him."

"Eh, can I ask who you are?"

"I'm Sholto Douglas, this is Darian Ross."

"Oh, well, I'm afraid Mr. Kennedy isn't in his office at the moment..."

Sholto laughed and said, "Isn't it funny how the mention of our names reminded you of that. You're a good secretary; we could use someone like you. Couldn't afford you, though."

Sholto, in a rare moment of damned bad manners, turned and pulled open the double doors, wandering into the offices uninvited, Darian scurrying to keep up. There was an open floor, maybe seven or eight desks, only three of them currently occupied and Darian recognized Alan Dudley at one. At the back of the large room was an office on its own, and Sholto was already moving toward it with the certainty of a man who had complained here before. He pushed open the door, ignoring the staff closing in on them from behind, and found the man he was looking for.

Bran Kennedy stood up from behind his desk and said, "Douglas, what the hell are you doing in a proper investigator's office?"

"I've come to ask you a series of very awkward questions."

Sholto and Kennedy stood opposite each other and glared waves of wary hate across the room, like a washed-up bullfighter who'd forgotten to bring his sword and a malnourished bull with no heart, facing off in the arena after the crowd had gone home and the lights had been turned off.

The three employees who had been at their desks, two men and a woman, surrounded Darian in the doorway, one of them grabbing his arm before Kennedy said, "Leave him, lads; let's hear what Oopsy the clown and the boy blunder have to say before we chuck them out. Go on, Sholto, tell the nice people what's gotten your blood pressure all riled up? I never saw you this red in the face when you were a cop except out of embarrassment."

"I'm just here to tell you what you already know."

"Well, that is a huge surprise, I'd better sit down before I faint."

One of the men behind Darian sniggered but Sholto ignored him and said, "You know that a letter you wrote was found in the possession of William Dent, and that it provided him with the reason, no, the advice, to target us, which in turn led him to his death. I know you've claimed it was a general update to the security department of the bank, but you also know as well as I do that the police aren't buying that. A case like this, Sutherland's being questioned about it, no way your updates just went to the security chief. The police are coming after you, Bran. Me and Darian, we'll be after you too and I suppose you think you can handle us, but the police, Bran, the whole vicious, seething lot of them, you know what it means when they smell blood. That letter painted a bloody great big target on your back, and a lot of people with good aim are ready to take a shot. I hope you've got a good shield to hide behind. So, who did you deliver the letter to?"

Kennedy had grown angrier the longer Sholto went on, but he took his time before he answered. In a voice that seemed too small for his large, ugly, totally bald head he said, "I gave it to the security officer, as I always do. I would never lie to the police about something like that. Now, lads, if you'd like to escort these trespassers out of the building."

The three employees shoved them all the way down to the front door and out into the street with practiced precision and glee. They walked back to the car and Sholto said, “He’s nervous about the police, which means he’ll run for the cover of whichever Sutherland is paying him the big bucks. Let’s see which one moves first.”

37

IN THE office Darian had several messages from Vinny, telling him what he'd heard at the station, which was nothing more than DC Vicario had already told them. The sense underlay each conversation that Will Dent was the guilty party and he had worked alone, the guilty man gone and nothing left to do but find Freya so Vinny could organize a funeral. It wasn't a positive thought, but it was an inevitability they were prepared for.

The phone call they had been waiting for was to Darian's mobile and it came from Phil. Darian answered and said, "Hello?"

"It's Phil Sutherland. Listen, I've had a call from my cousin, Simon, and he wants to talk to you and your boss, wants to talk to me as well. Can you get round to his house straightaway?"

"Yeah, we can."

"Me and Vinny are already on our way, we'll see you there."

Darian hung up and looked across the room at Sholto. He said, "That was Phil, Simon Sutherland wants to see us at his house right away."

Sholto raised his eyebrows and then raised the rest of himself from his chair. They drove up to Geug Place, Sholto viewing this first step by Simon as a sign of his guilt, a man worried he was about to be rumbled so making defensive maneuvers. Darian couldn't quite find a way to disagree with that, whatever his gut said. They parked behind Vinny's car outside the gate and the four of them congregated.

Sholto said to Phil, "How did he sound when he spoke to you, your cousin?"

"Scared. The police have been here to talk to him early this morning and I don't think he's handling it well. They haven't got anything against him but he's not used to having all these people rummaging through his life."

Sholto said, "No, he's not. Might be a good thing that it's changing now."

The gate began to open and the four of them walked in and up the drive. Olinda Bles was waiting at the front door. She looked as if she'd been crying and her expression said she blamed them for it. They approached and Vinny offered his condolences for the group.

She said, "Never mind your sympathy. Simon will see you, come in."

Olinda held the door open for them and they hiked in, Phil going first and heading straight to his right without being told, along the corridor and through the door to the empty room. He walked with the confidence of a man who belonged in the mansions of the quirky rich. Simon was waiting, standing back toward the door that led to one of the wings filled with the junk that had at various times passed through his life. The four men came in and stood facing him, lined along the wall opposite.

He said, "Thank you for coming, I'm sure you're busy."

While the other three nodded politely, Darian took the opportunity to speak first. "Can you tell us what you know of William Dent?"

Simon looked to the floor, hurt. "I couldn't believe it when I found out that he was dead. And how it happened, I couldn't believe it. He was doing what he did for me. I didn't tell him to, I didn't know why but he thought he was helping me."

"Row back a length. What was he doing for you?"

"Breaking into your office. It wasn't just himself he was trying to find any information about, it was me, too. He was convinced we were both being framed. Someone put the bra here to make it look like I was involved, and you might know something about it."

"Why did he think that?"

"He said you had been following him around and investigating the case. I said it was good because you'd find who did it, but he said you would help set us up. He said someone else had brought that bra here and you were going to help them get away with it. You'd blame us for the Short woman and Dempsey, even when you knew we were innocent."

"Why on earth would we do that?"

"Because he killed his ex and you want to protect your friend."

He was looking at Vinny, and so was everyone else now. Vinny scowled at him and said, "Are you off your fucking head? I mean, obviously you are, but this is really pushing it, pal."

Phil said, "Simon, Vinny didn't kill Freya, that's absurd."

Sholto said, "And if he had we would never cover it up, not a chance."

"Then you'll accept my offer to work for me now to find the person who did. I have money, I want to hire you."

Sholto shook his head. "We're already working the case for Vinny, who admittedly has much less chance of ever paying us but still, it's first come first served. If you care about us finding the truth then you have nothing to worry about, we're looking hard. It would help if you told us everything you knew about Dent."

"He was a friend. I don't have many, you know that already. He cared about doing the right thing, but, I don't know, he just couldn't trust people. I struggle with trusting people, too, I suppose, but I don't have to live among them. He was a better man than you think."

Darian said, "After Ruby-Mae Short was killed Dent repeatedly searched for information about the case on his tablet. If he had no interest in it then why would he do that?"

Simon stared blankly and said, "I don't know why he would do that. Maybe it was all over the news, I don't know why else."

Sholto said, "Simon, if it turns out you're lying to us about any of this you'll end up in court and you could even end up in prison."

Darian reached into his pocket, and stepping forward, he said to Simon "This card has my number on it. If you remember anything, if you find something out, call me, any hour of the day or night, doesn't matter. William Dent has too many connections to bad things to be the man you're trying to tell us he was. If you think of something that would explain that gap then call me."

Simon Sutherland took the card and Darian could at least be certain he was one person who wouldn't throw it straight in the bin as soon as they left. As they started to file out Darian noticed Phil give a small nod to his cousin, as if he was trying to reassure him. They walked out and left Simon in the empty room.

On the way down the drive Vinny said, "This isn't moving us forward. I need to find out what the hell happened to Freya and this is nothing to do with that. Much as I want to catch who killed Short, Freya is my priority."

Sholto said, "Someone bought Freya expensive gifts before she disappeared. Then William Dent decides to play with a train rather than be caught by us. Calling us here, accusing you to your face, that's not a dumb ploy."

Phil shook his head and said, "He was being genuine, surely you could see that."

"I'm older than you lads, I've met more liars than you have, this city is overflowing with them. I'm not saying he's one, but the best actors are so good you don't even realize they're doing it. Sometimes they're so damn good even *they* don't realize they're doing it."

"He's not acting. He's not."

Phil and Vinny left because they had to get back to Whisper Hill while Sholto drove them down to the corner of Geug Place.

Adopting the tone he used when he wanted you to think he was just goofing around but he was actually making a serious point, Sholto said, "There is another person who could have bought Freya expensive presents, and who definitely met her more than once. And he had potential access to Simon's house to plant evidence. And he knew we'd be away from the office last night. Wee Phil's been right by our side all the way, helping us get at his vulnerable cousin and flashy uncle, but how innocent is he?"

"Shit, Sholto, you're not serious. First you accuse Vinny and now Phil."

"I'm not accusing him, I'm pointing out that he fits the profile, nothing more. He's not even the person I'm most interested in right now."

"Who is?"

"Olinda Bles."

FROM THE NEW WORLD TO THE OLD CITY

A LOOK AT THE ABUSE OF CALEDONIAN IMMIGRANTS IN CHALLAID

It's a testament to the sensitivity of the issue that when I met the first immigrant I interviewed for this piece it was in private and they agreed only on the assurance that their identity would not be revealed. That, says Leonor Daza from the charity Caledonians in Challaid who help people moving here for the first time, is not uncommon. Too many people, she says, are coming across the ocean for a better life and to get it they must first spend a year living in fear and suffering exploitation.

"I couldn't say anything," the young woman tells me. She's twenty and nervous, speaking to me in the Earmam office of Caledonians in Challaid. She's been in the country for eleven months and one more month of employment will entitle her to the dual passport she came for. It hasn't been an easy first eleven. "I know I get paid a lot less than the minimum but I can't say it. I have to work long, long hours and I can't complain because I know I will lose my job. They always say that, if you are trouble you lose your job and then you won't get another, no passport."

This is a story repeated by many mouths. With twelve months of employment required for a dual passport the threat of losing a job is the threat of losing the opportunity to become not just a citizen of Scotland but Europe. Many feel they are being held hostage by unscrupulous employers who see them as cheap and disposable labor, easy to mistreat and, when they leave after twelve months, easy to replace with more young people arriving in the city from the Caledonian countries.

"It's a fairly even split between people from Panama and those from Costa Rica," Leonor Daza tells me in the same CIC office, a small place that receives no government or council funding. "Even though there are more people in Costa Rica, Panama has longer and more ingrained links here so it balances out. Very few come from Nicaragua because the passport laws are so much more restrictive for them. The people who come are mostly young, in their late teens or twenties, and they have their whole lives ahead of them. They take jobs paying criminally low wages, often the jobs no one from Challaid would do, and they're forced to work in unacceptable, dangerous conditions. Most will share a flat in Earmam or Whisper Hill with six or seven other people, a one- or two-bedroom flat, and they say they're willing because it's only twelve months and at the end they can leave."

The young woman I've come to interview doesn't want to tell me where she lives, but she does admit she shares with five other people. "It's not great. It has one bedroom and three of us sleep there, three in the living room. The landlord knows there are six, he charges for six."

That too is a breach of the law, both housing and safety regulations, but landlords also see "twelve monthers" as a chance to make easy money. Knowing that this is happening, what are Challaid council doing about it? Eunan O'Brien, Liberal Party, is the council spokesman on immigration. "We have clear policies already in place to make sure that all people coming here, wherever from, are treated with the respect they deserve, and are protected by the same laws that we would expect all citizens of Challaid to enjoy." When I point out that these laws don't appear to be enough to protect the twelve monthers he half shrugs. "It's a problem, not of powers but of enforcement. If people don't report criminal activity then there's not a lot that can be done. We're committed to making sure people feel able to report these things, and we've always said that if immigrants have themselves done nothing wrong then they have nothing to fear from police contact."

It's a familiar promise with exasperating wording to Leonor Daza. "The council have been committed to improving the lives of Caledonians in Challaid since the CIC was founded nearly thirty years ago, what they haven't actually gotten round to doing yet is improving the situation for anyone from Caledonia. And the language has never changed either, always the hint that an immigrant might have done something wrong, that they must be scared of the police rather than an abuser."

Due to a delay in completing interviews this piece didn't appear in last month's issue as planned, so I realized that the young woman I'd interviewed at the CIC would have completed her twelve months. I managed to get back in touch with her. She told me that on the day she got her dual passport she quit her job, left her flat and got on a train that took her all the way down to London, despite the uncertainty of her status there as the British leave Europe. She already has a new job and a better life. Although she still doesn't want her name to be used in the article, she did give me the name of her employer in Challaid, Highland Specialist Plastics.

HSP have a factory making tailored plastic parts for export in Bakers Moor, using part of an old warehouse building that was once one of many belonging to the famed Challaid Whaling Company. I asked HSP for a comment and they stated that they were "committed to the best working practices and to ensuring that all employees from Caledonia were treated fairly and given the best chance to gain their passport." When I visited their factory security wouldn't allow me to enter and none of their employees were willing to speak to me. HSP, it seems, are one of many for whom commitment to rhetoric on the twelve-month question is not matched in reality by a commitment to the people at the heart of it.

38

OLINDA BLES left Geug Place at 1:32, and Sholto started the car thirty seconds later. It was an awkward drive because of her competence relative to Sholto's. While she was aggressive and quick on the road, as you have to be if you want to get anywhere in this city, Sholto still couldn't bring himself to put his foot down for fear of hurting the accelerator. Darian gave him a couple of looks but chose silence over arguments.

Bles drove south through Barton and into Cnocaid, heading down toward Gleann Fuilteach, the valley that leads out of the city. She had almost reached down to the university but turned instead into a quiet residential street. She pulled into a narrow driveway and went into a neat semi-detached home, the sort that in Cnocaid would set you back a couple of hundred grand.

Sholto said, "Well, that's the nicest home I've ever seen a housekeeper call her own."

"I'm not sure looking after Simon Sutherland counts as normal housekeeping. I'd bet the family pay her very well for her babysitting."

"Maybe he pays her well for her silence as well."

With that they made their way to the front door and rang the bell. Olinda Bles opened it and, with the least possible surprise in her voice, said, "I don't know why you had to follow me all the way from Simon's house like this is a spy story. Come in, I'll talk to you."

Sholto did his best to look sheepish because it's what she wanted to see but he didn't really care. They were getting to talk to her away from the Sutherland house and that was the aim of all this. Olinda led them through to the kitchen at the back of the house, a large and bright room. She started making three cups of tea while they sat at the table and waited politely, guests in another person's house and that meant conducting themselves with a certain decorum. They weren't cops, they couldn't assume a right to be there so they had to keep themselves welcome for as long as possible. They didn't start talking until she put their cups and a plate with chocolate digestives on the table in front of them. Darian took one and Sholto took three so Darian spoke first.

"How well did you know William Dent?"

She sighed and there was true sadness in it. "I didn't know him well. He was a friend of Simon's, so he was at the house now and again. I spoke with him, not that much. At first, you know, Will would come to the house and I don't think he wanted to be there. It was Harold's idea, to have someone else at the house, a man of around Simon's own age. I could get the shopping every time but his uncle wants him to see more people, to make the isolation less. I agree with that. We have to be careful not to make it too obvious to Simon, but getting him to interact with more people is important. It wasn't easy at first but eventually they would speak and then they would have proper conversations and then they were friends. Not friends in the way that a young man like you has friends, Mr. Ross, but in the only way that Simon can have friends, where every word he says to a person counts. For Will, I suppose, it was a way of doing work that involved no work, if you understand, so he liked hanging around the house."

"It doesn't look good for Will. The evidence the police have found suggests an interest in Ruby-Mae Short."

"I heard. I don't know what to say. Will, I think he was the sort of man who would do things in the moment, without thinking. He was reckless, he teased, he liked to play games, I think. Murder? It would be cruel to think that of him."

"But he was breaking into our office."

"And you chased him onto the railway tracks. I don't know why he tried to steal things from you, he was an unpredictable boy, I suppose. He must have had his reasons."

Sholto took a loud slurp from his cup and asked, "How did you end up working for Simon Sutherland?"

"I've been in Challaid since I was eighteen. Nearly thirty-five years since I came over. I was one of the lucky few because I had older family that had come before me, a brother and a cousin, and they were able to help me get a job looking after children. I was a childminder for a family in Barton for a while because I was cheap and rich people often pick the cheapest option, even to care for their own children. That's how they get rich and stay rich. After Simon's mother died his uncle Harold wanted someone to keep the house, but mostly to look after Simon. He was vulnerable, struggling a lot at the time, much worse even than now, so I cared for him. The family I had been working for knew Harold, their child was older by then, so they recommended me to him."

"He didn't just take Simon to live with him and his staff?"

"I do believe that Mr. Sutherland cares very deeply for Simon. I know that he was very close to Simon's father, his brother Beathan. He cared for him, but he didn't want a son of his own, not with the responsibilities he has at the bank. That came first. It always does for them."

Darian said, "You've been with them a long time. You must feel a lot of loyalty toward the Sutherland family."

"I am close to them and I care for them because while a lot of people see only the money I see the people. They have suffered like all God's children do, they have lost people and things that mattered very much to them, they have struggled like we all do in this life. All of this, it is more suffering, and it needs to come to an end. I hope that the police will find a way. Not you because you are not real police. I know how much use you will be."

Sholto smiled a little but Darian couldn't help his defiance when he said, "You know well enough the influence the family have over the police. The family will get what they want there. We might not be much use to you, but we're just trying to find Freya Dempsey."

"And I hope very much that you do find her."

Sholto grabbed the last biscuit off the plate and they got up to leave. He thanked Olinda at the door and her look told him exactly how much that was worth.

Back in the car Sholto said, "That was a funny one, that. She picked her words carefully. I don't know, something's troubling her good little Christian soul, but I don't think there's any way in hell she's going to tell us about it."

39

BEING IN the office when you wanted to be out in Challaid getting things done felt grim, but if there was nothing left to do then there was nowhere left to go. It seemed no progress could be made until the police came up with more information regarding Will Dent. If they could prove that he and he alone was guilty of killing Ruby-Mae Short and that he alone was behind Freya's disappearance then it was over. If they found evidence of others being involved then there might still be work to do. For now all Darian and Sholto could do was sit around and wait, maybe make a couple of phone calls along the way to pass some time.

Darian messaged Vinny to ask if he had heard anything just as Vinny was messaging him with the same question. Having six different police districts in the city with more history of competing with each other than working together meant information tended to flow more slowly between them than impatient people could stand, and those caught in the vice of a criminal investigation tended to be reasonably impatient. Sholto, having lived inside the machine, was used to the drag of waiting for another station to remember the existence of the telephone.

There used to be a lot more police stations in the city, local knowledge covering smaller patches. About fifteen years ago they reduced it to six, one in each major district, but that's misleading. Dockside in Whisper Hill and Second Station in Earmam just deal with local policing because there's plenty hot stuff there to handle. Bakers Moor station handles its local patch plus the anti-organized crime unit, which operates city-wide. The other three stations, Bank, Cnocaid and Piper Station up in Barton, all have multiple city-wide units working out of them, there being fewer local issues to occupy their time.

Sholto said, "There are four stations involved in this, so that's going to turn it into a crawl. Bank where Dent died, Bakers Moor because Dent's flat is there, Dockside leading the Short investigation, Cnocaid hunting Freya. If they start sniffing at Simon Sutherland again that'll bring Piper Station into it. We have to wait for them all to talk to each other before they talk to us and half the occupants of those places operate with their mouths sewn shut. The fact it concerns Vinny, one of their own, that might speed it up."

Darian nodded noncommittally, both because he couldn't believe any force could be so slow in this day and age and because he wasn't convinced even Vinny's involvement would quicken the pace. That was Sholto trying to throw the hangdog a bone.

The knock on the door caught them both by surprise. The one good thing about the heavy wooden stairs was that no one, or almost no one, could sneak up on them because the office door was right at the top and every step echoed off the bare walls. They both jumped in their chairs and Sholto got out of his and opened it, hoping to find someone as likable and helpful as DC Vicario and instead being confronted by the sight of Bran Kennedy. The chief officer of Raven Investigators had not come alone, because Daniel doesn't wander into the lions' den by himself if there are others he can force to go with him. There were two young men tucked in behind him, ready to throw their bulked-up muscle around should tempers be roused. He had taken two with him because he knew Sholto would only have Darian by his side and Kennedy liked the comfort that superior numbers brought.

Sholto said, "What do you want? Here to try and bully us or buy our silence? I'd be more receptive to buying than bullying but you can stick your money up your fat nose as well."

Kennedy smiled and said, "Oh, Sholto, don't leave someone who brings good news standing out on the doorstep. Invite me in."

"You a vampire that needs an invite to cross the threshold? All the stories of ghouls at the standing stones and a monster at the mouth of the loch but you're one I would believe in."

Kennedy chuckled as Sholto stepped aside to let him in but Darian could see and hear the stiff acting behind the mirth. "I've come to share some news with you. I do this as an investigator, because I believe in doing what needs to be done to get to the truth of the matter."

Darian was on high alert for a lie to follow as Sholto said, "What the hell yarn are you spinning now?"

"The Sutherland case. It's not our case anymore. I've stopped working for Harold Sutherland, stopped reporting to him, stopped gathering information on his behalf. The bank still has its own security department but they're far more concerned about financial goings-on than life or death. That whole place isn't concerned about personal or personnel issues, just political and financial stuff. When Britain voted out of the EU they were having kittens because their value took a big dip being right next door, but some little dead girl doesn't rock them one way or the other. I don't like that. We were the ones Sutherland had poking around in all this and we're done with it."

Sholto looked at Darian and the frown they shared showed neither was willing to believe in this sudden outburst of moral standards. Sholto said, "Raven Investigators ended their relationship with the Sutherland Bank."

Kennedy smiled and said, "It's more complicated than that, Sholto my boy, you know it always is. I'm sure the big chief on his throne down at Edinburgh HQ has already been on the blower to some chinless wonder on East Sutherland Square making sure the bank knows there's still a lot we can do for them. Just won't be working with Harold Sutherland anymore, that's all."

Sholto said, "Don't bring me a red rose and not kiss me at the end of the night. Tell me why you walked out on Harold Sutherland. It must be significant."

"I already told you, Sholto, I'm an investigator. Just because you're a tin-pot operation in this little hovel with one childlike acolyte and we're a professional outfit with a real office and staff doesn't mean you have some sort of moral high ground. Honesty matters to the successful as much as it does to you. If we're working with someone who would rather protect family interests than do what's right then I'm not willing to work for them, and the bosses down south, who have an even nicer office than I do so you'll hate them even more, agree. Now, that's all I'm going to say because I have no more words that would stand up in front of any of our city's talented and logical judges. I've already said more than I should and I'm leaving now. Good luck, Sholto, and believe it or not I really do mean that. What happened to the Short girl, and maybe the other one, no one at Raven takes that lightly."

Kennedy turned and left, and his silent companions, looking disappointed at the lack of violence that had been waiting for them on Cage Street, followed. The door closed and the men who had ghosted up the stairs clattered their way back down, the game over. Sholto looked at Darian with neither sure how to react.

Sholto went first, saying, "He walked out on Harold Sutherland. Bloody hell, what reason could he have for shooting himself in the wallet like that?"

"He said Sutherland was protecting family interests rather than doing the right thing."

"He did, aye. Family interests."

SCOTTISH DAILY NEWS

WHERE THE MONEY CAME FROM

AN ASSESSMENT OF THE ORIGINS AND EVOLUTION OF SCOTLAND'S BIGGEST COMPANY

The Sutherland Bank wants you to think it's always been here, which, given that it was founded in 1632, is a very easy thing to believe. The Sutherland Bank wants you to believe that it only ever does the sensible thing, and its dour and steady approach to everything it does in public helps make a persuasive case. More than anything else the Sutherland Bank wants you to believe they'll always be around, and that that's a good thing, and they've carefully crafted a sense of inevitability to that effect. Despite their seeming omnipresence, the Sutherland Bank is a business like any other, and when you treat it that way its vulnerabilities come further into the light. Just as there are challenges in its future there are stories in its past, some that they have spent centuries keeping to themselves. In this two-part essay we will seek to bring just some of them into the open.

The power of the Sutherland family in Challaid stretches far back beyond the bank they would eventually found, with the clan involved in the twelfth-century wars of independence that would bring Scotland its nationhood and the family its first taste of real power. The Sutherland clan was given extensions to its existing land holdings on the north coast as reward for their role which included Challaid, then a port town with a reputation as wild and unpleasant, less than a century removed from bloody slaughter over its control that ended with the ragtag army of Raghnall MacGill saving it. It was in this moment that we witness the first example of the Sutherlands' brilliant instinct for politics. Rather than attempt to impose control over his new domain Dand Sutherland indulged the unruliness of its people, and so won them over, a stepfather who turned a blind eye.

For generations thereafter the Sutherland name pops up only occasionally, rulers of a large swathe of the northern Highlands that they didn't really control, obviously wealthy and politically influential but never at the forefront.

It's always been assumed this was simply a family trait, a genetic quirk in a clan that loved power and money but loathed the attention it brought. Instead we should look at the Sutherland attitude of secrecy, of being the power behind the throne and never sitting on it, as a product of their environment. The family didn't become who they are in a vacuum; they were shaped by Challaid, a city that has, since its very beginning, cherished its isolation from the south, its separateness. The family have lived for centuries in a culture which stubbornly clings to the Gaelic language to be different from the rest of Scotland, that has its own poetry and storytelling and songs and sports so that it can look in the mirror each morning and see nothing of the rest of the nation. The Sutherlands, like almost all the people of Challaid, don't want to be like us. They have always looked at anywhere south as bad and suspicious, the Gaelic word for southern, deasach, being appropriated for use there as a mild insult. Those from what we call the central belt, and they refer to sniffily as "the south," have always been seen not as countrymen or friends but as rivals or obstacles. Even Inverness, barely ninety miles of rail line south through the glens, is viewed as being suspiciously Anglo these days. Challaid has always looked north and west for allies. North to the northern isles and Scandinavia, west to the Western Isles and Ireland. It has, as a quirk of its early involvement, been an enthusiastic home for large numbers of Caledonians. Anywhere but south.

The key to their current influence lies in the century and a half between the arrival in Challaid of Queen Iona, The Gaelic Queen, in 1545 and the first Caledonian expedition in 1698. The additional power gained by the family's support of the queen's bloody power grab made them rich to the point that, in 1632, Lord Cruim Sutherland formed the bank we know today. The official story, as told in the subtle and sometimes rather dull advertising the bank engages in that's supposed to foster that sense of reliability, no bright colors or whacky taglines for them, is that Cruim wanted to help several local people in Challaid to set up businesses trading with the rest of Scotland and other North Atlantic nations and so set up the bank as a temporary measure to help them out. What a noble, gracious and friendly chap that makes him sound. The story tends to stop there, simply a man fortunate enough to be able to help some friends and nothing more to see, the bank's subsequent success presumably an unrequested reward for his goodness. Taking a closer look at the few companies he initially bankrolled and what they meant is difficult because the Sutherland Bank doesn't share that sort of information from their extensive archives and extracting any secret from Challaid is virtually impossible. What we can see is what people in the south thought those deals were by accessing the previously private Buchanan collection, a collection of letters and files from the desk of the long-serving seventeenth-century leader of the house in the parliament, Lord Buchanan of Stirling.

In his letter to Prince Robert, Lord Buchanan speculates that the Sutherland Bank derived much of its income in its first ten years from four deals, one with Brochan Campbell, one with the Portnancon Shipping Company, one with Einar Asbjornson in Iceland and another with the Purcell family in Ireland. Brochan Campbell was, to put it generously, a notorious swindler and crook based in Challaid, the Portnancon Shipping Company made its fortune shipping slaves, Asbjornson was at the time a wanted man in both his own country and ours for murder and theft and Gerard Purcell was a pirate turned land grabber. These people may well have been friends of Cruim Sutherland, PSC and Campbell were based in Challaid, Asbjornson lived there for at least two years when on the run and Purcell docked there often in his seafaring days, but it's easy to guess why the story of the bank's early clients doesn't go into any detail about who they were.

The first fifty to sixty years of the bank's existence can be separated from the rest because of a reasonable difference in attitude. In those first two generations almost everything they did seemed to be full of risk, while almost everything since has been centered on the steady consolidation of those successes. Having created a bank that quickly came to dominate Challaid commerce, in the 1650s it expanded south in a brazen attempt to place its wealth close to the throne and parliament in Edinburgh. Priorities and policies began to evolve again as the bank's influence grew, and it's almost possible to see the strings of history being pulled when we look back through the records of laws passed in that era. A law in 1662 to place a tariff on money loaned from outside of Scotland of sixteen percent. A law in 1664 to limit any financial institutions lending in relation to its holdings. A law in 1669 stating that no financial institution should be given lending power in Scotland without parliamentary permission. That last one was crucial, meaning that no new bank or institution could be formed without all of the Lords in parliament being given full details of it, which meant the then Lord Sutherland knew what everyone else was going to try to do before they could do it. It was said these laws were passed to protect investors from a series of banking collapses that happened in the central belt in the decade previously. Letters in the Buchanan collection suggest at least two of those banks collapsed because of aggressive moves of the Sutherlands, costing many small investors and businesses in Glasgow and Edinburgh their livelihood. Buchanan's letters also suggest that the family had been making significant donations to the crown since the days of The Gaelic Queen and had never stopped.

It was in 1698 that the bank pulled off the last of its great gambles. An expedition to Panama had been proposed to create a passage from the Atlantic to the Pacific and was viewed in Challaid as a risky investment that the government, who backed it, could scarcely afford. Many thought they were playing with the nation's future, the economy already close to ruin, and records suggest Lord Niall Sutherland was one of the doubters. Two debates were held on what became the Caledonian expedition and Lord Sutherland spoke against it in the first and didn't attend the second. Not long before the mission was set to depart the Sutherland Bank, at remarkably short notice, stepped in and funded a massive expansion to the numbers sailing, assigning its own people. As we know, those people included the likes of Alexander Barton and Gregor Kidd, brutal former pirates, or privateers if you prefer the official version, who would lead the ships to their violent and ultimately successful conclusion, earning themselves knighthoods and legitimacy and the bank untold fortunes.

The Sutherland Bank was set. Political power was guaranteed, and a constant flow of income merely needed to be protected by keeping up with the times, the need to gamble on the future now behind them. In part two we'll look at the bank's more recent history, including the power it continues to wield over what is supposed to be an independent parliament. While their political influence has been somewhat curtailed by the abolition of the Lords in 1952 and its replacement with an elected second chamber in Edinburgh, other routes to influence have been found. We'll also examine how the Sutherland family themselves have changed in the modern world, but how in many ways they, and the city they still call home, have hardly changed at all.

40

YOU NEED to go home. Go and get some sleep and we'll take another crack at this in the morning when we might know more than the nothing we know now."

Darian said, "That's more hours we're wasting. We should be out there..."

"Where, Darian? There's nowhere out there for us two to go. Do we go to Geug Place or Eilean Seud? To do what? Do we go to the police and if we do, what do we tell them? They're the ones with access to the Sutherlands and their legal team, so we wait for them. Rushing just gets us to the wrong location faster."

"Rushing? Freya Dempsey is out there somewhere and we're going home to get some sleep because we're a bit stuck. That can't feel right to you."

Sholto wasn't programmed for confrontation, least of all with people he liked. When faced with this sort of conversation with Darian he liked to treat it as an opportunity to educate. He assumed his most scholarly expression and leaned back in his seat, the desk in front of him once again covered in piles of papers that seemed to have somehow found their own way back to their original places.

Sholto said, "When Vinny brought this to us she had been gone for, what, five days. At that time she was missing and there was a chance, however slim, that she had left of her own accord. We were looking for someone who might have run, so we were hurrying because the more of a head start a person has the less likely we are to catch up. Then we found the connection to Ruby-Mae. It was chasing Freya that brought us to that, and if they're connected then I think we have to assume that the urgency has gone from our investigation. It's likely that the only difference between Freya and Ruby-Mae is that we haven't found Freya's body yet. It's likely to be the same killer and the same outcome. We have to recognize that the best speed to go at is the one that will deliver the correct result, not the fastest result. I want to catch this bastard, Darian, just as much as you do, and that's going to mean us both being awake and alert enough to pounce when he passes in front of us, if he's still alive enough to do so. I know you're young and full of enough fire to burn the city down, but you're also smart enough to know that rest matters."

There were moments in his speech when Sholto was so certain of his accuracy he began to sound smug, but Darian couldn't disagree with him. It was hard to admit but there was every chance they had been too late to save Freya before they even started.

"It's just rotten, you know. The fact she's probably dead, that Finn will never see his own ma again. Doesn't seem right that we weren't able to do anything to help her."

Sholto nodded. "Powerlessness is a horrible and cruel thing when you realize it applies to you, too. When I was a young cop I thought I was going to be able to help so many people, but the truth was that I was mostly just cleaning up after other people's horrors. There are four hundred and seventy-nine thousand people in Challaid, if you believe the census, which I don't, and we have no influence over the behavior of any one of them. If they choose to do something appalling all we can do is react to it, and that makes us feel weak. Thing is, Darian, cleaning up after the bad guys, it still matters. It's how we stop them from doing it again. We want the power to stop them the first time but as that's not possible this is the next best thing."

Darian thought about that a lot on the way home. He picked up a meal from The Northern Song and got the train through the tunnel. It was crowded but he got a seat opposite a couple arguing loudly, in Gaelic so it sounded like they were spitting on the floor half the time, about a gas bill. Darian was still lurching toward maturity. For example, he was immature enough to feel resentment toward the people on the train because none of them were acknowledging the traumas happening in the city around them. On the other hand he had recently acquired the maturity to understand how childish that resentment was, demanding a person recognize the pains of strangers as well as their own, a burden no one should be asked to carry.

He walked with his bag of food to the flat. It was in these moments of quiet misery that he wished he had a girlfriend, as bad as his taste had proven to be, or a close circle of friends away from his work. He could have picked up the phone to his sister Catriona or his brother Sorley but he didn't feel comfortable with that. Instead he took a plate from the kitchen through to the table by the window in the living room and sat looking out at the loch, eating slowly.

His mind returned to Bran Kennedy, a greedy person walking away from good money. He had said Sutherland was trying to protect the family. Any Sutherland had the money to give Freya expensive gifts she didn't want. Simon couldn't have met her outside his house unless he was lying about who he was, and for that to be the case he would have had to fool a lot of very clever people. If he was lying then why leave the bra to be found? It was unlikely, but it wasn't impossible. Harold had met her but there was nothing to suggest he had any wish to meet her again and nothing to link him to Ruby-Mae. If Simon didn't leave the house then he would need Dent to do a lot of the work for him. Harold had been at a Challaid FC match at the time Freya went missing, so he too would have needed Dent to do the dirty work. There was a third Sutherland. Sholto had mentioned Phil and Darian drifted mentally back to him, the quiet young man of money who had met Freya several times and who could command the same undue protection from his uncle and uncle's driver that Simon did.

As he watched a small yacht make its way to the south harbor in the early evening light Darian picked up his phone and made a call.

DC Vicario answered and said, "Hello?"

"Hi, DC Vicario, it's Darian Ross, from Douglas Independent

Research. Listen, uh, we've hit a bit of a dead end on this, but we've collected a few interesting pieces of information along the way. I wondered if we could talk, compare notes."

"Tonight?"

"Are you free?"

There was a laugh in her voice when she said, "I am. You can buy me a drink. You know MacCoy's, on Wodan Road?"

He smiled at the thought of a cop wanting to drink in a pub named after an infamous bank robber. "I know it, I'll see you there in, uh, three-quarters of an hour."

41

DARIAN TOOK the train to Mormaer Station in Earmam and from there a Challaid Cabs taxi up to Wodan Road, a curving street named after a possibly fictional mercenary said to have helped The Gaelic Queen. DC Vicario had picked an amusing drinking spot. She worked The Hill, so it made sense that she would want to live somewhere nearby, so this might have been her local.

A long narrow building, the back of it looking out onto the loch, a view of the docks: the kindest thing you could say about MacCoy's was that it tried its best. Maybe thirty years ago, when it was built, it might have been pretty nice, fashionable, raising the tone of the grotty neighborhood. The surroundings had since dragged it down to their level, and it looked scruffy, only hints now of what the owners had once aimed for and given up on.

Inside the decor was dated and gloomy, not many patrons to liven it up. That would have been another reason she had picked the place. The bar ran along part of the wall on the right as you went in the door; the few drinkers in the place were either lined up at it or at the tables way down the back where the large windows gave you a view of the water. All except one, sitting on her own at a table against the wall on the left, out of earshot for everyone else.

Darian walked across and said, "Hi, DC Vicario, thanks for meeting me."

She said, "Angela. These are drinking hours, not working hours. I got you a pint; there isn't a hell of a lot of variety round here. I had the choice of two wines, the red or the white."

He sat down opposite her. Her black hair was curlier than before, as if she hadn't had time to straighten it with all that was going on. There was a smile on the edges of her dark eyes when she said, "So what's the big news that you had to get me to buy you a drink for?"

"Not news, questions. Did you know that Raven have stopped working for Harold Sutherland?"

Now she was interested. "What? They're giving up Sutherland money? Why?"

Darian took a swig of his pint, horrible it was, as if the barman had reached out of the window to dip the glass in the loch, and said, "We don't know. Seems to have been a falling-out. Could Harold have been the one sending Freya gifts? Maybe Raven found proof."

"Well, if they did they're a step ahead of us, because we have nothing."

"I, uh, I don't want to piss you off here, because I know that you're doing everything you can in this case, everything..."

"But..."

"We had a visit from a colleague of yours to the office, DS Noonan, you know him."

She grimaced and said, "Yeah, I know of him."

"He was dropping hints like they were hot, telling us we're going to get shut down, all smug and jokey about it but, you know, he's dangerous. The Sutherlands are involved in a criminal case and everyone, I mean, absolutely everyone, knows that they have connections in the police force. We both know they have cops in their pocket, senior ones, high enough up the chain that they can shut down areas of investigation, make evidence go walkabout if they don't like the look of it. Noonan's the weapon they sent to shut us down when we wouldn't be bullied or bought."

Angela didn't look annoyed. Instead she nodded and said, "Yeah, they have connections. Clever about it, too, the way they do it. I've seen it. The security department of the bank, they're the ones that come and create the contacts, help out cops so they can get favors, build a relationship with you, give it a year or two and they have you wrapped round their middle finger, sticking it up at the rest of the city. They're bloody good, but, no, they're not going to stop us this time. No one's told us to back off. Noonan's an ugly piece of human garbage; I'll make sure he doesn't get too close to you again. Evidence going missing, I don't know about that."

Darian gave her a look that cut her off and she smiled her wide smile.

"Okay, yeah, I know it does happen, I'm not saying no, we're still a force with…problems…"

"Ha, that's a hell of a polite way of putting it. I heard things were getting worse, not better. The Anti-Corruption Unit in chaos as it gets rebuilt and the inmates running the asylum."

Now she looked a little annoyed, but covered it well. "No, you're getting carried away. Things aren't worse, they're just about the same. You're believing the worst of us, and, frankly, I'm a little offended."

Her smile took the sting out of what might have become an argument. Darian said, "I just worry about the dead ends we keep running down. It shouldn't be this hard to find the truth."

"It's been tough. Is that what you wanted to see me about, to break the news that you think some of my colleagues are still corrupt and that neither of us has a clue what we're doing with this case?"

He laughed. "No, not just that. It would help us to have Noonan held back. Plus, I feel like I need to talk it through with someone, get a fresh perspective. And, uh, I kinda wanted to see you again."

"Oh, you kinda did, did you kinda?"

Darian was beginning to turn a fetching shade of red at this point and said, "Okay, I'm not good at this sort of thing, but, yeah, I did."

"You're right, you're not good at this. Look, I do like you, but right now we're both tangled up in the same net and we need to get out of that first. When this is over, soon, I hope, I think, then you can try and bowl me over with your sparkling seductive conversation. I think when this is done I'll be interested in being bowled over."

They walked out together onto Wodan Road, an ugly place that looked menacing in the dark.

Angela turned to face him and said, "I'm walking home from here, you have a car?"

"I'm not driving after taking a drink, officer. I'll walk up to the ferry terminal at the docks and get a taxi to the station from there."

She smiled and said, "Good answer. And don't worry, Darian, I won't count this as a first date. We'll have another one of those later when you can raise your game."

She reached up and kissed him briefly on the lips, a soft peck that was full of promise, and he wished his breath didn't smell of the crappy beer he'd just had. He smiled as he watched her walking off down the street. His record with women had been, to be polite about it, shite, and he knew it was foolishness to fall for a cop, but she was the good kind of trouble. She was the best kind.

42

WHEN DARIAN woke it was to a distant noise and a certain sense that he hadn't had enough sleep. He rolled over and opened his eyes. What had it been? Something familiar, he thought, and through the fog of his half-sleeping brain came the memory. His phone.

He reached across and picked it up from the bedside table. None of his furniture had cost anything. The Ross siblings had kept very little of what had been in their parents' house and what hadn't been worth selling had been shared between the three of them, which didn't leave much each. Most of the rest of Darian's belongings had come from charity shops and secondhand places, some of it not built to last much longer.

It was three fifty, according to his phone when he looked at it, confirming the reason for his tiredness. The number was new, no name to identify it, and his mind raced ahead of the finger reaching out to drag the answer icon. It could have been anyone, including some time waster with a scam to run. More likely it was someone from the police or from Raven or Sutherland Bank's security department. The timing was more important than the number because that told him it was an emergency. Only the drunk and the urgent call you at three fifty in the morning.

He answered and said, "Hello."

"You have to come to my house, please. Someone is in here."

It was said in a whisper, a desperate hiss from a man filled with so much fear he couldn't stop it snaking out his mouth when he opened it. Two seconds into the plea Darian realized he was talking to Simon Sutherland, panicked and alone with a stranger in his house.

"Call the police, Simon, and I'll be right round."

"I will, I will. You have to hurry."

There was a second after hanging up during which Darian paused and tried to understand the feeling creeping up on him. There was some excitement there, the feeling that this could be it, the vital moment. Someone had broken into the house before to plant Ruby-Mae's bra and implicate Simon and now the same person was trying again. This could have been an attempt to repeat the trick and implicate him in Freya's disappearance. A person who thought they could get in and out unseen and unheard, or a person who didn't care because they were sure Simon had no one to call for help. A person who didn't know he had Darian's number and perhaps didn't understand that the last few days had changed Simon, just a little. People had been in his house, strangers he had allowed in and spoken to, and he had been dragged out to the police station. He had Darian's number and was willing to call it, to call the police, too.

Darian scrambled out of bed and began to pull on clothes that should have gone into the wash basket ahead of the next time he was close enough to running out of clothing that he was compelled to switch the washing machine on.

A thought pricked at him, the underlying part of that feeling he hadn't been able to identify before. If Simon Sutherland had killed Ruby-Mae and Freya then this could be part of his plan. He feared that Darian and Sholto were getting too close so he lured Darian to the house to get rid of him. If Dent had been working for him then he died trying to find out just how close they were and that had sent Simon into a panic. It made only a fraction of sense, which was a little more than most alternatives.

Darian called Sholto, waiting a frustratingly long time for an answer. Sholto typically woke up in stages and the first two were long and groggy and usually a few hours away. Eventually the phone was answered with a croaky "Sholto Douglas."

"It's me, Darian. I just got a call from Simon Sutherland saying someone is in his house and he wants me to go up there. He said he'll call the police as well. I'm going to go up in a taxi and see what's going on."

In a split second Sholto skipped to the wide-awake phase and said, "No, you will not. That could be a trap; you don't know what's going on here, Simon calling you up in the dying hours. Stay at the flat and I'll pick you up, we'll go up together and we'll tip off our friends in the police before we go anywhere as well."

He hung up before Darian could argue back. The risk of a trap was low because Simon was smart enough to understand that Darian would call for backup, and the police, himself. If it was a genuine emergency then he couldn't wait for Sholto to trundle his way through the city to get there.

He pulled on his shoes and tied his laces and on the way to the door of the flat he called Vinny. Through to voicemail. Vinny would either be fast asleep or out on a shift, so Darian left a message.

"Vinny, it's Darian. I just got a call from Simon Sutherland saying that someone's in his house and me and Sholto are on our way up there. You might want to swing up and join us if you get the chance."

Darian slipped the phone into his pocket and went downstairs to the front door of the building. He stood out on the street, shivering in the cold, waiting for what he knew would be an interminable length of time for Sholto to get there. These hours, so late or so early depending on which way round you look at a clock, are the moments when Challaid is at its most beautiful, the sun threatening to take the world back and the gray of the moon across the still loch, clinging to the surface. It's quiet, and it feels like a city with no evil, just a place any person would want to live their life. Those are the least honest hours of the day. Darian waited, edgy.

CHALLAID CITY COUNCIL PLANNING DEPARTMENT—PRIVATE FILES

PLANNING APPLICATION

11/10/12

Address: 5 Geug Place, Barton, Challaid, CH1 2LS

Owner: Simon Sutherland

Application: Application for extension to existing property. Two-story, north facing, ground floor approximate floor space 1,150 square feet. Design submitted separately.

Comments: Extension to be built on existing property in large, private garden. Walled and tree-lined, will hide construction from all view. Concern about noise in area, large new build in traditionally maintained area, large vehicles using narrow lane for access.

Update: Challaid City Council planning committee pass application 5 votes to 0.

PLANNING APPLICATION

19/06/14

Address: 5 Geug Place, Barton, Challaid, CH1 2LS

Owner: Simon Sutherland

Application: Application for extension to existing property. Two-story, west-facing to rear of existing property, ground floor approximate floor space 2,000 square feet. Design submitted separately.

Comments: Extension to be built in large private garden. Walled and tree lined will hide construction from public view. **4 existing complaints** from neighbors regarding noise while project is underway and objecting to design of exterior, considered out of place in traditional area, and to heavy vehicles using narrow lane to access property. During previous extension build, road was damaged, trees damaged with several cleared for vehicle access, road blocked on multiple occasions for residents.

Update: Challaid City Council planning committee pass application 4 votes to 1.

PLANNING APPLICATION

16/08/15

Address: Auri (14 Geug Place), Barton, Challaid, CH1 2LS

Owner: Simon Sutherland

Application: Application to add basement to existing property. Approximate floor space 210 square feet, accessed from within property. Design submitted separately.

Comments: Low risk of disruption for popular form of extension. 4 properties on same street have had similar applications approved in last 3 years, no objections formally raised for any. Some risk of heavy vehicles using lane but recent road upgrade makes that acceptable.

Update: Challaid City Council planning committee pass application 5 votes to 0.

43

SHOLTO ARRIVED on Havurn Road quicker than expected, which left Darian with the image of his boss hunched over the steering wheel, knuckles white, eyes bulging as he watched the road ahead, pushing the car as fast as forty miles per hour. It stopped at the side of the road and instead of getting into the passenger seat Darian walked onto the road and round to the driver's side.

He opened the door and said, "I'll drive."

They had made this mistake before and weren't going to repeat it. Sholto unclipped his seat belt and got out, stumbling into the road and running round to the passenger side. Darian noticed how rumpled his boss looked, even by his standards, shirt hanging down at the back, hair all over the place so it almost covered the baldness on top. This was Sholto in a state of rush Darian hadn't seen from him before.

He got into the driver's seat and as soon as Sholto pulled the passenger door shut behind him Darian accelerated away with a screech, the momentum forcing them back in their seats.

Sholto said, "Whoa, Nelly, calm it down and put your seat belt on as well, we're no use to anyone if we're wrapped around a lamppost."

Darian pulled the seat belt round in between changing gear and trying to work out the quickest route from Bank to Simon's house. In the daytime it wouldn't be the obvious one, using the main streets that looked the quickest route on a map but would be clogged, but at this hour of the morning when the roads were much clearer it made sense that the shortest route should indeed be the fastest.

Sholto, with one hand on the door and the other gripping the side of his seat, said, "What did Sutherland say to you, exactly?"

"He said someone was in the house and he wanted me to come round. He was talking in a whisper and he sounded terrified."

"I suppose we're about to find out if he's as good an actor as I think he might be. What did you say to him?"

"I told him I was on my way round and to phone the police."

Sholto mumbled something under his breath and said, "Well, if he did call them I wouldn't rely on him to get the message across, and if you don't nail the point with that lot you'll be lucky if they show up at all. Who else did you call?"

"I left a message with Vinny but I haven't gotten an answer yet."

"Not your girlfriend?"

"My...? Vicario? I wish she was and, no, I haven't."

The conversation was annoying Darian because he was busy reminding the car that thirty miles an hour was a legal limit but not a technological one. They were in Cnocaid already with the yellow light of lampposts flashing past outside, occasional bursts of white from twenty-four-hour shops standing out among the darkly sleeping buildings. It was disorientating but Darian could find his way on instinct.

Sholto mumbled something like a prayer under his breath and then said, "A message won't do it, I'll make a few calls. I don't want us being at the house alone, getting caught with our pants down. We need some honest backup."

Darian focused on the road while Sholto wriggled unpleasantly and pulled his phone from his pocket. He held it in one hand as he scrolled unsteadily through the numbers. Darian had caught a glimpse of the list in Sholto's contacts before and it was Tolstoyan in length, seemingly everyone who had ever committed, investigated, witnessed or heard a rumor about a crime in Challaid in the last twenty-five years and owned a phone. It was the benefit of experience that Sholto liked to point out: if you stick around long enough you'll learn who to talk to.

He pressed dial and Darian heard one side of a short conversation, Sholto saying, "DS MacNeith, it's Sholto Douglas here, sorry to wake you. We've just had a call from Simon Sutherland to say that someone's breaking into his house, you'll want to get your people there . . . Yes, of course we are. Goodbye."

Darian said, "That sounded like you hung up before she could tell you not to do something."

"Aye, well, I have other people to call and not a lot of time to call them, the speed you're going at."

The next person he phoned was DC Vicario, a call containing the same information but in a friendlier tone.

That ended when he hung up, and in his grumpiest voice, Sholto said, "She told me she would come straight round, and to say hello to you. There isn't something going on between you two, is there, Darian? Tell me there isn't, not you and a cop."

"Concentrate on your calls."

A third call went through to Sholto's contact at Piper Station in Barton, the nearest to Simon's house and the ones who would handle any investigation into a crime there. That was a confused conversation, Sholto having to try and explain that it was a Sutherland, that he never left the house and that he might have been involved in two murders, or might not have done anything wrong and could be a victim himself. That the cop Sholto was talking to didn't know who Simon was and what he had recently been accused of showed how little communication there was in the force.

He hung up on the last call and said, "Right, at least when we go in there'll be a battalion of nice uniforms on our heels, although I'd prefer a few of them to be in front of us."

They passed shops and restaurants far too expensive for either of them ever to frequent and turned onto King Robert Street, a few businesses and a couple of blocks of very expensive flats and a triangle of grass at the corner with black railings that acted as a private park for the people living hereabouts. It was small but it was flat and that gave them a view down toward the loch and the back of Geug Place. Reaching out of the dark sky a finger of black cloud seemed to have stretched down to the ground, touching a glow at the bottom.

"Is that smoke? Chee whizz, that's smoke."

Darian nodded. A column of thick black smoke, and as they headed for the corner with Geug Place, they didn't have to guess where it was coming from. They were driving straight toward it.

44

THE CAR sped down Geug Place and stopped with a shudder that left them almost sideways outside the gate. They both got out, seeing the flickers of orange through the trees and the billows of smoke carrying the souls of every item Simon Sutherland had ever owned into the night.

Darian ran to the gate and gave it a hard shoulder barge, but it didn't move even a fraction. He shouted, "We have to get in. How do we get in?"

Sholto said, "We have to get in and open the gate from the inside so the fire brigade can get in. And I have to move the car out of their way."

Sholto ran round to the driver's side of his car to move it clear of the gates. Darian was still holding them, trying to shift something he already knew he didn't have the strength to budge.

He shouted, "Simon, Simon, are you there?"

There was no reply, no movement but the dancing shadows. He looked quickly up and down the street, hoped to see a part of the tall railings and wall around the garden that might be more accessible than the rest, but there was none. What he did notice was that none of the neighbors had come to try and help, and, given the smell of burning that had settled over the street, the growl of the fire and smudge against the sky, there was no way they could all be ignorant of the emergency unfolding. Darian cursed the lot of them, unaware that many of the people who lived there were aging or positively elderly and could do nothing more than call the emergency services, which, telephone records would show later, three already had. Darian had no obvious route into the front garden.

Sholto slammed the door of the car as he got out and stood back, staring at the gates and the railings and trying to come up with a plan.

"We need a ladder. You won't be able to climb that and I'd have a heart attack just watching you fail."

There was no time, given that it was possibly already too late. Darian moved down toward Sholto and kept going right past him to the car. That dainty little thing couldn't hope to smash its way through the gates. It would have been sliced to bits trying, but Sholto had parked it right up against the railings to keep as much of the lane and house entrance as possible clear for more important people. Instead Darian walked round to the back and put his hands on it, pulling himself up so that he was on his knees on the roof, and then standing.

Sholto shouted, "Here, what are you doing? You'll break your neck and my car."

Darian ignored him, stepping back carefully and taking a one-step run-up. One stride and a jump and he was grabbing on and pulling himself up to the pointed tip of the railings.

He said, "I'll try and get the gate open for you."

Sholto was looking up at him and shaking his head. It was high at the top of the railings and he could see a terrified bald-headed man in the street on one side, the blackness of the garden below and the undulating light from the house on the other. Darian swung his leg over and lowered his weight, feeling the flaking paint dig into his fingers before he let go. There was a swoosh and a feeling of weightlessness that gave a tempting sense that everything was bliss, and then he hit the ground. It was enough of a thud to provoke a shout from him and an echoing one from Sholto on the other side.

Darian shouted, "I'm okay."

That was a guess when he said it, but confirmed when he stood up. He had landed on his feet, fallen backward and rolled onto his side and now that he was standing again the only pain was in his ankles and neither was badly damaged. He picked his way past branches outstretched as if to block him and onto the drive, running up toward the house.

It was not, at that point, a home any longer because a home envelops a person and their existence. It was now an incubator for a fire desperate to burst out and engulf the garden it could see beyond the cracked windows. The heat was fierce, as if it were a hand pressed hard to his face to try and stop him from getting any closer, and the house and light made the scene difficult to process, an attack on his senses. Darian stopped and took a step backward, not out of fear but because instinct told him not to step beyond that range and because he hoped to find Simon without burning to death in the search.

He saw a figure move. Black against the building but it turned to see him, to look at him. Not Simon, but Harold. The older Sutherland stood closer to the house, looking back over his shoulder at Darian, a look of shock, eyes half-shut against the heat. He was breathing heavily, there was a black smudge on his face and two buttons had been ripped from his coat.

Darian stood beside him and said, "Simon?"

"He's still inside. I tried to get him out, I tried. He's still in there. He called me, he was scared, but he won't come out."

Darian put his hands to his mouth and shouted, "Simon, where are you? Simon, can you hear me?"

His phone. He reached into his pocket and found Simon's number in the call log, calling him back. There was no tone, no voicemail and no answer, the phone dead. Darian was about to shout again when he caught movement out of the corner of his eye and saw Sholto coming up the drive, limping heavily and red in the face. The drop from the top of the railings had not been so kind to him, and there were tears in his eyes as he joined Darian and Harold.

"Bloody hell, this whole place is murder. We can't get in there, but we can still help, we can get that gate open for the fire engines. They'll be coming; we have to get the gate open."

He was right, of course, because if the fire engines were delayed then Simon's already tiny chance of survival would be wiped out. Darian was close to agreeing when he looked up at the house and saw it, movement this time more solid than the swaying fire. In a window on the first floor of the new wing he could see the black figure of a person silhouetted in the glow. A man stood and looked down at them, not shouting or trying to escape. A man who would rather stay and burn.

Darian shouted, "Simon, open the window. *Simon*."

Harold screamed, "Simon, come down, please, for God's sake."

The figure stood motionless, and then moved away out of sight. They paused, silent among crackling chaos, expecting him to return to the window, but he didn't. Simon Sutherland had walked into the fire and he hadn't come back.

Darian looked at Sholto and opened his mouth to speak but before he could Sholto said, "No, Darian, no. I will not let you go in there. We will do all we can to help him but that does not include dying by his side."

Darian didn't want to defy his boss, and he knew Sholto was almost certainly right, but he couldn't stop himself.

Darian nodded to Harold and said, "Don't let him leave, Sholto. The gate was locked. It was locked with him on the inside."

"What?"

"It was locked and he was here. Just don't let him go."

Darian bolted away from him and ran for the front door of Simon Sutherland's burning house.

Sholto shouted, "Darian, don't, Darian."

By then Darian was kicking in the front door and ducking his way inside as flames and smoke drawn by the draft from the new opening swept past him.

DIARY

16/05/18

With all the hard times there have been I find myself thinking of mother a lot. So many of the things she warned me about have now happened. All she said makes sense to me now. There were so many that I didn't take seriously but should have. The more time passes the more I realize how wise she was. I wish I had realized at the time. I wish I could have told her she was right about it. No one should have to wait so long to understand the cleverness of a loved one. We should know instantly. We should be able to recognize and benefit from that great wisdom. Sometimes I feel ashamed when I think of how I used to believe mother was overreacting. I thought maybe she was hysterical and I had inherited whatever's wrong with me from her. That was stupidly unfair. She understood this family. She warned me well.

When a person takes the long walk up the road they leave parts of themselves behind. You'll carry those parts with you for the rest of your journey, so you have to hope that they aren't heavily weighted with bitterness or anger, making your path harder to walk. Instead you want them to be light, to illuminate and add a skip to your step. For the first few weeks and months you won't understand what you've been left, and that's when the confusion of grief can overwhelm you. Time goes past me in ways I can't ever comprehend or control. A big lump of it is in my hands and then falling through my fingers as I flail about to try and catch it. The harder I squeeze the more pops out, and then it's gone.

This family is poisoned. Time is no antidote. Those were her words. She understood them all. Even the ones you think you can trust. The ones that seem so honest and normal. Every one of them. No one is untouched. The Sutherland clan can't be saved from itself. It will all come crashing down some day. I hope it's soon. The longer it stretches the worse it'll get. It's the money's fault. The lesson that a lifetime of wealth teaches you is a lie. It tells you that, because you have it, you must be superior. It says you can do what you want. There are different rules. You can test them. Push the boundaries hard. What other people say can't be done becomes a fun new challenge. No wonder our large family tree has been filled with thrill seekers. So many died young.

Mother warned me something like this might happen. She told me to be ready for it. Told me what to do when it started. I was always ready. It didn't surprise me. That was why I bought number fourteen, Auri. It's why I had the basement put in. I know I managed to keep it secret because if I hadn't they'd have come to question me about it. The police don't know. The family don't know. I bought it with the money that mother left me from the secret account she had. Father set that up. He didn't want all his money being held in the family bank. He wanted his secrets. He left detailed instructions for her about how to use it safely. She passed it on to me in turn. I did only what needed to be done. It's cost so much. Maybe doing the right thing is always expensive. I think that both my parents understood that. There's no cheap goodness.

It's so much pressure. Uncle Harold and Phil. Ross and Douglas, the two pretend private detectives. Detective Sergeant MacNeith and the other cops that have come after me. I've done nothing wrong. Perhaps none of them will understand that fact. I'll show them all. I'll make it clear to them, I hope. Hopefully it'll be safe. I hope it's soon. I want things to go back to normal. My life is stretched. I can feel it. The strain of everything just waiting to snap. Nobody else really understands. They still think it can somehow help me to leave the house. Soon I'll tell them. I'll have to, whether I choose or not. It feels like things are ready to fall. It's about time too.

I think I heard someone in the house. It must be him.

45

THE HEAT hit Darian hard, a stifling punch that had him gasping and made him want to turn around and do the sensible thing. Instead he gulped in some air and pushed ahead, into the hall of what had been the original house.

He shouted, "Simon, where are you?"

He had hoped that Simon had left the window and made his way to the stairs, trying for the front door, but there was no sign of him. Instead there was smoke and, pushing out through a door at the top of the old stairs that led toward the new extension at the back, fire. He had to move fast because the exit was seconds away from being closed off to him. Darian had been in the house before and that gave him a chance. He went right through the door to the empty room, little chance of fire in there because there was nothing to burn except Darian. He ran through to the extension and saw the beast waiting for him.

The huge room was full of it, rich in fuel with the collection of a life lined up on shelves just waiting for their chance to burn. The smell was of plastic and something else, something chemical he couldn't identify, and the smoke seemed to be running back and forth across the ceiling in rippling waves. This was a room a smart person would stay in for seconds, a minute if they were brave and two if they were stupid, only staying longer than that if they wanted to share the fate of the crackling items that filled the place.

Darian chose the less sensible of the two options and ran toward the stairs when the smart choice would have been to turn around. He ran through smoke trying to choke him and found himself in a section of the room where the items seemed to be mostly metal and little of it burning, just wavering under the heat. Darian inhaled deeply there and instantly regretted it as his lungs filled with a sharp taste he wanted rid of but would have to live with. He ran on and up the stairs.

It was worse on the first floor, thicker smoke and more fire. This wasn't the growing crackle that downstairs had been but a full-on roar, a fire that had as much control as it could want and was ready to make hay with it. Here there were clothes and magazines and bits of cardboard, a selection of items that almost seemed to have been picked with flammability in mind.

There had already been times in his life when Darian had felt very afraid, had been threatened, but he'd happily admit that to that point the fire was the scariest thing he had ever witnessed. Something about fire separates it from other threats. Perhaps it's the relentless and thorough nature of it, but to Darian it was the slowness that scared him most. A bullet or a knife are evils either to be dodged or which provide very brief suffering, but fire likes to take its time, to make the experience as agonizing as possible, as if it's reveling in the power it holds, drowning you in heat. Flames were climbing from the top of the shelves to the ceiling, tendrils jumping out from the sides and trying to get at anything it hadn't yet cornered, always looking to spread, to claim more. In the middle of it all stood Simon Sutherland, eyes wide with terror, motionless.

Darian half shouted and half coughed, "Simon, come on, we have to go. Simon."

He ran to him, a hand over the side of his own face to try and protect it from the ferocity of the heat, feeling the back of his hand burn red as he went. He reached Simon and stopped, putting his hands on the young man's shoulders.

He said, "Simon, *move,* you have to move."

Simon Sutherland was tearful as he said, "I do want to."

This was more than just the memories of his life, this was his whole world burning around him, every part of who he was and who he intended to be turning to ash, and the same instinct that made him collect it all was convincing him to stay and turn to ash with it. He wanted out, but on his own he wouldn't have been strong enough to fight for the exit.

Darian said, "We're leaving."

He moved behind Simon and shoved him, not so hard that he might knock him over but enough to force him to take the first step. Darian kept his hands on Simon's back but it was hardly necessary now, Simon moving freely when he felt the choice was no longer his to take. He had needed someone to break the spell.

They could both feel their clothes begin to melt into their skin as they got to the top of the stairs and the rage followed them down. Darian was struggling to hold his breath and he could hear Simon cough and gasp, but they didn't slow down, not until they were across the floor and into the empty room. There was smoke there now but still no fire. Darian could feel his shoes sticking to the tiles as the soles melted, and through the door he could see the corridor ablaze.

Simon, his voice a wheeze, said, "We can't get out."

The fire blocked the front door, carpets and wallpaper and banisters helping it along. They were going to have to run through it, which would certainly cause them pain, but it would be a few seconds and Darian felt sure he could make it. Simon didn't seem convinced. Darian was about to try and talk him into running when he heard the noise outside and noticed the flash of blue coming in through the front door and windows, puncturing the orange and grays. The fire engine was at the front door and people were shouting, getting themselves into position.

There was a lull, and above the fire and the movement, through the burst window closest to them, Darian heard Sholto's voice straining at its highest as he screamed, "Don't just wave it around, get in there and get them out."

Darian was about to shout back, to let them know they were close, but then a strange thing happened. It started to rain in the house. Out in the hall water started to fall into the fire, the hose shooting in through windows burst to pieces by the heat and in through the front door. This was the moment to move.

Darian shouted, "Now."

He grabbed Simon by the arm and held particularly tight as he pulled him out and across the hall to the exit. As they reached the door two figures in sand-yellow outfits and with breathing apparatus covering their faces came in and they all but crashed into each other. The firemen grabbed them and helped them out, beyond the smoke and the fire and back into the world of air and life.

Darian and Simon stumbled out, coughing and retching, Sholto running to Darian and holding him by the shoulders until he got his breath back, both of them relieved.

A fireman ran up to them shouting, "Is there anyone else in the house?"

They all looked at Simon and he said, "No, no one else."

Darian was breathing in lungfuls of cold air like a man dying of thirst diving into a pool of water, so it was only at the last moment that he saw the figures running up the drive toward them. Vinny and Phil were in uniform and both looked panicked. Phil ran to his cousin to check on him while Vinny stopped at Darian.

Above the roar of the fire he shouted, "Someone get a bottle of water, he needs water."

Darian nodded and Phil shuffled away to find something for them to drink. Darian said, "Thanks."

Vinny said, "Thank Christ you're all right. Do you know what happened, how it started?"

Darian looked at Simon and then across to the figure of Harold, still standing on the grass, looking uncertain, moving slowly toward them. Darian said, “I don’t.”

Vinny looked at Simon too and said, “Do you know who did this?”

Simon nodded sadly. “I do, I know. And Freya Dempsey, I know where she is.”

46

THERE WAS a second when Darian thought Vinny was going to swing for Simon, staring at him and reaching out a hand to a terrified man with lungfuls of smoke. Simon pulled back but Vinny only put a hand on his shoulder. From a distance it might look like a friendly gesture, but Vinny Reno had been a cop in Whisper Hill long enough to know how to make things look like something they weren't. Vinny was a barrel-chested bruiser and the hard grip of the shoulder was a reminder of how close the big hand was to Simon's throat.

Vinny looked him in the eye and said, "Where is she? What happened?"

"Nothing happened to her. Nothing happened because Will and I weren't willing to let it happen."

He was shaking his head and looking scared, a man with an answer to a question that hadn't yet been asked. Simon Sutherland wanted to explain everything despite Freya being unaccounted for. Vinny wanted his ex before the story.

"Where is she?"

"I own number fourteen. She's in number fourteen, Auri, just down the street on the other side of the road. It's smaller, but it's, I suppose, reasonably okay. I've never been in. I own it, though. She's in the basement."

Vinny looked at him and then at Darian and Sholto.

Darian said, "We'll go, come on, we'll go."

Simon said, "Wait, there's a lock, it's a security thing. I had it put in on the basement. You'll need the code. Three, zero, zero, one.

That's to the basement. There are keys for the gate and doors but they're in there."

They all followed his watering eyes back to the only place he had called home, the only place he had ever accepted and ever wanted to be, now turning to charred steel and ash in front of him.

Sholto said, "Go, you two, go, I can't handle falling over any more fences. Go, and I'll keep an eye on..."

He trailed off. His eyes flitted across to Harold Sutherland, to Phil Sutherland standing near his uncle with an uncertain look.

Darian and Vinny set off running down the drive and Darian was, within ten yards, reminded that he had just breathed in a lot of smoke and been burned and was exhausted. He coughed when his legs tried to go up through the gears and he had to slow down and spit some dark and ominous-looking phlegm onto the drive. He turned to see Sholto stopping Phil from trying to join them: no Sutherland welcome. Vinny didn't have enough sympathy to slow down but thundered on past the fire engines and down to the gate. Darian picked up the pace and turned left to head down Geug Place, narrow and with high trees and bushes on either side. In the daylight it was a picturesque way to make it feel rural, the walls shrouded in greenery, but at night it made identifying the numbers on the gates difficult. Darian saw Vinny ahead, slowing to check the number on one of them, then running on to the next.

They had turned the slight curve in the road and were toward the bottom of the lane when Vinny stopped and said to Darian as he caught up, "This one. This is it. Give me a leg up and I'll pull you up after me."

"What? I can't get you up that high."

"Aye, you can, stand against the gate, back straight, knees bent. Hurry up, Darian."

He cursed under his breath, but he did as he was told. Darian did his best, which wasn't easy because he was weakened and Vinny was a heavy old beast. It hurt like hell, Darian could feel his legs begin to buckle. Vinny stepped up onto Darian's shoulder, Darian wincing in pain. Then nothing. Vinny was up and grabbing the spikes at the top and pulling himself up.

Now for the reason that Vinny had gone first. He reached a hand down for Darian, who had to take a run-up to grab it but when he did it was as if he was weightless. Vinny lifted him up in one swinging movement and then Darian was grabbing the spikes and pulling himself over. They both lowered their weight and had to drop the rest of the way, hitting the cobbled ground and falling over.

They ran up a short drive to a house smaller than Simon's. This one was two stories of traditional gneiss, a little smaller than the original Sutherland home would have been before the extensions. The size mattered nothing to them, but they both noticed the darkness and emptiness of it.

Simon Sutherland had said he owned it and that he had never been in it, and it didn't look like anyone else had either. High walls surrounded the garden and that was just enough to hide the jungle it had become from the neighbors. The grass was thigh-high and the weeds taller, and even in the moonlight Darian could see the clumps of moss sticking out of the drainpipes and clinging to the roof, more weeds reaching out between the cobbles beneath them. They went to the wooden front door and Vinny looked in the small window before trying the handle to find it was locked.

He said, "What do you think?"

"I think you're a cop and you put doors in all the time. Add another to your list."

Vinny had never lived his life waiting for second invites, so he put his shoulder to the door and hammered into it. It didn't budge an inch, didn't even rattle.

He grunted. "That's not a normal door. Reinforced, I think."

"We need something to smash it with, force our way in."

If there was anything useable in the front garden it was buried under the grass and in the darkness they couldn't go feeling for it. They ran around the side of the house. Nothing there. Then to the back, a long garden running down toward the edge of the loch, a mesh fence around a large flat stone at the water's edge, a piece of history few understood and they had no time to look at.

"There. Birdbath."

Darian had spotted it, the top peeking out over the long grass around it, a stone circle that looked weighty. Vinny went across and grabbed it, tried to lift it but struggled. Darian helping, they shoved it, rocked it back and forth until it came loose and Vinny picked it up. With it on his shoulder he started running, straight to the back door of the house and charged it, assuming it was as secure as the front door. The first time it buckled but it didn't open. It needed a second run-up, all of Vinny's weight and the impact of the birdbath to smash the door around the multiple heavy locks and get them in.

The second the door burst open an alarm started screaming, loud enough to wake the dead in Heilam cemetery across the loch. Vinny tossed the heavy birdbath onto the pavement running around the side of the house. Ignoring the alarm, they carried on into the house. Vinny was a cop and they were doing the right thing so neither feared the law.

They found themselves in a long, empty, dark corridor with a hard wooden floor that seemed to stretch the length of the house with a staircase at the head and doors on either side as you went along it. In a horror movie it would be the scene where a door would suddenly open and something awful would leap out, and Darian wasn't ruling out that happening here. The whole house had the atmosphere of a trap. With the pulsing screech paining their ears they walked halfway down the corridor until they saw a small light: a security box on a door that surely led to the basement.

They stood beside it and Vinny pressed three, zero, zero, one and then enter, and everything changed. The alarm shut its damn mouth and the door clicked open a fraction, enough to show them a line of light. Vinny pulled the door open and they were standing at the top of a flight of stairs leading to another door. They walked down and found it was heavy, metal, but the same code that had unlocked the one at the top of the stairs had opened this one, too. They pulled it open and they found her.

The basement was large and well furnished; they could see a sofa and a TV, a table and a bed, and a small kitchen, all in the one open space. There was an open door through which they could see a shower, and they could guess a toilet, too. A light was on and a woman was standing in the middle of the room looking nervous.

She recognized Vinny and said, "Oh, thank God."

Freya ran across to him and they hugged. Darian was taking in the room and trying to examine Freya without it being obvious. There were no noticeable marks on her, cuts or bruises, but that confirmed nothing.

Vinny said, "Are you okay?"

"Yes, I'm okay, bored and frustrated but I'm okay. What the hell took you so long, I was expecting you ages ago?"

"What the hell...? I've been turning the city upside down trying to find you, that's what."

"Twelve days, Vinny. Some cop you are."

Darian smiled. "Come on, let's get out of here."

Freya said, "Oh, yes, I could use some fresh air."

"Won't be that fresh, it's full of smoke out there."

On the way to the door Vinny paused and looked behind at the basement, saying quietly to Darian, "Bloody hell, it's bigger than my flat, and a lot better equipped apart from no phone or wi-fi, and even with them my signal's patchy. I mean, I'm not saying I'd ever want to be kidnapped, but if it had to happen this is where I'd want to go."

"Yeah, they were well prepared."

They walked up the stairs and through the darkness to the front door. In the vestibule Darian found the keypad to unlock the front gate and they made their way down the lane.

AN CAILLTE

The sea had been rough and that was what they had wanted, had been why they sailed. It calmed as they entered the mouth of the sea loch and continued to sail south, the two men in the thirty-foot open boat wet and cold but filled with nervous optimism. Both were tall and heavily bearded, Ranulf "Ruadh," twenty-eight, and Tormod "Ciùin," twenty-seven, and both carried the scars to display the bloody work they had done in their lives, on land and at sea. Battle had brought them relative riches, but had also taught them that respect should be earned and not given, and those who wished to impose laws upon them had earned nothing.

"Further, back to the flat rock," Ruadh said to his friend, and as he looked over the side of the boat added, "it's deep, all the way in so far."

"The hills keep tall on both sides so the loch will be deep," Ciùin said in his low voice, the same gruff accent of a Leòdhasach as his friend.

They had returned to their island and found the king's men demanding loyalty, demanding a share of their violent earnings to take their coin and use it to further the glory of another man. Gèbennach was a fiercely ambitious man, a king of small throne who wanted more, and expected their help to take from those they had given nothing to. Others on the island accepted it, but others had not traveled as widely as they had, did not know how different the world could look. Others had not learned the hard lessons they had learned. People with titles would always take from them unless they took the titles.

In their previous visit to this loch they had found stones in two spots that might once have been buildings, but small and far apart, no hint that there had been a community. All that still stood to tell of man's time here were the standing stones, tall on the peak of a hill to the east and a reminder of a lost home. The hills protected them from prying eyes on the north coast, those who controlled the lands looking always for an advantage, a way to gain valuable favor or to steal from others. As they sailed toward the southern end of the loch they saw the valley that opened in the hills there, leading into the mountains. Their plan was not to stay so even a break in the ring of high protection was of little concern.

They sailed beyond an outcrop on the east bank and an island toward the west.

"There," Ruadh said, "the rock is as good a spot as any."

On the west bank was a protruding rock, flat on top with a small overhang at the edge of the water. They lowered their sail when they were close and used oars to pull up to the bank, the water shallowing here but their boat built for this. Preparation was most important, and it was why they were here.

They secured the boat and Ruadh used both hands to carry out the cloth bag they had with them, filled heavy as it was, and placed it on the rock. They put two short swords and an ax pressed to the side of the rock, out of view of the water, in case their negotiations went poorly, and were both reassured by the knives they carried. Now they sat on the rock, feet in the heather, in the rain, and waited.

It was hours later when a single boat came into view toward the mouth of the loch, its sail drifting toward them. When it was close enough they could see Egill "Halfeye" on board, and with him his little brother, Vali "Two Eyes." They knew both men well, the blond hair and wide faces and broad shoulders the same, the sibling look marred only by the long scar that ran from the middle of Halfeye's forehead, splitting his eyebrow in half and ending just below the empty red socket where his right eye had been. They reached the rock and Halfeye stepped off the boat onto the bank.

"This is a good place," he said in his rough and amusing attempt at Gaelic.

Ruadh spoke a little Icelandic but Halfeye's Gaelic was better so it was what they used.

"It will do," Ruadh said. "The hills for shelter, deep water all the way to the south bank. We shall make use of it and you should, too."

"We shall," Halfeye said, polite to the offer of a thing he didn't need, rainwater dripping from his neat beard. "And we start today. There are as many as you asked for, as good as you need," Halfeye said, "but I tell you again you are wasting time and blood you have little of to spare. An island on the western edge? What can you build there when others claim it as theirs, all these kings fighting? You will spend a lifetime defending what you have rather than taking more. Look at this place. Here is where you can build a stronghold to call your own. Sail ships north and east, and not a hard sail to Ireland either."

"This," Ruadh said, "is not home."

"Home is not where you were born; it's where you choose to be."

Halfeye helped his brother carry out the delivery, dozens of longswords wrapped in thick blankets. Ruadh took the bag of coins across and placed it beside the weapons. This was the moment when a deal could turn rotten. Old friends or not, new priorities could persuade one side they were better off with the swords, the payment and two dead bodies. Halfeye picked up the bag with more ease than Ruadh had and looked inside. All of the coin had come from a man now dead, stolen by Ruadh and Halfeye just months before. It had made both men, and others, rich, but great wealth led to great problems. Halfeye recognized the coin from the chest they had taken.

The Icelander smiled. "Good fortune to you, friends, I hope you wet the swords."

As Halfeye put the bag on the boat beside Two Eyes, Ruadh and Ciùin checked what they had bought, the blades sharp and all of the quality agreed. As they drifted north from the bank they saw Halfeye take a coin from the bag and flick it into the water of the loch, offering his payment for good fortune to the sea that had killed so effortlessly so many good men he had known. Never forget to honor its power. Ruadh and Ciùin watched the brothers sail beyond view before they began to count out the swords, sure that the Icelanders wouldn't return. Halfeye was a hard man to trust around money but perhaps his brother calmed him, or the coming winter persuaded him that the easiest money was the best. Ruadh ran his hand along the side of a blade, thinking of the men who would soon arrive from Ireland to be armed, the blood they would spill to name a new king of the isles.

"This is a good spot," Ciùin said. "What shall I mark it?"

"We shall call it An Caillte."

47

VINNY LED the way with Freya by his side, her looking around all the time. Darian could see that she hadn't known where she had been taken and still didn't know where the hell she was because she'd never been on Geug Place before. As they walked the slow tilt of the lane they could see the blue lights flashing and the orange glow, the thick plume of black smoke yawning into the sky. For someone who hadn't been outside that basement room for twelve days it was an assault on the senses and Freya was holding onto Vinny's arm to make sure it didn't overwhelm her.

She said, "Finn? Is he okay?"

"He's fine. Worried witless about you, but he's doing okay. We can go see him, right after this."

"Where are we going now?"

"To see the person who did this and if he doesn't tell me why he did it I'm going to throw him back into the fire Darian just got him out of."

Darian already suspected something close to the truth, but he wanted to hear it from Simon. They turned into the drive and walked past the fire engines and onto the grass where Sholto was keeping watch over Simon, Harold and Phil. They stood looking at each other, Simon sheepish, Freya unsure. Harold raised his chin slightly, defiant.

Before Freya could utter a word, Harold said, "Whatever you are about to accuse my nephew of you should be very careful. He is not a well man, and he has just been through a terrible trauma.

Our family has sympathy for whatever has happened to you but we will defend ourselves. I have already contacted people to that effect."

He spoke fast, breathlessly. He was a man rowing against the waves. Freya glared at him and said, "I know what happened. I know."

Sholto said, "You contacted people? You contacted Noonan? Must have been before we got here, and he hasn't turned up yet. You're about to find you have fewer friends than you thought."

Vinny looked back and forth and said, "Hang on, what? This is about Simon, right? It was Simon."

Freya shook her head. "Will Dent told me it was Harold behind it all. Dent was the only one I saw and I didn't know if I could believe him, but he was right. Where is he?"

For a few seconds the group fell into an awkward silence before Vinny, with no hint of sympathy, said, "He died yesterday, probably trying to stop us from finding you. Tried to break into Sholto's office, got chased, ran across the railway lines and had an argument with a speeding train. He lost."

Simon Sutherland said, "He did everything because I asked him to. He did it for me, so, I'm sorry."

Harold grabbed his nephew by the shoulder and said, "Say nothing, Simon. Not a word. They'll use it against you."

Simon looked at him. There was a moment where Darian wondered, where it seemed that the strength of his uncle's hold on him might be enough. Not this time. Simon stepped away from Harold and Phil and moved over to stand next to Darian. Vinny was watching, the bulky, menacing presence. When Harold took a step toward Simon, Vinny moved between them.

Freya glared at Harold and said, "Will told me he was trying to stop me from being killed. He said it had happened before and that him and his friend were going to stop it happening again. I take it you're the friend."

Simon nodded when she turned to him and said, "Yes, I'm the

friend. Harold is my uncle; he killed a young woman called Ruby-Mae Short. Will was able to tell me about it because he was there. Uncle Harold told him they were going to pick up a girl he was dating but they went to Earmam and picked a drunk girl off the street. Will drove them to a flat Uncle Harold had in Bakers Moor and left them there. He didn't like it, the young woman didn't know what was happening. He didn't stop it. Then Uncle Harold called him two hours later and made him come up to the flat. He took her dead body and dropped it at the railway line. It was only when Uncle Harold put the bra in my house that Will decided to tell me what happened. I know I should have told the police but he's family and the bank needs him. He looked after me when my mother died. When Will told me about you, about the accident and Uncle Harold saying he liked you, we decided to keep an eye on him. If he was going to make a move we would be a step ahead of him. When he started sending you gifts we knew we had to act."

Harold was shaking his head and laughing. "This is nonsense. No one believes this. Simon, I know you're ill, God knows I've done more to help you than anyone, but you need to stop talking. We'll get you help, okay. I will."

While Harold spoke, loud above the shouts and actions of the firemen, the rest of them looked at Simon and at Vinny. Simon held the truth. Vinny held the violence.

There was a short lull before Sholto said, "Why kidnap her? Why hold her there?"

"I thought if we kept her out of reach for a week or two he would realize what had happened. He would know that we were onto him, or someone was, and it would stop him. Instead, when he found out it was me, he came round and burned down my house. He thought I would stay inside and be burned with it, and that no one would try to rescue me."

As he spoke he made eye contact with Darian and there was a nod between them.

Vinny, with a snarl, said, "Why the hell didn't you just tell someone this bastard was on the prowl?"

Harold stepped back at the fury in the look Vinny gave him. The big man was flooded with relief and energy he hadn't had much chance to use yet. When Harold moved back it was Phil who put out a hand and grabbed his uncle by the arm. He held him tight. Harold turned and glared at him. Shocked. Two family members turning on him. Sutherland against Sutherland.

Vinny turned to Simon. "The police are going to have a lot of questions for you, what you did was still rotten. Kidnapping her and then accusing me to my face of killing her, you wee bastard."

Phil said, "Actually, Simon didn't take her, Will Dent did, and there's nothing to prove Simon ordered it or had any control over it. The worst you could say is he knew about it and he did nothing, but he had reasonable motives for that."

Sholto, in a high whine, said, "He just bloody said he ordered it and we all heard him."

Vinny gave Phil a sideways look that suggested he wanted to put a fist through his young partner and said, "Aye, you're still a Sutherland all right."

A car turned into the driveway behind them with a screech, drove up toward the house and pulled recklessly onto the grass to avoid going into the back of a fire engine. Harold looked up hopefully. It could have been Noonan. But Harold would never see his pet cop again. Noonan only backed the winning team. You always backed the Sutherlands because they always won, that was common logic. The police knew that. The Sutherlands were in control. Maybe, just maybe, he would have been able to solve the problem. The Sutherlands had bought their way out of plenty of scandals before. Defend the family. Protect the bank. Those were the rules and as long as all the family stuck to them they had a chance of surviving any scandal. Not this time. The car door opened and DC Angela Vicario got out.

48

ANGELA APPROACHED the group and introduced herself. Harold tried to get his story in first.

"You can't charge Simon with anything. He's mentally ill, demonstrably so, it's care and protection he needs, not this, not a squad of policemen bullying him into lies. And don't think I won't be pressing charges for this..."

It was Vinny who stepped toward Harold and shut him up. "You're going to let the boy speak and you're not going to say a word."

Nerves were rising. The flood of relief at finding Freya and now the determination to stop whoever was responsible. The heat from the house and the shouting of the firemen, the roar of the fire, made every word jangle with nerves. Behind them more blue lights as a police car from the local station turned into the drive and found itself confronted with more people and vehicles than it knew what to do with. Behind it an ambulance joined the throng.

Angela introduced herself to the new arrivals and one of them said, "So who are we arresting?"

Vinny pointed at Harold and said, "That one."

The uniformed officers hesitated. One of them said, "But what for?"

Darian said, "He set the fire. We got here and the gate was locked, no cars around, but when I went over the railings he was inside, on his own. He slipped in, locked the gate behind him and set the fire."

Harold was laughing again and shaking his head but Phil said, "I saw your car round the corner on King Robert Street."

Another family betrayal. Harold looked with horror at Phil and Simon, but the two uniformed officers stepped in and led him away to the car. There would be many more charges to follow.

Angela turned to Simon and said, "You're the one who knows what's going on here. Why don't you share it?"

Simon nodded. "Okay, I'll tell you. It was Will who told me about it. Uncle Harold had always been, I don't know what you would call it, a ladies' man. But he only liked to have short-term relationships. He didn't let Will see the truth until he was sure that he could trust him. Then he could have Will drive other men's wives to one of his flats around the city for the night. He started sending Will to bars to pick up girls for him. He was getting more forceful about it, too. Then he had Will drive him around on weekends, late at night, and would offer drunk girls a lift in his luxury, chauffeur-driven car. When they had gotten into the back he would try his luck. Will said sometimes Uncle Harold got aggressive, and other times the girls were too drunk to know what was happening. Then one night they picked up Ruby-Mae Short. Will dropped them at the flat in Bakers Moor, on Normandy Road, he said, and left. When he was called back she was dead and Uncle Harold told him where to take her, like he'd planned it, told him how to get to the tracks without being seen. Will was convinced they'd get caught but it never happened, the police didn't come after them. He told me everything. Uncle Harold had put the bra in my house, I think as a warning to Will. I should have called the police then but Uncle Harold has looked after me since my mother died and I knew what it would do to the bank. Then there was a while when everything seemed to calm back down to normal, like he had been sated by what he'd done, and then the crash happened. Uncle Harold started sending you gifts after that, and Will found out because he had to go and collect them when you refused them. We had already planned what we would do if we thought it was definitely going to happen again, so we put it into practice. Will was convinced that he would get years in The Ganntair for what happened to Miss Short, and I don't think he believed he could survive that long. I think that must be why he didn't step out of the way of the train. I thought when all this happened Uncle Harold would speak to me, tell me he wouldn't do it again and everything would be okay. I honestly never imagined that he would try to kill me, too."

He had spoken quietly throughout, face still smudged by smoke, the group around him straining to hear his voice over the fire and the people fighting it.

Angela said, "Thank you, Simon, that's helpful. You'll have to tell that again on tape, and you might have to go to court."

"Oh, yes, I know."

Phil said, "He's doing all he can to help and he'll continue to. I'll contact the chairman of the bank, have him send out a legal representative for Simon."

It was an attempt to negotiate complete honesty in exchange for favorable treatment, no charge of withholding information and, if he could sweet-talk Freya, which seemed unlikely, no charge of kidnap. Phil had spent years steering clear of the upper branches of his family tree and here he was promising to call the patriarch personally. The very mention of the most powerful man in Challaid subdued the aggression Vinny had shown and promised a prosecution-defying defensive wall was about to be built around Simon. Phil was sacrificing a little of his normal life to protect his cousin, who had no one else to look after him now.

Angela said, "I'll have people head out to the house on Eilean Seud and try to work out what other property in the city he owns, which is probably a lot. The very least we can be certain of convicting him on is setting fire to the house, but I think we have enough to get a whole lot more. We've been trying to get justice for Ruby-Mae for a while, and we will now. I'm going to the station to prepare for the interview. Simon, we'll want to talk to you right away."

As more police cars pulled up Phil said, "I'm coming with him.

Freya, it's good to see you safe, and Darian, Sholto, well done on everything tonight, you saved Simon and stopped a killer. Thank you."

There had been a stiffness in Phil's delivery that made it sound obligated and not heartfelt, and he led Simon to a waiting police car. Angela said to Darian, "They'll take him to Piper Station first, this is their patch. It could be a while before we get to question him. We'll need to talk to you all as well."

Darian nodded. "Of course."

Angela brushed his hand and, before she walked down the driveway, said, "I'll call you."

There were four of them left now, Darian, Sholto, Vinny and Freya, and they all breathed a sigh of relief.

Darian looked at Freya and said, "How are you feeling?"

"Relieved. Tired. A bit hungry. Annoyed it happened. Glad it's over."

Vinny said, "All because one bloody Sutherland didn't want to call the cops on another bloody Sutherland."

Sholto said, "No matter how good his legal team are and how much your partner wants to help him, Simon Sutherland is looking at a conviction here."

"He is, but we all know how these things work around here. He's rich and his family will pull strings, he'll go to court and say he was scared of his uncle and that he has mental health issues so if he does get convicted there's almost no chance he'll spend a single night in a cell. They'll send him back to his rebuilt mansion to hide from humanity forever more."

Darian said, "Aye, well, the more I see of humanity the more I think he might be onto something."

It was at that point that Vinny smiled and said, "Okay, hands up, who among you had me pegged as the most likely suspect?"

Sholto slightly raised his hand and then pulled it down again in case Vinny wasn't making a joke of this, and then said, "DS MacNeith did for sure."

"I know she did, and she was right to. It's usually the ex."

Freya looked askance. "You? They thought you would be able to kidnap me? They thought you had killed me?"

"I know, I could never win a bloody argument with you, let alone get away with bumping you off."

"The only thing you ever made a half-decent job of was Finn, and now I want you to take me to him."

"Yeah, let's go. I can smoke out the window of the car. Been desperate for a San Jose for the last hour but I don't want to light up in front of firemen and paramedics. I feel like I'd be on the end of a double-barrelled lecture. Let's go see the boy."

Vinny and Freya said goodbye to Darian and Sholto and left, knowing Freya should have stayed to talk more to the police but feeling this was more important. Vinny would take her to the station later, but for now they were heading to his flat in Whisper Hill to see their young son. That, Darian felt, was the most gratifying moment of the whole thing, watching them going to give a young kid the surprise he had been praying for. That happened far too rarely. There would be children in the city, other family members, too, desperately hoping that a lost parent or child or sibling would return. Most would be disappointed.

Darian and Sholto walked slowly out to the car, both tired and sore, and Sholto made a three-course meal of making a three-point turn to get them out of Geug Place.

On the way south through Barton, Sholto said, "A Sutherland will never call the cops on another Sutherland, that's what Vinny said."

"We knew that, didn't we?"

"I suppose. I just wonder if it applies to his partner, too. He's a Sutherland. How early did he know about his beloved uncle? How early did he know about Ruby-Mae?"

"You think he knew and said nothing, even when Freya was missing? That's a hell of an accusation."

"I know, that's why I only put it to you in the car instead of in front of the rest of them in the garden. I won't repeat it either, because

I'll never be able to prove it, but it's always worth remembering that even people you think are good folk have their own moral code. Everyone does. You think someone is decent because they have most of the same standards as you, but then you spot a difference and it shocks you, but it shouldn't. Nothing would surprise me about the moral code of another person, even if it meant believing Phil could have put a stop to this earlier."

Darian mumbled agreement but didn't dive into dirty detail. One of the very first pearls of wisdom Sholto had rolled his way was that no case was perfect, and most would leave behind a selection of unconquered question marks, even after the main point of the investigation was solved and the file closed. Nothing as complicated as a Challaid criminal could give you an easy answer.

As they stopped outside Darian's flat, the sun making its lazy way into the sky, Sholto said, "Go and get some proper sleep. I don't want you in the office before lunchtime. We've got a big report to write and no one to read it, and you'll have to give more statements to the police. If you're lucky it might be to DC Vicario, and you'll want your beauty sleep before you see her again. Go on, get out of my sight."

"Thanks, Sholto."

Darian walked slowly up the stairs and took the key from his pocket. He opened the front door and went into his small flat. There were times, sitting at his desk in the office looking down at Cage Street, when he felt jealous of big operators like Raven, and when he resented his father for robbing him of the chance to follow his dream of becoming a real detective. Nights like this one changed it all.

ABOUT THE AUTHOR

Malcolm Mackay's novels have been nominated for the Edgar Award for Best Paperback Original, the CWA John Creasey (New Blood) Dagger, and the Theakston's Old Peculier Crime Novel of the Year. *How a Gunman Says Goodbye* won the Deanston Scottish Crime Book of the Year Award. Mackay was born in Stornoway on Scotland's Isle of Lewis, where he still lives.

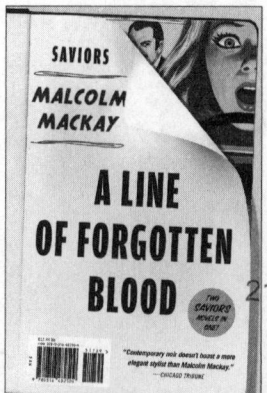

Books by Malcolm Mackay

The Necessary Death of Lewis Winter

The Sudden Arrival of Violence

How a Gunman Says Goodbye

The Night the Rich Men Burned

Every Night I Dream of Hell

For Those Who Know the Ending

SAVIORS

IN THE CAGE WHERE YOUR SAVIORS HIDE

MALCOLM MACKAY

MULHOLLAND BOOKS

Little, Brown and Company
New York Boston London

Mulholland Books / Little, Brown and Company
Hachette Book Group
1290 Avenue of the Americas, New York, NY 10104
mulhollandbooks.com
Twitter @mulhollandbooks
Facebook.com/mulhollandbooks

First United States omnibus edition: August 2019
Originally published in Great Britain by Head of Zeus, London, as *In the Cage Where Your Saviours Hide,* April 2018

Mulholland Books is an imprint of Little, Brown and Company, a division of Hachette Book Group, Inc. The Mulholland Books name and logo are trademarks of Hachette Book Group, Inc.

The publisher is not responsible for websites (or their content) that are not owned by the publisher.

The Hachette Speakers Bureau provides a wide range of authors for speaking events. To find out more, go to hachettespeakersbureau.com or call (866) 376-6591.

Also available as an ebook.

ISBN 978-0-316-48250-9
Cataloging-in-publication data is available at the Library of Congress.

10 9 8 7 6 5 4 3 2 1

LSC-C

Printed in the United States of America

For my father

IN THE CAGE WHERE YOUR SAVIORS HIDE

PROLOGUE

A DROP of dirty rainwater fell from the guttering and landed with a splash in the open eye of the dead man. He lay with eyes wide and mouth open, arms close to his side and legs together. The body had lain there for three hours and not a soul had cared to notice. The alley was narrow and unlit, with large bins pushed against the walls on both sides. Navigating from one end to the other was an assault course and that was what had slowed him down and killed him.

The dead man had run into the alley at ten past one in the morning, gasping, bleeding and limping. The ground was wet and he slipped against a green industrial bin placed beside the plain red rear door of a struggling restaurant. His hand reached out instinctively and hit the top of it with a thump, sliding it backward a fraction, feeling the thick raindrops that had settled on it wet his palm. He pulled away and the lid slid shut with a hollow knock. Running was already beyond the man with the knife wound, and now he had to weave between bins and boxes stacked against bare brick walls. The effort ensured that twenty-five seconds later he was on the ground, dying.

A little before two o'clock in the morning a waiter came out of the back of the restaurant and pushed open the lid of the bin a dying hand had touched. He held two plastic shopping bags filled with food scraps, the bags knotted at the handles. He slung them into the bin in a looping movement and pulled the lid tightly shut to deny the rats a meal. He took a cigarette from his pocket and lit it, standing by the bin for two or three relaxing minutes, ignoring the familiar,

rotting smell. A shout from inside the building, a woman's voice, the waitress he gave a lift home to each night. He dropped the cigarette on the ground and stubbed out the orange glow with his shoe, blew out the last mouthful of smoke and walked quickly back into the restaurant. He said he saw no body in the alley, that there was light enough to spot it so it can't have been there.

At twenty past two a police car sped down Somerset Street and past the end of the alley. Its siren knifed the silence, its lights flashing blue into the darkness, bouncing off the walls and briefly down the alley. The city had many emergencies for its police to tackle, and no one had realized another victim was lying, waiting to be discovered, nearby. From the alley, beside the body, you could hear the siren fade away into the distance, looking for a new horror. They wouldn't have to search long.

At four o'clock in the morning another man entered the alley from the Morti Road end. This one was walking more slowly, carefully, picking his way and watching his footing with unnecessary care. He went past the bins and saw the body lying flat, so he stopped. He moved slowly beside it and nudged the still arm with his boot. He knelt down and slapped the face gently, held a hand over the nose to try to feel breath. There was nothing. His medical expertise exhausted, he stood and took his mobile from his pocket and called the police. Two and a half minutes later sirens were loudly announcing their return. The dead man had been found and reported, and now the investigation would begin.

1

WE'LL START before the obvious point because the real beginning of this story comes a couple of days earlier than that. Instead of opening with the gorgeous dame walking into the office on Cage Street we'll instead go to a flat on Haugen Road, over in the Bakers Moor district in the east of the city.

There were forty people in a room that could hold twenty, in a flat that housed six and was designed for three. That's always the way on the east side of Challaid, too much life for the space. The music was loud and indistinguishable from the general racket, shite, to be succinct; the crowd packed so tight it was hard to tell who was dancing and who was waving for help. It was hot and, boy, was it sweaty, the movements slow. A young couple were kissing with the passion of people who had uncovered a new art form and wanted to perfect it, fast. Darian Ross stood back against the wall by the door, on his own, and watched.

Girls in vest tops and shorts and boys in T-shirts with unwitty slogans printed on the front, shimmering brows on blissed faces.

A constant and aimless sway of bodies in the absence of actual dancing.

A pill passed discreetly from one hand to another.

A shout and then a bottle breaking, the crowd pausing in anticipation of a violent follow-up and then carrying on, disappointed, when they realized it wasn't coming.

Someone was trying to make themselves heard close by and failing, the music screaming and the babble of voices always rising in the

battle to be heard above it. This was what other people's joy looked and sounded like. A gap just large enough for him to raise his hand cleared and Darian took a sip from his warm beer can.

His eyes never wavered, fixed on the same couple.

The girl had black hair in a bob and big teeth, but he couldn't see the rest of her. They were deep in the crowd, Darian catching occasional glances of their heads as they looked into each other's eyes, the man doing all the talking.

He was older than her, older than most of the people in the room. She and they were teenagers; the man she had her arms around was twenty-seven. Brown hair combed back, average height, an ordinary, clean-shaven face and small, dark eyes that always seemed to have a light trapped inside them. Not a lot to look at, but his charisma held him above the ordinary mass of boys that usually chased her.

Two young girls had offered Darian a body to lean on earlier in the evening when there had been more room to approach but he had turned them both away, not interested. The only person he was there to see was the man with the unremarkable face. As the crowds filled the flat and the temperature rose, the light had faded from the room, too. Darian was handsome, light brown hair, feminine features, large brown eyes and full lips, six feet and slim with an intense look. In the dark he could lean back against the wall by the door and play the detached observer, still just young enough at twenty-two to slot in and not look like a creepy bastard. He'd picked his spot to make sure anyone who left had to parade right past him. More coming than going, and it had reached the point where a couple arrived and instantly decided that being crushed in a sweaty crowd was not actually the best available option for a Friday night. In this city there were always, always better options.

The beer in his can was flat and had lived long enough to rise to room temperature but he didn't notice. Darian sipped from it only so that he wouldn't be the only person standing still. In this room the man not moving was the man who stood out, so he'd occasionally nod his head self-consciously to the thudding music he hadn't yet

identified. He found his excitement in silent moments, but this crowd was looking for something else. Most of them wanted more from life than peace and quiet, and one of them wanted everything.

Darian lost sight of the couple for a few seconds, a wave of bodies rising in front of them. Where the hell did they go? Shit, lost them. No, wait, there, he saw them again. Picked them up, walking toward the door beside him, politely nudging past partygoers to reach the exit. The ordinary face leaning down to speak into the ear hidden by dark hair. She smiled, buzzing, eyes wide and too alert, looking forward to being somewhere else. They managed to escape the scrum and passed Darian, out of the flat.

He let them go and counted slowly to ten, then counted a second time to make sure he had it right. He put the beer can on the floor for someone else to kick over, spun off the wall and walked out through the door, not looking back at the crowd that had barely noticed his presence and didn't spot his departure at all.

THE CHALLAID GAZETTE AND ADVERTISER

14 JANUARY 1905

32 DIE IN TUNNEL COLLAPSE

Tragedy struck Challaid yesterday morning with a major collapse in the rail tunnel being dug under the Bank district of the city which killed thirty-two men working at the site. It is believed the men drowned when the tunnel ceiling collapsed and mud and water poured in from above, filling the tunnel and preventing escape. A large rescue operation began immediately but no survivors have been retrieved, and it has now been confirmed that bodies will not be recovered until the tunnel has been drained, which may take several weeks.

Concerns had previously been raised regarding the digging of the tunnel as part of the rail extension with unions arguing the boggy land close to the docks was unsafe. The project, funded by Sutherland Bank, has been controversial since its announcement, with the tunnel proposed as an alternative to an above ground line, reducing disruption in the city center during construction and afterward. Lord Sutherland, chairman of the bank, has stated his shock and sadness and added his hope that work can begin again on the tunnel in quick order for the good of the city.

Glendan Construction—who are building the rail line from Barton to Whisper Hill—have confirmed that thirty-two of their workers are missing after the collapse but will not confirm the identity of the men until families have been informed. It is thought that most or all of the men were from Challaid and Glendan has stated that its senior engineers were leading the tunnel excavation at the time.

Further questions have been raised about the proposed underground rail system that would connect various parts of the city not served by the new main line. The underground designs are before the council planning committee and it was hoped construction would begin next summer with parts open to passengers by 1908. This is now likely to face delay while the safety of all proposed lines is assessed.

POLLA CLOTHING SALE

Polla Clothing New Year sale.

Large reductions on menswear and ladies' clothing in both South Sutherland Square and Sandpiper Road stores.

Sale lasts until January 31st

KING BEGINS TOUR OF CALEDONIAN STATES

His Royal Highness King Kenneth IV yesterday docked in the port town of New Edinburgh in Panama for the first day of his three-week tour of the Caledonian states. King Kenneth, traveling without Queen Margaret, was greeted by large crowds happily waving saltires and Caledonian flags, with all suggestions of unrest in the region surrounding his visit proved false.

King Kenneth will give a speech to parliament in Panama City on Monday and will attend a banquet in his honor on Tuesday in the city. His tour will continue north to Costa Rica and Nicaragua. It is the longest visit by a reigning monarch to Caledonia in more than seventy years and comes against the backdrop of growing demands for full independence for the three states. Recent elections in Costa Rica saw the independence party finish second with almost thirty percent of the vote. The Scottish government has denied his majesty's visit is a reaction to the rising volume of the independence movement, and have reiterated that the visit will boost trade and opportunities for both Scotland and the Caledonian states.

2

DARIAN LEFT through the open front door and made his way to the stairs. He could see them ahead, both pulling on coats as they moved out of view, walking side by side, leaning against each other out of lust and a need for balance. The stairwell they skipped down was dark, streetlights coming through the full-length windows giving a dull orange tinge to the deep gray surroundings. Darian lurked at the top to play voyeur, listening to them go down together.

The girl said, “Hold on, I can’t see properly.”

A squeal followed as the man said, “Don’t you worry, I got you.”

She sounded too young to be playing this game. She started to giggle and that noise was smothered quickly by a kiss on the landing a floor below Darian. Thirty seconds passed before it turned back to movement, shoes clacking on bare concrete stairs as the couple moved further down. Darian kept up the stalk, making sure they couldn’t hear him, walking slowly on the balls of his feet. He only needed to be close for this early part of the journey, just until he was sure his guess was right.

He was on the first-floor landing when he heard the front door click shut behind them. Darian sauntered down, pushed it open and stepped out into the cold, clear night. They were, as we said, on Haugen Road, dirty lamplight showing the four-story flats on either side of the long street, their dark brown brickwork hugging the shadows tight, the road curving downhill toward Bakers Station. One man, he looked middle-aged, was walking up the street, and seemed to be struggling to keep his feet on a flat pavement inconsiderately not

designed with the stumbling drunk in mind. The young couple had crossed the road and were walking down toward the station, the man with his arm tight around the girl. Darian stayed on the other side and walked more slowly than them.

It was a careful process, staying far enough behind to make sure his footsteps couldn't be heard. He didn't need to stay close now, but it was hard to walk down the hill to the station any slower than the lovey-dovey, hands-on couple were going without tying his feet together. They went into the brightly lit, century-old, gray stone station at the bottom of the road ahead of him, so now he could take his time, let them get ahead, let them disappear. They entered through the large arch to the concourse and Darian followed slowly, dragging his fingers along the bumpy surface of the stonework on the outside.

The couple used their travel cards to get through the barriers and hopped onto the next train heading north to Whisper Hill. Darian was, technically, working, so he went to the machine and bought a ticket with money he could claim back the cost of with a rare proof of expenses. The purchase killed four minutes; made sure he missed the train north they were on but got him to the platform in time for the next.

A short detour from the tale here, but anyone who's ever been to Challaid will know the leading pastime of the populace is not football or camanachd or the theater or, unfortunately, books or any other noble pursuit, it's complaining about the transport system. Ignore the stadiums and grand halls and libraries the other hobbies occupy, nothing can compete with the scale of people whinging about travel. This is a port city, founded over a thousand years ago as a fishing and trading town, or so your history teacher would have you believe, and centuries later boats remain the only vehicles we're any good with. The roads are clogged because we're a long but narrow city, U-shaped round the end of a sea loch, and because the rail system is a calamitous joke. We have no underground trains, and a single line running round the city above ground.

Look, we all know the reasons; a lot of people died when the original line was being built, probably more than was ever admitted because immigrant workers were never properly counted, and the companies involved were tone-deaf in their response. People protested against further development. It was dangerous back then, and by the time engineering skill caught up with public demand to make building an underground system safe it was prohibitively expensive. We're a reasonably rich city, but there's no appetite to spend the many billions something that big would now cost, so instead we complain. It's cheaper. There had been a suggestion in recent years that a monorail should be built, running over buildings instead of trying to dig under them. Funnily enough this idea had met with little support from communities who would have trains rattling above their heads every ten minutes and the odds of it ever happening ranked somewhere alongside the chances of everyone in Challaid being provided with a jetpack.

Darian was on the next train up to Whisper Hill, the carriage a mix of people silently annoyed with the others who were drunkenly loud. He was content to let the couple get ahead of him. It took fourteen minutes before the train stopped at Three O'clock Station in Whisper Hill and Darian got off. He walked out through the eastern exit of the sprawling station, each expansion adding a new architectural twist to the last stop on the city line, a glass and steel frontage on old brickwork on the east side of the tracks, a long, thin, white-paneled extension on the west and the back end of the building twice the height of the front.

There was a time, probably, when Whisper Hill would have been attractive. The hills, the narrow stretch of moor and then Loch Eriboll; who wouldn't find that pretty on a rare day of summer, midges the only pollution? Now this area of the city was dominated by the large industrial docks built in the thirties around an inlet, and the "engineering marvel" of Challaid International Airport built on top of Whisper Hill itself, the hilltop mostly leveled to accommodate it. No one in the last century has put the eyesore area on a postcard.

The lights up the steep hill shone bright, and Darian walked that way. Along Drummond Street, the long road that ran from the docks to the airport, the first half flat and the second a steep climb out of the tangle of concrete and up the heather-clad hillside. Darian turned right before he reached the bottom of the hill to walk down Gemmell Road, a narrow street with ugly brown three-story flats on each side. This was low-cost housing built for people working the docks in the thirties and forties. Short-term housing for temporary residents. It was the sort of area, buildings tightly packed together, a squash of inhabitants with a high turnover of tenants, in which a person with secrets could live a life unnoticed.

Darian knew he was looking for the second building on the left; he had spent time on Gemmell Road already, and went in through the front door and up the stairs to the first floor. There was no need to creep around now; they would have been inside the man's flat for more than five minutes.

Darian pictured them, kissing intensely, hurried, all that energy bottled up since meeting at the party cracking the glass with its intensity now.

Tension racing wild as soon as it was let off the chain.

Clothes being pulled off as they moved into the bedroom, onto the bed.

The girl underneath, that was the pattern.

The man licking and then biting, the girl getting scared as he forced her to roll over.

She would try to push him off, slap him, and he would ignore her. When she moved too much for him, made his mouth's work too difficult, that was when he would reach for the knife, that's when he would want blood.

Darian stood outside the front door, eyes closed, trying to calculate the time that pattern would take to play out. There was a scream from inside, quickly muffled. Darian took a step back and kicked, aiming for the lock of the front door, knowing how cheap and feeble such fixtures were. It was the smash-and-grab burglar routine;

kick, damage, repeat, the same methodical impact taking three kicks before the door cracked open. Darian was into the corridor and pushed open a door to find a bathroom, pushed open the next one to find his target.

A lamp was on beside the bed, showing the walls painted a dark blue, the bedside cabinet and a wardrobe opposite, no other furniture. The girl with the black bob was sitting up on the pillows, her eyes wide, a single drop of blood tickling down her left breast. The man, Darian knew his real name was Ash Lucas, whatever he was telling the girls, was standing at the foot of the bed, naked and excited. He had a large silver knife with a serrated edge in his hand and he spun to face the door when Darian walked in.

It took a glance for him to see it all, to understand that the pattern was indeed being repeated. Not pausing because delay gave the knife an advantage, Darian took a step toward Lucas and swung hard with his right fist, aiming accurately for the bridge of the nose. He hit the smaller man hard but he didn't hear the crack he was hoping for. The tactic was to hurt the bastard, and fast. Lucas stumbled backward, gripped the knife harder and reeled forward to his front foot to try to make a thrust at Darian. A second punch caught Lucas around the left eye, Darian's longer arm jabbing over the knife before he danced a step away.

That punch hurt both of them, Darian's index finger cracking, but he didn't show it, didn't react to pain in a fight. Lucas dropped sideways onto the bed. Darian took aim, his boot this time, the girl shouting as Darian stamped down on what we'll chastely call the man's excitement, scuffing down the skin. Lucas opened his mouth and instead of screaming he gasped loudly for breath as his eyes bulged, dropping the knife onto the floor. Darian picked it up and pointed it at Lucas.

He said quietly, "Got you, you piece of shit."

He was about to say something reassuring to the girl when she bolted across the bed and out of the room, scooping up enough of her clothes in a bundle to cover herself as she ran down the hallway,

struggling to dress as she hopped and stumbled out through the broken front door.

Darian shouted, “Hey.”

She didn’t come back and he didn’t chase, couldn’t leave Lucas unguarded. Another punch, this one to make sure Lucas didn’t kid himself by thinking he had the same freedom to run his victim did. Unlikely that he could have moved fast anyway, hunched over and crying quietly as he was, hissing through his teeth. Darian took his mobile from his pocket and scrolled down through his contacts. He knew the nearest station was Dockside, and he called his contact there.

3

HIS CONTACT came round in minutes in a police car with another uniformed officer. They used to say that all the toughest cops in Challaid were based at Dockside station because Whisper Hill was by far the shittiest area, populated by people who saw violence as another form of exercise. It might not be as brutal now as it was in more casually violent times gone by, but the Hill remained the home of the darkest nights in town.

It was two reassuringly large coppers who stood in the bedroom doorway of the flat, looking at Darian standing over the prisoner. Darian's contact was PC Vincent Reno, a barrel-chested bruiser in his thirties and the sort of honest rogue who made the ideal friend in the force. Vinny had a wide, smiling face, pale skin prone to flushing red when he was talking energetically as usual, and he looked like he'd been born in the uniform. Darian didn't know the other cop, he was very young and quite tall, narrower than Vinny, and looked like he'd borrowed his uniform from his father to play dress up.

Vinny was looking down at Lucas, relishing his discomfort, pleased to see the smudge of blood under his nose mingling with tears. He looked at Darian and said, "So this is how Darian Ross spends his Friday nights, is it?"

"Aye, very good. There was a wee girl with no clothes on as well, but she did a runner."

"Happen to you a lot, does it?"

Darian gave him the classic don't-push-it-too-far-pal look, and

Vinny knew him just well enough to take the hint. Knew him enough to know this was a mixed blessing. Darian had no business chasing after this now-naked bastard, not legally, but Vinny was among a group of coppers who knew exactly what sort of arsehole Ash Lucas was, what he had been getting up to and getting away with. He'd take any chance to put a stop to it, even a bloody awkward one.

Vinny said, "Right, get some clothes on you; I'm not looking at that ugly wee willy of yours all night. We'll take you for a drive to the station."

Lucas looked up at him through teary eyes and, with spit on his lips, said, "Fuck you, I need to go to the hospital."

Vinny smiled and said, "That's not really for you to judge, that's for me to judge. They won't have much room for you at A&E in the Machaon on a Friday night anyway, better off trusting yourself to doctor professor Reno. That's me, by the way."

Lucas groaned a lot as the younger cop threw a random selection of clothes at him to put on and Darian and Vinny stood in the doorway and watched. Vinny wasn't gentle as he led Lucas down the stairs and out to the police car. Challaid cops seldom are. It was a short drive, nobody speaking a word in the car on the way.

Whisper Hill rattled past them, gloomy and menacing where the high buildings faded above the lights, figures walking through a welcoming night in search of easily found fun or fleeing from the amusements of others. Countless stories that would never be told. They went down past Three O'clock Station and left onto Docklands Road. It was a long street filled with large, irregular buildings, on one side the backs of the huge warehouses whose fronts looked onto the dock itself and on the other a line of large buildings intended to serve shipping in other ways; among them the much-needed police station. They drove up the side of the whitewashed block and round to the walled car park at the back.

Vinny led Lucas by a well-gripped arm to be booked in, shouting happily to the sergeant at the desk, "Ash Lucas, assault and

attempted rape. Suffered a few cuts and bruises to the face, but I believe most of the damage was done to the, uh, front of his rear end. He'll live, just at a higher pitch."

Before the smirking sergeant responded the young cop, still remaining nameless, put Darian into an interview room to await interrogation. If the young cop looked nervous it was because he knew this might turn out to be uncomfortable for Darian. They all knew who he was, knew who his father was, and they knew what Darian was doing for a living.

He sat in the small, windowless room, just the table and two chairs on each side of it, and waited for eight minutes. He ran his finger along the ridge in the light blue table top where someone had tried to gouge something—likely a name because people are stupid enough to do that—on it but had stopped before they'd finished an identifiable letter, maybe a p or B, presumably after being caught.

The detective who came into the room introduced herself as DC Angela Vicario. He didn't need the name to see her ancestors had sailed across from one of the Caledonian countries, but her accent was purest Challaid so she was a few generations rooted. The young PC came in and sat silently next to her, but she didn't bother to introduce him either. Poor bugger seemed doomed to never get a namecheck. That told Darian this wasn't going to be a formal interview with a witness but a casual chat among people who could help each other out. He'd never met her, she looked too young to have worked with his father before things went sour, so he had no idea what her approach would be.

DC Vicario had long dark hair, tied back, black eyes and a large mouth that smiled easily at him. The Hispanic look was quickly overwhelmed by the Challaid accent when she said, "I'm not sure I should thank you for a gift like Mr. Lucas, like a cat bringing a half-eaten mouse to my door."

"It's the thought that counts, and I thought getting him off the streets was a good idea."

"Why don't you start by telling me how you ended up in his flat, booting him in the unmentionables?"

"I was at a party in Bakers Moor, house party. I noticed him there with a girl, remembered that the company I work for had been hired to track him down regarding money he owes. He and the girl left the party together and I went after him."

"All the way to his flat?"

"All the way."

"You didn't manage to catch him up between a party in Bakers Moor and his flat on Gemmell Road, protect the girl before the attack began? Must have taken a series of remarkable quirks to prevent you, falling down open manhole covers, shoelaces tied together, that sort of thing. Did you take the train or did you decide it was such a nice evening you would walk?"

"Him and the girl must have been on the train ahead of mine."

"I see. So you got to the flat…?"

"I got to the flat and I heard the girl shout as I reached the front door. I didn't know what to do, call you guys and wait or try to help on my own, but I decided I should try to help. I kicked open the door and went in, stopped him from attacking her with a knife. Then I called you."

DC Vicario nodded and smiled again. "Could you identify the girl if we find her?"

"I think so. Young, mid-to-late teens I would guess, black hair in a short bob. I'd know her if I saw her. The party was on Haugen Road, the flats on the left just where the road straightens on the way up. Someone there should be able to identify her."

"And you just happened to be at the same party? What are the odds?"

"You never know your luck."

"Are you still working as a private detective with Sholto Douglas?"

"We're a research company, not private detectives."

"Right, because private detectives have a long set of rules they have to operate by, like not kicking in doors, stamping on cocks and

arresting sexual assault suspects. Research companies have a little more leeway."

"Douglas Independent Research, down on Cage Street in Bank, that's us."

She looked like she was enjoying this now, the two of them batting back and forth and ignoring the young PC beside her. She said, "So you have someone hunting Lucas for money?"

"We were asked to research his whereabouts, if he had left the city. Just happened to spot him at the party and I'm glad I did."

"I'm glad you did, too. I'm sure you'll be called to give evidence, probably be interviewed a few times more before then, but you can go."

Darian got up and walked out the way he had been led in, to the car park at the back. Vinny was leaning against the wall just outside the door, smoking a cigarette, a San Jose by the smell of it. He dropped it on the ground and crushed it under his boot, reached into his pocket and took out a packet of mints.

Darian said, "Last time I spoke to you you'd quit smoking."

"Last time you spoke to me all was quiet on the western front."

His ex-wife lived over on the west side of the loch, in case that comment needs some explanation.

Darian said, "You see much of the boy?"

"Every weekend, we all get on all right, it isn't as bad as all that. I wouldn't weep if someone threw her in the loch, but... You need a lift up to the train station?"

"Thanks. You need to wait for your ten-year-old pal?"

They had started walking across to the police car they'd arrived in, a Volvo that was probably the most expensive thing anyone had ever trusted Vinny with. "Nah, I'll run you up the road and come back. He doesn't need to work anyway, that one, he's a Sutherland."

"Not an actual one?"

"An actual fully functioning one of the bastards, and not some distant wee branch at the bottom of the family tree either, mainline.

Wanted to be a cop instead of a banker, whizzed through training and into the force, got sent here."

"You're pulling the piss out of me. A Sutherland and they sent him to Dockside."

"I reckon it's what the family wanted, put him somewhere they think is the arsehole of humanity, hope it scares some sense into him and he goes screaming back to the family bosom. The kid's all right, he'll stick it out."

"Won't be too hard if he's working next to you with your effort avoidance techniques."

Vinny, aghast, said, "Are you insinuating I don't work hard? Do you remember that gathering of wee fascist fuckwits with goofy haircuts they had and only six people showed up? Do you know how hard I had to work to come up with an excuse to belt the leader of that rabble? Don't tell me I don't make an effort."

Darian said, "You smacked him? Won't that get you another complaint?"

"Oh sure, people like him are always the whiniest, and the disciplinary panel will file it straight into the shredder. We're getting more and more of those pricks crawling out of the internet and into daylight, bunch of half-witted, shrieking virgins. Let me tell you something, Darian, punching a fascist in the face will never be prosecuted in this city."

He was right. Our city lost almost a third of its young adult males in the Second World War, and on top of Stac Voror we built a tower that can be seen from every corner of Challaid as a constant reminder. Out beyond the mouth of the loch, a few miles to the east, you can still see the metal mast of the *Isobel*, a destroyer docked in Challaid during the war and sunk by a German U-boat as it left with two hundred and six men lost, the ship wedged in the rocks underwater with the radio mast breaking the surface, a maritime grave untouched by man and left to nature, a reminder of the danger of worshipping power and identity more than the rights of the people. Many of the young men who fought in the war came

back to a broken city, an economy held together by the women they'd left behind, and few jobs available to them, so a lot were fast-tracked into the police service, itself a struggling mess at the time. They could easily have slipped the other way and fallen in love with the uniform, seeking to protect those who aggrandized their power, but instead turned their violent power against those who tried. You can accuse, accurately, the woefully corrupt Challaid Police Force of many, many, many indiscretions, but forgetting their history is not one of them.

Vinny dropped him in a no parking zone outside Three O'clock Station and Darian rode the train down to Bank. It was an eight-minute walk up Fàrdach Road to his flat on the corner with Havurn Road. He was moving slowly, full of himself after what he considered a good night's work. Fàrdach Road is on the edge of the Bank district, which is the city center and full of old-money businesses and pubs, clubs and venues, but this little knot of residential buildings was usually peaceful.

It was an expensive place to live, even a flat as small as Darian's, and it was unusual that a young man on his own could afford to buy there. The flats were old and sturdy, all well-maintained three-story, sandstone blocks with large bay windows and ornate black railings out the front. Darian was able to afford his place because of the ugly way his family fell apart, but more on that later.

He lived on the top floor, right on the corner of the building, and from the living-room window he could see the long sea loch, and the lights of the city up both sides of it. It had a living room, a tiny kitchen, a bathroom and one bedroom; the smallest flat on the block because it was on the corner. It was as much as he needed, living alone. The furniture was cheap and basic and there was little enough of it to make the floor look work-shy. The living room had a couch, a chair that didn't match and a TV. That was it.

Darian had always wanted to be a police officer, but he couldn't

follow in his father's footsteps because of where they stopped. If things had been different, well, that's not a sentence there's much point in finishing, is it, because things weren't different. There were still moments, like that night, when the good outweighed the bad, and he believed the future, while not the one he had hoped for, could belong to him.

THE PRIVATE SECURITY INDUSTRIES ACT 2004

This act states that all companies/individuals involved in private investigations should be licensed. Under this act you will require a PSI license from the domestic security office of the security department of the Scottish government if you are involved in any surveillance, enquiries or investigations that are carried out for the purposes of:

– gaining information about any individual or about the activities or whereabouts of any individual; or
– gaining information about the circumstances in which property has been lost or damaged.

Anyone involved in providing contracted private investigation services will require a license. This includes employees, employers, managers, supervisors and directors or partners of private investigation companies.

According to this Act, the following activities will not require a license:

- activities solely for the purposes of market research;
- activities solely concerned with a credit check;
- professional activities of practicing solicitors and advocates;
- professional activities of practicing accountants;
- professional activities of journalists and broadcasters, and activities solely relating to obtaining information for journalists and broadcasters;
- activities solely relating to reference to registers open to the public; registers or records to which a person has right of access; and published works;
- activities carried out with the knowledge or consent of the subject of the investigation.

PENALTIES

The penalty for operating as an unlicensed private investigator will be:

- upon summary conviction at a Sheriff Court, a maximum penalty of twelve months' imprisonment and/or a fine of up to £10,000.

The penalty for supplying unlicensed staff will be:

- upon summary conviction at a Sheriff Court, a maximum penalty of twelve months' imprisonment and/or a fine of up to £10,000;
- upon conviction on indictment at High Court or Sheriff and jury trial, an unlimited fine and/or up to seven years' imprisonment.

4

DARIAN ROSS might have been the only person who enjoyed the commute to work in Challaid, or at least admitted it. A short walk down to the crowded Bank Station, making his way through the bustle of bleary-eyed miserablists at half-eight. Onto the train and east through the tunnel, off at the next stop, which was Glendan Station. That was the closest stop to the tunnel where all those people were killed digging it, so they claimed they would name the station in honor of those lost. Their choice? The title of the company the dead men worked for, that had sent them to excavate in treacherous conditions with no thought for their safety. Apparently the people of influence who picked the name couldn't understand why none of the families accepted their invitations to the opening. Anyway, that was also the closest stop to Darian's work, and it was a twelve-minute walk through the morning to Cage Street. On a nice day, admittedly rare, the stroll through busy streets could be pleasant.

Here we'll talk a little about what Darian did for a living. He was, in truth, a sort of private detective, but if you asked him about his job those would be the last two words that would fight their way through his lips. He worked for a man called Sholto Douglas, a former detective now running Douglas Independent Research. How Sholto had managed to last fifteen years as a detective was one of the great many mysteries he never solved, and he was relieved to get out of it. Now he was in a single-room office on the second floor of a building in need of repair on a narrow old street in the city

center, pretending his company limited itself to market research and credit checks.

When he started, Darian asked Sholto about the fact he was a private detective dressed up as something else and nearly provoked an aneurysm. Sholto growled and said, "It is research, really, when you think about it. That's what all of police work is, or detective work, or whatever you want to call it."

Then the conversation would switch to who was to blame, and while Scotland hadn't had a proper war with England since the Trade Wars of the eighteenth century, Sholto was all for kicking off another.

"And the licenses, and the restrictions, they're all nonsense anyway, just there to stop you doing the work. They only did it because the English put the same stuff into law so they thought they had to copy it. Just copying another country because they couldn't think of anything better to do with their time, that's all it was. Bloody English. Bloody Scottish government. You look at the two laws; they're almost identical except ours are harsher. Also, it's Raven's fault... Don't get me started on Raven..."

Raven Investigators was a large firm of private detectives based in Edinburgh and with offices in our own fair city who were raking up more muck than a landscape gardener. Their respect for the law was considered inadequate, so the law was tightened hard and Raven Investigators shrank accordingly. Companies like Douglas Independent Research existed so that people who couldn't afford the shiny corporate professionalism of Raven had someone to pester small-scale criminals for them, or that's how Sholto liked to present it, anyway. So that was the not exactly noble world of half-truths and delusions that Darian walked into each morning, including this Saturday.

Sholto was at the office before him, which wasn't always the case. Darian had a key for the days when his boss was late. He used to be DC Douglas, and he had struggled to escape the comfort of the marital bed and get in to work those days as well. The one piece

of timing he got right was retiring early before they invited him to do so, and that left him as a man in his late forties with nothing to get up for. He started Douglas Independent Research, and needed someone to help him, someone young enough to do most of the heavy lifting. Sholto had worked with Darian's father, so he knew him already, knew he had wanted to be a cop, so offered him the job. He never said it out loud, but there were probably days he regretted it.

Both of them spent too much of their lives on Cage Street. Darian turned down onto the short and narrow pedestrianized street, slipped in between two larger ones. There were three buildings on each side of the walkway, and the office was in the middle on the right as you went down. It had all become quickly familiar to Darian, a place of comfort, the gray three-story building with the entrance to the stairs at the side.

Their office was on the top floor.

The ground floor was a Chinese restaurant, The Northern Song. It was owned by Mr. Yang, and Darian and Sholto lived on his rather fine grub.

Mr. Yang and his family lived in the flat on the first floor, the other room on the first floor an office for an entertainment agency that never seemed to be occupied and can't have been entertaining anyone but the taxman with its creativity.

There were three small offices on the top floor. Sholto's not-quite-a detective agency was the first door on the left at the top of the stairs, and the third office was occupied by a data services company that had no nameplate on their door but had told Mr. Yang they were called Challaid Data Services, which didn't expend much of their imaginative powers. The room in between had never been occupied in the three years Sholto had been there. He and Darian occasionally heard people from the data company coming and going from it, and it sounded like they used it as a storeroom.

Darian had asked, "What does a data services company need to store?"

"I don't know. Data, I suppose."

They bumped into the three men from that company in the corridor often enough and they were all polite and likable fellows in their thirties, well dressed and groomed. If ever there was an issue with the building, those three were happy to chip in and prove themselves good neighbors. One day, Darian was going to have a deeper look at them and their work, try to figure out who they really were and what they were up to, but there were so many other more urgent things to do first. Taking a look at the owner of the building could be one of them.

The building was owned by Randall Stevens, a man in his fifties, no more than five feet tall. Darian had never met him, or even seen him; he never visited the place. Sholto was half sure he'd seen him at a distance once, but he'd never spoken to him. Apparently, he lived in the Cnocaid district, somewhere near the Challaid Park football stadium, and took his money from this and two other buildings. Didn't seem like enough income for the house he had, but Darian hadn't dug any deeper. If he'd just Googled the name he might have realized something was amiss, but he didn't care to look when there were cases already on his desk to tackle.

Darian went in the side door and up the stairs, in through the office door to see Sholto at his desk, reading what looked like a good old-fashioned letter.

Darian said cheerfully, "*Madainn mhath*."

"Is it?"

"We got anything interesting today?"

He didn't mention Ash Lucas because he wasn't supposed to be chasing after the man. People came to them and asked for their help but Sholto, with the wisdom of many years dodging difficult cases, didn't always choose to get involved. There were cases, like Lucas, which he felt should have been left to the police and would risk his cover as a "researcher" if they got involved. Sometimes Darian would accept that, sometimes he wouldn't, and Ash Lucas had been a target he couldn't stop himself aiming at.

Sholto put the letter down and looked at him. He was sitting at a mess of paper that everyone assumed had a desk underneath but you could only ever see the legs; there might have been nothing but a gravitational miracle holding up the paper, laptop and phone. He was just inside the door on the right, a short bald man, gray hair at the sides. He was chubby in a way that filled in all the worry lines he ought to have had, and he always tried, and just as often failed, to dress well. He wore a shirt but it was typically too small or badly tucked in, or he'd have tied his tie on wrong so the thin half was noticeably longer than the wider half. Darian's desk was a less frantic affair, over by the window, looking down onto Cage Street.

Sholto said, "Nothing exciting, just back to the south docks. Take a look at the warehouses again; see if you can find them importing drugs or people or plotting the downfall of decent society, something like that."

Darian scoffed. "They're not importing drugs. They're trying to run a legal business at the old docks and Glendan just wants to push them into the loch so they can build more flats normal people can't afford."

"Yeah, well, abnormal people need places to live as well."

Darian sighed and Sholto sat and stared at him, not saying a word. He struggled to understand what Darian's problem was. A small, family-owned, long-standing company was refusing to sell its two warehouses at the south docks, the last buildings down there still used for their original purposes. The rest had been turned into flats and trendy waterside bars years ago. Glendan, the building company, wanted to play with those last two buildings, but the Murdoch family had been there since they arrived in the city a hundred and fifty years ago and weren't in the mood for budging.

Douglas Independent Research was investigating it because some rich and powerful people had told them to, not because there was any suspicion of a crime. They were acting as intimidators, not investigators. Challaid was a city founded as a trading port in which authority was granted only to those who knew how to look the

other way, and it had been occupied by an assortment of Vikings, pirates, mercenaries and crooks in the centuries since. The modern world had reached Challaid, but it hadn't changed it.

Sholto was a man who went to church every Sunday morning with Mrs. Douglas, and she went every Sunday night and to a bible study on Wednesdays as well. Sholto seemed to feel his mortal soul didn't need such a deep cleanse, just a regular wipe down. He was a person without malice, but he needed to make a living.

"Just go and watch them, they might surprise us and we need the money."

Sholto always thought they needed the money. The last big payday had been three months before, £46,000 for three weeks' work. They had been hired by Challaid FC to go down to London and investigate a player they wanted to buy and whose team were suspiciously keen to sell. The two premier league clubs in the city were fairly regular customers. In this case Challaid were planning to spend big money on a twenty-three-year-old called Arthur Samba and they wanted to know what sort of human being went with the footballing talent.

Darian did most of the work, being young enough to move in the same circles as the target without looking ludicrous, and he stumbled across some alarming behavior, even by the standards of a professional footballer. Sholto delivered the dossier to the club and assumed they would pull out of the deal. Instead they used the revelations to knock the fee down from £4 to £2.8 million. Saved themselves a fortune for the sake of a forty-six-grand investigation, and now they just had to hope that when they inevitably sold the troublemaker on, the buying club wouldn't be as curious as they were. That's how "research" works.

Darian left the office and walked down to the old docks on the south bank. The new, much bigger ones, up in Whisper Hill, had been built for modern industrial ships in the 1930s, but there had been some sort of dock on the south bank of the loch, they said, since the city was founded.

The sort of history lessons you get in primary school will tell

you the city was founded by warriors, regrouping at the loch before they defended their fair lands from invading Norsemen or other enemies.

The sort of history lessons you get in secondary school will tell you it was founded by a group of Hebridean pirates who needed safe shelter from which to raid boats sailing to Ireland or further north.

The sort of history lessons you get in college will tell you Challaid was founded by groups of Highland and Norse traders who needed a safe bay to exchange goods, and the city grew from there.

The last is the most likely but nobody knows because we're a thousand years old and the first thing you lose in old age is memory. The one thing every story agrees on is that the south bank was the original port.

Boats still landed there, Darian could see them from the glass-fronted café he stopped at twenty yards along the dock from one of the Murdoch warehouses, but they were mostly yachts. Pretty white things that rich people played with because other rich people did, and few of the well-to-do liked seeing two big ugly brick buildings right beside their dock otherwise lined with sleek architectural show-offs. Those old buildings belonged up in Whisper Hill these days. Darian liked the dirty things for their defiance, for the way they summed up what the south docks had always meant to Challaid. That was why he made so little effort to watch them. The owners were doing nothing wrong that mattered, but the hope was that he or Sholto could spot a molehill that Glendan could spin into a mountain. It wasn't work to be proud of.

5

IT WAS the middle of the afternoon when Darian started to walk back to the office. The only things going in and out of the two warehouse buildings were the employees, only a handful and all of them Murdoch's. They'd had a shipment the day before, and Darian was sure they had another two on Monday, but it was always small drips of the tide of goods that washed into Challaid. There was a persuasive economic argument that they should sell the warehouses to Glendan and move up to Whisper Hill. It would be easier and cheaper for them to do business in the bigger docks and without a major property developer poking them in the side every day, but their bloody-mindedness was amusing.

When he turned the corner onto Cage Street, Darian saw the man standing just outside the door to The Northern Song, eating one of Mr. Yang's spring rolls. Darian had never met the man in the suit and wannabe smart coat, but he recognized what he was from a distance and who he was when he got closer. DC Alasdair MacDuff, a young detective working in the anti-corruption unit at Cnocaid station, and where he went you could be certain DI Folan Corey was a few steps further ahead.

It should tell you all you need to know about our city's commitment to tackling corruption that the unit dedicated to the task had only a dozen or so officers and was led by a detective inspector instead of someone more senior, a man allowed to run the unit in whatever way pleased him and the people of influence in Challaid. There had been a time, back in the late nineties, after the Three

O'clock killings, when the force made a very public effort to clean up its act, but that was a long time ago, and old habits had returned.

Darian didn't acknowledge DC MacDuff, a tall and plain man, light hair cut short and small features. He seemed awfully hungry, leaning against the wall by the restaurant doorway. He was waiting for someone. Darian went in the side door and ran up the stairs, stepping into the office to find Sholto behind his desk looking red-faced and angry, a man in his forties sitting across from him with wavy dark hair, beady eyes and an easy grin. The guest was DI Corey, now and always in control of his conversations.

He looked at Darian and said, "Ah, you must be the young Ross, I can see the resemblance. I knew your father. He seemed like such a good man. It's actually you I'm here about."

"Oh, why's that?"

The dirty look Sholto gave Darian was the opposite of encouraging.

DI Corey, legs crossed, hands in lap looking comfortable, said, "You were involved in the arrest of Ash Lucas, I'm led to believe, which is strange given that you're the employee of a research company."

The mocking tone of the last two words made Sholto visibly wince; he wanted no part of anything in the world that would blow his thin cover. He was an ex-detective who could be convicted of running an illegal business, and was now faced with the sort of former colleague who would take cruel pleasure in making that happen.

"I was asked to find out about his finances, for that I had to find out where he lived. I just happened to be at the same party as him, ended up outside the flat and heard the girl scream."

DI Corey's attitude blunted every clever thing he had to say. If your intelligence lives behind a sneer it's unlikely to be quite as sharp as you think. He smiled happily and said, "All just a big happy fluke, huh?"

"Good luck and good timing."

"Odd thing, though, that you wouldn't be able to find his address without following him home. I'd have expected better of you. I

mean, what the hell sort of research is that? We're getting very close here, dangerously close, I think, to straying into police business, and I'm sure neither of you would want that to happen."

Sholto said quickly, "Of course not, course not; we go out of our way to avoid anything that might interfere in an active case. I know how it works, Folan, don't worry, I know."

"You know, but does your boy here?"

"He knows."

Darian stood uncomfortably beside his desk. He was being talked about rather than to, mockingly by Corey and angrily by Sholto, and that raised his hackles. He should have said nothing but instead he said, "I'm surprised you have any interest in Lucas, Detective. Last I saw of him he was at Dockside, being well looked after. I'm not sure I see how a rapist fits into the anti-corruption unit's remit."

Sholto's eyes were wide now, and he was sitting bolt upright. Terror was the one workout his posture ever got.

DI Corey remained impassive when he said, "There are a lot of things about my department, about policing and about this city, that you do not understand. I know you want to hate me because I'm a detective, and we were the ones who put your father away, which means we absolutely must be the bad guys. All of us, all the time. It's going to come as a grievous shock to you when you realize that even those of us who aren't terribly pleasant are still trying to do a good job for the right reasons. Some people have a lot more value than you realize."

"People like Lucas?"

"Even the worst people have the ability to do good. You're young, you're idealistic, you're ignorant, and because of that you made a mistake. I'm a forgiving man, but I expect a higher level of professionalism from this office in the future or we might have to ask some questions about whether your behavior on the street matches the description on your registration sheet. No more mistakes."

Darian said, "I'll learn."

"Too late for learning, boy, you learn before you leap. You jumped into the Lucas situation because you thought you knew it all, thought you were doing what us dimwitted policemen and women couldn't, and now Lucas is back out on the streets. He won't go to trial, and the only way he ever will is when a police officer, a senior police officer, gets involved. Someone like me."

"Someone like you."

"Yes, and not someone like you."

"What's wrong with someone like me?"

"Apart from the fact you're not a cop and never will be? You're an idealist. A hero. The savior of the downtrodden, bringing justice to all those in peril. You go chasing after bad guys and to hell with the rest of it, right? You give your life to being something noble. That's fine, I'm not mocking it, there's nothing wrong with wanting to be someone's hero, we're all arrogant enough to want that at some point. Thing is, this city doesn't need people to be heroes, it just needs them to use an ounce of common sense now and then. Real police work is about something less gallant. It's about doing the dirty grind that people think you should be doing anyway, about doing work nobody ever finds out about so they curse your laziness because they're ignorant of your efforts. It's about keeping your head down and your mouth shut when ignoramuses shoulder-charge their way into your business and spoil years of effort. It's no place for heroes."

"I'm not trying to be a hero."

"You are, and you'll keep on trying, I know you will. It's written all over your righteously offended face. But you will learn, just like Sholto here learned, back in the days when he used to spend his life hiding in an office at the station instead of hiding in this one. You'll become like him, looking to get through another day without tripping up, praying for no fuss, no challenge. Your ambition will shrink to fit your talent and position, and when people come here looking for your help, for you to be their savior after exhausting every other option, you'll pretend you're not home. You'll learn, all right. I do not expect to bump into you again."

Without looking at either of them he walked across the office and out, down the stairs where his acolyte MacDuff was waiting for him. Darian looked at Sholto and Sholto looked like he wanted to sprint down the stairs after his former colleague and boot him up the arse, but he didn't have the courage or agility. Instead he looked furiously at a spot on his pile of papers until he calmed down enough to talk, although it still came out as a voice raised high.

"You went chasing after Lucas when I said not to, when I told you to stay away from him."

"He was attacking a schoolgirl with a knife, and Corey's let him go."

Sholto was a decent man, so he hated that he was shouting at Darian instead of DI Corey, but his voice would never have the strength to attack the cop. He said, "Don't you understand what this could mean, going up against a man like Folan Corey? I'm not saying you crapped the bed here, but there is an awful lot of crap all over the bed you were using. He is dangerous. Every cop can be dangerous to us, but him a hundred times more than the rest because he'd enjoy it."

"I didn't know he had a connection with Lucas, and I still don't understand what the connection is. How can you be relaxed about him letting Lucas out when you heard what Lucas has done before?"

"I'm not relaxed, don't say I'm relaxed, do I look relaxed? Never been less relaxed in my life. I'm at best a heartbeat and a half ahead of a coronary right now. I know what Lucas did, and he should be locked up for it, but he must be valuable to Corey. Him, Corey, he's the sort that has a thousand dodgy contacts up his sleeve, anyone he needs help from falls on the floor as soon as he shakes an arm. That's why I could never make it and people like him always can. He'll have Lucas on the rack now, willing to do anything for him."

"That's not..."

"I know it's not right, you don't have to tell me, but it's how it works round here. This city, it's always been the same, always about

the least worst people getting out on top. Just promise me, Darian, promise me you'll stay clear of Corey from now on, and from Lucas. Corey's good at what he does, and what he does isn't for you and me."

He paused and didn't say anything.

"Darian."

"Fine, I promise you."

WHISPER HILL

He had lived on the hill all his life and he didn't know how long that had been, but he was certainly an old man now. His parents, oh, they'd died when he was young and that had left him alone. He had wanted a different life, back in his youth when he would watch the town from the hill with envy. Down across the loch there was a world of activity, people running along cobbled streets, boats sailing out to sea, noise and chatter.

He could see that it had changed over the years, the routines of the place different now. He remembered when he was a boy and the boats used to go out first thing in the morning but now they waited until afternoon. He always saw them leave when he took his break. He lived the way his father had wanted the family to live, separate from the people, alone.

He followed the same routine each day, getting up around sunrise to scavenge on the hill, going through the forest on the far side looking for things to eat. He always walked the same route, checking traps he had laid for small animals and taking a separate bag for vegetables. He had been doing it for more years than he remembered. The old man would get round to the front of the hill in the afternoon where there was a flat stone among wind-stunted trees that had a clear view across the loch. He liked to sit there for a few minutes, maybe eat a piece of fruit, and watch the town.

Then he would return to his shack on the far side of the hill, a single-roomed small wooden building with a stone chimney. There was a time when it had been clear of the trees and had a small garden around it, but not now that he wasn't strong enough to cut them back and they had overwhelmed the plot. They didn't threaten the shack yet, but they kept it in deep shade. Not that he minded because the dark, the trees and the hill itself, these were things he knew, they were reliable and constant, and he had lived his whole life among them. He trusted them, and he trusted nothing else. He pulled the

ancient, filthy blanket around him, lying on the floor of the shack, and thought nothing of the life he led.

* * *

The boy had always been intrigued by the wind, but nobody seemed to know anything about it and that troubled his inquisitive mind. He asked his parents and his grandparents, he asked his teachers and his neighbors, and none of them knew. That couldn't be right. How could all these grown-ups not know the answer to such a simple question? Where does the three o'clock wind come from? They knew about the rain and the tides and the sun, but they didn't know about the wind.

On Saturday he was going to walk around the harbor, over the moor and take the track up to the hill. He had been before with his friends, but this time he was going alone. He gathered a few things in a bag, slung it over his shoulder and set out. He didn't tell anyone else, he was too smart for that because they would try to stop him. Little boys weren't supposed to go onto the hill alone; they had all been told that. His teachers and his parents had said it to him in that stern tone they used when they actually meant something.

It was fun, getting through the streets and past the harbor and out round the bay, sneaking down backstreets, hiding behind trees, making sure nobody saw him. Not just an expedition of discovery but a secret one. He was glad he was on his own; it was so much better this way, more dramatic. He didn't want to have to share the credit when he found out where the wind came from.

He pushed on into the trees, slowed down by branches and bushes nobody had had the good sense to cut a path through. Maybe he would suggest that when they were all marveling at his soon-to-be discovery. It did make the truth of the wind, whatever it turned out to be, all the more special that he'd had to fight his way through the trees to get to it.

* * *

The old man had made his way round the front of the hill and up toward the stone where he took his daily rest. It was getting harder to keep this pace and he knew in coming years he wouldn't be able to make the walk every single day. That thought filled him with fear. He had never found rabbit burrows near the shack; they were all on this side of the hill. He could get some mushrooms nearby, but even they required an effort he might one day not be capable of.

He sat on the stone, letting the relief of rest sweep through his weary muscles, and he opened the bag to see what he had collected so far. One dead rabbit that he would skin back at the shack, a few berries and some mushrooms he'd made the effort to gather today, having not done so for a couple of weeks. He took some of the berries out and wiped them clean on his dirty shirt. He put a couple in his mouth and looked down the hill and across the harbor at the town.

The boats were idling in the harbor with their sails loose, waiting for wind, and the old man could just see the movement of people in the streets, more than usual. There were days like that, a few a year, where there seemed to be an awful lot more people running around the town. From the top of the hill you could catch a glimpse of one end of the large town square, and you could see the celebrations. They held them every year in the winter, you could see the fire barrels and decorations they had up. It was nice to see them happy and it made him feel warm.

He took a deep breath and sighed because all this happiness belonged to other people. The boats in the harbor shot forward, sails billowing against the wind that carried them out to sea. He couldn't hear it from so far away, but there were even a few cheers followed by laughs from the jovial crowd.

This was what he enjoyed, sitting on the stone, watching the town spring to life and become the sort of busy place he had always dreamed of being a part of. He'd had his five minutes of rest and it was

time to go. As he stood he heard a rustle in the trees that made him pause, thoughts flashing automatically through his mind. It sounded too heavy to be any of the animals he usually encountered here, the old man knew he was the largest thing living on the hill. He was uncertain, a little afraid, when he watched the boy step forward.

* * *

He came close to the edge of the clearing, walking on soft moss, and saw the man. He hadn't sat down yet, coming from the opposite edge of the clearing and walking across to the stone. He looked old and had white hair that appeared dirty and long, and he had deep lines on his face. He looked like the boy's grandfather if the boy's grandfather didn't wash for a few months.

This old man could be dangerous, some sort of wild man. What a wonderful thought! Fighting through the trees and encountering a wild man in the woods, a chance to prove his courage. He knelt down beside a tree and watched, waiting for the man to do something wild, except he didn't do anything. He sat on the stone like a normal old person, and then reached down into a bag. The boy watched as the old man pulled some berries from the bag and started to slowly eat them. Wild men didn't eat berries slowly, they ate birds with their wings still flapping, ripping them apart with broken teeth and eating the feathers as well. This was just some old man the boy had never seen before.

Then he sighed. From his spot in the trees, the boy could see the old man do it, could see the dying leaves on the ground rustle in front of him as the wind ran down the hill and across the harbor. The boy grinned happily. He had found the wind. He studied the old man, watched him sit there staring down at the town. He only took a few minutes to rest and watch, and then got up.

This was the moment, time for the hero to confront his discovery. He stepped out of the trees and stood a few feet from the old man, looking up at him with a smile on his face.

"Hello," the boy said.

"Hello." The word sounded uncertain coming from the old man who wasn't used to speaking out loud, or speaking to other people. The last conversation he'd had was, well, he didn't know how long ago but it was decades, certainly.

"I saw you," the boy said, "I saw you sitting there and making the wind. You did, didn't you? You made the wind."

The old man looked at him, afraid of the boy and what he was saying.

"I don't. I just sit there. It's not me."

The boy took a step forward, moving to the stone. He looked back at the old man and out across the harbor to his home town.

"Can anyone?"

The old man looked at him and shook his head slightly as the boy sat on the stone and looked to the loch, smiling. He put his bag down and cleared his throat and then suddenly the boy blew out hard. Leaves kicked up on the hill and the few boats still tied in harbor rocked on the sudden waves.

With a grin on his face, the boy was about to say something joyous when a hand grabbed him and pulled him roughly off the stone.

"Careful. You have to be careful."

The boy paused and looked up at the frightened old man. "I understand. Too much wind and you damage things, too little and it's not useful. Yes, I understand."

The old man nodded, relieved.

"Okay," the boy said. "Is it just you?"

The old man nodded again.

"I can help you. I can come up here with food and clothes because you really need them. I can blow the wind sometimes, but mostly I'll leave it to you. And you're old, so you have to stop working soon, because that's what old people do. Then I can do it. Yes! I can do that, and it'll be our secret, I won't tell anyone."

The old man smiled gently, and nodded again. There was someone to take over from him, to give the town the wind it needed.

He didn't want to be responsible for ending it. There would be clothes, the boy had said he could bring him new clothes, and maybe even a new blanket. All these years he had sat on that stone and delivered the wind, and it had finally brought something back.

6

NOW, THIS is the point where the damn sexy woman walks into the private detective's office looking like five feet five inches of pulp-novelesque seductive trouble. Her name was Maeve Campbell, she had long brown hair, dark eyes, a small mouth and when she smiled her cheeks dimpled. She was wearing a dark blue skirt under a dark coat and she sat with her pale legs crossed in front of Sholto's desk. He cleared his throat and his dirty mind and welcomed her.

"How can we help you, Miss Campbell?"

She tried to look decorously sad when she spoke, but there was too much anger and it spoiled the impression. She said, "My boyfriend, my ex-boyfriend, I suppose, was murdered, about a month ago. The police have been investigating, but they haven't found anything and I'm certain they won't. They don't want to. I do. That's why I'm here."

Sholto said, "I'm very sorry about your, uh, ex-boyfriend, but I don't think there's anything we can do to help you. That's a police matter, it has to be left to them. We can't interfere with that sort of case, a murder inquiry; it would be criminal for us to do so."

She scowled and said, "There is no inquiry to interfere with; they've given up on him. Not that they broke a sweat in the first place, because they don't want to find the person who killed him."

Darian asked, "Why wouldn't they?"

Maeve looked across the room at him, Darian sitting behind his desk at the window. She appraised him in a heartbeat, a woman who always knew what her best chance looked like. He was seething,

the kind of anger that would trick a smart person into making misjudgments. Darian wanted to do the right thing, to bring a morsel of justice to a city that wallowed in a lack of it. He was too good a man to avoid bad decisions. The fire of anger inside him had cooled, but he was still hot to the touch and Maeve Campbell touched him.

He had taken the train up to Three O'clock Station in Whisper Hill that morning to tell the woman who had hired them to catch Lucas that her attacker was untouchable, thanks to the Challaid Police Force, a hellish conversation.

It's worth a detour to point out that the names of the station, the hill and that district of the city, the furthest north-easterly side of the loch, came from an old folk tale about Bodach Gaoith. It started as a story from the late seventeenth century, before it was updated in the nineteenth, fleshed out a little. That's the version local kids get spoon-fed in primary school. The moral, they're told, is that being adventurous is good and the elderly have great knowledge and much to offer. A better message might be to keep a closer eye on your children before they wander off and meet weird men up a hill.

It's also worth mentioning that the story first became popular when Scotland was trying to create its own little empire in Central America, and came back into fashion when we were thinking of war in the early twentieth as the three Caledonian countries were gaining independence. Through that prism the message that bold adventures are a good thing looks a little more cynical, doesn't it?

Maeve said, "My...ex, his name was Moses Guerra; he was involved in some things. He was a crook, that's the truth of it, and his crookedness was probably what got him killed. He was the sort of criminal who made money for people who want the world to think they're saintly, and that's why the police don't want to dig any deeper. The bones of credible people are down there, and they don't want the scandal of finding them. They brought in the anti-corruption unit and they did a damn good job of shrinking the investigation until it was small enough to focus only on me."

Sholto was already shaking his hands in the air in front of him

like a man in a foreign country who couldn't verbalize his distress. "No. No, no, no. I'm sorry, but that's not an investigation we can have any part in. That's a case that only the police can handle, and any other research or investigative company will tell you the same. I'm sorry."

Maeve looked at him and then across at Darian, the target that mattered. "It was clear from the start they weren't interested in catching the killer. A Detective Inspector Corey has been leading the investigation, and all I've had from him are sly hints that he thinks I was involved. That's what he's aiming for, to persuade the world that I was the main suspect but never actually arrest anyone. It keeps people's eyes focused on me and off the truth."

"What did your boyfriend do?"

"Ex-boyfriend. We had split up, although, I suppose, there was still a chance for us. Moses handled money, took in dirty cash and rehabilitated it. He was a sort of accountant, but not really, he wasn't qualified, just talented, and he used qualified people to add legitimacy. He connected people in possession of money they shouldn't have to people who'd take a small cut of it to make the rest look like it had always belonged to the original owner. He dealt with real accountants and businesses and banks. He was the point of contact for the people needing to use the service; they'd deliver to Moses and after a long journey of cleansing it would be filtered back to the original person by him. It was Moses who created the network in the first place, and it seemed to work. He met a lot of people that way, a lot of people who are more important than this city cares to admit."

She had turned in the chair to face Darian now, Sholto behind her still waving his hands as if semaphore was making a comeback. Darian said, "There are a lot of people fitting that description. Why does Corey think you might be responsible?"

"He doesn't. Moses and I had an argument, I hadn't seen him in a couple of weeks, Corey has tried to make that tiff seem big enough to kill a man. I'm convenient, that's all. My greatest crime was

proximity to the victim. Corey doesn't have to prove I've done anything wrong, he just has to persuade enough people with innuendo that I probably did so they have an excuse to stop looking elsewhere. I get to be the clichéd femme fatale so he can cover bigger beasts' tracks."

Darian nodded, both to her and to Sholto behind her. "That's a very serious accusation. I'm sorry, Miss Campbell, but a murder investigation really is a police matter and if we were to get involved we would be breaking the law ourselves. You can make an official complaint about the current investigation and try to force a change in the investigating team."

She had an angry smile now. "So you won't help me? A man is murdered and nobody gives a shit about finding out who did it? My God, this is some city, it really is."

Maeve got up and walked quickly to the office door. She stopped as she opened it and looked back at them both, thinking of something clever and cutting to say, but the anger that filled her and Darian both, it smothered things like wit. She slammed the door behind her as a petulant alternative.

Sholto started speaking as soon as the door stopped rattling. "Now you listen here, Darian Ross, please. You are not to go after her, you are not to get involved in anything, and I mean anything at all, that Folan Corey is at the heart of. That woman, she's only going to lead you down the road to ruin."

"I know."

"You know, yes, you do, but knowing is only half the battle. A young man, all hopped up on justice and anger and seeing a vixen with legs up to her arse and dark eyes that weepingly tell you she needs your help, you're likely to make a poor choice. It was a long time ago, but I've been there before and the scene hasn't changed a bit. That woman is grief in nice packaging, and you stay away."

Darian smiled and said, "I hear you, Sholto, don't worry. I'll stay away from her and I'll stay away from Corey."

7

A FEW hours later Darian went looking for Maeve because he wanted to get at Corey. He lied to Sholto about it, sure, but that was a frequent part of their working relationship and Sholto would have been disappointed in him if he hadn't. They lied to each other because the truth was the sort of whiny goody-two-shoes that got in the way of a useful arrangement. They were a generation apart but making money from working together, and whatever motivated one shouldn't weigh overmuch on the conscience of the other. Darian lied about Maeve because lying was best for business. And let's remember, when all this happened Darian was twenty-two, so while he may have been intelligent that didn't mean he was at all wise.

Finding out where a person lives isn't hard; there are so many companies and local government agencies that hold people's addresses and however much they say they'll protect people's privacy, their defenses are only as good as the will of their lowest paid, most disgruntled employee. One call to a contact at the council and Darian had her details from the electoral register—Maeve Campbell, twenty-seven years old, living at 44–2 Sgàil Drive, Earmam, Challaid. Darian, thank goodness, had a knowledge of the city that would make a taxi driver's jaw drop, every street and almost every building. A good memory and a nerdish dedication to studying the detail, that was why. He knew Earmam, the region on the east side of the loch full of low-cost housing, people packed upon people, and he knew Sgàil Drive, a street whose name had started as a joke among the builders putting up the flats there.

He got off the bus at the corner and walked down to her building, three blocks of flats on each side of the road, all in a cross shape that might have been part of the architect's graveyard humor. Hers was on the left side of the road, directly under Dùil hill, too close to the incline to be able to see the standing stones, An Coimheadaiche, above. He went in through the red front door and up the cold staircase because the lifts had stopped trying. These were buildings thrown up in a hurry and on the cheap within living memory, using a slice of land that had previously been considered inappropriate for development and had since proven that initial judgment correct. He knocked on the door to number 44.

Maeve opened it and looked at him, no surprise in her expression. She had known Darian would come trailing after her when she left that office, whatever he had said and no matter how long it took him to find her.

She said, "Come in."

Her flat was much more a home than Darian's. It was cared for, and there was the ticklish sweet scent from a candle. The living room and kitchen were the same room, a living area some lying estate agent would describe it as, and there were two couches that were different shapes but had similar blankets tucked carefully over them. There was a small bookcase with a TV on top of it and a vinyl record player that was supposed to look old but had a USB slot on the front of it sitting on the floor under the window, a row of albums lined up beside it. The light was on already.

She said, "Excuse the darkness, the sun doesn't climb the hill until late and then it comes all of a sudden before it runs away and disappears in the mid-afternoon. You get used to the dark, eventually. Can I get you a drink or something?"

Darian said, "No, thanks. You know why I'm here."

Maeve smiled a little because her dimpled little smiles could go a long way. She was strikingly pretty and knew it. She had changed since she was at the office, now wearing black trousers and a gray jumper that seemed shapeless, but when she sat on one of the

couches and crossed her legs it still sent a confident ripple round the room.

Darian sat opposite her and said, “I need to know everything you do about what happened to Moses Guerra.”

“Then I will tell you everything I know. He was stabbed outside his flat on Seachran Drive in Bakers Moor, chased from there to an alleyway between Somerset Street and Morti Road and killed. The police have found nobody they’re willing to call a real suspect and one they’ve decided to imply is a suspect because they’re lazy fucking liars. Moses helped people hide money, like I said at your office, so he spent time with plenty of law dodgers who had the ability to make a thing like this happen. He knew them and their secrets.”

“Do you have anything that would prove the sort of work he did, who he was working with at the time he was killed?”

“Come on, Detective…”

“I’m not a detective, I’m a researcher.”

“Fine. Come on, researcher, men like Moses don’t keep a paper trail for a jury to walk along, you should know that, whatever you say you do for a living. Once he’d read something that told him what he needed to know he would shred and chuck it. Only just stopped short of burning the shreds and eating the ashes. No phone messages, emails, anything of that sort about work, he was too paranoid about online security. You won’t find anything about his work which in itself should prove he was doing things worth hiding, but it’s why he was killed and it’s why the police did nothing. They’re protecting the people he worked for, and even if they weren’t, people with Moses’ reputation don’t get the same treatment. A second-generation Caledonian with his biography, there aren’t many who will pretend he mattered. Well, he mattered to me.”

“In which case he matters to me.”

Maeve looked at him skeptically. “I think you say things because you think you ought to, not because you mean them. It’s automatic, the way you say it.”

“I mean it. Moses might have been a criminal, but nobody

deserves to spend their last seconds in fear, lying in an alley, knowing they're a breath away from the end. I'll try to find out who did it, not just because you asked and because you're paying me but because the person who did it shouldn't be out there thinking they can do it again. Even in this city a dead man deserves at least a scrap of justice."

"Good."

That helped convince the employer of his commitment, always good to nail down early on, so Darian shuffled back to the awkward questions. "His personal life?"

"He wasn't on social media, didn't send texts unless they were very ordinary things, and even then he shuddered when he sent them. He had a small group of friends and most of them were people who moved in the same narrow circles he did, so they're not chatty sorts. The police have dug into it, I know they've tried to talk to anyone they thought would admit to being a friend of Moses, but they only got the minimum required by law in reply. Nobody wants to incriminate themselves, or others, which doesn't leave them with much to say."

"What sort of person was he?"

"Not the sort of person to jump into a hole without knowing there was an exit route at the bottom, or to pick a fight with anyone, not even one he could be a hundred percent sure of winning. He was passive. We met at a party, we had mutual friends who introduced us, and I liked him. He didn't ever wear a mask. All the actors you get in this city, trying to pretend they're tougher than they are or smarter than they are or more dignified than they are. So full of shit. He was open."

"Were your mutual friends criminal types as well?"

"I know a lot of people and some of them are on the shifty side of the tracks. If you know a lot of people in this city then you'll have friends your minister wouldn't love, but it doesn't make you a bad person."

"How long were you and him together?"

"Six, seven months. Long enough for it to matter."

"But you weren't living together."

"Are you in a relationship?"

"No, I'm not."

"I'm sure you've been in a relationship where having your own space was as important as sharing it with the other person. Just because you like being on top of someone doesn't mean you want to live there. I liked him a lot, might even have loved him. I think I did, and I'm fairly sure he loved me back, but it wasn't the sort of relationship that made you rush for a marriage license. Moses understood that, although he didn't always agree with how hard we should press the accelerator. He wanted me to live with him and I wasn't ready. It was one of the reasons we had a falling out."

"He was older than you?"

"He was, but not much and I don't think that's why he was in more of a hurry. He spent his life around people who thought might was right, thought they could be tough and dominant and everyone else would fall into line. It wasn't his natural way, but it was still hard for him to shake it off, even in a relationship where it wasn't needed. He didn't like pushing things along, but he thought he had to, thought that was how it worked."

"What do you know about his family?"

"Very little. He was second-generation; his father came from Caledonia in the mid-seventies, got married, had a kid, got divorced and didn't see his son again. I think his mother's alive somewhere, but I couldn't point her out for you if she stood right in front of me. He was an only child as far as I know, although I suppose his father might have created a half-sibling or two. He had left his family behind and didn't want to look back, not even to see his parents, forward all the way."

"Sounds a bit brutal."

"No, brutal would be the wrong word for him, he was sure. Moses decided that you had to live life moving in one direction and I

liked that, the certainty of it. He was always honest about it, that he would never let the past put up a barrier around tomorrow. It was one of the things I thought I loved about him, his honesty. It was a positive thing, I thought."

"You thought?"

"Perhaps he was denying himself too much, but that was his choice. He didn't like any of his past so he wanted to pretend it wasn't there anymore. Maybe it's the equivalent of a child closing their eyes and thinking the world has disappeared."

"You said you loved his honesty."

"Said it and meant it."

"When you came to our office you called him a crook, but he can't have been much of one if he suffered from honesty."

"I've known a lot of people in my life that weren't honest. Some were just built to be liars from the ground up, others were like you, honest in bits while trying to hide a lot of the truth as they went along. Did you tell your boss, Mr. Douglas, that you were dropping in to visit me at home? Did you get my home address from an above-board source, because I didn't give it to you? There are different kinds of honesty. Moses was genuine. I called him a crook because he was, but he never lied to me or to himself about it. You're lucky if you don't realize how rare that sort of honesty is."

"I know how rare it is."

"Then I'm not sure why I'm sitting here trying to explain it to you."

Darian paused, realized her tone had grown a steel spine and decided that if he was in for a penny he was in for a pound. "Was he rich when you started your relationship?"

"I was actually under the impression he was a lot poorer than he turned out to be. Is this your strategy, to come in here and try to coax something juicy out of me with petty insults, rile me up until I spill my guts? DI Corey tried the same thing, with a lot more skill I might add, and got nothing, because I have nothing to give."

"Are you looking to hire me to clear your name or to catch who killed him?"

"Both. Catching the killer will clear my name."

"It could be expensive."

"You tell me when the cost starts to hurt and I'll tell you when to stop."

"It could take a while."

"I have some money, and I want to know."

Darian had heard that sort of thing before, an investigation started while the raw emotion of loss pained someone into desperate action, but the hurt dulled and people began to move on with their lives. No matter how much a person meant to them, a life can't be lived standing still waiting for justice to be done. People wanted to know more about a dead relative, their financial affairs, their relationship with a woman who shouldn't have been in the will. People could be passionate with grief, but that's rarely a long-term motivation, and clients often grew out of the investigation they'd started and canceled the contract early. They wanted the battles of their past in the history books, not raging alongside them. Sholto called it the distance clause, the dead becoming less important the smaller they got in the rearview mirror.

He said, "How long will you be mourning him?"

"Just as long as he would have wanted me to. No looking back, remember. I won't be wearing black into my thirties, but I won't forget him either, which is why I won't let you walk away from this when the going gets tough. You're going to find the person responsible; I'll make sure of that."

She gave him the names of some of Moses' friends and the few people she knew worked with him. It was an unimpressive mob, some of whom were familiar to Darian and most could be safely ruled out straight away. Petty conmen that had found their way into Douglas Independent Research's files, low rate and nonviolent, the only money they were interested in was the easy kind. Killing a man did not make for easy cash. That left him with a shortlist to investigate. Armed with that, Darian walked to the front door.

Maeve opened it for him, the two of them standing face to face, holding eye contact.

She said, "I wonder why you wanted to know when I would stop mourning."

Darian walked out of the flat.

8

BEFORE FOLLOWING the trail of bread crumbs Maeve had thrown his way, Darian had to bake a few of his own. The first trick in avoiding the police was to get all the information he could about their investigation into Moses Guerra's murder. It had been handled by DI Corey, which meant Cnocaid station, so he called up his senior contact there.

A good investigator makes sure they have someone in each of the six police stations in Challaid, preferably more than one. Darian didn't often pay them to talk; it's important you understand how it worked. There were rare occasions where money changed hands, but typically it was a favor for a favor, one scratched back for another. Darian did things for these cops, typically gathered information they couldn't reach, which helped their own investigations along, so they did the same for him.

His senior person at Cnocaid was DC Cathy Draper, a woman in her early forties and one of his earliest and most willing contacts. Her story is for another time. For now we'll mention only her very small role in the story of Moses Guerra, meeting Darian to provide information, and to gain a favor from him by so doing.

Meeting with DC Draper was an elaborate operation, Darian assumed because she worked in the same station as Corey and so had more reason to be careful than most. It was early in the morning, half past six, and she wanted to meet in the back office of Siren's record store on MacUspaig Road, just north of Sutherland Square,

so it was only a fifteen-minute walk from home for Darian. It meant he had to get up at an ungodly hour. The fact she wanted to meet there, the back office of a record store run by an incalculably dubious former record company boss, was cause for surprise, but not necessarily concern. Cops were entitled to keep strange friends, too. She would have parked out front on the long, shop-filled street, just about the only time of day you could find a spot in the whole Bank district. Darian cut down the alley from the back and went in the side door, next to the entrance for From Cambalu, a clothing store that sold the finest, handcrafted items twelve-year-old Indonesians could produce.

She was there ahead of him, in a windowless storeroom filled with plastic containers, looking nervy, a small, tanned woman with short, dark hair. Her arched eyebrows and downturned mouth gave the look of a constant frown, and mood often matched appearance. Contacts all had to be handled differently. Someone like Vinny was a pal; you could joke with him, chat about shared interests and family matters, have your meetings somewhere you could get a drink and relax. Others, like Draper, had to be handled like a bottle of nitroglycerine, so there was no sarcasm in his voice when he said, "Thanks for meeting me."

"You shouldn't be sniffing around Corey."

He had mentioned that he needed to know about Moses Guerra to make sure she was armed with the right information when they met. "I'm not; he's finished with the Guerra case. I know Corey took over the murder investigation and didn't get very far, and I need to know exactly where he did go with it."

"It's still his case and you're still taking a risk."

"It isn't through choice, trust me."

"I should be staying away from the bastard, too."

"You work with him."

"He'll crush you, if he finds out. That's his way with people who go against him. You and your family. Anyone he can get at you through, he will. He's smart, as well as dangerous."

"I'm not going after Corey, just whoever killed Guerra. The worst I'll do with Corey is annoy him, not attack him. I need to know what he found out about the killing."

She sighed but didn't try to discourage him further; it wasn't in her best interests. "He didn't find much, but he doesn't always look for much. He has his own priorities. I know Guerra was a lifetime criminal, but he stood close enough to legality to get away with it. They found connections to very clean financial people that didn't go far. They decided it was probably the girlfriend. She knew about the money and wanted some."

"They talk to anyone interesting?"

"Nobody in Guerra's building heard anything, and they don't think it started inside the flat. Might have been someone jumped him outside when he arrived home and he ran for it, ended up dead in an alley when that same someone caught him up a few streets over. He didn't get far. There was a waiter, the restaurant backs onto the alley, he said the body wasn't there when he went out for a smoke, but he must have been lying, body would have been there for a couple of hours by then."

"That's it?"

"That's it from me. I wasn't on the team. I'm not one of Corey's people. He has his own group in the anti-corruption unit, cops that are all loyal to him. Mostly younger detectives, they owe him their rapid rise. Even when they're moved out of his unit to other stations or leave the force, they're still Corey's detectives before they're Challaid Police Force's."

"It's not a lot."

"It's more than you'll get from anyone else. No one inside his unit will talk to you. They're a team, and you're an outsider. They don't even talk to other cops, so your family connection won't help. Corey will hammer you for sticking your nose in, and he'll hammer me twice for helping."

"I know. I owe you one."

"A big one."

"Fine."

The thought of another favor acquired seemed to satisfy DC Draper and she left through the front of the record store. Darian left by the side door and went to the office, first one there, for another day of watching warehouses that had nothing to show him.

A BRIEF REVIEW OF THE CALEDONIAN EXPEDITION—SCOTLAND 1698

Just two months before the voyage, at that point referred to as the Darien scheme, was due to depart from Scotland, the Sutherland Bank made a late decision to invest heavily in what had before been viewed as a fanciful lowland idea. The then chairman of the bank, Lord Niall Sutherland, added significant funds and four additional ships to the five planned. He also appointed Alexander Barton, a man previously accused of piracy but who claimed to have been a privateer, to lead the expedition with Thomas Drummond. The nine ships left in 1698.

There remains much debate about what happened when the ships arrived in what was to become New Edinburgh. It is known with certainty that two weeks after arrival Drummond was dead, and Alexander Barton was declared commander of the remaining group. It was he who made the decision that the previously chosen site of New Edinburgh was inappropriate for the group's intentions, and that they should move inland. At this point the differing intentions of the original group of five ships sent by the Company of Scotland and the four sent by the Sutherland Bank became clearer. The Company of Scotland had sought to take and hold the land that would allow the passage of goods from the Atlantic to the Pacific, with ports on either side of the narrow stretch, while the Sutherland Bank had given Barton and his chosen crew orders to take much more.

The exact movements of Barton and his men in the months that followed is still unclear, but that they survived by establishing a defensive base further inland while ranging out to pillage local villages seems clear. While the settlers from the original five ships who stayed behind faced starvation and disease in New Edinburgh and saw their numbers dwindle fast, Barton and his men expanded their land grab, and gained new members

from the indigenous population. While the stories of the time suggested those local Indians joined with them as a preferred alternative to Spanish rule, there is better evidence, in the form of large graves, to suggest Barton and his men gave them little choice. By the time Barton returned to New Edinburgh he had a small army, well fed and with a stable base inland, which they named Fort Sutherland, and had reached the Pacific coast and founded Port Isobel, named after his own wife. It is not disputed that they could have returned to New Edinburgh sooner with food and supplies, but chose not to. They argued this was impractical and would have put their own success at risk, and by the time they did return the population of New Edinburgh had dropped to fewer than a hundred.

From this point forward the remaining members of the original five ships joined forces with Barton, accepting that his ruthless ways were their only opportunity for survival. The buildup of his army continued until barely a village covering the route from east coast to west wasn't under their control, as men were pressed into service. The New Edinburgh project, that was to have been the centerpiece of the original plan, was practically abandoned by Barton. He led his group from coast to coast, and although many lives were lost in the jungle it was, many said, fear of Barton that pushed them on. By the time the second expedition arrived, seven more ships, this time all funded by the Sutherland Bank in Challaid, Barton had achieved what he set out to do. On his return to Scotland he was knighted by the King in Edinburgh and lived well, the Sutherland family rewarding him generously. That he was successful only because of his cruelty toward the local population was written out of history at the time.

More ships sailed to Caledonia, bringing more settlers and boosting the population of Scots. New Edinburgh was developed and linked with Port Isobel on the Pacific coast via Fort Sutherland.

Towns and villages were built along the line of what would become the Caledonian trade route. Scotland would expand throughout Panama and north into Costa Rica and the south of Nicaragua, creating what we now know as Caledonia. In the centuries since 1698 the bloody role of the Sutherland Bank and Alexander Barton have been romanticized, as has the often shocking behavior of Scottish troops in Caledonia, but the links forged in those early years remain.

9

THE DOWNSIDE of hiding his clandestine work from Sholto was that he had to spend all day on the Murdoch warehouse case. But working the Guerra case at night meant seeing the scene as it had been a month before, when Moses stumbled into it to his death. Darian started at the block of flats on Seachran Drive where Moses had lived. It's a narrow and short road, made skinnier by the cars parked there, long rows of flats along both sides. It's in Bakers Moor so we're not talking about the heights of luxury here, but it's a neat enough street, the four-story buildings relatively modern and well kept.

It was after ten o'clock, earlier than Moses had been killed but still dark and cold enough to make sure conditions matched. DC Draper had suggested Moses was jumped on the doorstep, probably getting out of his car, and had run for his life, not quite fast enough. Darian stood and looked at the door to the building Moses had called home and understood why he hadn't gone that way. A gate leading to steps leading to a locked door, a man without a second to waste would have to go another way. From the flat where he had lived to the alley where he died was a five-minute walk, two minutes if you were running to try to keep up with the life that was seeping out of you. Darian tried to track the route a man with death at his heels would use.

He walked to the corner and across the road to confront the first conundrum. If Moses was just looking to create distance then he would go over the fences and round the backs of the houses there,

cut across their gardens and save time. That meant running into unlit gardens, going where nobody would see him, where the potential killer would have no witnesses to his crime. Surely if he thought he was going to die he would stay in the bright areas where someone would spot them and help him. Darian shook his head; he needed to think like Moses, the career criminal. What was he carrying that night that he might want to hide?

Darian went through the gardens, trying to keep to the most logical route of a desperate runner, keeping his head down so the occupants wouldn't realize a young man was skulking across their property and think they were about to be burgled. Now he was on Somerset Street, and the alley where Moses bled to death was in view, but so were better places to run. Again, Moses had chosen the one route where he could be sure he wouldn't be seen, by the attacker and by other witnesses. He had passed many buildings on the way where he could have found help.

The alley was unremarkable but for the fact that a man had died there a month before. It's a narrow stretch behind buildings, a shortcut from Somerset Street to Morti Road, but it was mostly a place to store bins, boxes, crates, filth and rats. It was a place to hide, not a place to run. Darian walked down to where the body had been found, far enough away from either end to have been missed by people walking or driving past on adjoining streets. Not so well hidden that someone standing in the alley could possibly miss it.

"I must have missed it."

Darian and the waiter were standing in the alleyway. He was in his mid-twenties, dark skin and dark eyes, nervous about this conversation. He was wiry and his movements were all sharp and jerky. His name was Benigno Holguin and he was taking his ten-minute break to speak to Darian. It took five of those minutes for Darian to explain who he was.

"Are all the lights that are on now on at two o'clock in the morning?"

"Yes."

"So if you stood here..."

"I did stand here, for my cigarette. I come out with bags for the bin, I put them in the bin, I stop here to have cigarette, two, three minutes, I go inside."

"So if the body was there you would have seen it, you couldn't have missed it."

Holguin shrugged.

Darian said, "They think he may have been dead before two o'clock, so the body should have been there."

"I said this to the policemen, the body was not there, it must have come just after, I don't know. They must have their time wrong. I thought this was finished."

Darian could guess why he was so worked up. "Where are you from?"

"El Roble, Costa Rica."

"How long have you been here?"

"Ten months. I have two months to go, I said that to the detective, he said this was finished and it was okay."

Holguin was two months away from a fast-track dual passport, Caledonian and Scottish. Anyone from two of the old colonies, Panama and Costa Rica, can get a dual passport after twelve months working in Scotland. Used to be you just had to live here for a year but some bored politicians with fear to spread got that changed to twelve months of legitimate employment.

That was going to change again soon enough, a clamor to keep people who wanted in out, blame them for things that couldn't yet be their fault. It would go to two years of employment. It was already much harder if you came from Nicaragua, because we only ever had the south of it, it was the last colony we captured and the first we gave up and the people spent the entire time in between fighting for their freedom.

For every good-hearted soul we sent across there was a murderous thug like Gregor Kidd or a scheming conman like Joseph Gunn, dark stories too long to tell here. Knowing what Kidd did to the

people of Sambu you might wonder why any immigrant would want to live in a city that named one of its largest streets after him. The way we treated people in Caledonia, many think they should all get a dual passport if they want them, but it's more complicated than that. Once he had a Scottish passport Holguin could go anywhere in the EU, he didn't have to stick around if he didn't want to, so those tighter limits were on the way. He was two months from all of Europe opening its arms to him as a fellow citizen, and a man like DI Corey could put a stop to that.

Darian said, "You couldn't have missed it, could you? Come out and looked the other way the whole time? It was near the wall so..."

"No, I don't think...No, I am not blind. I would have seen it, but it wasn't there. They say he died before then, I say no, he must have come here after. He was not here. Why is this not over?"

Darian tried again to reassure him, not wanting the waiter to go running for comfort to Corey or any other cop from the anti-corruption unit. The longer they were in the dark about Darian's work the fatter his slim chance of success got. He said, "It is over, it is, I'm just trying to work out everything the police worked out. I don't think there's any chance of them wanting to speak to you again. Thank you, Benigno."

"Okay."

Darian let Benigno go back into the restaurant, working for less than minimum wage for a year because Challaid pretended he would be rewarded at the end of that time. Men like Corey were itching to use his vulnerability against him. His status as a Caledonian was a weakness. Challaid only existed so our boats could trade and raid with the Scandinavians and Irish, so they were our first immigrants, then the Caledonians and the Polish and anyone else we could make money from. They gave to our city and it mostly took from them.

Our past teaches us as many bad lessons as good ones. In this city we have a problem understanding what's telling us to change and what's telling us to stay the same. It comes, probably, from our

desperate need to remain distinct, different from the Scotland of the Anglicized south and from the world beyond. We hang on to our language and our culture, our sense of difference, because we know these things to be good, but we allow that to spread to areas where cosmopolitan modernity is, frankly, a hell of a lot better. People in the south whinge incessantly about our Gaelic road signs, but it's the old prejudices underneath that pose the real problem here. We don't like outsiders unless we're dominating and exploiting them.

Darian left the alleyway, hoping Holguin wouldn't get caught up in any of this, but not sure. People like the waiter, a bystander who didn't deserve to suffer, were the first to take a hit because they didn't see it coming. Darian made the long walk down to Glendan Station and went home. He knew more about Moses Guerra's death, but he didn't know any better.

10

HE WAS late enough turning onto Cage Street the following morning to know Sholto would be there before him. It was wet and cold because this is Challaid and you can assume that any time the weather isn't mentioned it was drizzly and there was a nip in the air. Darian could feel the water trickle down the back of his neck because he wasn't dressed for it, which is a sign of stupidity in a city where the rain and wind stand beside death and taxes as life's certainties.

A man was standing across the lane, pushed back against the wall of the Superdrug store opposite The Northern Song. He had the last bite of one of Mr. Yang's breakfast dumplings from a foil tray and stayed where he was, staring ahead and pointedly not looking at Darian. Darian pointedly didn't look back and went in through the door to the stairs and up to the office. Sholto was, as expected, there first.

Darian walked across to his desk by the window, looked down into the lane and saw the man still there, seemingly nailed to the spot. He said, "There's a man…"

Sholto interrupted him. "I know there's a man watching the building, and I know who he is and I know why he's here."

"Who is he?"

"That's Randulf Gallowglass, stupid bloody name, and he used to be DC Gallowglass along at Cnocaid station, one of the anti-corruption team. He left the force, I don't know why but probably because he was the baddest egg in the carton, got elbowed out, and

he's now doing work for Corey, off the books. Right this very now he's standing across the way because Corey will have told him to. That's Corey's old-fashioned version of a warning shot, Gallowglass the bullet that lets you know that he knows you're working for Maeve Campbell and he wants you to stop."

"Oh."

"Oh, aye."

Darian looked down at the man in his thirties, light brown hair and a square face, big ears sticking out the side of it, a tall and blocky frame. He said, "He does work for Corey?"

Sholto sighed and said, "Yes, he does. Corey's very loyal to any cop that works with him, anyone he considers a protégé. There's a whole generation of them that he made sure he taught, and he keeps them all around, somewhere between apostles and bodyguards. They hero-worship him to a laughable degree. If he tripped up an old lady in the street they would hail him for inventing gravity. Just because a man like Gallowglass is outside the force doesn't mean the string from the back of his head to the end of Corey's finger has snapped. Never mind him, come away from the window and look at me."

"What?"

"What do you mean what? You went wandering off after the Campbell girl, all googly eyes and bulging trousers, and you're digging about in that Moses fellow's bones."

"You knew I would."

Sholto shook his head and said, "I thought this time some of my good sense might have rubbed off on you. How many hundreds of times have I told you not to get involved with a client?"

"It's less than fifty so, to the nearest hundred, none."

Sholto huffed and said, "Well, that's because I should only need to say it once, and even then you should have guessed it before I opened my mouth. We should be swerving around Corey like he's poison, and that Campbell girl isn't much healthier for you. You know they think she did it."

"Do you think she did it?"

"I don't know who did it, it could have been her. Recently split up with the man, knows where he keeps his money, bloody hell."

"Why would she be waiting for him out on the street, though?"

Darian was getting excited and Sholto wanted to put a stop to it. "Never mind trying to talk yourself into believing her innocence. Never mind any of it. Could have been King Alex in his castle in Edinburgh that did it for all I care. Moses Guerra is dead and buried up in Heilam, it's not our case and there's every chance we'll never know who killed him. I've seen enough investigations like that, too many suspects and too little evidence; they never amount to anything but wasted sweat. It's not worth the dust up your nostrils that poking around in his background will get you."

Darian paused for a second and said, "How do you know he's buried up in Heilam?"

"Never mind what I know or how I know it, just assume I know best and tell me you'll keep away from this thing."

Darian never wanted to pick a fight with Sholto. He liked and respected the man too much for that, but there was often fun and sometimes profit to be had in it. There were any number of places Moses Guerra could have been buried, or cremated, and while the graveyard in Heilam, just beyond the end of the urban gray in Whisper Hill, was by far the biggest, that didn't mean you assumed he was there.

Darian said, "You've been doing some digging of your own, haven't you?"

"Well, I knew you would so I thought I might as well do it properly just to show you how. A pretty girl comes looking for help; I knew what you'd do next. Lack of blood flow to the brain, that's the problem around girls like her. And I'd bet Mrs. Douglas's finest jewelry, which isn't up to much, I admit, that you've been round to see the lovely Miss Campbell at her flat, haven't you?"

"You're throwing mud at me when you had your own spade out digging holes."

Darian was close to laughing and Sholto was close to blowing up. They both paused for ten seconds and drew breath. Sholto said,

"You'll never find out who killed him, you know that, don't you? There are too many gaps that no one can fill without incriminating themselves. If this was to do with his work then it's over because no one he worked with will talk. Sometimes you can't clear the blur of a case and that's the hardest thing for a young cop to learn."

"I'm not a cop."

"Neither am I anymore, but we still think like them. This is a job for the police, and it's one they can't finish either. Leave them to it."

"You looked at it because you thought you might be able to work it out."

"Doing anything that upsets Corey is a gamble with our own future, and I'm not a gambler, Darian, I never was. Corey, he's . . . Ach, it makes me mad thinking about him, coming in here and talking down to me like he does every other cop, but I worked hard to get this company started and we do some good work. I don't want that ended by him."

"If we were careful."

"We're always bloody careful, and the whole world tiptoes around that man and it doesn't help."

"If Maeve Campbell hired us because Moses Guerra owed her money, we would be entitled to examine his financial background to try to work out where all his money came from and where it went. We would be identifying cash that our client might be entitled to. If it just happens that his financial work was behind his killing and we stumbled across information that proved it, well, that would be a coincidence within our remit."

"Maybe."

"You went looking for information about Guerra, which means it might have been you that Corey found out about."

"Unlikely."

"But you do want to find out who killed Guerra. You want to get one over that bastard Corey."

"Language, and maybe."

That meant he did.

11

THE FIRST step in a joint investigation was to share information. Darian told him everything he had been able to uncover so far, which was a short recap. Moses Guerra must have been attacked outside the building, not inside, and when he ran he picked a route that carefully avoided anyone else seeing him or his attacker.

Darian said, “Not much, is it?”

Sholto smiled and said, “Well, you’re young; I keep telling you you’re young. A big part of policing is hanging round long enough to know who to ask. The police think Moses was attacked outside the flat as well, chased to the alley and he was stabbed there multiple times, enough times that them clever psychologists might start to think there was a personal element involved, although it might just have been that it was dark and rushed and the attacker struggled with it. Suggestion of a personal element doesn’t help the pretty piece of work that was in here cooing to us about her innocence.”

“Could be someone he worked with before, knew where he lived but couldn’t get in. She would get in, surely, and how would she keep up with him if he decided to sprint? How would she knock him down?”

“Don’t you get caught up thinking the little woman couldn’t possibly attack the big man, that’s foolishness. If she has a blade and an inclination to use it and he has no willingness to fight back then she wins every single time. And if he still loved the girl, daft sod that he might have been, maybe he tried to talk her round.”

"So you think she could have kept up with him and then got him after a chase?"

"Maybe, maybe not. He was stabbed six times, and he covered some ground from the flat to the alley so the person who went after him was fast and determined, willing to stick with the chase in public for minutes instead of seconds. That might well be someone scared of the consequences of failure. We need to work out who he was working with; the people who might have put money into him and not gotten as much back as their imaginations expected, or just people who knew what he was handling, maybe carrying that night, and thought they could carve a slice for themselves with that knife."

"How do we find out who they were?"

Sholto smiled and said, "Well, I took a little shortcut and found out all the names the police have on their list of known associates. He was a quiet sort of criminal, which is all too rare, someone who facilitated other people's wrongdoing or tidied up after them. The anti-corruption guys put this shortlist together of all the crimes they believe he was involved in and the people he probably worked with on them. One of them, from the early days, died four or five years ago in a car crash, so unless this is *The X-Files* we can probably stroke him off our list. The rest of them? Murder's not just out of their league, it's playing a different sport, which is probably why he worked with them. That's what the unit think and I agree with them. Crooks, not killers. Money does make people daft, though."

"Maeve said there was no family."

"Maeve, is it? Miss Campbell no longer. Aye, there's no family in this country. Father long disappeared into the ether, no siblings, mother back living in Panama as of last year. It's the work, that's what killed the boy. Someone he worked with or against decided to put a stop to his mathematical gymnastics. There's not much for us to grab a hold of, though. He hung around some bad folk, but so what? There's a lot of people out there to label bad, depending on your definition, and none of us can avoid them all. The police

investigation went round in a couple of circles and then fell down dizzy. No pressure from family or media to catch the killer, and they can tell the neighbors it was related to his criminal work and not anything they need to worry about so everyone's happy."

"Not everyone."

"Well, no, not everyone. Now we've got Miss Maeve trying to clear her name and muddying the water."

"She says she thinks she loved him because he was honest."

"Honest? He might have been honest about being dishonest but that's as honest as he got. You believe that's why she was with him?"

"I don't know, women are strange."

"And getting stranger all the time. Now, Mrs. Douglas, she married me because I had a steady income and no visible scars, and I married her because I had a steady income and she had no visible scars, and we've rolled along just fine for a quarter of a century. These days people think a relationship should be like something out of a movie, or a dirty movie at least. It isn't like that. And that's the other thing I want you to think about. We're taking a risk going up against the devil's wee brother and we're doing it with a job from Maeve Campbell as our paper-thin cover. When Corey tries to punch a hole in our defenses it'll only take one swing of his claw, so how dedicated is she? Right now she's angry and she's sad and she wants to know who really did it, partly for Moses and mostly for herself, to clear her name. What happens if she stops caring? We get two weeks into this and she finds herself another boyfriend and doesn't want to rock the boat with the new love so she tells us to stop. It happens. She finds some other lucky sod to bounce around on and we're left with all the aggro and no way of finishing the investigation."

Darian said nothing. He wanted to argue but he knew it might be true.

Sholto said, "See if our pal is still singing in the rain out there."

Darian looked out of the window and saw Gallowglass, who hadn't moved a half-inch. "He is."

"Good. You're going to go to the Murdoch warehouses and stare blankly at them for a while and I'm going to stay here. We'll do what we normally do and see which one of us he thinks is more interesting. If we're doing anything at all for Maeve Campbell, we're doing it when wee George Smiley down there goes home for his tea and a sleep."

Sholto was right, and Darian went to the warehouses to sit and watch nothing happening there, the place going through its boring routines, and no sign of Gallowglass having followed him. It was good to have Sholto on board. The bald man at his desk could seem like he'd dosed up on tranquilizers at breakfast, but when he had his tail up he still showed flashes of the talent he'd started his police career with.

FROM THE SMOKE

It was built in a U shape and it was seven stories tall. The intentions had been better than the budget and the flats had ended up small and the building thrown up quickly with cheap materials. The cobbled courtyard was left bare of the once-planned furniture. The only stairs were in the center of the U so more space was saved to cram people in. The large storeroom had been placed on the ground floor on the left side of the courtyard inside the U.

The janitor's tools took up the shelves around the door and most of the rest of the space was usually given over to the sacks of coal that were distributed round the building to those who could afford to pay. The coal delivery had been due the following morning so there were no more than a score of sacks stacked against the back wall at the time.

They were fighting the fire on the right side of the building with a chain of men passing wooden buckets back and forth in the early evening. More men were at the stairs trying to get people out, with a few venturing into the burning building to search for anyone who might be trapped. They were risking their own lives to do so. It was chaotic in the courtyard. There was water splashing onto the cobbles and making them slippery as men bellowed deafeningly along the line. Smoke poured out the upper-floor windows where flames had broken the thin glass on the fourth and fifth floors and drifted down in the still night to blanket the courtyard. It was unlikely that anyone still on the upper floors of the building would find an escape.

He was the only one who saw her. He was standing in the middle of the line passing a bucket forward, and as he let it go to the next man something made him turn his head. He saw just a glimpse of her. She wore gray clothes and had gray hair and was moving through the smoke of the courtyard before disappearing in through the door to the storeroom.

He broke from the line and started to walk across the courtyard. Someone called his name but he waved a hand behind him and kept walking. Nobody would follow him on this night when there was so much to fight for. Many had died in the other fires that struck buildings in this area so every man and woman knew the urgency of this one. The others went back to fighting the fire while he moved into the smoke and out of their view.

The door to the storeroom was ajar and he entered knowing what it should look like inside. It was always dark in there as the row of small windows at the top of the wall were filthy with coal dust. It took a few seconds for his eyes to adjust and when they did he saw her.

She was sitting on a wooden chair he didn't remember being there before in the middle of the floor. She was watching him and waiting. Her mouth wasn't smiling but her eyes were. She was trying to seem serious. The woman was trying to pretend that this wasn't a game for her. He took two steps toward her and paused as he was reluctant to be further from the door. The air was already heavy in the storeroom and he knew it wouldn't get better. He was breathing heavily with the mixture of nerves and smoke. He stood looking into her eyes for what seemed only a few seconds and then took a few more steps forward.

"She's here!" he shouted.

He turned and looked at the high windows behind him as though expecting to see some reaction. It was dark still but there were dancing lines of light visible from the fire. As he looked at a window a flicker turned to a burst of flame as a fireball exploded from the other side of the building and into the courtyard. The roar of fire covered the shouts of men to begin with but when the flames settled the men didn't. They were still shouting in the courtyard as they battled fire and fear with volume.

He turned sharply and looked at her. Now she was smiling. Not a joyous smile but a satisfied one. The smile of someone whose effort had just been well rewarded. He couldn't keep the fear out of his face. He moved toward her and was now only three steps away. He

opened his mouth to talk and coughed in surprise at the thick smoke that ran into the back of his mouth.

"Stop that," he tried to shout, but he was coughing and croaking the last word as he felt the soot on his tongue.

He lunged the last couple of steps to her and reached down to try to grab her wrists. She hadn't moved since he'd come in and was still sitting in gray with her hands on her lap almost lost in the folds of her long skirt. He grabbed them with no intention. They seemed at once light and impossible to move. They were frail but powerful. She looked at him in silence. There was no need to say anything.

He started to cough and gasp but the more he did the tighter he grabbed hold of her. If he could stop her the others might have a chance. If he could just hold her in place. He could feel the heat on his hands and could feel the smoke trickling down his throat. He realized as he dropped to his knees that he should have let go. He was still holding her. She watched him drop. She seemed curious but didn't move. He coughed and gasped but only more smoke found its way in. He collapsed on the floor and let go of her wrists.

She sat and looked down at him for a full minute and continued to ignore the sounds of shouting from the courtyard. It took no more than a minute for her to grow bored with the sight of his dead body and to forget why he was lying at her feet. She stood and made her way to the side door beside the tool shelves that led further into the building. She wanted to find more people.

12

IT WAS the first test of Maeve Campbell, Darian asking her if she had a key for Moses' flat. They sat in her living room, and she nodded her head slowly.

"I do. I didn't tell the police that I did because they had already started to hint I was a suspect by that point. I don't know, I just thought it would be better if they assumed I didn't have one."

Darian said nothing. She hadn't understood that Moses had been chased from outside his building, so her having access to the flat would have made her less of a suspect.

"I want to get in and have a look around, see if there's anything the police might have missed, or that they might have seen but we don't know about. Have you been in the flat since he was killed?"

"No, God no. I'll get you the key."

"Thanks."

She handed it over to him and said, "Can I get this back when you're finished with it?"

Darian said, "Sure."

Sholto picked him up from Glendan Station and asked him about the key.

"She had it, says she hasn't used it since before he died."

"Police didn't take it off her?"

"She didn't tell them she had it."

"She didn't, did she not?"

"She did not."

Sholto didn't say anything else, but they both knew what that

meant. She had kept the key because she intended to use it; there was no other good reason. At some point she would have made her way back into the flat. Neither Darian nor Sholto needed to say that it was a poor reflection on her, or that it was also understandable. Maeve would know where the money was buried, and there was no one else to claim whatever cash reserves Moses had hidden away and left behind.

As they drove toward Moses' flat Darian said, "You're going the wrong way."

"We're not going in the front. People with an unhealthy interest are more likely to be watching the front door because they can sit in the warmth of their car to do it."

"Who?"

"If Corey has a pet watching the office then he might have another from his kennel watching the flats. We'll go in the back, I know the way. We'll go through the Lady in Gray flats and out across the garden behind them, in through the back of the flats on Seachran Drive."

They parked and Sholto led the way. He knew the area like a man who had arrested a lot of people round there back in the day, and led Darian across the square of grass where a courtyard had once been and into the front of the U-shaped building. It was one of the few that had been set on fire by someone way back in the 1870s, and the suspect had been a woman seen fleeing the scene of a previous fire. It was always factories she'd targeted, and in this case flats owned by a factory owner and occupied by his staff. She'd killed a few people, if it was a she and if it was even a single person because many think it was a sequence of insurance scams during troubled economic times, but was never caught and may have died in the last fire she'd set. In the end she drifted off into legend and became the Lady in Gray, now shorthand for a fire-starter or just a madly dangerous person in these parts. It is rather typical that a woman with a place in our local cultural history is seen as something wicked, a mysterious killer who was presumably driven mad by something the factory

owner had done to her. These days most people don't remember the original story, the factories are long gone and the flats were now just a renovated modern block in an old shell.

Sholto led him in the front door, along the broad corridor, past the stairs and straight out the back. It was dark and it was raining but neither of them could spot a watcher as they walked across the narrow stretch of grass and in through the unlocked back door of Moses' former residence. The stairwell was unlit and Sholto banged his elbow on the banister as they made their way up. He was still inhaling through his teeth and rubbing it when they got to the door. Darian let them in and they started to search, fast.

Sholto had said, "Anything that gives us a lead on who he was working with. Paperwork, receipts, anything. Let's just try to get a picture of the man."

Sholto had told Darian to look at pictures of Moses, as many as he could grab ahold of. It was one of his things, the parcels of wisdom he wanted to pass on to his young apprentice. You see a picture of a person and you can read a lot into it, how they stand, the expression they have, the difference between when they're posing alone and when there are other people there. Sholto had decided from the few he'd seen that Moses put on a false face when others were there, being cheerful to fit in, and that he was quieter and more relaxed when it was just him and whoever took the photo, presumably Maeve. Darian had decided that Sholto's theory was charming quackery. To Darian Moses looked like an awkward but likable fellow, light brown skin and a round face that made him look fat when he wasn't.

They were in the bedroom of the flat, and they were two men not bound by the limits of great wisdom. Sholto said, "Just think, Maeve Campbell slept in that bed. Probably did a lot more besides."

"Hard to picture her here."

"Oh no it's not, son. You need to get yourself a more potent imagination; it'll see you through the cold nights of a long Challaid winter."

"I mean it's hard to picture them together, acting like a normal couple. Him seven years older than her and he wasn't much of a looker. Plain and a bit podgy. Even if he was handling a lot of cash, it wasn't his money. He wasn't a rich man."

"Ah, but she might not have known that when it started. Maybe she thought she was climbing into the bed of a millionaire."

"No, she's too smart for that; she knew what she was getting into. Girl like her, she would have looked at his life before she leapt into it."

"Mm. Must have had talents that went beyond his much vaunted honesty, our Moses Guerra."

They walked back through to the living room. The place was small but tidy, sterile. It was a boring flat, no flair for living on show. Nothing on the walls, a TV but no consoles, no sign of a tablet, no bookcase. If the flat was a reflection of its occupant then it was another mark against Moses.

Sholto said, "Never trust a man who doesn't need to buy a bookcase. All this stuff is paid for, didn't have a penny of debt so life wasn't a struggle, even if he wasn't drowning in luxury."

Darian walked into the kitchen and opened a cupboard, looked at a full bottle of whisky and another of Coke. Three glasses stood beside them, and that was all the cupboard held.

Darian said, "He lived here eight years and you couldn't guess at who he was by looking around. Don't you think that's odd?"

"Odd how?"

"Odd, like a man should leave a shadow behind in the place where he spent his life. You couldn't describe this flat to a stranger, there's nothing distinguishing here, no sense of who he was."

"Some people don't have a shadow to leave. Maybe Moses Guerra had nothing to distinguish him, no interests or personal touches. Some folk only have their shadow for entertainment, and they take it with them when they go; it's why most people are soon forgotten. Plus, he was a youngish man living on his own, working and living in criminal circles. He had reason to hide the things other people could strip him of."

"Maybe he was just really boring."

"Maybe. Is your flat bursting with fun and games?"

Darian said, "You couldn't fit fun and games into my flat."

They spent another five minutes searching for signs of life in the dead man's flat. No paperwork that told a person what Moses had done for his money, no personal items that hinted at friends or a girlfriend.

Sholto said, "So?"

"So I can't get a picture of the guy in my head at all."

"We've spent long enough looking for it. Let's go before some busybody notices the lights on and knocks on the door. Key or not, we shouldn't be here."

Sholto drove them both to Sgàil Drive and Darian ran up to Maeve's flat to put the key through the letterbox. It was deep into the night, no need to wake her up for the sake of returning the key. He ran back down and got into the car.

Sholto said, "She didn't get rich in that relationship."

Sgàil Drive was not populated by people who had married well. It was the sort of place that someone desperate might reside, and that was Sholto's double-edged hint.

13

THE COLD fingers of worry squeezed his heart when he saw the motorcycle parked outside his flat. It was a 1952 Vincent Black Lightning, and it belonged to his older brother Sorley. His one bold extravagance. Darian didn't mention it to Sholto, let him stop the car and say goodnight as he got out. He watched Sholto drive away and then went into the flat.

He loved his brother unconditionally, but there was a wall between them. Clear enough that they could see each other through it, but too firm to knock a hole in. Theirs wasn't a sibling problem akin to The Waiting King and The Gaelic Queen, no violence and hatred, but it was awkward. Darian owed his brother too much, he and his younger sister Catriona both did. Sorley had been seventeen when their father had gone to prison. He had, with minimal help from their aunt Ann-Margaret, raised his curious fourteen-year-old brother and whip-smart twelve-year-old sister. Their aunt was, technically, their legal guardian, but she was a walking screwball comedy and chose not to even live in the same house as them.

The children's hearts had been cracked by their mother's death from cancer three years before, and a hammer was swinging toward them with their father gone, too. Sorley had thrown himself in front of it; let his heart break and prospects crumble to protect his siblings.

He had been an intelligent boy who excelled at camanachd, loved design and had talked about a career in architecture, but instead he dropped out of school and went to work. Odd that Darian, so

inquisitive even then, hadn't worked out that his brother was living a life of crime to pay for them. On reflection he could see that he hadn't wanted to know. Sorley brought enough money back to the nice family house in the Cnocaid district to carry on the comfortable life their parents, a teacher and a detective, had given them. Then Darian grew up and moved out when he got a job with Sholto, and Cat went to university. It annoyed Sorley that they both stayed in a city he thought was poison, but he never mentioned it. Instead he sold the family house on Treubh Road and split the money evenly three ways so Cat wouldn't have to worry about student debts and Darian could buy his new flat. Darian and Cat did both wonder if he really split it evenly, or if he gave them both some of his share.

Darian went into the building and up the stairs. He smelled the wisps of a San Jose cigarette before he turned the corner up to his floor. Sorley was sitting on the top step, looking bulky and bored, the cigarette dangling loose between his fingers. Sorley was the only one of the kids who got his looks from their father's side of the family. Where Darian and Cat were both feminine, pretty, Sorley was a solid block with dark hair and eyes, thin lips and a square jaw, a long forehead and nose just slightly too big. He had a moody expression so often it had to be deliberate. He stubbed the cigarette out on the tiled floor beside him when he saw Darian.

"Getting bored waiting for you. I hope your late night was fun."

Darian smiled sheepishly and said, "I'm on my own, so..."

He stepped past Sorley, making a note to pick up the crushed cigarette butt when his brother had left so the other residents on his floor wouldn't complain. He unlocked the door and they went inside, through to the living room. Sorley had never been to the flat before so he took a good look around.

"Good job I wasn't planning on swinging any cats."

Darian got defensive and said, "It's perfect for me. Good location, near the station, view of the loch. And the value's going up all the time, every place in Bank is."

"Aye, well, good. Still, about time you got something with an engine in it to get you around instead of using those shitty trains. They're always late and dirty and miles away from everywhere. Only reason the bloody things don't get lost is because they can't. You should get a bike."

"I'd be pretty easy to spot on some old classic."

"Aye, well, you can get something a lot more boring than mine that would still let you slice through the traffic."

The inevitable silence fell, two young men who should have had plenty to say to each other but couldn't hold a conversation down and force it to talk. They were brothers, three years apart, and they cared deeply about each other, which was why Sorley was there. It was him who ended the quiet.

"I hear you're sniffing round after the fragrant Maeve Campbell. That true?"

"Where did you hear that?"

"It true?"

"We have a job on. Her boyfriend was killed and we're following the money trail, that's all. What's it got to do with you?"

"Doesn't have a damn thing to do with me. I heard about Moses Guerra, and I know Maeve Campbell is worse news than the weather forecast. You should stay away from her, and from any investigation the anti-corruption unit are driving before they run you over with it. You and that fucking amadan Sholto, you'll get splatted if you're not careful."

"We know what we're doing."

"No, you don't. You're following a good-looking girl and you got this huge sense of justice right in your face so you can't see much past the end of your nose. She's using you for something, it's all she ever does, and the ACU won't stand for someone like you sticking a finger in their pie. Just leave them all to their bullshit, go back to hassling poor people for rich clients, that's safe ground."

"They never found out who killed Guerra, but he deserves the

truth being known. Don't give me that look, everyone deserves that much."

"If it was the girl then she wouldn't have hired you, if it was for his work then it was heavier trouble than you can pick up. Either way you're fucked."

Darian said nothing. He spoke so rarely to his brother and here was Sorley bringing grief to his door in the dark of night.

"If you know something about who killed Moses..."

"I don't. It was probably his work and it was definitely something Corey's unit has a better chance of uncovering than you and Sholto do. Big-time criminals, that's who you're looking for. If you want to see what honor among thieves looks like you can usually find it lying in an alleyway covered in blood. This is out of your league, both of you. I remember Sholto, when he was working with Da; he never had the balls for it then and I don't think he could grow them this late in life."

Darian frowned and Sorley would have realized, a second too late, that he had offended him. Sholto had been good to Darian, giving him a job after their father went away, keeping an eye on the family. He may never have been the world's most competent detective, but Sholto was a decent man and rarity gave that value. Sorley saw too little of good men in his world to recognize the worth. It went quiet again so the older brother took a different route, aiming for shared interests.

"Did you ever play the game *Brothers: A Tale of Two Sons*?"

"No. It good?"

"Yeah, it is. It's about these two young brothers and their mother's dead and their father's dying and they have to go find the cure for him. I know you're making contacts that can help you prove Da is innocent; get him out of The Ganntair. I'm doing the same, just coming from the opposite direction. You the cops and me the criminals."

"Meaning?"

"The game, *Brothers*, it doesn't have a happy ending. All the stuff

you've been doing, a man like DI Corey can ruin all of that, prevent you from ever getting Da out. Or you could lose more in the journey than you get from the destination. One error of judgment can make it all worthless, that's the point I'm making."

Darian said nothing to that either. He did try to make contacts with all the cops he could, journalists and businesspeople who might help him uncover the evidence he needed to prove their father was no killer, no thief. He had always known Sorley was doing the same thing using very different methods.

Sorley asked about their little sister before he left. "How's Cat?"

"Good, I saw her last week. She was saying the three of us should get together a lot more often, Sunday lunch or something like that, make it a regular thing."

"Yeah, she said something like that last time I saw her, last month. She came down to watch my camanachd team play the university side at Barr Park; she was full of big ideas that'll never happen."

"You win?"

"Against a bunch of middle-class university nerds? Hammered God's green snot out of them."

"You wish she'd left the city, don't you?"

"I'm proud she's at university, but I wish it was somewhere else. We should all have gotten out of Challaid first chance we got."

"Then we couldn't help Da."

"We might not be able to help him from here, and spending our lives trying might be a bad idea."

Sorley left and Darian struggled to avoid crying. Sadness ran through him every time he talked to Sorley, his big brother who was so clever, so strong, and reduced to running second-rate scams with bit-part gangsters. He was a talented young man, but he lived a life wasted to give Darian and Cat what they had.

14

THERE WAS a narrow gap in the thick curtains when he woke, a dusty line of daylight filtered through a smudged window. Darian blinked and shut his eyes again. He was beginning to dislike the sun, his best work often done in the darkness and the day reserved for resting. He struggled out of bed twenty minutes later, looking at the clock beside his bed. It was half-eight and he was going to be late for work.

He had a shower and got dressed, jeans and a warm sweater. He had to dress in a way that would allow him to pass unnoticed in the areas he was working and daylight hours meant watching the old warehouses at the marina. He took the time to shave, not bothered that it cost him more minutes and Sholto would whinge about it. No aftershave, because Darian didn't like to drench himself in cheap smells and couldn't afford expensive ones. Then he made himself a cup of tea and sat at the small table by the window in the living room, thinking about a different flat and another man.

Moses Guerra had handled cash for dangerous people, which instantly made the always treacherous money the most likely motive for his murder. There was little chance the dead man would have tried to keep people's share from them because he didn't seem that stupid, but that didn't matter. Moses could have honored all his fellow thieves and one might still have got it into his numb skull to kill him. People got jealous or paranoid, convinced someone they'd trusted with their secrets knew too many of them. Darian had to find out what Moses had been involved in lately, and if any bad souls had been hunting stolen money. One crook steals from another and

hides the money with Moses; when the money gets tracked down the person holding it is punished beyond the last inch of their life.

Darian finished his tea, got up and went to wash his cup in the sink with cold water. He dried it and placed it on the worktop. He had one of everything: cup, spoon, knife, fork. Few people had been in his flat since he'd moved in and none had stayed the night, none had been given a drink or a meal. This is said not to make him sound pathetic but to point out the obsession he had with his work, and the damage it did to him. His relationships were as brief as he could make them, and that wasn't healthy.

He'd wanted to be a detective since he was a small boy watching his father going off to work in the morning. The dream of being a good cop, finding the worst people in a rough society and cleaning them off the streets. The uniform was pulled beyond his reach when his father was accused of murdering a petty crook who had helped him steal precious gems from the criminal gang illegally importing them into Challaid. Darian was fourteen when his father was arrested and charged, fifteen when he was sentenced to life. The son of the disgraced former DS Edmund Ross was never going to find a role within the force, so he had to focus his ambition somewhere else.

The day his father was arrested he didn't come home as usual; instead it was DC Sholto Douglas who came round with their aunt Ann-Margaret to try to explain what had happened. What Sholto said that evening remained true to Darian now; his father was innocent and it would eventually be proven. It was taking too long, but their determination as a family to show he was wrongfully convicted never dimmed.

You might think Darian's desire to be a cop would have died the day he saw the police lead his father into court to convict him of a crime he didn't commit. Accused of working with a known thief to steal illegal items and then killing the thief to cover his tracks and take his share. The diamonds were never recovered and the evidence always seemed flimsy and carefully constructed.

Sorley had needed money to support his siblings, so he went to

work for people he should have body-swerved, the sort of monsters the hysterical media like to tell you have a grip on the whole east side of the city, Bakers Moor, Earmam and Whisper Hill. That's a preposterous exaggeration, but those criminals are strong enough for a smart young man to make a living out of, and Sorley did. That gave people who didn't like their father the chance to claim the apple hadn't fallen far from the tree, when in fact it had traveled miles.

Darian left the flat and walked out into a morning as cold as his mood. Challaid has always been a city obsessed with itself, concerned that it needed to upgrade to keep pace with the rest of the world but stay the same to respect its identity. The isolation that was originally one of our greatest defenses has evolved into insecurity, a fear of being forgotten in an interconnected world, and the city is always trying to wedge bits of the future into the few gaps the past has left. Rebuilding, rebranding and waving our oh-so-individual identity in people's faces. But life for Darian was about his work, and, no matter the era, crime in Challaid has always revolved around booze, drugs, money, sex and power.

15

SHOLTO WAS up on his feet the second Darian came through the door. "Where have you been? You're late. Never mind, don't distract me. I've got it, I've done it. Cracked the whole thing with a phone call on day one."

"Cracked it?"

"Smashed the bastard to smithereens. I know who killed Guerra and I know why."

It came, as many of the best tip-offs do, from a barman, listed as contact #S-39. He worked in a pub called The Gold Saucer, not far from where Moses had lived and died, and Sholto had brought forward the usual monthly update he got from him in case there was something relevant to this investigation. There was, although Sholto didn't tell him it mattered in case the contact decided he wanted to be paid more than his usual pittance.

"My contact overheard a whispered conversation between two very drunk men, which means it wasn't nearly as whispered as it should have been. The man we're looking for is called Randle Cummins; he was the one doing the mouthing off. He was talking about his old pal Moses Guerra, and how he had gone round to Moses's flat to get money from him because he knew Moses was holding a lot. Said things turned nasty but he got into the flat and got the cash."

Darian didn't know where to go with that. "He just blurted this out in some pub?"

"He was talking to his pal, lending him cash, didn't know the barman could hear them. Drunk people, if they're stupid to start

with, well, they'll let it all out. It works, though, doesn't it? If Cummins knew Moses then he might know when he had money he was supposed to clean. Cummins goes round, there's an argument and a chase, he stabs Moses, takes his key and goes back to the flat for the dosh. They didn't find much cash in the flat of a man who handles money."

"Is this barman reliable?"

"A hundred percent, always has been, who can you trust if you can't trust a barman? I'm more concerned that Cummins was just mouthing off, trying to sound like a big man. Wee men with the drink swirling inside them can get imaginative and macho when they want to be."

"Then we need an address."

Sholto smiled and said, "Got one already, that's why I've been so patient waiting for you. Our watcher on the wall, Gallowglass, he's not out there, or he wasn't. Stick your head out the window and make sure he didn't turn up in your wake."

Darian went over and looked down into Cage Street, saw no sign of the former cop. "Looks clear."

"Good, we'll drive round and see if we can wake up Mr. Cummins. He doesn't have a job, according to my barman, and he'll know which of his regulars do and don't work. If I had no job and a lot of someone else's money I would be treating myself to a few lie-ins. If we're lucky we'll have him nailed to a jail cell by lunchtime."

They left the office and walked round the corner at the bottom of the lane onto Dlùth Street where Sholto always parked his six-year-old Fiat Punto. He drove them at his typical sleepy snail's pace. You couldn't get through a journey of more than ten minutes in the daytime with Sholto behind the wheel without hearing the sound of someone else's horn. One of the benefits of his anti-speed policy was that it gave them the opportunity to talk.

Sholto said, "You don't think this is our guy, do you?"

"I don't want to talk it down, but this sounds like a drunk who read about the murder in the papers and decided he wanted to put

himself in the middle of the scene. He wouldn't be the first infamy whore in this city. And I've never heard of him, have you?"

"Well, no, but I've never heard of everybody at some point. No one starts famous."

"But to go from some pal of a crook that we'd never heard of to killing that same pal for money? That's a pole vault."

Sholto went quiet and concentrated on his awful driving. They had to get to Jamieson Drive up on the northern edge of Bakers Moor, the old council houses where Cummins lived. Darian didn't want to piss all over Sholto's new shoes, he really didn't, but the sort of man who whispered loudly in a pub about killing someone wasn't typically the sort of man who avoided detection for over a month after the crime. Any lead was worth pursuing, and anyone who might have known about Moses and his work was worth the effort of chasing down, so Darian said nothing else to put Sholto off. It was rare enough to see the old man with this sort of enthusiasm.

16

CUMMINS LIVED in a semi-detached house that looked desperate to fall over. The street on both sides was in groups of four houses, all from the forties or fifties, many looking like a giant ruffian had given them a bit of a shake. None was in quite as much disrepair as Cummins'. Beside the front door there was a huge crack up and a small chunk out of the whitewashed wall, about a quarter of the slates seemed to be missing from the roof and the chimney pot had somehow been sheared in half. It wasn't obvious how any of this had happened, but it must have taken a concerted effort. The small front garden was an overgrown obstacle course they traversed before they reached the door. They could hardly see the path for the weeds and the never-cut grass.

Sholto said, "The state of this place. Wouldn't want to be living next door. Someone should arrest him for this if nothing else."

He was nervous and sounded it, worried that this shambolic house was a reflection of its owner because when people were this broken down they became unpredictable.

"Maybe he's not in."

"Only one way to find out."

Darian knocked on the door and the two of them took a step back, waiting twenty seconds before it was slowly opened by a short and wiry man with a narrow face, blotchy skin pinching at the cheeks, dark hair all over the place, two chipped front teeth chewing on his cut bottom lip. He was wearing a baggy T-shirt that showed a handful of amateurish tattoos and tracksuit

bottoms. He looked at them both through sleepy eyes and said, "Yeah?"

"Mr. Cummins? I'm Darian Ross, this is Sholto Douglas, we're here to talk to you about..."

"This about that old bitch next door, uh? The fuck did she call you about this time? She saying I'm the Lady in Gray, or The Taisgealach? Eh? She'll have me trying to bump off King Alex next. What is it this time, you old cow?"

Darian raised a hand to stop him shouting at the house next door. "We're not the police; nobody called us to come here. We want to talk to you about Moses Guerra."

The anger slipped from his expression and confusion took its place. He said, "Well, I don't know anything about that, do I?"

"But you knew Moses."

"I suppose, sort of, yeah, I did. I knew him but I don't know anything about what happened to him, nothing like that. Nothing I would tell you anyway."

Cummins sounded cocky now and Darian liked that, it would make him more likely to talk. Darian said, "We're not cops, but we're looking into what happened to Moses. Can we come in and talk to you about it? We'll make it worth your while."

Cummins laughed and opened the door a little wider. He said, "Sure, aye, come in then."

The outside of the house was an ineffectual prologue for what lay inside. The mess of the exterior was a Herculean effort for an insignificant return, but the real blood, sweat and tears were splattered all over the inside. There were holes in walls, no carpets on the floors, broken furniture and every surface was a canvas of stains in an abstract style. Avoiding the ones that still looked damp was a game that might never end. A few of them looked like blood, a lot were drinks and food, and some were better left unidentified.

Cummins led them into the living room where there was one chair, which he sat in. "You want to sit on the floor or something?"

Sholto said "Mm, nah."

Darian took the first step in the questioning because he was more confident of his footing. "Moses was killed and there was no money in his flat. You knew him, does that seem strange to you?"

"I dunno. Maybe. I don't know what he did with his money. Didn't spend it anyway, fucking cheapskate."

"You don't know if he had cash stashed in the flat?"

"I suppose he had some. That was his work, wasn't it, the dough."

"What about you, what do you do for a living?"

"I'm not working."

"You making ends meet?"

"Yeah, I'm all right. I pay my debts."

"You had debts?"

Cummins shrugged.

"And you paid them off?"

Another shrug.

"Did you pay them off recently?"

Cummins looked up at him from the chair, the expression of a man who wished he had a gun in his hand to shut their mouths with. He had let them in because there had been mention of being paid. Now the talk had switched to his money, not theirs.

"How much debt did you pay off?"

"None of your business, that."

"Who did you owe it to?"

Cummins said nothing, looking down at the floor.

Sholto said, "Did you owe money to the Creags?"

We'll break away briefly for another detour to tell you who the Creag gang are, because they matter. The name has existed in Challaid, mostly working out of Earmam and Whisper Hill, for at least a century, a multigenerational concern. It started out as a group of low-income tough guys running protection rackets and the like, and with each generation it's evolved, different people using the identity. Sometimes the Creags have been small-scale, a disparate bunch of gangs the police have identified under one badge for simplicity's sake, but sometimes one person, or a small group of people, come

along who are strong enough to morph it into a single, functioning unit. That's what it was at the time Moses was killed, a small council running it. If you borrowed money from a lender on the east side of Challaid, whether you realized it or not you were borrowing from the Creags and if you valued the blood running through your veins, you'd better pay them back.

At the mention of the Creags, Cummins looked sharply at Sholto and back at the floor.

Darian said, "You owed the Creags, and they were leaning on you to pay back?"

"Hey, you want me to answer your questions you arrest me, okay. I got rights."

"We're not cops, I told you that already. You had the Creag gang leaning on you for money and you knew Moses had cash in his flat. You said you paid your debts, so you must have found money somewhere. Where were you the night Moses was killed?"

Cummins said nothing.

"Can anyone vouch for your whereabouts on the night Moses was killed?"

"I want a lawyer."

"We know you told someone that you took the money from Moses around the time he died."

"I want a fucking lawyer."

Darian and Sholto went out into the corridor and whispered to each other while Cummins stayed sitting on the chair in the living room, looking miserable. He still hadn't grasped that the people questioning him weren't actually cops. If he had he might have tried to find a way to talk himself out of the sewers.

Sholto said, "It was him. We have to call it in now. It was him."

Darian nodded, but he didn't say anything.

"You're disappointed, I understand. He's pathetic and someone who took a life should never be that pitiful, but most of them are. This is it, Darian, we got it. A month Corey and his lot spent chasing this and they got nowhere, we've been on it a couple of days and we

got it. They should give us a medal for this, or at least a certificate. We call it in."

Darian nodded. "We call it in."

It was ten minutes later when the two cars arrived. There were two uniformed cops in one and two detectives in the other. One detective was a young woman with short, dark hair and a frown that Darian didn't recognize but Sholto said was one of Corey's people, a DC Lovell, and the other was DC MacDuff. The uniformed officers took Cummins away, and MacDuff stood in the corridor with Sholto and Darian.

He said, "You shouldn't be involved in this."

It wasn't the threat Corey would have delivered. It was a nervy, miserable warning. Sholto nodded and said, "We didn't mean to, we just sort of fell arse backward into the whole thing, working for a client looking for lost money. Led us to this guy. We're done with it now."

MacDuff said, "Good, I hope so."

Sholto drove Darian back to the office. They weren't done yet, but very nearly. Darian would have to tell Maeve about it, and they could expect a huffy visit from the police to find out what else they knew about Cummins, questions that wouldn't take long to answer. Essentially the work was done, and it was an anticlimax. Randle Cummins was a poor excuse for a killer, and paying off a debt he might have the shite kicked out of him for was a lame reason, but Sholto was right, that was how humanity worked. Sholto was buzzing with relief that it had turned out well, that he had proven himself as an investigator again. Darian sat looking out of the window, wondering where Gallowglass had gone.

A SECOND FIFTEEN MINUTES?

FORMER KNICK GORM MACGILLING ON HIS HOPES OF AN NBA COMEBACK

When the car stops outside the Colina Hotel at the top of Stac Voror, the steep hill that overlooks the Scottish city of Challaid, you can see the love of sport down below. Looking across the sprawl that loops round a sea loch you can see multiple stadiums and pitches for soccer and for camanachd. What you won't see, anywhere, is a basketball court. "I wanted to play camanachd," Gorm MacGilling tells me, with his deep voice and nervous smile. We're sitting in the café of the five-star hotel, the table and chair too small for him but he doesn't complain. "It was a teacher of mine in high school that said I should try basketball, so I did." He did, and for one week in May last year he was the center of the basketball universe, not that you'd realize it now.

If you follow the NBA, the play that made MacGilling famous hardly needs to be retold; it was the subject of a million vines and gifs, a hashtag and a frenzy of media attention. "It was pretty mad. We were up in Cleveland for the game and by the time we got back to New York I had gone from 5 thousand followers on twitter to about 30 thousand. Crazy." It sounds like he's talking about someone else.

So, the play. The Knicks had brought MacGilling to the club in February on a short-term deal, not expecting him to play much. "I'd been playing in Ukraine but things were bad there so I was out of contract, and my agent got me the chance in New York." He didn't play a minute in the regular season, and watched without playing as Kristaps Porzingis led the Knicks to the Eastern Conference Finals, and a shot at the no. 1 seed Cleveland Cavaliers.

The series went to a deciding game seven, the game tight going into the last two minutes when Willy Hernangomez fouled out and injuries meant the only big body left on the bench was the Scot. "I thought we might just go small for the last couple of minutes, but they put me out there."

Four seconds on the clock, the Knicks down by two. Lee inbounds the ball to Carmelo Anthony, MacGilling sets a screen for him at the top of the key and Melo uses it. The crowd expects a shot but Melo spins to kick out to Porzingis in the corner, but as the

ball leaves his fingers it's tipped by Tristan Thompson. "I saw the ball change direction. I saw it coming toward me and I knew there was no time left. I had to throw up the shot." With Thompson and Lebron James racing toward him, MacGilling took the shot. Swish, and his world changed.

It hardly seems to matter that the Knicks lost the finals in 6 games and MacGilling got nothing more than garbage time throughout. If you add up all his minutes across the five appearances he made for the Knicks, he was on court for fifteen minutes and twelve seconds. Still, in a world of instant media he hit a shot that mattered and became a sort of legend. "There was all this attention, but it didn't feel like it, not really. I was right in the middle of it, and the club was preparing for the finals, so I didn't really get the chance to experience it much."

And after the anticlimax of the defeat by the Golden State Warriors, the Knicks didn't offer MacGilling the chance to come back. "That was disappointing, I would have loved to stay, I loved New York. They wanted all the cap space they could get for the summer though, I understand that." There were no concrete NBA offers for him, and as he prepared to try to win a spot on a summer league team, hoping to make a strong impression, he suffered the injury that's kept him out for nearly a year. "That was tough, the timing of it couldn't have been worse. I came back home, I've been working out every day, getting myself into shape. I've never been fitter than I am now, never."

He's recognized a couple of times while we chat, both times by members of staff. At seven foot tall and two hundred and ninety pounds he's hard to miss. "I'm not famous here," he tells me with a smile. "I can do normal stuff. I went to New York for a holiday in the summer and got recognized everywhere, but not here. Here I can just be me. Go to camanachd matches, hang out with my mates." He talks of life here in a way that suggests the NBA is behind him. "No, no, no way. I'm only twenty-six still, I have loads of time. I need to get a new agent and get onto people's radar again, but I'll be back in the NBA again, I'm sure of that. Might have to go back to Europe first, or the D-League, but I'll make it." He hasn't given up, and he doesn't want to be forgotten. Gorm MacGilling is a legend for one shot, but he wants to be famous for more.

17

THE JOB was done, the case was closed, it was time for life to trudge on somewhere else. The police would charge Cummins with the murder of Moses Guerra and the case, and this story, was done. At the end of the working day Darian should have gone round to Maeve Campbell's flat and told her the goodish news. That was what Sholto told him to do, but once again he chose to defy the orders of his chief. Darian went looking for his brother instead.

There were two places Darian could think of to find Sorley at that time of night. He went round to his flat on Freskin Road up in Earmam but there was no answer. It was a bit of a plod from there to The Continental café on the corner of Kellas Road and Parker Street. Presumably the intention for that café when it first opened was to be a normal, run-of-the-mill place, but it had become a hangout for Sorley and his mates, and they organized a lot of their dubious work from there. It had large windows facing the two sides that looked out to the streets; it was a single-story, flat-roofed place. The neighboring buildings were mostly divided into flats, so the dinky little café looked like it was in the wrong place. At night, when the café was lit up and you could see the bar and the tables by the windows, it seemed like stepping into a gruff, cheap plagiarism of *Nighthawks*.

Darian came along Parker Street and could see the lights from the window, the figures moving around inside. The usual suspects, looking ready for their usual night's trouble. There were four motorbikes and three cars parked in front of The Continental, and one of the bikes was Sorley's. If you'd walked past, looked in the window

and seen the mob of hardy bastards within, you wouldn't have gone anywhere near them. Darian, being a man of reasonable good sense, wouldn't have either, not if Sorley wasn't one of them.

He pushed open the glass door at the corner of the building and went in. The volume of the music playing in the background was low but he recognized it as local band The Overseen. That would have been Sorley's choice, the man who paid the wages picking the tunes. There were empty and emptying beer bottles all along the counter, but nobody seemed drunk and the talk wasn't boisterous. It was early in their night. They would still have work to do before they started really to enjoy themselves. As he let go of the door, a couple of the people closest stepped toward him. They wouldn't have done it if they thought he was a random guy looking for a drink; they crowded him because they could see he was here on purpose, searching the faces for one that fitted. They were both exceedingly big. One was about six two and built like a professional wrestler, which he had tried to be, and the other was seven feet and built like a professional basketball player, which he had been.

The wrestler said, "You in the wrong place, pal?"

Darian opened his mouth to speak but someone else beat him to it. A voice from one of the tables at the side said, "Let him in. He's my brother."

The two men, Jake Cayden and Gorm MacGilling, stepped aside at their boss's orders. Cayden, head shaved, thick-necked and with small features, had gone down to Glasgow to try to fight for SWF under the name The Last Man, but he lasted two months and came back up the road muttering about contractual issues. Sorley told Darian he'd heard Cayden had gone down there and belly-flopped, just wasn't up to the job. They offered him coaching but he never took well to being told he needed help. That was when he decided the smartest thing to do was start a wrestling company in Challaid instead, fill a gap in the market. It had been a year and a half and he hadn't started yet. The only thing that told you he had tried wrestling was his nickname, TLM. He said he was a born-again

Christian, Sorley said he was a psychopath; it's just possible he was both. MacGilling, with his long chin and protruding eye sockets, had actually been a basketball player for some team in America, he had the height but no talent to complement it, and his career looked over as well. He was working a very basic racket for Sorley.

The laundry scam was simple and small and one of many Sorley ran. They went and collected the laundry from the hotels for washing and ironing and took them to the same depot that had been doing the job before, only now they were doing it for 70 percent of the value while Sorley took the extra 30. The only cost to Sorley was sending Gorm MacGilling in the van to collect the goods instead of the employee the legit depot had sent.

He would go and pick up the laundry in the big van and be recognizable, be every inch the Sorley Ross employee. Darian would later suggest to his brother that the big man didn't seem scary at all, and Sorley agreed.

He said, "He's not tough, couldn't handle himself in a fight with a toddler, but that's not the point. Guy that size, he doesn't get into fights at all. Nobody who isn't seven foot tall ever picks a fight with someone who is."

Sorley was sitting by himself in the café, at a table by one of the windows. He had a board and a few stacks of cards beside him. Darian recognized them; Sorley had been playing *Gwent* with someone. Darian sat down opposite him and saw the smile on Sorley's face.

"Didn't think this was your sort of place."

Darian said, "I'm not here for the fun of it. I'm here to ask you a favor."

"So you're going to take the fun out of it for me, too. Go on."

With his voice lowered Darian said, "I need to find out if someone paid off a big debt to the Creag gang. I need to know who to talk to about that."

"What's it about? This isn't still Moses Guerra, is it?"

"That case is closed, the police have arrested a guy me and Sholto led them to. This is about tracking money."

"Moses Guerra's money?"

"Fine, yes, Moses Guerra's money. This isn't a big deal, though, not to the Creags, it's just to prove whether the person who killed him took his money or not."

"Every little thing is a big deal to the Creag gang. They don't like people talking about the money they lend. It would be too dangerous a conversation for you to have."

"I'm not a little kid, Sorley. I've spoken to big, bad people before. I know how to talk to someone without threatening them. I'm not one of your pals."

Sorley looked round at the others in the café, about twenty people, an even split of male and female, all young and all looking well acquainted with giving and receiving a fist to the mouth. He was growing his gang, and not to help gather evidence for their father's release. This was Sorley being pulled deeper into a world he should have been trying to climb out of.

"I know who it is you need to talk to. You want to know, fine, I'll play you for it."

Darian said, "Great, we can play The Organization. I love that game."

Sorley frowned at the mention of the card game based on a popular TV show about Glaswegian gangsters, which was a little too close to home. He said, "We'll stick to *Gwent*."

Darian picked one of the four *Gwent* decks on the table, Northern Realms it said, selected his hand of twenty-five cards and glanced at his older brother.

He said, "Not exactly *Casino Royale*, is it?"

Sorley laughed a proper laugh. That raised a few eyebrows along the counter. They all respected their boss, some of them probably liked him and a few feared him, but they all believed he had well earned the nickname Surly. None could remember laughter like this, but the spontaneous joy was the difference between knowing someone as a friend and knowing them as family. What Darian and Sorley had, and the relationship both had with their sister Cat, ran far

deeper than anything these co-conspirators could develop with him, and with that depth came greater pain and joy than any of them could bring to Sorley.

The next ten minutes were spent in a tactical battle, a best of three rounds between Darian's Northern Realms deck and Sorley's Monster deck. Sorley loved these sorts of games and this was one of only two he could play with Darian because he knew his little brother would be familiar with it from the PS4 game it came from, *The Witcher 3*. You can be 100 percent sure Sorley would tell you it was luck, but Darian dominated their match. He won the first round with a lot of spies and doubled siege units, let Sorley win the second and waste some of his better cards in the process, and had more than enough in reserve, with the use of medic cards, to overwhelm in the third.

"Huh, I was hoping you wouldn't have as good a grasp of the game as that. Fair enough, I'll tell you what you need to know. You want to speak to Vivienne Armstrong."

"A woman?"

"Yeah, an actual female woman. You're not getting all misogynistic are you, Darian? Must be hanging around with old Sholto Blowhard that's doing it. What would Cat say if she could hear you?"

"I'm just surprised, that's all. Is this Vivienne Armstrong high up in the Creags?"

"Pretty near the top, one of the few that get to make decisions instead of follow orders. Viv keeps a crushing grip on the money-lending side of it, so she'll know if your suspect has settled his debt or not. Not that she'll want to tell you, won't speak a word to you, but that's a problem you'll have to solve yourself. You can tell her I sent you, but I doubt it'll help."

"She a friend of yours?"

"Viv? Friend would be the wrong word. She doesn't have anything as useless as friends. Our paths have crossed a few times, that's all. Don't get on the wrong side of her, Darian, she's tough, treats people like shit because she can wipe them all out. If she says it's midnight and the sun says it's midday, you call the sun a liar."

"So where do I find her?"

"Get out of your bed early, get to Sigurds pub on Caol Lane at eight o'clock."

"Will it be...?"

"It'll be open. They open early so she can get her morning whisky there, so it'll just be her and the bleary-eyed barman. The drink is part of her mystique, people think she's a mad fucking boozer but she just uses the pub to collect messages. She won't thank you for gate-crashing, but she wouldn't bother thanking you if you donated an organ to keep her alive, so..."

"Thanks for this, Sorley."

"Uh, huh, just make sure this is the end of you and Moses bloody Guerra, all right? Time for you to go back to being someone I don't have to worry about. Pick something nice and safe to spend your time on and save me the gray hairs."

Darian smiled and said, "Sure, and good luck finding someone dumb enough to lose to you at *Gwent*."

"Get out of here."

Darian left the café smiling.

18

VIVIENNE ARMSTRONG was standing alone at the bar of Sigurds. Darian had walked down the narrow lane in the fading gray of early morning and pushed the door, expecting it to be locked, but it wasn't. The bar was directly ahead, running off to the side, with round tables against the front windows on either side. It was dark in there. What light survived the brave fight through the clouds struggled to then find a route to Caol Lane, four-story buildings on either side of the cobbles. Darian stepped inside and let the door close, the noise enough to alert Vivienne. She didn't turn round.

She stood straight, wearing dark, tight trousers and a black coat, her black ponytail over the back of the large collar. She was about five feet eight, slender, and when Darian stepped beside her he could see her narrow face and thin lips, small bags under her eyes. She was pale in a way that her dark hair made look unhealthy and her makeup didn't hide it. Darian didn't know how old she was, but he was indiscreet enough to guess at mid-thirties. There was nothing in her general appearance that told you what sort of person she was, but when she glanced back at Darian her look suggested violence was a friend she cherished.

"Morning, Miss Armstrong."

She looked across again, raised a thin eyebrow and said nothing.

"My name's Darian Ross, I'm Sorley's brother. I wanted to talk to you about a man called Randle Cummins. I heard he owed you a lot of money and I heard he was good enough to pay you back."

"You're Sorley's brother?"

"Yes, his younger brother."

"Sorley, Darian and Catriona. Ha, your parents didn't want to give you much of a chance."

Darian threw her a look that was supposed to be silencing.

Vivienne scoffed. "Don't get precious about insults toward your parents. You're on the east side. Go take a walk in any direction from here and you'll find a bunch of kids with greater tales of woe than you have. One parent dead and another in jail? They don't hand out awards for that round here; too common."

"I'm not here to talk about my family; I'm here to talk about my work."

"Aren't you some sort of cop?"

"No, I work for a research company, but we do investigations into some people's finances. This is nothing to do with you, though, just Cummins."

"You probably know a lot of cops, don't you, Sorley's brother?"

There was a sneer in her voice and he had to chase it out fast or lose the conversation. "This will help you. I'm not doing it to help you, that's a side effect, but I'm giving you a warning. DI Corey has arrested Cummins and he's going to charge him with murdering Moses Guerra. Cummins is linked to you through money, through his motive, which means you might find yourself in a courtroom."

This time her silence was contemplative, not dismissive. This was bad news and it was taking its time to go down. There was a glass of whisky on the bar in front of her, a few drips left. She picked it up and emptied it, put the glass back down.

"Corey's been looking for an angle to take my scalp for months. He has a particular objection to women."

"His unit doesn't cover what you do."

She looked at Darian and smiled. This time it was mocking and perhaps rather pitying. "You might be Sorley's brother, but you

don't know the world like he does. Corey's unit covers whatever Corey wants it to cover, and he wants it to cover me so tight I can't breathe."

"So, Cummins?"

"He paid us back. He owed eighteen and a half thousand, and he had time to pay. We leaned on him a little, not a lot. Not for the whole lot, just a part of it. Suddenly he returns every penny."

Vivienne stopped because the barman had emerged from the back. He moved toward her, saw the look she gave him and turned like a gale had blown him sideways. He marched back to wherever he had come from.

She went on, "He paid in cash. As far as we were concerned that was the end of the matter. The debt was on the books, a registered lender. If he's putting the word around that I, or anyone else, forced him to get the money or suggested he steal it or kill for it then he's a lying little shit with a short lifespan."

Darian said, "He's not saying that. He's denying he had anything to do with it, but it doesn't look clever for him. The evidence says he killed Moses Guerra to get the money to pay you off."

"Evidence has a habit of saying what you want other people to hear. Your family should know that."

"But he paid you the money in cash?"

"He did, and it would have been a day or two after Guerra last breathed out as well."

"You should expect a visit from DI Corey then."

"I will. You were right to deliver the warning, but don't think this means I owe you a favor. Say hello to your brother, and tell him to remember what I said to him the last time we parted."

Darian didn't ask what that was; the tone suggested Sorley should remember and if he didn't he was in trouble. It was enough to make him pause and ask, "Did you ever work with Moses Guerra?"

"No, and I better not hear you repeating the suggestion that I have."

Darian turned and walked out of Sigurds. The door banged shut behind him and he was on the uneven cobbles of Caol Lane again, no brighter than when he had gone in but as sunny as it was going to get all day. He walked back to Mormaer Station and took the train to work.

19

DARIAN SAT at his desk at the window of the office and stared out into the street. Gallowglass was nowhere to be seen. The Cummins case was in the bag, there was no more intimidation for Corey's man to throw around, no more unwelcome investigation to silence. It didn't feel right, but it didn't have to. A man was guilty and that man was going to pay for it, so the job was done.

Sholto was at his desk, writing out an update for Glendan about the activities spotted at the Murdoch warehouses. There was little to report, but he could spool almost nothing out into six or seven pages and make himself look terribly busy. Darian did much of the work on Murdoch, but Sholto wrote the reports. Had it been left to Darian the wording would have been unhelpfully honest, telling Glendan there was no criminality to find there. Sholto kept the possibility alive because that was what the client wanted, and getting what they wanted would persuade them to extend the investigation.

The stairs leading up to the office were bare wood and Sholto's desk being next to the door made it easy for him to hear anyone approach. That was deliberate; he didn't like people sneaking up on him. Occasionally he would hear what he thought were steps and then nothing would happen. That always got the same response, a pause to listen to silence and then, "Must have been Bodach Gaoith."

This time, at half past midday, there was a knock at the office door following the footsteps. Sholto got up and answered it because

Darian appeared to be dreaming. It was DC Alasdair MacDuff. Sholto recognized him.

"What can we do for you, Detective?"

MacDuff entered the office and stood midway between the two desks looking uncomfortable. He was young, but he didn't have the brashness Darian would have expected from a protégé of Folan Corey.

MacDuff said, "We've charged Randle Cummins with murdering Moses Guerra and stealing money from him. We thought it would be right to tell you. Chances are you'll be called as witnesses, so you'll have to explain how you got involved in the whole thing. I don't know if that'll be difficult for you."

Sholto paused while he tried to identify sarcasm. His detector wasn't great but there was none to find. MacDuff wasn't Corey. Sholto said, "It's good news that you've charged him, good, good news."

"He hasn't confessed yet, but that might just be a matter of time. The evidence is piling up, especially the money side of it. It all fits, so we'll get a conviction."

"Well, it's good of you to come round and tell us, we appreciate that."

"Yeah, well, you were involved so . . . And you should expect to be called as witnesses. Anyway, I'll let you get on with your work. I'm going to pick up lunch at the takeaway downstairs."

MacDuff left and Sholto looked across at Darian. He had turned back to the window, looking out at Cage Street and the few shoppers walking by, mostly using it as a shortcut to somewhere better.

Sholto said, "Go on then, tell me why this isn't good enough for you."

Darian turned and looked at him. He had to answer Sholto's frustration. "He seems guilty, but a lot of people aren't what they seem. I don't think Cummins has the wit or the fury to kill, not even with the wolves scratching at his door."

"You don't know him well enough to know that. And he confessed."

"Not to anyone that matters, and not sober. He confessed when he was drunk and trying to sound like a big man in a private conversation. We've both heard plenty of people talking crap when they've got the drink splashing around inside them."

"The money, Darian, the money. How does he pay off that stonking great debt to those thugs without stealing it from the man he killed?"

"I know. The money."

"You're judging a book by its cover. Cummins is a small man in every way. You want a killer to be big and impressive and striking because murder is all those things, but maybe he did just go round there to mug Moses and things got out of hand, he panicked and pulled the knife. It's nice to think that the man you helped catch was a killer who might strike again and so you've saved someone by stopping him, but getting justice for Moses will have to be enough."

Sholto was often smarter than he sought or was given credit for. He could be wimpish and old-fashioned and he often seemed motivated by a desire to make as much money as possible by doing as little real work as possible, but the embers of the fire that had pushed him to be a cop in the first place were still warm. Thirty years of chasing after the worst of Challaid had given him instincts worth following.

Darian had to get out of the office, so he went to the south docks again to watch the warehouses. There was nothing to see, but he didn't care. Darian wanted to stare into space.

Summary report: Dockside Police Station, 40 Docklands Street, Whisper Hill, Challaid, CH9 4SS

Summary of reported incidents at 13 Long Walk Lane (Misgearan) for January

Jan 1st—Fight started in bar, spilled out to lane. At least fifteen involved, dispersed when police arrived. Two arrested—James MacPherson (25), William Armstrong (31). Attending officers—PC Vincent Reno, PC Philip Sutherland.

Jan 2nd—Three men entered bar and attacked victim, hospitalizing with serious injuries. Victim—Vasco Nunez (40). Possible revenge attack, Nunez identifying witness in previous night's arrest of William Armstrong. No arrests. Note—William Armstrong younger brother of POI Vivienne Armstrong. Attending officers—Sgt Seamus MacRae, PC Carol Lis.

Jan 8th—Knife fight in bar, two men injured. Two arrested and taken to The Machaon Hospital—David Carney (34), William Gow (23). Attending officers—PC Najida Azam, PC Zack Stuart.

Jan 12th—Body of Ruby-Mae Short (20) found on railway tracks behind 13 Long Walk Lane. Miss Short seen drinking in bar with several unidentified people, male and female, earlier in evening. None of fellow drinkers identified. First attending officers—Sgt Seamus MacRae, PC Vincent Reno.

Jan 23rd—Man dragged from building against will, taken away. Victim and perpetrators unidentified, motivation unclear. Probably crime, other witnesses in bar claimed it was a joke. One perpetrator described as "a giant." Attending officers—PC Zack Stuart, PC Sam MacDonald.

Jan 25th—Fight culminating in attempt to set fire to neighboring building. All but one involved party had fled scene before police arrived. One arrest—James MacPherson (25). Attending officers—PC Vincent Reno, PC Philip Sutherland.

20

HE MUST have taken the train to get up to Whisper Hill, although he couldn't remember afterward. It was destructive instinct that led him there. A young man who didn't know what else to do with his heavy misery so he tried to drown it. If you wanted to kill a few brain cells with a bottle, there was nowhere better than Misgearan.

Sandwiched between Fair Road and the train tracks there's a narrow lane with a collection of shabby-looking buildings on either side. Number 13 is Misgearan, a drinking den with a reputation and a half. Long Walk Lane apparently got its name because so many drinking dens around the north docks were shut down during a crack-down in the fifties and the sailors had to walk or wobble over a mile to the lane for some booze. It's well known for its drunken violence, but most of the crimes are never reported. The few the police hear about are because of the reputation that draws visitors and students to see if it's as grim as the legends suggest, to test themselves against the sort of hard-core alcoholics to whom drinking the city dry is a serious aspiration, not a witticism. Innocent people don't realize that you aren't supposed to call the police. They also don't realize that the police, particularly at Dockside station, use Misgearan as their own private club, and they're not going to let the council shut it down, no matter how much our elected representatives on Sutherland Square would love to try.

Darian had been there a few times before, usually to meet Vinny. He knew he'd be let in when he knocked on the side door. There were people out in the lane, there were always a few shuffling

around, waiting for trouble to join them. He could go in the front and sit at the bar, but that wasn't the sort of drinking he wanted. Being among other people and their noise, the inevitable fights breaking out, getting jostled and questioned, someone putting an arm round him and trying to lead him in song or tell him a long-dead joke, that wasn't for him. Darian wanted to sit alone, in silence. That meant a private room and that meant knocking on the side door.

He waited as a train clacked past loudly, invisible behind the corrugated fence. Darian knocked when he knew he would be heard, and the door opened within seconds. The woman looking back at him was short and in her sixties; Caillic Docherty had run the place for nearly twenty years. She had short brown hair that was thin enough to show scalp, deep frown lines and yellow teeth, glasses hanging from string around her neck. She remembered everyone, and who everyone drank with, so she would have known Darian was a friend of the police and wouldn't have considered turning him away. She was a woman in possession of many secrets, and her job depended on her keeping them.

"You wanting in?"

"I am."

She nodded and held the door open for him. Experience had brought with it both the knowledge of who people were and the understanding of what people wanted. She said, "You after a room?"

"Aye, and a half-bottle."

Every private room was tiny, little more than a box you could stand up in. There was a small, round table and two chairs, never more than that. People used them to drink miserably, and they were designed to be too small to allow misery the company it needed to turn violent.

Docherty was back inside two minutes with a half-bottle of Uisge an Tuath, cheap whisky from a local distillery. Nobody went to Misgearan for the quality on offer. A night there tended to deliver an

experience akin to being hit on the head with a shovel, and was only marginally more expensive. She put the bottle on the table; Darian passed her a twenty for that and the room and she left.

Darian drank steadily and with commitment until the bottle was empty. He hadn't spent the time thinking about anything because thinking wasn't part of the mission. He got up and shoved past the table, opening the door. He wasn't steady, but he wasn't quite ready to fall over. He got out into the lane and moved through the small crowd without bumping into anyone, which could easily have led to a fight he wouldn't win and injuries he wouldn't quickly recover from. He got out onto Fair Road and started walking, not thinking a damn about where he was going. The streets of Whisper Hill and Earmam were all familiar; he never had a sense that the darkness of the night could trick him into a dangerous wrong turn.

She opened the door and looked at him, at first uncertain of this man standing out in the corridor. Maeve took her time to compose herself before she said, "Darian. Can I help you?"

"I'd like to talk. We should talk. Can we?"

He sounded drunk, although the walk to her flat had taken some of the weight from his tongue. Maeve held her door open and let him in. Darian had to make an effort to walk straight in a confined space, and the effort of dodging the walls showed. He later convinced himself she was amused by him turning up at her flat in the early hours of the morning pissed out of his skull, although he couldn't actually remember something as subtle as the expression on her face, and drunk people tend to incorrectly assume they're hilarious. Maeve would be an unusual woman to have been thrilled by the evil o'clock arrival of a drunk man she barely knew. She let him in, though, and they went through to the living area.

Maeve said, "Take a seat."

Darian sat and looked round the room, taking it all in. He was either too drunk to notice any changes from his last visit or sober enough to recognize that there were none. It might be telling that he

didn't remember what she was wearing when he went round to her flat at two in the morning.

He said, "They got someone. Randle Cummins. He knew Moses. They're going to say he stabbed Moses and then stole money from the flat because he needed to clear a debt."

"They told me. A cop came round a few hours ago to let me know. He said you and your colleague were the ones who identified Cummins and proved his guilt, even though I don't think he enjoyed giving you the credit. You said you would get the man who killed Moses and you did."

"Ha. Yeah. I said I would get him and I got someone. Wait, did I say I would get him? Did I not just say I would try?"

"Okay, you tried and you got him."

"I went and I found him. We both did, me and Sholto. We talked to him and we tripped him up because he's not clever, Cummins, not the sort who can talk his way out of bother. Can talk his way in and you lock the door behind him. He talked, but he never said he did it, not to us, and not to the cops either...I don't think. Never said that."

"The detective told me he definitely did it."

"There is no definite, never is. There's a chance, that's all it ever is really. Your man was killed and Cummins had the motive to do it and he knew where Moses lived and he would know how to get at him. It might be that easy. Like dropping all the pieces of a jigsaw on the floor and they all land in the right place for you to see the whole picture. It could happen, but what are the odds?"

"Wait, do you think he didn't do it?"

Just at the point Maeve got interested in his drunken ramble, Darian hit the wall. The more he talked the more his jaw wanted to stiffen into a yawn, but he said, "I'm saying nothing is definite. If everything's in the first place you look for it then you're either really lucky or you don't know what you're looking at."

He had leaned back on the couch as he was speaking and tiredness was pushing his eyelids down. It was only when sleep wouldn't take

no for an answer that Darian realized how late it was, and that he must have got her out of her bed. He hadn't intended to come here. It was unprofessional. It took a couple of seconds for him to realize his eyes were closed. He opened them sharply, and didn't remember them closing again. He thought he heard Maeve saying goodnight.

21

HE OPENED his eyes and found dim sunlight stinging his eyes. Not as much light as he was used to, but any was too much. He blinked heavily, trying to ease the discomfort.

"Morning, sunshine."

A female voice and that caused him to sit up fast. He wasn't in bed, he wasn't in his flat and he wasn't alone. Darian turned to look through the sleepy blur at the female figure standing a few feet from him. It took a few seconds for his fractured memory to convince him this was Maeve Campbell, but that was as much information as it could compute so quickly. There was no memory of how he had ended up there, not at first.

He said, "I'm sorry."

"Don't apologize. You came round here to tell me the truth because you were too drunk to lie. I find most people are braver drunk than sober."

He nodded but that rattled his brain so he stopped. He had struggled to keep up with her comments. "I don't know what got into me."

"Ha, I know exactly what got into you, I could smell it the second I opened the front door."

"I shouldn't have come."

"You were right to come, although you won't win any prizes for your timing. But, then, if you'd waited for daylight and sobriety, you probably wouldn't have made the journey."

Maeve took a few steps and sat on the other couch opposite him.

She was wearing a short skirt, her long hair down. She was amused by his discomfort, smiling her dimpled smile. Darian watched her cross her legs.

He said, "I should go."

"You know, my neighbors already think I'm a classic example of the moral decay of this city. A young woman on her own, the man I was sleeping with murdered. Then you come banging on my door in the dark and leave a few hours later. You're not helping me to make a good impression."

Darian looked across the small room at a woman who had never consciously tried to make a good impression in her life.

"Sorry."

"You can make it up to me by explaining what you said last night. If Cummins didn't kill Moses then who did?"

"I was havering; I was wrong, ignore me."

"No, you want me to ignore you now because you were right last night. All the people I've met since Moses was killed, all the people investigating it, there are only two I've seen prove they're intelligent enough to listen to, you and Corey. If Corey told me aliens don't exist I'd start looking out for little green men. You're the only smart one I can trust. You were honest last night and I want you to shame the devil and be honest with me this morning as well."

There was no threat in her voice, but there was the demand of a woman who had a right to know. Darian had sacrificed his right to keep his opinion to himself at the same moment he had abandoned the policy of keeping his big mouth shut late the previous night.

"I don't know who killed Moses but I'm pretty sure it wasn't Cummins. That guy, he's not capable of much, murder included. He's the sort of guy who runs up a debt, not the sort that pays it off."

"So it's a hunch?"

"No, not a hunch, it deserves a bigger name than that. You get to understand people when you study them enough, get to know the types. Cummins is a loudmouth but he's weak. If he had done

it there's no way he would have gone a month and dodged a large police investigation without it being known."

"When DC MacDuff came here yesterday he said there was more than enough evidence to confirm and convict."

"There's evidence. All very neat and just enough of it to be sure Cummins gets a long sentence."

"What does that mean?"

"It means all that evidence and a man with a brain like DI Corey didn't spot it, but me and Sholto found it within two bloody days of looking. Not to talk our talent down, but I don't find that convincing. They'll put him in a court and they'll get a conviction and that'll be that."

"That'll be that? If the person who killed Moses is still out there then you don't get to stop looking for him just because Corey and his mob say so. I'm hiring you and I'm telling you to keep looking."

Darian looked at her, the magnetic fury on her face, and smiled. Someone willing to fight for the dead, long after the final bell had tolled. He said, "I'll keep looking, but I don't know how much I'll be able to find."

"You'll keep looking and you won't do it alone because I'm going to help you. I know people that were close to Moses, the sort that might know who he was working with around the time he was murdered. A lot of them wouldn't talk when there was a police investigation going on, didn't want to be tangled up in that unpleasantness. They won't talk to you either because they'll see you as a cop without the credibility."

"Hold on, no, this is not okay, you would be putting yourself at risk."

"I'm going to do this, so talking me out of it is a waste of your boozy breath. If I do it without your help I'll be less effective and at greater risk. So you'll help me, won't you?"

When she smiled in triumph she was a woman Darian couldn't say no to.

He said, "I'll do what I can."

SCOTTISH DAILY NEWS

A LESS EXPENSIVE FAILURE

WHY GOVERNMENT CLAIMS OF BANKING SUCCESS HIDES AN ALTERNATIVE FLAW

It happened again over the weekend, the Scottish government's finance secretary telling a collection of business leaders that sidestepping the worst of the banking crisis that engulfed the world in 2008 was down to their policy and regulation. Its true policy and regulation were a major factor in the shallowness of our recession, but it wasn't their policy and it wasn't their regulation.

No government in the modern history of Scotland has admitted it, but their dirty little secret is that the Sutherland Bank has dictated finance policy, from taxation to regulation, for more than a quarter of a millennium. Every major finance policy that has passed through parliament, from every major party, has been written to fit the austere philosophy of the Challaid-based bank that has dominated the Scottish financial sector since its inception in the seventeenth century.

We don't, in the south, think of Sutherland Bank that way, because we don't think of Challaid that way. It's the remote city, hidden on the north coast, barely accessible and culturally separate. They speak Gaelic, they keep themselves to themselves and the tentacles of their local businesses tend not to reach into our lives. Except for one, the bank that's always been there, that's always presented itself in the way we see the city it sprang from, distant. Talk to people who work in Challaid and they tell you a different story about the power that pulses out of the grand building by the park, not coincidentally next door to the equally grand council headquarters in the city.

Things went bad fast in 2008, but Scotland's recession was shorter and shallower than many. It was not, contrary to the PR nonsense of the politicians at the time, good planning and rigorous regulation that saved the day, it was a fluke born out of a different kind of corruption. Sutherland gets to decide how every other financial institution in the country operates, because they've been the lender of last resort to the Scottish government since the mid-eighteenth century. They're a company with a

long history, a patient and conservative bank that sees gambling as beneath them, so they drew up a set of rules that forced every other bank to operate the same way.

It means that nobody else can ever grow enough to challenge them in their domestic market, and allows their influence to smother Scotland and reach out beyond. That legally enforced financial conservatism meant we didn't get as high a boom as they had in London and elsewhere, and didn't get the crushing bust either. Sure, our economy took a big hit, but not as bad as it could have been. It's often reported that Sutherland actually profited from the wreckage of its rivals. One or two scallywags have even suggested they played a small part in making the crash happen, so they could look strong and pick over the carcasses of their former challengers.

The real shame of it, though, is not a large bank controlling financial policy, that's simply a more crystallized version of what happens in many countries. The shame is that this distant bank has had undue sway over social policy to boot. They have believed, throughout their history, that progress is made slowly, that risks are for the graceless and that a decent society is always tightly controlled. The progressive agenda in the south has been resisted, and the amount spent fighting poverty has been reduced, because of a banking corporation that won't allow money to be spent on something as frivolous as tackling poverty and social injustice.

At some point in the next few months a politician will address business leaders in Challaid or Edinburgh or Glasgow and they'll call the Sutherland Bank one of the greatest success stories in Scottish history. One or more of the bank's board, all members of the founding family, will be in attendance, and they'll nod politely, trying to look humble. They should. They have more to be humble about than the people they so powerfully influence would ever admit.

22

IT WAS tempting to throw the rest of life overboard and sail wherever Maeve pointed the boat. Darian found himself thinking about her as he walked to the office on Cage Street after going home for a shower and change of clothes. Her strength, her boldness, pushing for difficult truth and willing to take the risks, even enjoying it. He couldn't abandon every other case just to obsess about Maeve; he had to help Sholto pay the bills.

Sholto was in the office ahead of him, the smell of Chinese food from the container on his desk that had held his greasy breakfast.

"Good, you're here."

Darian said, "I thought you were on a diet."

Sholto said, "Mrs. Douglas is trying to get me onto a diet. She's convinced that one day she's going to see me in a news report about obesity. You know the ones where they film fat people on the street and you never see their faces, just wobbles in tight clothing. Got me worrying I'll recognize my wobbles on TV."

Darian looked at the takeaway and said, "I applaud your discipline."

"It's stress release, we've got something and I don't know if I like it or not. Well, I don't like it, I know I don't, when I'm uncertain it always means bad news."

Darian sat at his desk by the window and said, "Go on."

"Some kid, eighteen or nineteen, got the holy smokes beaten out of him last night. He's at the Bob, they kept him in overnight."

The King Robert VI Hospital is in Cnocaid, which meant he

was beaten on the good side of town. It sounded, on the surface, like Sholto's kind of case, easy and uncontroversial. Young man gets leathered on a night out and lands in the hospital, not likely to become a headscratcher. Just find the drunken kid that used the other drunken kid as a punch bag.

"So what's the bad news?"

"Well, he got knocked about last night, he was found alone in the alley behind Himinn nightclub on Malairt Street. They called an ambulance, he told the police he saw nothing, they said they'd investigate. His father's decided that's not enough, that he doesn't trust them to make a job of it, so he called me."

"So turn it down. It's a police case."

"I would, I would, but the father, he, eh, he works for Sutherland Bank. He's not a Sutherland, but he's senior."

Sholto had a policy of not turning down anything that came from the bank. You do good work for those people and they use you a lot. With their wealth you can charge them eye-watering amounts without them complaining, so saying no was bad for business.

"Who are they, the father and son?"

"Father is Durell Kotkell, son is called Uisdean. The father, I Googled him while I was talking to him, he's a senior executive with some control over their operations in Caledonia. Sort of guy with a big office at HQ and the ear of the family in the boardroom. If he recommends us to the company, we're set."

"And if we stand on police toes we're screwed into the ground."

"Well, yes, there is that. Come on, I'll drive us to the hospital and we'll talk to the boy while it's fresh in his mashed-up head."

Sholto drove them to Cnocaid in his Fiat and complained ferociously at the price of parking. As he jabbed the coins into the machine Darian stood beside him.

"I spoke to Maeve Campbell."

"Oh, right."

"Yeah, she still wants us to keep looking for the person who killed Moses."

"She wants us to keep looking for Randle Cummins? He's in the bloody police station, we know where he is, and soon he'll be in The Ganntair. Does she want a photo to prove it? She should be happy with how this worked out. Well, not happy, her man's still dead after all and we're not Jesus enough to bring him back, but she should let it rest. It's finished, and we're finished with it."

Sholto had stopped at the machine to rant and a woman was standing behind him, waiting to pay for the luxury of switching off her car to visit a sick relative. She cleared her throat and he started, nearly dropping the hard-earned coins in his hand. They didn't speak about the case again as he got the ticket and went back to put it on the dashboard of the car. They went into the large, L-shaped building. Its many facelifts didn't hide its age, and some would suggest the attempts to make it look less nineteenth century only damaged it. There are a lot of buildings like that in Challaid, patched up in the name of modernity because we instinctively don't like rebuilding and they would have been better off left alone.

The boy's family were round his bed in a private room on the second floor. His injuries didn't warrant a room of their own, but his father's status did. His influence had also pulled a bored-looking uniformed officer into its orbit in the room and kept him there for no good reason.

"Hello, I'm Sholto Douglas; this is my colleague Darian Ross."

The father stood up from his bedside seat. He was short and thin with dark, receding hair and the expression of a man who didn't have to work hard for respect. All the action in his face was around the small eyes, thick eyebrows in a V to show his anger and the deep lines cutting his tan showing that this was his usual expression, a small mole above his right eye. His suit was stylish, and no doubt expensive, but he wore it like an obligation, not a pleasure.

"Finally. I'm Durell Kotkell. It's about time we got some proper investigators here; we've been waiting for hours with just this clueless wonder for company."

The young officer rolled his eyes but said nothing.

Kotkell said to him, "You can wait outside, there's nothing for you to add here and I'd like to speak to these gentlemen in private."

That was an idea the cop liked, and he left quickly. Leala Kotkell was sitting at her son's bedside looking uncomfortable, a darkly tan Caledonian, straight dark hair tied back out of her way, too-thin eyebrows and a button nose. Darian noticed the expensive rings on her fingers. The boy in the bed looked bruised and embarrassed. He was boyishly handsome, a mop of brown hair that needed a brush put through it, small eyes that were the opposite of his father's in their innocence, the beauty spoiled slightly by a line of spots along his poorly defined jawline. The few visible injuries suggested it had been by no means the worst pasting handed out in Challaid that night.

Sholto said, "So, Uisdean, why don't you take us through what happened."

Before the boy could open his cut lips his father said, "My son was brutally attacked is what happened. Unprovoked, followed out of a nightclub and battered senseless for no reason. The police have done nothing of any use; they've made it perfectly clear they don't think it matters much. That's not good enough, so you're going to find out who did it."

Darian realized that Sholto had already committed to playing the obsequious yes-man so he spoke for the first time. "We'll need to hear it from your son so we can have as clear a picture to work from as possible."

Durell Kotkell frowned like a man trying to decide how best to win a fight no one else realized had started. Sholto shuffled, cleared his throat for no reason and said to Uisdean in the bed, "Can you run us through what happened last night, as much detail as you can remember?"

The boy, and he looked younger than eighteen, spoke like it hurt. His accent was the epitome of posh Challaid, the phlegmy style of a working-class accent designed for Gaelic replaced with silky care,

less roll on the r's, a lighter touch on the l's and less spittle all round. "I honestly don't know what happened. I was having a night out with some friends, we were at Himinn, had a few drinks and we left. I went to use the alley to cut across to Cala Street and get a taxi home from the rank there. I remember going into the alley, I could see the lights from the buildings on Cala Street, and that was it. They must have attacked me from behind because I didn't see anyone waiting there."

"Uh, huh, and you didn't hear anything or see anyone on Malairt Street when you came out of the club that looked like trouble?"

"No, nothing."

"There was no bother in the club last night, no arguments or funny looks?"

"Nothing."

Durell had been silent quite long enough for his tastes and, still standing, said, "Of course there was no trouble; if there had been then even the clowns masquerading as policemen in this city would have known where to look. You need to find out who did this."

Sholto said, "Of course, of course. Was anything taken from you, money or your phone?"

"No, nothing."

"Do you know if they went through your pockets looking for anything?"

"I don't know."

"Were you wearing a watch, Uisdean?"

"Uh, yes."

Sholto leaned toward the bed and said, "Is that it there, the one on the bedside cabinet?"

"Yes."

"No scratches on your wrist or anything where they tried to take it off?"

"No."

"And there was no one you've fallen out with, even ages ago, and

you didn't think it was a big deal at the time? There's no one who might have been half-cut, outside the club, saw you come out and thought they'd try to settle a score you forgot they were keeping?"

"No, no one."

"Right, good. Can you give us the names of the people you were with at the club?"

He looked reluctant but one glance at his father set his tongue running. "Leandro was there, Leandro Oriol. He's at the university with me, lives in the accommodation there. Others came and went but it was him I went to the club with."

Darian had stayed silent since his first intervention, letting Sholto show that his years of ducking real work hadn't blunted his talents completely. He'd asked the right questions politely enough to keep the father from raging again. They each shook hands with Durell and Uisdean, nodded to Leala on the other side of the bed, and walked back down to the car.

When he pulled the passenger door shut behind him Darian asked, "What do you make of it, inquisitor?"

"I wish his father didn't work for that bloody bank so I could have told him to stick his job up his arse and jump out the window with it."

"Aye. And the boy?"

"Well, it had nothing to do with money. There was good money ticking away in that watch, that really was worth mugging someone for, tempted by it myself. The posh always have fancy watches, it's the only thing they have the imagination to give each other for Christmas. He knows more than he's letting on, and he only gave us the one name because he knows that lad will back him up."

As the car putted into life and Sholto looked over his shoulder to reverse out of the space, Darian said, "We'll have to talk to him when he's on his own, when the father isn't there to play stifling defense. I think he'll tell us the story then."

"Aye, but it might not be the story the father wants to hear, and

that doesn't help us much. We're done with Maeve Campbell, by the way. We found the killer and I'll write up a bill for her and stick it in the post. Might even get this one wrapped up as fast as that one. You're bringing me good luck in challenging circumstances these days, Darian, and I'm a big fan of good luck."

23

IT WAS tempting, when Sholto went home, to make a start on the work Maeve Campbell wanted him to tackle. She needed to know who had killed Moses Guerra and Darian wanted to help her. Of course he wanted to catch the right killer because getting it right mattered to him, but he had been thinking about Maeve all day, the smile and the legs crossing, the fierceness. She was a distraction. If he did some digging on the Moses case then he would have the excuse he wanted to go and see her again.

Darian shook his head as he walked up Cage Street on his way to Glendan Station. He had to prove to himself he could resist the girl. He wasn't in control of the case if he couldn't recognize the need to go home and get a good night's sleep. Maeve had hired him, but if he wanted to be professional then he couldn't let her control him. The Moses case mattered far more than Uisdean Kotkell taking a few slaps on a night out, that's why the police had shrugged their collective shoulders in the face of his father's demands, but Darian had no hope of helping either if he was less than half-awake. A night at Misgearan demanded abstinence for the next two.

The train was busy on the short trip west through Bank. His radar was switched on as he walked, not scanning faces but alert to any movements that fell into sync with his own. Darian had lived in that flat on the corner of Havurn Road and Fàrdach Road for over two years and he had made that walk to and from the station at least twice a day every day since. He could see every crack in the pavements and picture every building with his eyes shut. He knew

the people that usually hung around outside the doors of the station, the familiar characters he passed on the walk now and again. It took very little for him to notice someone out of place.

The first trick to being followed is to never let your tail know you've spotted them. Darian needed this person to get close, to show themselves, because he didn't recognize him at first glance. He was good at what he was doing and he was well covered, the hood of a puffy jacket pulled over his head; the weather does make tracking a person in Challaid without showing your face easier. Darian walked home, going at the same pace he usually did, making no deviation from his well-worn route. The same footsteps day after day; with paint on the soles of his shoes he would have marked out a very narrow trail. If this person knew he always got the train home and exited through the north door of Bank Station then he probably already knew where Darian lived.

Only when he got into the building could he do something about it without giving his knowledge away. He ran up the stairs to his flat, went into the kitchen and took the bag out of the bin. It was only half-full but that didn't matter. He pulled it shut and bolted back downstairs with it. He was back to being casual, moving at a sedate pace as he opened the front door and stepped out, walking along Havurn Road to the gap between his building and the next where the bins were stashed. He opened one and chucked the bag in, turning quickly and catching a split-second glimpse of his follower, just the side of his face as the man turned away and started walking out of view, but it was definitely Randulf Gallowglass.

Back in the flat Darian sat near the living-room window with the light off, looking down into the street. There was nothing to see there, but he kept up the vigil. Gallowglass wouldn't know for sure he'd been identified, but he had been seen and that would be enough to send him scurrying back under his rock. A good tracker, who doesn't want to be seen, isn't going to risk being picked out on the same street twice, hours apart. Even unidentified, his purpose would be understood. Darian kept looking in the hope that he would spot

a car going past with Gallowglass or Corey in it, but that wasn't necessary to confirm his suspicions.

Gallowglass wasn't back on his tail because he'd found a new hobby he liked. It hadn't been a day and already Corey knew Darian was still working the Moses case, and maybe knew Maeve was going to try to help him out. Darian had spent many evenings, when he first moved in, sitting at that window, watching the lights of boats leaving and entering the loch, the view between the buildings down to the water. Now he sat looking down at dark gray tarmac lit yellow by artificial light, contemplating what this meant. Gallowglass hadn't wanted to be seen, so this wasn't a thuggish warning. This was Corey fishing for information before he tried to put a stop to Darian's efforts. This was Darian putting the research company at risk by picking a fight he couldn't win.

THE BUST OF ACAIR DUFF

It was the story of the year at the university. It was a crime that the police had very little time for. In the bubble we live in it can be hard to appreciate how meaningless some things are. When Michael Watson, the first-year student who was the star of the university camanachd team, and Ben Gauld, the fourth year who was vice captain of the side, were assaulted returning to the halls of residence after a match, it was the only topic of discussion among us students. Michael Watson was in hospital for two days and missed three months of matches; Ben Gauld was only slightly injured and missed no matches. In a city where forty-one murders were reported last year, this was not a priority for the police. That would be why their investigation involved a few easy questions and nothing more. Because it was such a big deal to us all, I dug a little deeper.

To understand why it matters it's worth explaining why the university's camanachd team matters. It's the cheerfully brutal sport of the city, and the university team plays in the national league and cup. It may be the one thing that draws all students together, a flag to rally around. Only current students can play for the team, which has meant success has been, to be polite, occasional. Players may not make a lot of money from the sport, but they can become heroes in the city. The university hasn't won the league since 1988, and only twice in a century, and hasn't won the cup since '96. Even a passionate support can lose its verve in the face of ingrained mediocrity. Then, along came Michael Watson. A first-year student studying mathematics, a likable black kid from a working-class background, and one of the best camanachd players the university has ever had. With a solid supporting cast already in place he represented our best shot at silverware in a generation. Then he was attacked.

Watson and Gauld had been playing a match that afternoon, beating An Fiadh-Chù, or Earmam Athletic to give them their proper

name, 4-2 with two goals from Watson. It had been played up in Earmam, at their Sgleò Park ground, and the Challaid University players had made their own way home after the game. Some had gone for a few drinks, because that's what students are prone to doing in the wake of everything. Watson and Gauld had got the train back to Ciad Station, the largest in Challaid because it's where you get a train south out of the city, and walked down from there. As they made their way up the main approach to the halls of residence they were attacked from behind by three men. Watson suffered a broken ankle as well as facial injuries and two broken fingers, and Gauld suffered facial injuries and a cut hand.

Now, this is where I, Catriona Ross, come in. The police had asked a few questions and then wandered off, leaving speculation in place of answers in their wake. I wasn't satisfied with that, and felt there was more to learn. The place was swirling with rumors about scumbag Earmam Athletic players being behind the attack, and, as my brother Sorley was one of them, it was personal to me.

"They were followed home from the bar they were in," one student said to me with zero evidence to support the claim. "Everyone knows it."

I prefer not to accept what everyone claims to know. They might have got hit in the head with sticks occasionally but they weren't numb to the brain. There was no way Earmam players would have risked being seen leading an attack on campus grounds, where the security was obsessively tight. I know how insane some people are about camanachd, and I know Sorley can be huffy in defeat, but this seemed like a big stretch.

At times like this it pays to be pushy. I didn't know either of the victims, I was a second-year student at the time so didn't share any classes, but I sought them out. I saw Watson on the east green and made a beeline for him. Even on crutches he seemed energetic, tall and lithe.

"Hi, Michael," I said with a cheery smile. "My name's Cat Ross, I just really wanted to say how terrible it was what happened to you."

"Oh, thanks," he said, and started to move away. He'd have heard enough expressions of sympathy for mine to mean very little.

"I was wondering if you saw who did it, the three guys? I know some people up in Earmam, a couple who play for their team; they might be able to help identify them."

"I'm sorry; I didn't see them at all. They jumped us from behind."

"So Ben saw them? What did he say about them?"

"He didn't really see them either; he got jumped and saw the figures running away after. I'm sorry, but I'm running late... Hopping late."

"Oh, sure, go on," I said.

The next step was to visit the security room on the ground floor of the halls of residence. The building is rather grand; a spectacle is how it was sneeringly described when it was built. Most of the university, like many other elements of Challaid life in the last three hundred years, was funded by the Sutherlands. The hall of residence was instead paid for by a donation in the mid-eighteenth century by a shipping magnate called Morogh Duff, who was, in every way, the opposite of the Sutherland family. To say Duff led a full life would be to undersell it criminally. He was wild, gregarious and loved to thumb his nose at the conservative establishment in the city of his birth who called him a pirate, hence the ostentatious building he paid for and the scholarships for the children of his working-class employees.

The security room for the building was on the left side of the main entrance hall, across the colorful tiled mosaic of a ship crashing through waves and in through a small, arched doorway. There were two computers on a long desk and one young man in a shirt with a badge on it saying he was the security officer for the building. That was Nassir El-Amin, and if you were nosy enough to want to know what was happening in the building then Nas was a man you made friends with. It was easily done; he got awfully bored in that office. As resident nosey parker we knew each other well.

"Hey, Cat," he said when I walked into the office.

"Hi, Nas. Listen, can you help me out, I'm digging around in what

happened to Watson and Gauld and I wondered what you'd heard. What did the cameras show?"

"Cameras didn't show anything but blackness. The ones at the front were down on that night because of a software shambles; they'd been down all day. We didn't pick up anything of what happened, or who did it."

"They'd been down all day?"

"Yep, since the early morning. The police weren't impressed either when they came looking. I think that was the final straw for them. They asked a few questions of a few people, but I think they're done poking around in this already."

I was about to leave but not before I mentioned something unusual in the office. The bust of Acair Duff, son of the man who paid for the building and himself a significant donor to the university, was on the floor in the corner of the room. It had been outside, atop his pedestal on the approach to the main entrance, but now it was in the security office with a chunk out of the back of its head.

"What happened to your new roommate?" I asked Nas.

"Poor sod was the third victim of the attack, not that he's getting any sympathy. They must have pushed him off the plinth when they attacked; he was all over the pavement. Not the first fellow we've found all over the pavement here after a wild night out, mind you."

That intrigued me, and I found myself out at the entrance, hood up against the rain, looking at the plinth where the bust had been. There were four, two on each side of the path, of people who had put good money into the university, all men with epic beards. I walked over to Acair's father, Morogh, and gave the bust a gentle push. There was no movement. It was firmly in place, which meant whoever knocked Acair off his perch had hit him with real force. This was no pushover. The bust at head height, held in place with wires firmly enough to stop the Challaid wind blowing it over.

I found Ben Gauld in one of the common rooms, watching his pals playing snooker and looking grumpy. He was sitting alone, so I gave him some company. He gave me an unwelcoming look, and I

noticed the plaster on the side of his hand and bruises on his face. He was the sort of leader who could inspire great passion in a very small number of people. No one would build a statue of him, or name a ship after him, but someone might take it upon themselves to engrave his name on a small plaque and screw it to a university bench without permission.

"Terrible business that," I said, nodding to the hand.

"It was."

"You can't have expected that to happen."

"I didn't."

"You getting hurt, I mean. When you jumped Watson you must have thought it would be clear and easy. You knew the cameras were down, had all day to find that out. You go and play the match and then you go drinking. Watson was probably all over the place on the way back, easy enough for you to drop behind without him noticing. You jump him and go for the ankle and hands because that's what he needs to play, and then you try to run. Turned and sprinted right into poor old Acair Duff, didn't you? It was him that roughed you up from beyond the grave."

He stared at me, and his friends had stopped playing to listen, standing with snooker cues in their hands, but I must say I wasn't scared. There were other people in the common room that had nothing to do with them, and being a Ross means picking fights with people who deserve it.

"Why did you do it?" I asked him.

"Ben?" one of the snooker players said. That was what did it, me putting the pieces into order for one of his friends who hadn't realized what he had done.

"We've been in that team three years. Three fucking years. Every time we win a bloody game it's him at the bar, the hero, getting the pats on the back and the drinks. Does he do it alone? He's hogging it all for himself and he's only just in the door. He hasn't earned any of it."

So that was it, one of my first investigations. It never came out

publicly that Gauld was behind the attack, but he never played for the university again, claiming a hand injury. Watson made it back, but by then the season was a washout, and Challaid University would have to keep waiting for the drought to end. A month later Watson stopped me in a corridor and took me aside to whisper a thank-you. He was a polite kid, not the sort who wanted trouble, and I think he was struggling to find his place at the university. I believe he knew who attacked him that night, and he was glad someone else had proved it for him.

24

"THIS ISN'T going to be worth our valuable time."

Darian was sitting in the passenger seat of Sholto's Fiat. He said, "You don't think?"

"Nah, no chance."

Sholto enjoyed speaking as a master to his apprentice, letting Darian know he'd done this all before. It was an act of basic kindness to let him ramble on about it, even though Darian already knew why the boss was right.

Darian asked, "Why not? He's Uisdean's friend, he was with him on the night. If anyone saw something it's bound to be the friend."

"Well, first of all, that beating the boy took, whatever it was for, it was a setup. They knew he was in the club and they tiptoed up behind him when he came out. The friend didn't go with him down the alley, so he wouldn't have seen the attacker because the attacker would have made sure he didn't. Place as busy as that and no one saw him? This person knows how to play the game. Second of all, Uisdean doesn't want us to know what really happened, so there's a good chance this reliable pal he's willing to name will have his lips sewn shut as well. They'll look out for each other."

"So why bother at all?"

"Passes the time, and Kotkell's paying by the hour."

It wasn't just their own time they were passing, it was Darian's sister Cat's as well. Leandro Oriol lived in the halls of residence at the university in the south end of Cnocaid, in the same large building she stayed in. They were sticklers for security, so Darian and Sholto

needed someone with a pass to get them in. He had called Cat and asked if she could help. She had said yes, but only if she got to sit in on the interview, because seeing them at work promised to be entertaining and maybe even educational.

She was waiting for them at the main doors. The building was old, finished in 1762, and came with a high, arched entrance and doors thick enough to make an invading army pause for thought.

Darian smiled when he saw her, walked over and gave his sister a hug. "Good to see you, Cat."

She was always the little sister to him and Sorley, with her thick, red hair, wide smile, pale, freckled skin and slight frame they thought she needed all the protection they could give. That was complete nonsense, of course, and especially so by the time they arrived at the door of the university halls. She was twenty, already planning to be a journalist, and knew her way around the worries of the world without the need of a guiding hand.

Sholto smiled, shook her hand firmly and said, "Catriona, it's lovely to see you. Goodness me, you have your mother's look if ever I saw it."

A lot of people who had known their mother said the same, and Cat never quite knew how to react to reminders of her. Death chips a small corner from you, leaves you a different shape than you were before, a less complete person.

Darian knew any mention of their parents would make things awkward so he said, "Thanks for helping us with this, Cat."

"I'm just getting you in and watching the show, it's no big deal."

She led them through the hall and across to the side. The security didn't really kick in until you left the main hall and tried to go down one of the corridors to the rooms. That was where you needed a swipe card to enter, which was where Cat came in handy. She held the door open for them and led them along the wide corridor and round to room seventeen. She had checked the register to find out what room Oriol had.

She said, “Here we go. These are some of the better rooms; you usually have to be pretty well connected to land one down this end.”

Sholto knocked and the three of them waited. The door opened and a middle-aged woman looked back at them. Cat didn’t recognize her so she wasn’t a lecturer or member of staff, and it was a fair bet she was a parent. She didn’t look surprised. She was tall and blonde, bright red lipstick against pale skin, and she looked at them with the irritated expression Darian and Sholto were used to.

Sholto said, “Hello, love, my name’s Sholto Douglas, this is my colleague Darian Ross, and Catriona Ross. We’re from Douglas Independent Research and we’re needing to speak with Leandro Oriol. Is he at home?”

“What is this about?”

“Don’t worry now; he’s not in any bother at all. A friend of his was knocked about like a crisp packet in a tornado and we were hoping young Leandro might be able to tell us one or two things about the stormy night in question.”

She frowned more deeply still and said, “You’d better come in.”

She stood at the door and the three of them walked past her. It was obvious they were expected, and that, whoever she was, she was there to deal with them. The rooms were bigger and better than Cat’s, basically a small flat with large windows and nice views of the side gardens. Cat was two floors up in tiny rooms she shared with two other people and several patches of damp that had lived there a lot longer than them.

The room she led them into was the kind of living room that every student wanted but very few could afford. Gadgets galore, gaming consoles and a bookcase full of games, VR headsets and framed movie posters on the walls. There was a cabinet that had an assortment of bottles in it, many of them still full, which meant it must have been restocked often. They weren’t cheap bottles either. On the couch, which had remarkably few stains and no visible rips in it, sat an eighteen- or nineteen-year-old boy. He was darker than

the woman, but there was a resemblance there. Where she had the pasty look of a local, the boy's father was presumably Caledonian. Leandro was chubby and he needed a haircut because the long style he was aiming at wasn't working for him. He had a double chin, a fuzzy attempt at facial hair and small glasses, and he was wearing the sort of jeans and hoodie combination that looked like a sarcastic impression of a working-class kid.

Sholto looked at the drinks cabinet and said, "Hoo, I could get half-drunk on a year's salary on that lot, eh?"

Leandro didn't smile and the woman just frowned again. She said, "Mm. My name's Kellina Oriol, this is my son Leandro. I'm a lawyer, so if you don't mind I'll be sitting in on this interview."

Sholto said, "Oh. Good. We're not police, just so you know."

"I already do know. You're a private investigator pretending to be something else, I've checked. So go ahead and ask your questions."

She sat on the couch next to her son and Sholto and Darian sat on the second couch in the room, Sholto slumping back and saying, "*Ohh, ohh*."

There was a spare dining chair against the wall by the door, presumably for when their gaming sessions got crowded, so Cat pulled that beside the second couch and sat on it.

Sholto said, "You don't mind if we take the weight off, do you, Leandro? No point wearing out our feet while our brains are working."

He half nodded and then looked at his mother to see if he was giving the right answer. It was too late; bums had already hit the seats.

Sholto pushed on. "Now, Leandro, seeing as Uisdean's already been in touch to tell you we were coming you can crack on and tell us what happened the other night outside Himinn and we can get out of your mother's lovely hair."

"I don't know what happened; I didn't see any of it. I didn't know it had happened until this morning."

Leandro had a deep voice that sounded like it was coming from

somewhere else, and his tone said he didn't like having to use it in this company.

Sholto said, "Oh, we know that, but walk me through the things you do know. You weren't so blootered you can't remember, were you?"

Kellina Oriol tutted and Leandro said, "No, I remember. We went out for a few drinks, stopped in at Himinn and stayed for, I don't know, a couple of hours. We left at the same time, but I went up the street because I was going to stay at my parents' house, so I went up toward Ciad Station. I think he was coming back here so he went down the street to use the alley to get across to the taxi rank on Cala Street."

All said in the clipped tone of an over-rehearsed performer scared of mistakes. Sholto nodded cheerfully along and said, "That was it? There was no one at the club trying to turn the dancing into something more physical, or even just keeping an eyeball on you?"

"I don't think so."

"A nightclub in Challaid and there was no one there looking for a rumble? That seems unlikely."

"Nobody approached us, or spoke to us. We had no trouble at all."

"Uh-huh, uh-huh. And what sort of mood was Uisdean in?"

"Mood? He was fine, normal."

"Good, right. So when you left the club I suppose there would have been some people out on Malairt Street, always busy out there in the festive hours. Did you notice anyone on their own, anyone taking an interest in you?"

"I didn't see anyone I can remember recognizing. There were a few folk there, but just ordinary groups of people."

"So Uisdean, a good enough looking lad, money burning a hole in all his pockets, probably a wee heartbreaker, am I right? Got a tidy wee girl or three on the go, maybe picked one of them up from another lad who didn't want to let go, something like that?"

"No. That's not Uisdean. I don't think he has a girlfriend. I don't know."

"You don't know? You're his mate."

"I don't think he does."

His mother said, "Really, Mr. Douglas, they're young men in college together, they're not Siamese twins."

"I think they prefer to be called conjoined. So, Leandro, you probably don't know him well enough to know of anyone who might have it in for him."

"No."

"No. The big N O. Nothing else springs to mind, nothing that might help us find out who tried to use your not-as-good-a-pal-as-we-thought-he-was as a *piñata*?"

"No."

Sholto glanced at Darian and they both stood up, so Cat did the same. She had come to see Darian at work but it was Sholto who had made an impression on her. He had always seemed so bumbling, her father's former colleague who had become a byword for sloth. The way he handled that interview, and the lawyer present, was far more impressive than she'd expected. If you wound him up, like Leandro's mother had, he still had some life left in him to spit out. This was the moment Cat realized her brother was in good hands.

Sholto said, "We won't take up any more of your expensive time, Mrs. Oriol. Or yours, Leandro. This card here has my office number on it, just in case a flash of memory hits you and you need to get in touch about it."

Cat led them back out and through the hall to the cavernous entrance. Darian said, "Well, that card will be in the bin by now."

"Aye, and I bet the bin cost more than Mrs. Douglas's weekly shop. Imagine a student having all that gear. A student. I could have gone swimming in his carpet. Did you feel it? The kind of people that go on skiing holidays and sail boats around the Mediterranean with no cargo to deliver, they are. Closest I've gotten to a foreign holiday in the last five years was chasing a debt dodger down to Carlisle."

Cat said, "I'm sorry it didn't work out."

Darian said, "It wasn't worthless. Leandro's obviously holding

back, he knows something about what happened to Uisdean. His friend and his mother both told him what to say and he picked the best-sounding answers from their short list of options."

Sholto said, "Aye, a couple of well-brought-up liars, that pair. That's the thing about posh people, the rest of us tend to think they stick to the law better, don't duck under it for a quick buck, but they're actually worse because they think they deserve to get away with it."

Cat said, "As long as it's keeping you busy."

"Oh aye. We caught a killer this week, did Darian tell you that?"

"No."

Darian said, "It's complicated; I'll tell you in proper detail some time."

"I look forward to it. Say hello to Sorley if you see him before me."

They parted, and Darian and Sholto walked back to Sholto's car. Darian said, "Will we hit Himinn then, see what they have to say there?"

Sholto looked at his watch. It was half-four in the afternoon. "Nah, better to leave it to tomorrow morning. We've done enough work for one day so I'll drop you back at home if you want. You take my advice, don't become a workaholic, it's one of the worst aholics you can be; it can be the end of you. Nearly happened to me."

"Did it?"

"Oh yeah, when I was your age I worked all the hours they would pay me for. You get wiser as you get older."

Darian said nothing to that, but he was thankful for the lift home. It meant he would dodge Bank Station, where Gallowglass would be waiting.

25

WHEN HE left the flat, he did so carefully. Darian had been looking into the street for hours, checking for Gallowglass and not seeing him. He went out the back, onto a large square of grass that served as the shared garden of the four L-shaped buildings that surrounded it. Every time he reached the corner to go onto a street he looked carefully first, worried about Gallowglass seeing him. He didn't take the usual route to Bank Station, or use the usual entrance on Fomorian Road, but instead used the bridge to cross the tracks and onto Sloc Street to enter from the far side of the building. He hadn't seen Gallowglass, and he'd tiptoed through the shadows with enough skill to be sure Gallowglass hadn't spotted him.

Darian took the train up to Mormaer Station and got a taxi from there. It was already after eleven, late enough to be a nuisance, so the long walk to Maeve's flat would have left him too late to be decent. The road was visible in the lamplight as the taxi pulled up, but the flats on either side of the road and the steep Dùil hill behind trapped the light between them, the tops of the buildings and the hill a collection of ominous shadows. On Sgàil Drive you could easily believe these buildings existed in a void, no world visible in the blackness beyond.

He knocked on her front door and it took a while before a response arrived. Maeve pulled the door open, looking sleepy and flustered, wearing just a T-shirt.

Darian said, "Oh, sorry, I should have called ahead first. Do you want me to go?"

"No, no, come in."

They went through to the living room and Maeve stood in the doorway. It was cold, and Darian could see her nipples press against the thin T-shirt. She walked across to the record player and picked something up from beside it. When she bent down the T-shirt rode up and, although it was only a split second, Darian had the certainty of hope that the T-shirt really was all she had on. Maeve walked across with a small notepad and passed it to him.

She said, "You look through that while I put some clothes on. I didn't expect to have to look respectable at this hour."

"Sorry about that. I don't always keep sociable hours."

"Well, these hours can be very sociable with a little warning."

She went to her bedroom to change and he opened the notebook. It was mostly a list of names and numbers, a couple of addresses and a few phone numbers. It was people she knew had worked with Moses and there were educated guesses at the amounts of money he had handled for them. It was mostly small numbers, and there were a few names of committedly mediocre criminals Darian recognized and immediately dismissed.

"You need to keep in mind that he didn't handle big sums of money very often, not the size that a person would kill for."

Darian looked up at Maeve. She had pulled on a pair of trousers and a raggedy jumper over the T-shirt that had seen many better days.

Darian said, "People have killed for tiny amounts of money before. Or for no money where they thought some would be. Or a lot of small amounts added together. Could the money he was handling have added up to the eighteen and a half grand Cummins paid his debt with?"

"It could, but he would have had to get his timing just right. Rare for Moses to have that sort of money in the flat, as far as I know. And if he had, Cummins wouldn't have known. I don't think any of his clients would have known and I don't think any of them would have killed him for it."

"Do you know them well enough to be sure?"

"No, but I knew Moses and I know the only people he handled small accounts for were people he knew and trusted, people he'd known his whole life, and the people with big accounts wouldn't need to kill him for the cash."

"So what exactly did he do for them?"

Maeve sat and said, "He would hide the money they shouldn't have had in the first place. It wasn't always in cash; it depended on who it was and how they were receiving it in the first place. If it was cash it would be in the flat, but not for long. If the person who killed him knew he had a lot of money then they must have known that it had either just been delivered or was about to be collected, so they could have found out from the previous or next link in the chain. He would put the money into businesses and they would put it into their books. It was like investing money, that's what he used to say, sometimes more or less would come back than had gone in but what came back was always clean, and it now had a backstory to protect it after traveling through the business world."

"So he must have had a bunch of businesses helping him?"

"Of course, but I have no idea who they were. Say what you want about Moses but he respected the privacy of the people he was breaking the law with."

"If we could identify the businesses or the high-value clients then we might find our killer. One of them might have decided Moses was too well informed."

The lights in the flat flickered and cut out for a few seconds before they came back on. Maeve said, "Ignore that, it happens a lot. The electricity cuts out a lot under the hill, they say they're going to fix it but…"

"Okay, so, his clients."

"I think the most likely candidates will be one of the people near the top of that list, the ones I know he handled decent money for."

Darian looked at the names, some he recognized and some he didn't. A couple of known criminals and a few businessmen of notable standing that Darian hadn't known were dirty but really

should have guessed. Neither of the criminals he'd heard of had been identified as working at a level where people died on their orders.

He said, "Do you know which of them worked with him most recently?"

"No, he didn't give information like that away, I wasn't even supposed to know this much and he didn't realize I did. I overheard whispered conversations, caught a glimpse of receipts he was reading by hovering over his shoulder in passing."

"We need to be very careful with this. The sort of people we're dealing with won't take kindly to being questioned about the killing of a man they knew, and I don't just mean the criminal types either."

"Please, just because some of them dress up in nice suits and sit in expensive offices in Bank or Cnocaid doesn't make them less criminal."

"You're right, I know, and those people will go a long way to protect the image they've built. Lawyers, to start with, and they're dangerous enough, but there could be more after. If one of these people did kill Moses then we have to consider that they might be prepared to silence anyone who shows the inclination to catch them."

"I know the risk, but I'm going to give chase anyway. I can't just move on from Moses being murdered, not until I'm sure the person who did it is in jail. It would be an insult to him, and I cared too much about him to let that insult pass. And you, Mr. not quite a private detective, you wouldn't let an innocent man rot in jail for this, would you?"

"No."

"So I need to do something. I'll pick the lowest-risk person on that list and have a chat with them, see what falls out when I lean on them."

"Okay, how about this. You pick someone on that list that didn't give him huge money and knew him well, you see if you can find out from them who else he was working with lately. The bigger a picture we can build the better a chance we have."

"I can do that, a casual chat with an old pal."

"Good, because right now we don't want anyone else knowing what we're up to, so don't interrogate anyone. Try to get the little things, details that often seem irrelevant but can provide a small answer to a big question. And keep your eyes open, because Corey isn't going to like either of us working an investigation he's twice decided the book is closed on. He's had one of his pets, a guy called Gallowglass, following me for the last couple of days and I think it's because of this."

"Well, I didn't tell anyone what I'm doing."

"I'm not saying you did. I'm just saying, be wary, because if Corey's coming after us he will eventually catch up, and we have to have the truth to defend ourselves with when he does."

There was a pause for a few seconds before Maeve said, "Gallowglass, that's not a common name. Is he the one who used to be a detective?"

"He is. Do you know him?"

"Know of him. He used to move in some grubby circles, back when he thought he could get away with it. A girl I knew went out with him just long enough to know she needed to run a mile. When she ran, I picked her up from his house. I can show you where it is, if you'd like. We can take my car."

He so enjoyed being with her, both because she was beautiful and because they were going to catch a killer together. He couldn't decide which reason thrilled him more. They left the flat together as the lights on the street flickered again.

LIGHT PLAYS ON THE SEA

The lighthouse keeper stood outside the door, wrapped up warm in his thick coat, bonnet pulled tight on his head. The wind was loud but he knew its tune and he could hear what lay underneath it. The cracks, the splintering, and the shouts. He was a man of experience, he had heard those sounds before, and he knew what his responsibility was now.

The lighthouse keeper lived alone in the tall building, in his lighthouse north of Heilam. It showed the way for sailors coming into the sea loch, going to the port of Challaid. He was so close to the city, but he couldn't go to it, his job demanding absolute commitment. For months he would sit alone and wonder if any in the world knew his name, if they spoke of him or thought of him. A name unspoken was not a name, a man unmentioned was nobody. His work made it possible for so many to safely arrive at and leave the city, but all of those people thought nothing of the one who helped them. Sometimes he was angry to think of it, but on other days it was to his benefit.

The weather had been poor all day, a fog that was swept away by strong wind and heavy rain. There had been few boats coming into the loch. In the night he sat by the window and looked out to sea, watching the light of a boat rocking back and forth, rising and falling, moving slowly toward the lighthouse. The lighthouse keeper watched for a time as it got closer, able to identify the boat as a large cutter, making a run for shelter. The lighthouse keeper could see what was going to happen, knew the water and the weather, knew the rocks and knew the wrong light that shone.

Now he stood outside the door to the lighthouse and listened to the noises underneath the wind. There was the sound of the wood breaking on rocks, of a mast cracking and falling into the water. The song of a boat breaking apart in the sea was one the lighthouse keeper had orchestrated often enough to know well. The cutter would be mostly underwater, none of its crew on board. They would be in

the cold water, the swell pulling them under or pushing them onto the rocks. The sea always claimed its share.

He had the musket tucked under his arm as he walked carefully to the edge of the cliff and picked his path down toward the small shingle beach. The lamp was still shining on the post by the cliff edge where he had placed it, a lying substitute for the lighthouse light. He knew the cliff and the beach; he knew every path and climbing route that could be used in this area. While a stranger would struggle to find their way up in good weather, there was no danger for him going down in the storm.

His boots crunched across the shingle as he made his way to the rough water's edge. The lighthouse keeper hadn't heard a human shout for some minutes, but he heard one now. As the cold water rolled as far as the toe of his boot, the lighthouse keeper made out the figure of a man trying to stand, desperately crawling in the water as he made his way for shore. The man saw the lighthouse keeper, struggled forward until the water reached only his knees. He stumbled the last few feet and landed heavily beside the lighthouse keeper, looking up at him. "I am the only one," he said in shaking gasps. "The sea took the rest. It is only me." The lighthouse keeper smiled, aimed the musket and shot the man in the head.

Over the following two hours the lighthouse keeper carefully moved all valuables that washed ashore to the small basement of the lighthouse. It was a good haul, interesting items he would examine carefully over the rest of the week. He took two hours and stopped, even knowing there were some boxes left on the beach. He switched off the lamp and put the lighthouse light back on. Enough time had passed for people to miss the cutter, so he began the long walk down to the north of Challaid to raise the alarm. The little-known lighthouse keeper, doing his sad duty.

26

IT WAS an excuse to spend time with Maeve, nothing more than that. There was no benefit to Darian in seeing what hole Gallowglass slithered into of an evening; it was something he could have uncovered for himself if he'd cared. Doing it alone would have meant doing it without Maeve. The two of them together in a small, battered old car, trundling north through Whisper Hill. The heater was on but it seemed to be blowing cold air, and Maeve kept looking at the needle to check how much petrol she had.

She said "We won't run out...I don't think."

They drove in the shadows of the hills until they reached Drummond Street at the north tip of the city and turned onto Heilam Road going north out of Challaid. They were leaving the bright lights of what could generously be called civilization behind and going off into the moors toward the mouth of the loch. The day will come when the city sprawl will reach up there, too, you can be sure of that, but so far the landscape has held it back. There's only a narrow passage between the steep hills and the loch at the very top of Whisper Hill, and the road north out of the city almost filled it. That stopped anyone developing up there, because everything had the ominous, or comforting if you like that sort of thing, sense of being cut off.

There was a dark gap through the moor before you saw the few lights of Heilam. It wasn't much to look at, a council estate in the open that was supposed to be the first step in developing the area and turning Heilam into the seventh region of Challaid. Another of

the council's grand plans that went awry, started by one party with big dreams and a big budget and ended by the next. The houses, all white roughcast, had gone up in the early seventies when Labor led the council, the expansion stopped when the Democratic Party took over and was talked about without effect now that the Liberal Party was in power. It was probably only because they were out of sight and out of mind that these houses hadn't been pulled down.

Late at night was the best time to visit Heilam. With the moon on the loch lighting the view out to sea, and with the hills rising darkly on the other side, the brooding graveyard behind you, you could almost believe it was beautiful. It was the sort of scene in which a songwriter would set their folk tale of heartbreak. It was the smudge of old council houses in the middle of it all that spoiled the picture. Remember that we're talking about a village whose biggest selling point was the large number of bodies buried on its outskirts. You could make a sturdy argument that the dead had better accommodation than the living. The only building of any age was the old lighthouse at the north end of Heilam and no one lived there anymore.

Maeve said, "It was along here somewhere."

She turned onto a short street with houses in blocks of two on either side of the road. They all had small front gardens and they all looked cold, huddled together against the weather on the moor like lost sheep. Maeve stopped the car across the street.

She nodded across at two houses and said, "It was either one of those two. My friend texted and told me to come and get her from here, she was standing outside that gate when I arrived. From what she told me, Gallowglass is hooked on madness. He was always looking for trouble and creating some if there was none around. Maybe he's calmed down now he doesn't have the police shield to hide behind, but he doesn't seem like the sort who would. He'll keep pushing his luck until life pushes back."

"If the protection of the force let him run wild then he still has Corey looking after him now."

They sat and watched in darkness. After half an hour a car pulled up and stopped, a little too close for comfort. Gallowglass got out of the driver's seat and went into his house, not bothering to look around as he went. From where they sat he looked very ordinary. Mediocrity, when wrapped in the right kind of skin, can travel a long way before anyone thinks to challenge it. He slammed his front door shut with a bang that would wake the neighbors.

Maeve said, "Looks like someone didn't find what they were looking for in the great city tonight."

"It's nice to be missed. Come on; let's get out of here, bad enough he's following me without him thinking to get on your tail as well."

Maeve started the car and drove Darian back south. They chatted as she drove, a journey shorter than Darian would have liked. He hadn't had a girlfriend for a while, too wrapped up in being a pretend private detective to have a relationship, and Maeve was reminding him how pleasant the sensation could be. Not because she was beautiful or sexy, although she was both, but because she was someone to talk and laugh with, to share time with away from work. She dropped him outside Three O'clock Station and he took the train home.

27

MALAIRT STREET early in the morning is not the same as Malairt Street late at night. At night it's filled with middle-class students and an array of careful fun-seekers. The main party area in the city used to be over on the edge of Bakers Moor, a little closer to the working-class east side. Over the last twenty years or so party central has drifted west toward Cnocaid, where a safe night out can be had amid gentrified surroundings. During the day it was populated by quiet shoppers, and, on this morning, Darian and Sholto.

They were outside Himinn, Darian leading the way because Sholto was old enough to call a nightclub a discotheque and would rather have spent his morning in the McDonald's next door. The doors to the club were open, but the interior was silent. They walked along the hall, ignoring the doors that led to the balcony stairs, and went into a small bar area tucked away from the main floor.

It was a gloomy little nook in which a heavily bearded man was kneeling beside the bar, cleaning the rail that ran along the front of it. The place seemed to be a slapdash approximation of the sort of pubs your grandfather might have drunk in. Darian could smell the brass polish and there was a box of rags and bottles of cleaning products on top of the bar. The whole place had a genteel air about it, which none of the Challaid pubs of your grandfather's generation suffered from.

The man with the beard looked up at them and said, "You cops?"

Darian said, "No, we're not."

"Huh. So what do you want?"

"You in charge round here?"

"Maurice Gomez, bar manager for the time being. What do you want?"

"We want to ask you about an assault that happened in the alley at the side of the building a few nights ago. Uisdean Kotkell, was drinking here, went out, got taken apart. You hear about that?"

"Yeah, I heard about it."

"And?"

"And nothing. I heard about it when it happened, but it was peaceful in here that night, like it is every other night. We don't have trouble here."

"Well, that's super to hear but what do you know about the young man who was attacked?"

Gomez looked at them both and said, "You two ain't cops?"

"No."

"So I don't have to talk to you at all?"

"No."

"Good."

Gomez went back to his cleaning, ignoring Darian and Sholto. Darian glanced at his colleague, sensing he had lost his chance to make a connection so now it was Sholto's time to shine in the last-chance saloon.

Sholto said, "We're working for the victim's family, so you'd be doing them a favor. We can make it worth your while."

"No, you can't."

Sholto looked at Darian and shrugged. They had tried to find what they could here, but it was a poor use of time to chip away at a brick wall. Darian hated to walk, especially when there was nowhere else to go. They left the nook and walked past the arches that led into the club proper, that place in darkness. On their way through the entrance hall they saw a young man coming down the stairs.

Darian said, "Ally, you working here now?"

Alfonso Bosco saw who was talking to him and his expression collapsed into that of a man who can hear a favor being called in.

Nearly a year before, Darian had helped Ally out of a little jam when a former friend scammed a lot of angry people out of their money, laid a misleading trail to Ally's door and skipped town. Ally wasn't a man you crossed and stuck around. He was a bouncer of formidable renown, partly due to the eyepatch he wore. He had lost his right eye in a knife fight when he was nineteen and could have worn a glass eye with no discomfort, but he liked to be looked at. He was six-three and had a long goatee beard he tied in a ponytail with colorful bands, so he was tough to miss.

Ally said, "Aye, I do."

"So you'll know what was going on with Uisdean Kotkell when he was whomped round the back the other night."

Ally puffed out his cheeks and said, "Come on next door and you can buy me breakfast. I talk better with a burger in each hand."

The three of them sat in a booth away from the front windows of the McDonald's next to the club and Ally did his talking in a full-mouthed near-whisper between bites.

"That kid was at the club quite a lot, him and his posh mates. There's a bunch of them, little rich kids, I dunno. They drink somewhere else before they get to the club, I think they go on to their own little parties afterward. Richer stuff than I've ever been to. It wasn't anything that happened in our club, I know that, we'd have spotted something. I told the cop that came to ask about it. MacDuff."

"What was he asking about?"

"Nothing specific. Pissed off Gomez with a couple of questions, that's all it ever takes with that grumpy sod. Then he asked me and a couple of other staff who were working that night about it, general stuff, did we see him that night, did we see anyone looking for him? We had nothing to tell. The thing I didn't tell him, and I'll tell you because it's you, is about that boy's ex."

"Oh."

"Yeah. There was a while there when the Kotkell boy was coming in here with Dillan Howard. Now, Howard, he's got a short fuse and likes playing with matches. The story I heard was that they had

a big falling out, went their separate ways. Howard ain't the sort to shrug it off if he thinks he's been badly treated."

As Sholto had the expression of a man watching an alien invasion unfold, it was Darian who said, "You know where we could find Howard?"

"Pretty sure he lives up in Earmam somewhere, but I don't know where exactly."

"That's a good start, cheers, Ally."

If Sholto hadn't been there Darian would have slipped Ally some cash and added it to the client's bill, but Sholto objected to that sort of thing. Keep the bills as low as possible or the client goes elsewhere, like Raven Investigators with their detailed expenses and special offers. It was a shame, because the bouncer at a club where young rich kids partied was a worthy contact. Darian would catch Ally up later and slip him a twenty, seal him as an ongoing contact. Darian and Sholto walked out of the burger joint and down the street to where Sholto had parked the Fiat.

He said, "Bloody hell."

Darian said, "What?"

"The father didn't mention the boy was gay."

"So?"

"So what if the father doesn't know? He's not going to want to find out from one of my skillfully written reports, is he? I knew this case was bad news. Any case with young people is awkward because young people are terrible at life, keeping open secrets."

"We can find Howard, talk to him."

"Aye, and hope the whole bloody thing doesn't blow up in our faces."

The city of Challaid still has corners where Presbyterianism and Old Testament morals are extolled by influential people, like the Sutherland family who employed Kotkell, which made Sholto nervous. Any complication stood like a mountain before him, while the map in front of Darian showed a path to a possible solution.

28

THERE ARE a few streets in Earmam shabbier than Mòine Road, but the list is short. The whole area had once been dominated by factories, built in the nineteenth century and spewing out dirt nonstop until the post-war period. Then they became useless and unnecessary and were mostly pulled down to make way for cheap housing, like the flats Dillan Howard lived in. A few streets away, closer to the loch side, there were old factory buildings that had been converted and actually looked rather good, classic buildings allowed to age. These post-war shortcuts were ugly, and even the reasonable effort the occupants made to keep the area neat made no dent in the unsightliness.

It had taken them two hours to find Dillan Howard's address. Sholto parked the car across the road from the entrance to the flats, set back from the road. The council had laid some grass down where the floors of the sprawling factories would once have been. All sorts of stuff had been handled there back in the day: tobacco, whale oil, textiles and anything else the city could lay its grasping hands on.

Darian looked at Sholto and said, "You want me to handle this one?"

"No, no, I can do it. Better I do, try to make sure none of this gets back to Kotkell. A Sutherland executive getting upset with us. Can you imagine what that'll do for business?"

They got out of the car and went across the road to Howard's flat. It was on the ground floor, and Sholto knocked. The door was opened by a young man, tall and handsome, dark brown hair, and

not nearly as unhinged looking as Ally had led them to expect. He had light stubble over the sort of face you could tell would age well, only early twenties now.

The man nodded and said, "Yes?"

Sholto said "Dillan Howard?"

"That's me unless you're trouble or wanting money."

"My name's Sholto Douglas, this is my colleague Darian Ross, we work for an investigations company and we're looking into an assault in the city three nights ago. Could we chat?"

Sholto asked as though he hoped to be refused, but Howard was happy to disappoint him and held the door open. He led them through to a sparse kitchen where they sat at a small, round table. There wasn't much of anything to look at in the kitchen. It was small, with a window looking out at the side of the building next door, and a gap where a washing machine would go.

Dillan said, "Would you like a cup of tea or something?"

They both said, "No thanks."

"What's this about? Private investigation, so you're not cops?"

Sholto said, "No, we're not, so you don't have to answer anything if you don't want to. We're here about Uisdean Kotkell. You'll have heard he was beaten up outside Himinn the other night?"

"I heard."

"And what do you think about that?"

"What do I...? I think it's very sad, that's what I think. I was going to go and see him in the hospital today but I heard he's out, back home with his parents. It was a shame what happened to him, he's a good guy."

"And do you happen to know anything about why this great shame happened to this good guy?"

Dillan leaned back in his chair, his face getting harder and taking on the look of a man hanging onto the end of his short fuse. He said, "How would I know anything about it?"

"Well, what do you think happened to him?"

"I suppose he must have got jumped, someone got pissed and

wanted to be a hardman, or thought they could mug him and make a bit of money. No shortage of young men getting pissed and violent in this city. Surely your investigations have taught you that?"

"So you and him didn't have a big falling out, he didn't dump you? You weren't the one who got pissed and violent, waiting for him outside the club so you could give him a little bit of relationship counseling?"

Howard was smiling dismissively. He looked almost childish when he did. He said, "Do you think I got in a fight with him, or do you just wish I did so you could pin it on me, get an easy bad guy to point the finger at? That would make it nice and easy for you, go back to Uisdean's father with my head on a pike, because that's who you're working for, isn't it? Private investigation. The police would never be good enough for him; he would always want special treatment for his family and he could pay any price for it. He's a dangerous man, Uisdean's father. All that power. I hope you realize what his reaction would be if you tell him something he doesn't like."

"I can't tell you who we're working for."

Dillan laughed at the stiff delivery. "Oh, you are playing with fire if you're playing with that man."

This was going round in a circle so Darian interrupted and said, "Were you and Uisdean in a relationship?"

"A relationship? No. I've known him about a year, we partied together a bit, had some fun, but there was nothing more than that. Neither of us could have dumped the other. If you want a scapegoat you'll have to go look in another field."

"Do you know anyone who might have had it in for Uisdean?"

"He isn't the sort of guy that goes round making enemies. He's not flash, not a troublemaker, so don't try to blame what happened on him. Some drunk, I don't know, a random attack. I'm sure you'll find a way of wrapping it up without catching anyone and without embarrassing his father."

Sholto, with surprising force, said, "We will not wrap it up, we will not. A crime has been committed and we will investigate it fully."

There was a slightly stunned silence for a few seconds before Darian hurdled over it, saying, "You hadn't heard anything about someone threatening him, maybe trying to get money off him?"

"No, the only person Uisdean ever complained about was his father and by the time he was done whinging about him there was no time left for anyone else."

"All right, we'll leave it there."

They left the building and went back to the car. Sholto looked annoyed by a spiked dead end, no solution but a reminder of the danger that upsetting Durell Kotkell posed. He slammed the car door shut behind him. Darian gave him a look.

"Waste of bloody time, and he didn't need to get that chippy either, as if we're the bad guys."

He was flushed, looked unsure of himself. For Darian it brought back the memory of Corey in their office, telling them they were hiding there, that Sholto didn't have the guts for real police work and its dangers. He'd lost one verbal battle that didn't matter a damn and he was losing the rag about it. Maybe Corey had a point.

Darian said, "So what now?"

"We'll try to get the boy on his own, without the father or mother there. He's the last person left who knows more than he's told us."

They drove back to the office.

DOUGLAS INDEPENDENT RESEARCH

Douglas Independent Research
21 Cage Street
Challaid CH3 4QA
Tel: (01847) 041981
Email: Sholto.Douglas@DouglasIR.sco

Dear Miss Campbell,

I'm writing to inform you of the conclusion of the investigation regarding the financial affairs of Moses Guerra. You will by now be aware that a suspect, Randle Cummins, has been arrested and charged with murder, and that my colleague and I played an active part in uncovering the suspect and securing the charge against him. Overleaf you will find a sheet detailing the work carried out by us on your behalf that led to this conclusion.

Overleaf you will also find a separate sheet detailing the expenses incurred in pursuance of this investigation. I am pleased to say that as the investigation was relatively short the cost to you is much less than previously expected. All expenses are in line with standard practice, as presented to you at the beginning of the investigation, and if you have any questions regarding them then please don't hesitate to contact the office.

While the suspect charged has not yet been convicted, and a trial is yet to occur, I wish to express my relief that we have been able to aid you in this matter. If, as expected, Mr. Cummins is convicted then it will take a very dangerous man off the street, and your determination to not let the matter rest was the cause of that. I wish you well for the future.

Yours Sincerely,
Sholto Douglas
Douglas Independent Research

INVESTIGATION INTO FINANCIAL AFFAIRS OF MOSES GUERRA

BY SHOLTO DOUGLAS, DOUGLAS INDEPENDENT RESEARCH
—FOR MISS MAEVE CAMPBELL

My colleague, Darian Ross, began the investigation at your request, starting with information provided by yourself and another contact. No contacts will be named in this report as all receive strict anonymity as a condition of their assistance.

- Darian began by questioning the waiter, Benigno Holguin, who had been in the alleyway where the victim's body was found, on the night. No new information was gained.

It was at this point that Darian and I began to work together on this case, believing it required as much manpower as we could provide.

- I learned from a separate contact that Randle Cummins had stated that he had previously been a friend of Moses Guerra and had taken a significant sum of money from his flat, with the suggestion that violence may have occurred in the process.
- We carried out research to identify the address of the suspect and made our way there to speak with him.
- We gained access to the house of the suspect and spoke with him at some length about his friendship with Moses and whether he had taken money from the flat. While he denied that he had killed Moses, he did let slip that he had owed a significant sum of money which he had been able to pay off.

At this point it was clear to us that Randle Cummins was a suspect in the murder of Moses Guerra and that the police needed to be informed. They subsequently arrested the suspect.

- As a further part of our investigation my colleague, Darian Ross, was able to confirm that Randle Cummins paid a debt in the region of £18,500, within forty-eight hours of the murder of Moses Guerra.

The suspect has now been charged with murdering Mr. Guerra, and we believe the evidence against him is convincing and our work on your behalf concluded.

DOUGLAS INDEPENDENT RESEARCH

Douglas Independent Research 21 Cage Street Challaid CH3 4QA Tel (01847) 041981	TO	Maeve Campbell 44-2 Sgàil Drive Challaid CH8 6DG

	JOB	PAYMENT TERMS	DUE DATE
	Researching finances of Moses Guerra	Due on receipt	

QTY	DESCRIPTION	UNIT PRICE	LINE TOTAL
	Travel expense – petrol		£26.52
	Travel expense – rail card		£12.00
	Telephone		£4.60
	Office expenses		£8.00
	Labour		£205.05
		TOTAL	£256.17

Quotation prepared by: Sholto Douglas

To accept this quotation, sign here and return: ______________

Thank you for your business.

29

THERE'S NO parking on Cage Street, it's pedestrianized after all, so Sholto always parked on the road at the bottom, Dlùth Street. From there it was a short walk for him and Darian to the office. They came round the corner at the bottom of Cage Street and Darian stopped. Sholto kept walking, oblivious, but Darian grabbed his sleeve.

He said, "You see that guy outside The Song? That's MacDuff."

Sholto very obviously stared at the young man who was taking the opportunity to have more of Mr. Yang's spring rolls. He looked casual, like he wasn't watching for anyone and wasn't in a hurry.

Sholto said, "Maybe he's just back for the food."

"He came a long way out of his way to get it."

They walked up the street to the building, nodding to MacDuff in passing. He looked a little sheepish, Darian thought. They went in and upstairs, Sholto putting the key in the door and finding it already unlocked. That spooked him, and he went paler. He pushed open the door and stepped in to find DI Folan Corey sitting patiently on the chair in front of Sholto's desk, playing the role of the happy visitor. He'd probably been in that office a while and he'd have had a good look round before they turned up. Darian wanted to ask where he'd got a key but Sholto didn't and it was his conversation.

He said, "Folan, good to see you, how are you, what can we do to help you, would you like a cup of tea?"

Corey ignored the barrage and looked past Sholto to Darian. He glared at him for a few seconds, and then turned back to his former colleague. Sholto had taken his usual seat behind his desk, facing

Corey over a stack of folders. The DI ignored Darian completely now, focusing on the cage he knew he could rattle.

"I'm hoping you can help me out, Sholto."

"I'll try."

"You see, I have a problem with people harassing me at my work. It started out when they targeted a vital contact of mine."

"Oh, right."

"And then they tried to get involved in a large murder inquiry, and are still hampering that inquiry despite the fact a man has been charged with the murder in question."

"Gee whiz."

"And now they're getting involved in an assault inquiry handled by my station that has nothing to do with them."

"Blimey pink."

"I'm starting to think they're trying to provoke me, maybe hoping I'll do something that gets me into a lot of trouble."

"*Muirt mhòr*."

"Are you taking the piss out of me, Sholto?"

"What? No, Folan, no. You know me, I wouldn't do that."

Corey stared at him a while, watching the nerves twitch on the jowls of the former detective. He said, "You may not be doing it knowingly, but that doesn't mean it doesn't sit on your shoulders. You have to take responsibility for the things your staff do, Sholto. The buck stops right there."

Sholto looked down at the spot on his desk Corey was pointing at, and then said, "Okay."

Corey turned slightly in the chair to look at Darian, now sitting at his own desk. Corey said, "Oh yes, I can see a lot of your father in you. Perhaps not as much as is bubbling away in your crooked big brother, but still enough to be obvious. You know, I have a theory that ninety-nine percent of people under the age of twenty-five are insufferably boring. The thing about most smart young people is not how deluded they are, because most smart people get deluded by their cleverness, but how pretentious and worthy they think they

have to be to prove it, always trying to be superior. They haven't been beaten down enough by the world to respect its power. You may actually be a one-percenter."

It was a sort of compliment, the kind you weren't sure you had received, and Corey was skilled at giving.

Darian didn't bother pointing out that they had been hired by Durell Kotkell, because Corey would have known that already. He also didn't bother pointing out that he considered Cummins innocent, because Corey would know that, too. Instead he said nothing as Corey got up from the chair and strolled over to the door he'd already made his own uninvited way in through.

Corey looked at Sholto and said, "I'm sure a skilled investigator like you will find out who's been harassing me and put a stop to it, won't you, Sholto?"

"Yes, Folan."

"It's DI Corey."

He left the office. Sholto stared back at the spot on the desk where the imaginary buck was still sitting. It was obvious he was furious with Corey, but the cop was gone and, even if he wasn't, Sholto wasn't going to aim his guns in that direction.

"You're still working with Maeve Campbell? I told you not to, we're finished with her. I posted her report and bill this morning, so that's it, we're officially done with her. Tell me you're finished with her, Darian."

Darian looked at Sholto and then looked away without saying anything.

Sholto threw up his hands and said, "Ach, I don't know why I bother trying to teach you anything, all my years of experience and you won't listen. You're like a dog staring at a seagull on a chimney pot, convinced you can jump and catch it the second it takes off, and I can't make you understand."

There were a few hours of awkward silence in that office until the security officer at Glendan called and told Sholto they would pay for two more weeks of watching the Murdoch Shipping warehouses.

The promise of more easy money cheered Sholto up no end, and two weeks sounded like long enough to spot something that could be dressed up in the clothes of criminality. He remained convinced that it was impossible for any of those old shipping companies to be entirely clean; if Murdoch were, then they'd be the first in a thousand years.

"You go and sit and watch those warehouses. Don't get seduced by them if they show you a bit of leg, don't get led astray by their whispers, and don't go sticking your nose into Corey's business because they tell you to. Just watch them. Can you do that?"

"I'm going."

"Aye, good, and you can call up Maeve Campbell and tell her the party's over as well."

As Darian got up from his desk he said, "I'm going round to see her tonight. I'll talk to her about it then."

"Going round to... That's the problem, once you see her you're under her spell like that old witch with the snakes on her head. Just use the bloody phone so you don't have to get beguiled by her, it's what they were invented for. There's no helping you, there really isn't."

Darian left the office and headed for his usual spot in The Knarr café, watching the warehouses. He was thinking about Maeve, about Corey, and about how Sholto's attempts to educate Darian were really efforts at helping himself.

30

IT WAS dark by the time he got to Sgàil Drive, but it always seemed to be dark on Sgàil Drive. This time Maeve was ready for him, fully dressed and armed with information.

She opened the door, smiled, and said, "Come in."

He walked through to the living area and sat on the same couch he'd been on last time. He watched her walk out of the room and come back thirty seconds later with her notebook and a bottle of cheap wine clutched in one hand and two glasses in the other. She filled the glasses quickly and passed one to him. He took a sip and was careful not to wince.

"I got my bill from your boss today. You're not cheap for a day's work, you two."

"He said he sent it. He might round up the expenses now and then, but he's not a cheat, that's the going rate. I take it the report told you nothing you didn't already know."

"Not a damn thing. He wrote about it being an investigation into financial affairs and then talked about the murder without saying anything much."

"He's always careful with that. Doesn't like the client knowing too much, especially when the client is you. He told me to call you and tell you I'm finished helping you. We had Corey in the office today, warning us about this, and other things."

"Shit. Corey. So are you finished helping me?"

"I didn't call, did I?"

Maeve smiled and said, "Have you found out anything?"

"No."

"Right, so here's what I've got. The first thing I did was go and find out who the best friend of Moses from the list was. None of the big-money people, but I thought about which one he talked about most and I went to see him. I don't think now that he was that big a mate of Moses, but he was willing to speak to me. His name's Nick Palazzo. Have you heard of him?"

"Doesn't ring a bell, apart from being on the list."

"If you'd ever met him you would remember. He dresses to be seen from space and I'm pretty sure he's crazy enough to be locked up as a precaution. He'll burn the world down one day. So far his criminal life is just working for other people, so he's probably under the radar and he was just using Moses to clean up the small amounts of cash he got occasionally paid. There's no way Nick was involved, he knew nothing about it and he rabbited on for ages about Moses and how good a guy he was. Sometimes, the way he bangs on like that, I think it was sarcastic, but he was surprised by what happened, that much was true. I wrote down all the little things he said, like you suggested, but I can't see much to help us."

Maeve held up the notebook for him to see the scribbled writing across two pages. She was excited and her movements were jerky, caught up in the thrill of the chase. It made Darian smile, remembering that he had been the same way when he started out, not that long ago, Sholto always telling him to damp down the fire.

"So we can scratch Captain Crazy off the list?"

"Yeah, we can. But I had time to go to someone else on the list, Frang Hunter. Now, I know he's a proper criminal type, so you've probably heard of him."

"Yeah, I have, and he's exactly the sort of person that you shouldn't be talking to on your own. He's a violent criminal and he's sent people to Heilam for less than digging around in his financial affairs."

"Oh please, Frang was fine. You need to stop thinking that every criminal is a terrible threat to every decent person they meet, that's

naïve. And you need to stop thinking that a woman on her own can't go and have a conversation with someone without being in terrible peril. I didn't need rescuing and I didn't need you there to hold my hand. If I'd turned up with a private detective in tow then I might have needed rescuing, but so would you."

"I'm not a private detective, I'm an investigative researcher, but point taken."

Maeve smiled at his sulking tone and said, "So I went round and met him and his wife, Brenda, who was there as well, and they both told me how sad they were about what had happened to Moses. I asked Frang what he thought about the killing and he sort of clammed up, used the whole 'they've got someone for it so that must be who did it' argument. I said I wasn't sure, and Brenda, she gave him a nudge and then he admitted he wasn't sure either. The way he saw it, Cummins couldn't have killed Moses even if he'd wanted to because he didn't have the guts or the muscle. Moses wasn't big, but he could handle someone like that. And there were much better candidates that might have used Cummins and his debt as a shield. When he started talking he was going on about the kind of people who did business with Moses, how he didn't know who many of them were but some of them had to be serious. Then he said the people with the money to use Cummins as a shield, pay off his debt in exchange for him taking the spotlight for a while, weren't just the people that used Moses, they were the people that Moses used."

"Meaning?"

"The businesses that Moses cleaned the money through and the people who ran them. According to Frang, a lot of those people weren't just small-business owners looking for a quick buck on the side; some of them were major companies who want a slice of the dirty market. He thinks some might have been major companies working with criminals who use the legitimate to cover their criminal earnings, especially when it goes offshore to Caledonia and back."

"I thought of them, but, I don't know, the way it happened didn't seem professional."

"Maybe the person they sent botched it, or deliberately made it look amateurish. It makes some sense, doesn't it, that we've been pointing in the wrong direction with this? We've been looking at the people who used Moses instead the people Moses used."

"It does make sense, yeah."

Darian took another sip of wine, which reminded him how appalling it was. He looked across at Maeve and saw how excited she was by the progress they had made, her face flushed. She was looking down at her notebook with an intense expression, and then looked up at Darian.

She said, "What?"

He shook his head a little and said, "It's good to make some progress, but we have to remember that the chances of us getting where we want to go are slim. We have to find proof, real proof, that we can put in front of a judge."

"I know that, it needs to be something that can stand on its own two feet without us propping it up, but I think you and me can do it. I think you and me make a hell of an us."

"Yeah, I think we do, too."

He finished the glass of wine out of iron-stomached politeness and refused a top-up. Darian was tired; he needed some rest, so he got up to go. At the door Maeve gave him a brief hug of thanks. Her body pressed against his felt good.

31

LETTING MAEVE do all the work and take all the risks felt like a failure to Darian. That was why he was up early the following morning, taking a detour up to Earmam before he went to work. Down Caol Lane and into Sigurds to interrupt the morning of a woman he should have been sensible enough to avoid. If Maeve was meeting with dangerous people then the least he could do was match her daring commitment.

Viv was standing at the bar, in her usual spot, with no drink in front of her, which meant she must have just arrived. She was wearing tight trousers and a coat, looking tremendously respectable and refined to Darian. She looked like she was taking a drinks break halfway through the school run. He stepped up beside her and got an annoyed glance.

"I'll pay for your next one."

Viv said, "I don't pay for drinks here."

"Free drinks? Any tips on how you swing an arrangement like that?"

"What do you want?"

Darian took a look around at the pub. There wasn't another soul in there, not even the barman, although he could hear crates rattling in a backroom behind the bar. Seemed like the barman always found something to do in any other part of the building when Viv was there. Despite that, Darian kept his voice down when he spoke.

"I need to ask you a couple more questions, nothing that'll cause you any trouble."

She looked hard at him when she said, “You’re nothing but trouble.”

“Don’t be dramatic. I gave you fair warning of bad weather heading your way last time, and all I have this time are a couple of very minor questions. I want to ask you about the money Randle Cummins paid you. You said he paid it all off soon after Moses was killed.”

“I remember what I said; it’s a brain inside my skull, not a cabbage.”

“You said he paid it in full, in a oner, this guy who didn’t have a penny to his name beforehand, and he didn’t tell you anything about it? He wasn’t reading from a script when he handed it over?”

“I wouldn’t know.”

“What sort of state was he in when he delivered the cash?”

“You think I was there waiting for him, my heart aflutter?”

“Someone must have seen him.”

“No, he dropped it at the unit.”

“The unit?”

She sighed through her nose and said, “We have an industrial unit off Tobacco Road; we use it as a drop-off point.”

At that moment the barman emerged from the door behind the bar, wiping his hands on a dirty blue towel, finished with his crates and ready to serve the woman he dared not leave dry. As he moved toward the more expensive whisky bottles he nodded and said, “Morning, Viv.”

“*Thalla is cac.*”

Without any hint that he’d been offended, the barman turned quickly on his heel and disappeared back through the door.

Viv turned to Darian and said, “With a lot of people we pick the money up from them. If they’re hard to get to, or they suddenly find themselves with cash they want to be relieved of, there’s a drop point. The unit is open, there are lock boxes inside. You put the money and a message in the open box, close the box and it locks automatically. They’re welded to the floor, not that anyone’s stupid enough to steal from us.”

"So there was no one at the unit to see him deliver, and I guess no camera."

"Ha, good guess, Rebus. Of course there's no bloody camera at our drop-off point. We're trying to encourage people to use it, not chase them away. He left a note in the box with the money."

"Do you have the note?"

"Do I have the note? You think I keep notes from people like Randle Cummins? They're not love letters, scented and kept in a little shoebox, tied with a ribbon."

"What did the note say?"

Viv gave him a look and said, "You started this saying you were only going to ask me a couple of questions, we're past a couple now, in case you're innumerate. I don't remember what the note said, the same nonsense they always say. Here's your money, it's all there, the debt is repaid. They always put that last line in about the debt being cleared, as though we might not realize."

"All right, I'll leave you to your breakfast."

"If you think I'll ever repeat a word of what I've said here in front of a cop or a judge you'll be crying yourself to sleep."

"I expect nothing more of you."

Darian was halfway to the door when Viv said, "Say hello to Sorley for me, and remind him to remember what I told him."

It was the same instruction she'd left him with last time, so it meant something to her. Darian said nothing, and walked out of the bar.

THE CHALLAID GAZETTE AND ADVERTISER

07 MAR 2018

LETTERS TO THE EDITOR

THE GANNTAIR REPORT

Dear Sir,
I'm writing after reading in your paper the article *New Report Condemns Conditions in The Ganntair* (01/03/18) and being angry with the reaction to it. In your report council leader Morag Blake (Liberal Party) said that she supported the new leadership of the prison and would work with them to improve standards. Hasn't she said this before? Hasn't she said this every year for the last three?

I have experience of the prison through my family, and I know that what was in the Inspectorate Report was only the tip of the iceberg, everyone with family at the prison knows. No one wants to talk about it because no prisoner wants to become a target for the staff or for the gangs that really control the place.

The report said that use of force was high and records of it poor. That's because use of force by staff is routine and the prison leadership doesn't want it properly reported because it would show how little control they have over prisoners and how violence is the only answer they have to that lack of control. That's not so much the staff's fault, it's because there are far too few of them to begin with.

I know, and everyone who visits the prison more than once a year like the inspectors knows, that prisoners aren't safe in The Ganntair. The culture of violence is rife and the only way most prisoners can have any safety at all is to join a gang they previously had nothing to do with. Young men are going in there for offenses that had nothing to do with gang violence and they're coming out tied to gangs because it's the only way to survive. Again, the prison and its leadership know this and have done nothing to stop it.

Drugs are common in the prison, and criminal business is conducted in the open. There are men in there who would like to change their lives for the better, get rehabilitated, but they can't because the conditions make it impossible.

Convener Blake needs to stop supporting failing leadership in

the prison and start taking action. How many years will we keep seeing the same report and the same reaction from our political leaders? How bad does the situation have to get? The understaffing and completely outdated facilities mean that we will be talking about this as a tragedy before long.

I know there isn't much sympathy for families like mine, with members in The Ganntair. People are there because they broke the law and people want them to be punished, but how will anyone ever be rehabilitated when the environment they're going into is far more dangerous and criminal than the one they're being taken out of? That's the question the convener and the prison leadership have to answer.

(Name and address supplied)

THE NAME GAME

Dear Sir,

I read with some amusement your editorial (03/03/18) re the campaign underway to change the name of Bank district. Your argument appeared to be that as it has been called Bank for three centuries, and we don't know the origins of the previous Ciùin Brae name, it would be pointless to change now, but isn't that an argument to the contrary?

We know that it was called some variation of Ciùin Brae for far longer than three hundred years, and we know too why it was changed. The shift to Bank has nothing to do with the location on the south bank, every district in the city is on one or other bank of the loch, but an attempt to satisfy the industry (cont.)

32

"THROUGH HERE."

The man leading Darian wasn't in uniform, just a plain middle-aged man in a suit. He was involved in administration at the prison at a high enough level to get Darian an unrecorded meeting with a prisoner. He was a contact Darian and Sorley had worked together to cultivate, one of several in the prison they used to keep updated about their father.

He knew the prison in Earmam well, went to visit his father every month. The three kids all went on separate weeks, their attempt to make sure their father always had someone to speak to and a visit to look forward to. He was an isolated man in there, with very few people it was safe for an ex-detective to be around. He always told them he was doing fine, but they didn't expect him to tell them the truth when he was trying to protect his children from it.

The man, who we won't name because he shouldn't have been helping Darian, said, "Your father's still doing well, far as I can tell."

"Good."

"Wait here."

He had led Darian into a small office on the second floor, sparsely furnished and obviously never used. There was an empty desk with a chair on either side and a metal filing cabinet by the door with the top drawer missing and nothing in the others. There were no bars on the large window, but you'd have needed to learn to fly before you tried to jump.

Darian looked out of the window at the wing jutting out opposite

the one he was in, and then down at the yard between them. His father was in that wing somewhere, that sprawling place populated by some of the worst examples of humanity Challaid had produced in the last half-century. The female prisoners were sent down to the central belt, Cornton Vale. The minor offenders went to softer prisons, Huntly usually. The pedophiles were sent to Peterhead because they had a rehabilitation program there and any sent to The Ganntair would have had slim chance of leaving with the same number of body parts they'd possessed upon arrival. They protected the pedophiles, but they sent his father here, among men he had locked up. They had insisted, the prosecution arguing it was necessary to show that Edmund Ross wouldn't get preferential treatment because he was a former police officer. The family all saw it as an act of malice.

The door opened and a prison officer shoved Randle Cummins into the room with gleeful force. The prisoner looked over his shoulder and tutted as the door was closed, the officer on the outside, and then looked round at Darian.

"Oh, it's you."

"Yeah, it's all me. Sit down, Randle."

He did as he was told, a dirty look the extent of his protest. He was still as sallow and blotchy as before and now he was picking at a small cut high in his forehead with dirty fingernails. As he sat at the table he said, "What do you want? Come to try and throw more shite at me, have you?"

"Actually, no, I'm trying to wipe off some of the shite you're already covered in. They've charged you with murder because they know they can get a conviction. You don't have to be guilty, Randle, you just have to do a good job of looking like it, and so far it's uncanny."

"It won't get to court, I know that."

"If there wasn't enough to get you to court you would be sitting in your grim little house right now, instead of this relative luxury."

Cummins blinked heavily and said, "I know what your game is;

you're here to try and get me to say something stupid, try and trick me to make me look guilty. I'm not daft. You say you're here to help me but I got to help you first, and then you get me to say something that gets me in even worse fucking trouble."

"You've been charged with murder. How much worse do you think I can make it?"

"It won't get to court."

"I'm trying to help you here, Randle, but you have to be willing to help yourself."

"Uh-huh, here it comes, here it comes."

"I'm going to talk and you're not going to interrupt me, Randle, got that? They have charged you with murdering Moses Guerra and stealing money from his flat. Within hours of Moses being killed, someone went to the Creags' unit and paid off your debt in full, leaving a note claiming to be from you. I don't believe for one second that it was you who delivered that cash."

Cummins looked like a man whose brain was falling over its own feet trying to find an answer. There was nothing behind his eyes to help him, so he just scoffed and looked toward the window.

"Who paid your debt off for you?"

No answer.

"Someone came to you and told you to take the fall, didn't they? They'd handle your debts and make sure you were looked after in here, maybe get you out nice and early. Was that it?"

"What the hell are you talking about? You've lost it, pal."

"Someone is making a mug out of you, Randle, and they haven't had to work hard. What was it, huh? They pay off your debts and you spend a few months in here before they make sure you get released? Is that what they told you?"

"Oh, *dùin do chlab*."

"You're in here and they're out there and you still think they're going to come back for you. You've been left behind, Randle. The only way the case against you falls down is if someone knocks it over and right now I'm the only one trying. You can scream and bawl for

their help all you want but they've abandoned you. That was always part of the setup you fell for."

"You're more full of a shite than a farmer's field. I'll be out of here soon enough, it won't go before a judge."

Darian leaned back in his chair and shook his head. Sitting in a prison office, looking at an innocent man making a bad job of trying to look guilty. Whoever he had done the deal with, Cummins trusted them more than he was ever going to trust Darian. They had paid eighteen and a half grand for that privilege, and they were obviously still providing for their patsy. Cummins hadn't run up that debt on the outside paying for home improvement, and whichever addiction it had fed was probably being maintained in The Ganntair.

"I'm going to keep trying to get you out of here, because no one else will."

"Ha, you're priceless. It's your bloody fault that I'm in here at all."

Darian stood and led Cummins to the door. The man in the suit had been waiting with a prison officer out in the corridor, the latter leading Cummins back to a life at least as comfortable as it had been outside. The man in the suit led Darian back down toward the rear entrance the staff used and a long walk out toward a back gate that needed two members of staff to unlock. They'd gone to more trouble to help Darian than he thought his payments to them warranted, which made him wonder how much Sorley was doing to keep them loyal.

On the walk to the exit and the taxi ride up to Mormaer Station, Darian was trying to glue together the broken pieces of information he'd gathered. Cummins had wanted to be arrested. The drunken talk about Moses Guerra and taking money from him, the debt being paid within hours of the killing, that was choreographed to imitate guilt. And Cummins was so sure of his position. Darian got the train down to Glendan Station and went into the office for a long, slow day of boringly honest work.

33

MAEVE WAS waiting for him at her flat, looking more excited than he did when she opened the door. They went through to the living area in what was becoming routine.

As he sat Darian said, “I’ve had a couple of useful chats, although whatever direction they move us in, it isn’t forward. I do know for sure now that Cummins didn’t pay his own debt, someone paid it for him. That’s more evidence that he probably didn’t do it. I talked to him.”

“In prison?”

“Yeah, but it was off the record. I spoke to him and he didn’t speak back other than to point out that he doesn’t trust me. He was very confident that he’s going to get out, and quite soon. I don’t know if he was in on it from the start, but he’s in on something now. Someone killed Moses and then paid off the debt, maybe then they went to Cummins and told him he had no choice but to play guilty for a while.”

“He’s going to get life for someone else?”

“He doesn’t think it’ll be life, he’s certain it won’t even get to court. A few months and he’ll be back on the street, debt-free and able to return to the crumbling wreck of a life he had before.”

Maeve frowned and said, “If someone else clears his name, isn’t there a chance they implicate themselves in the process?”

“I don’t think that’s occurred to Cummins. Someone used him, got him to take a fall, and by the time he realizes they’re not going to bother getting him back out, no one will believe his accusations.

He won't know who was behind it all; Cummins will only have met a third or fourth or fifth party."

Maeve nodded and said, "Well, while you were digging those bones up, I was doing some handy work of my own. I've been writing down way more notes, the stuff that everyone has said to me about this, going right back to when the police were questioning me about it. I think it was MacDuff who mentioned Moses' paperwork, about how they hadn't found any. I shrugged it off because of course he wouldn't keep any when it was all incriminating to him and the people he was working with. But when I spoke to Frang he mentioned documents. It was just a passing comment, laughing about how complicated they were, but Moses always knew how to work it out. When the police went through the flat they didn't find anything, neither did you and your boss."

"No, we didn't, but we checked thoroughly."

"Maybe you did, but I think I know where his hiding place in the flat was. I thought it was just cash he kept in there. I was going to go check it when I knew the coast was clear."

Darian gave her a look.

"Oh, come off it, you think Moses would have preferred I left it for DI Corey to find and slip into his pocket, or for the next people who live in the flat to stumble across it and take a holiday on his efforts?"

He said, "Fine."

"No, not fine. Don't give me that look and say that as if you're judging me. That money would come to no good, but I could use it properly, the way it should be used. I can put it toward finding the person who did this. Isn't that a better use?"

Darian raised his hands to calm her. "Okay, I get that, the money would be taken away and used for no good, but you should have been honest with me. If I'd known he was hiding things in the flat me and Sholto could have found it earlier."

"I am being as honest with you as I can be. It's not that long since DI Corey was accusing me of being some deranged killer. It

could have been me instead of Cummins playing the scapegoat, only it would have been because the police round here can't be bothered looking past the first target they bump into."

She was close to tears. Darian got up and went across to the other couch and sat next to her. "That's not going to happen, not now. We're going to do all we can to find out who did this, and if the money can be used to help then I'm sure that's what Moses would have wanted."

He was speaking of a man he had never met, but Maeve didn't point that out. She looked him in the eye and put a cold hand on his cheek. "I need your help, Darian. I would do it on my own, but with your help I feel like we can do this. We're a good fit together, you and me. It works."

"It does."

There was a moment when they were half an inch apart. Maeve leaned in and their lips touched, but she moved to the side and turned it into a hug that lasted for thirty seconds. She was right, they were a good fit.

When she pulled back Darian said, "You still have your key?"

"I do."

34

MAEVE DROVE them south to Seachran Drive. They parked along from Moses' flat and sat in the car for a few minutes, watching for any sign of the charming Challaid Police Force. They had to hurry up the stairs, Maeve fishing the key out of her pocket to get them into the flat. She closed the door quietly behind them.

Maeve led the way through to the kitchen and opened the door to a shallow cupboard. There were shelves on the back wall and just enough room for a skinny person to step inside. Sholto had opened the door and glanced around when they were in the flat, but hadn't seen anything that surprised him.

Maeve said, "Hold on."

She stepped across the kitchen and pulled open a drawer, fished about among some utensils and came up with a curiously small screwdriver. She walked back over and said, "I know it was in here, and I know he used this, but I don't know exactly where or how."

It doesn't take long to find something odd when you know what odd thing you're looking for. When they moved a dustpan and brush and a small bag of tools out of the corner they saw the screws on the floorboards. The tops of them were painted with the same varnish as the wood, but you could see the scratches the screwdriver had made and could feel the dents they made in the wood with your fingers.

Darian unscrewed them and lifted the board, pulling out three envelopes from the small space underneath.

He said, "Here we go."

Maeve took them over to the kitchen table and they went through

the three of them. All the envelopes were open, some of the papers pushed in sideways or badly folded.

Maeve said, "He wouldn't have done that, no way. He was tidy with his work."

All of the papers were either letters or invoices, and the only name mentioned on any of them was Moses Guerra. The only sums of money mentioned were small and references to money he could easily have acquired legitimately. It implicated no one.

Maeve said, "This can't be right, it can't be. There's no reason why he would have this screwed down under a floorboard, there's nothing here worth hiding. There must have been something else."

She was upset and Darian knew why. She had convinced herself this was going to be a breakthrough and instead they'd found a raised middle finger.

Darian said, "Maybe he kept other things somewhere else."

"No, I don't think he had anywhere else. The person who killed him must have known about it, they must have cleared out everything that could implicate them when they killed him."

"Would he have told them about that place?"

Maeve shook her head. "I don't know...No, probably not, not unless it was forced out of him somehow, maybe when they were attacking him. Or if it was someone that was really close to him, but I can't think who that would have been. I don't know."

Darian said nothing. He took the envelopes and slipped the useless letters back into them. He wiped them with his sleeve before he put them back in their needless hiding place and screwed the single board back down and covered it again. Maeve was still sitting at the kitchen table.

Darian said, "Come on, let's go."

She drove him up toward Bakers Station so he could make his way home from there. It was busy outside the station, hard to find a parking space, and there was a lot of noise and light. Darian sensed the change in her mood. The excitement of catching a killer was waning as they stumbled closer to ugly truths and awareness of

their own limitations. The dirtier the case became, the less of a noble cause it seemed, the less of a giddy thrill.

When she stopped on a single yellow line he turned to her and said, “Will you be okay?”

“I’ll be fine. I don’t need the heroic private detective to hold me through the night, if that’s what you’re suggesting.”

She was looking at him mockingly, a hint of a smile as she got her composure back. Darian said, “I just thought you seemed rattled, that was all.”

“I was, but I’ve stopped rattling now. I just assumed it would be someone, I don’t know, distant. Now I think it might have been someone close to him and it upsets me that I don’t know who that could be. Maybe I didn’t know him as well as I thought. And I’m worried it’s going to be someone I know, and that’s a weird feeling, that I might be hunting down a friend. It doesn’t change anything, though, I’m just as determined to catch whoever did it.”

“So am I.”

Maeve touched his hand and then let go. It felt strange being so close while they talked about her murdered ex-boyfriend. It felt insulting.

“You noticed there was no cash in those envelopes either, so my chances of paying you Sholto’s going rate for this are pretty slim now.”

Darian smiled. “I’ll be generous when I put my bill together.”

He stepped out of the car and watched her drive away. Darian took the convoluted route home again, getting the train down to Bank Station and leaving by the south exit. It lengthened the walk home as a means of avoiding Gallowglass, who might not even have been there. It gave him time to walk in the cold air, trying to think about the case and the little more he had learned. His mind wasn’t playing ball. All he could think about was Maeve, the touch of her hand, the smell of her. It was unprofessional, but it made him feel happy, and sometimes that matters more.

THE CHALLAID GAZETTE AND ADVERTISER

17 FEB 2018

CONCERNS RAISED AGAIN OVER HOUSING CRISIS

In an endless echo of worries highlighted repeatedly over the last ten years, a housing charity has brought up the issue of affordable accommodation in Challaid. A recent survey has shown that rates of homelessness are continuing to rise, with the average house price in the city now exceeding £210,000, with the increase being driven by rocketing prices on the west side of the loch where average prices are now approaching £400,000.

The survey of house prices has again raised the issue of availability on the east side, with particularly acute problems in Earmam and Whisper Hill. Rates of homelessness there continue to be high, with the city council under increasing fire regarding its housing policy. With so few new properties being developed in those areas, landlords have been able to raise prices unchallenged, knowing demand vastly outstrips supply.

When we reached out to the council for a response to the survey they released a statement saying, "Challaid City Council takes seriously its obligation to improve housing availability and conditions for all residents in the city. We have already instigated a policy encouraging owners of brownfield sites to develop them for housing and this will begin to show results in the coming year. We have also made clear our determination to ensure that landlords charge fair rent for their properties, but do not accept that a rent cap will help solve a complex problem. Finally, we will soon put forward new plans to expand developments in Heilam as part of a long-term strategy for increasing housing stock and improving housing conditions in the city."

It has already been pointed out that this statement bears a striking resemblance to one released in the wake of a similar survey carried out two years ago. The problem of housing on the east side is one that has rumbled within Challaid for generations, too many people living in cramped conditions with the only people benefiting being the landlords. Solutions have repeatedly been sought but not delivered, and Fair Housing Challaid,

the charity who carried out the latest survey, has stated that it expects nothing to change. There is no will among large developers to build on land they own on the east side while there are sites on the south bank and west side that can provide far greater returns, with the marina development on the south bank a notable example.

There is another, less often mentioned, problem exacerbating the issue. With house prices going ever upward on the west side, the Barton district has become something of a super-rich ghetto, and the mere rich have been pushed further south. This has the knock-on effect of pushing up prices around the south bank, making it impossible for anyone on average incomes to think about moving off the east side. As prices continue to rise the inevitable consequence will be a creeping unaffordability, with Bakers Moor the next area to rise out of reach for most, and the crisis in Earmam and Whisper Hill will become even more acute.

35

THEY'D PARKED further down Parnassus Drive because Sholto didn't feel the Fiat was worthy of a spot in the Kotkell family driveway. From the street they could see a large garage on the opposite side of the driveway to the house, the sort of building that could hold at least three cars, and it was a fair guess the Fiat didn't belong among the company it would keep there. Not that it belonged out on the street either, mind you. Parnassus Drive is about the richest of the rich streets up in the north of Barton.

Sholto tried to comb what was left of his hair in the rearview mirror with his fingers, wanting to look presentable. He said to Darian, "I hope they don't have a dog. I get nervous around dogs and rich people."

They walked up the long drive, admiring the manicured front garden. Sholto took a guess at the gardening bill and puffed out his cheeks. He couldn't wrap his head around the money on casual display. He said, "Imagine having the money to stay here and then choosing to stay here. Give me enough dosh to buy a house round here and I'd be off somewhere sunny."

Darian pressed the doorbell and a dog started barking and a rich person opened the door. Leala Kotkell looked down on the two men her husband had hired and sighed, her small features crumpling into a frown. She said, "What do you want?"

Darian took the lead, saying, "We'd like to speak with your son, please, Mrs. Kotkell."

"My husband's not home."

"That's quite all right; it's just your son we need a chat with. He's in, I take it."

She didn't like being spoken to that way, and there was a moment when it looked like she was going to turn them away. Instead she opened the door for them. She led them through to what was presumably a study, a desk and two leather couches, no TV, book-cases against three walls and a large bay window looking out across the front garden. Leala Kotkell went to fetch her son, but not with-out a backward glance to show how reluctant she was to leave these two chancers alone with the valuables.

When she was gone Sholto, standing at the window, said, "A cop's salary was probably the best I could do with my life, but you're smart enough to have stuff like this if you'd picked a better career than working with me."

"Aye, well, I think I'd rather have the one-bedroom flat and a proper job."

"Mm, maybe you aren't as smart as I thought."

Uisdean Kotkell walked into the room by himself, still sporting a few fetching cuts and bruises that added a dash of purple to his boyish face. Darian and Sholto had both seen much worse injuries plenty of times before on people who insisted they were no big deal.

Darian said, "Uisdean, how are you?"

"I'm okay, fine. I'll be fine."

He sat on the couch opposite them and Darian and Sholto shared a quick look. Darian said, "Have you thought of any other details about what happened to you? Is there anything else you can tell us about the attack?"

"Uh, no, nothing. I told you everything I can remember at the hospital."

He seemed nervous, a young man trying to be polite but worried his good manners would invite more questions and prolong the ordeal.

Darian nodded and said, "So you haven't thought of a reason why someone might want to attack you?"

"No."

"One of the people we talked to in the course of our investigation was Dillan Howard. We suspected him for a while, but I don't think he did it, but I did wonder if maybe someone attacked you because of your relationship with him."

"I don't have a relationship with him."

"Friendship, then."

"We just hung around a bit, went to the same clubs, that's all. I don't see what that has to do with this."

"He's a bit of a lad, Dillan, from what we've heard. Maybe someone thought they could rattle him a little by rattling the hell out of you."

"That's nuts, he has loads of people closer to him than me."

"Someone was waiting for you, Uisdean, watching out for you. I don't think this was random and I think you know why it wasn't."

"No."

The door to the study opened and Leala Kotkell walked in and sat next to her son. Darian looked at Sholto and gave him the nod to take over. He was fresh out of questions and figured it was probably time to say a polite goodbye and leave this waste of time behind.

Sholto said, "What we'll probably try to do next is go public, get the word out about what happened and see if someone who was outside the club that night will come forward. It'll mean a lot of people finding out about it all, but that's what it takes sometimes."

Sholto looked at Uisdean and Uisdean looked back, silent. Sholto's expression suggested he didn't like trying to lean this hard on the kid, but it was one of the few remaining ways of tempting the truth out of him. It had no effect.

Uisdean said, "Good luck. If you'll excuse me, I have a headache."

Uisdean got up and walked out of the room. His mother stood and looked at the two of them with hatred and said, "Now that you've made my son ill perhaps you'll consider your work here done and leave."

Sholto said as he got up, "Sorry, Mrs. Kotkell, we certainly didn't

want to make the boy sick, we just want to try to resolve this as quickly as possible, for his own sake. I don't blame him for having headaches, though, it can be very traumatizing, getting beaten up and then having to go over it again afterward so carefully, so many times."

If her mood softened at the sound of an apology it was imperceptible. She led them out of the study and to the front door.

36

LEALA KOTKELL opened the front door for them and Sholto went out first. He stopped in his tracks on the top step, blocking Darian's exit. Looking over Sholto's shoulder, Darian caught a glimpse of what had caused the breakdown ahead of him. A large, sleek car was in the driveway now, its engine still running and the driver behind the wheel. The man who had been in the back was out and walking fast across to the front door, a furious look on his face, and Durell Kotkell did fury like a pro. If Leala had phoned her husband as soon as Darian and Sholto arrived, then that driver must have put Jim Clark to shame getting up from Bank in that time. Kotkell could afford the speeding fines, although how his driver found roads clear enough to speed on is an otherworldly sort of mystery.

"Why exactly are you here without informing me first?"

He stood with his hands on his hips, a hard expression that was supposed to convey rising anger and provoke the subject into trying to placate him. It probably worked on his many staff.

Before either of them could answer, Leala said, "They upset Uisdean, upset him terribly. He's had to go back to bed with another headache because of these men you hired."

There was venom in those last few words and it was directed at all three people in front of her, although the sneer in the word "men" was just for Sholto and Darian. Sholto turned and looked at Leala with a hurt expression, as though she had betrayed a confidence. He said, "We were just asking a few questions relating to our investigations, trying to do the right thing, that's all."

Durell said, “That’s all? The man who assaulted my son is still out there and the most you’ve achieved on my money is to upset my son further.”

His tone was mocking and Darian had heard enough of it. “We had a few questions for him to help us rule out things that related to what we’ve uncovered so far. We were hired to do all we could to catch the attacker, and that means asking questions, even if they’re sometimes uncomfortable.”

“Uncomfortable? What uncomfortable questions do you think you have the right to ask my son?”

Sholto said, “Well, I’m sure you don’t want to talk about this out on the doorstep.”

“I asked the question on the doorstep and you can provide me with the answer here as well.”

Given the gaps between houses on the street they would have needed a loudspeaker for the neighbors to overhear them, so Darian said, “We asked him about his relationships, whether he was still in touch with someone we had thought might have been involved in the incident, and we can now rule that out.”

“Relationships? You think if this was some strop over a boy my son wouldn’t have said? I can assure you both he is a very responsible young man; he would not be keeping it to himself if it was something as mundane as that. Bloody hell, I would expect even the halfwits in uniform at Challaid Police could have solved that little puzzle.”

Sholto breathed out a sigh of relief that Darian had to cover by talking over it. “As it happens, we agree with you. It has nothing to do with his private life. But our investigation led us in that direction and it’s right and proper that we gather all the information before we ruled it out. We need to be thorough.”

“Thorough enough to upset both my son and my wife, both of whom have been through enough of an ordeal without you piling in on top of it. I’m beginning to think I may have hired the wrong people.”

He looked at them with an expression that was designed to be

a challenge. Darian could feel his temperature rising, ready to snap back, when Sholto said, "Of course we're very sorry if you feel that way, Mr. Kotkell. We were hired to get a result, to make sure we found the person responsible, and we weren't going to hold back in doing that. I'm sorry it's arrived here."

Kotkell scoffed and said, "I should sack the pair of you, go and find someone with more good sense, which wouldn't require much of a manhunt, but I won't. You two need to buck up your ideas, start putting some proper effort into this instead of chasing easy options. I'll give you a week, and if you haven't made progress by then my reaction will be very bloody notable."

His tone made it clear it was time to get the hell off his front step and into the city to look for his son's attacker. They scuttled down the drive and along the street to where the Fiat was parked. There was another car along the road that actually looked like it was in the same price range, and presumably belonged to someone's cleaner. They got in and Sholto started driving, eager to clear out of Barton.

Darian said, "The man's an arsehole."

"Aye, but the thing about arseholes is that they can cause a terrible stink. We need to work out what the attack was all about and if it wasn't his bedroom business than we don't have a single lead."

"Why didn't he sack us? A guy like that, upset with us, thinking we've done a bad job, why didn't he sack us?"

"Bloody hell, Darian. Don't talk us out of work. You've brought us enough bad luck this week already."

Sholto kept driving, and Darian kept thinking about Kotkell and his surprising reprieve. A man who probably sacked people every day of his working life and could afford to replace them with any investigator of his choosing and yet he had kept them on. Darian thought back to the coincidence of Kotkell hiring them to investigate a case Corey's station had shrugged off.

37

DARIAN NEEDED a bit of help. For day-to-day work it was fine to take the train; he was rarely in a terrible rush and spent more time sitting stationary outside places like the Murdoch warehouses than was conducive to a healthy lifestyle. To do the job he wanted to do that night he needed a car, and that meant going to Tuit Road in Bakers Moor to visit JJ's car hire. It was a place you went when you had a sad lack of funds and didn't care what state the car was in, as long as it was basically mobile. It was a small building and patch of dirt tucked away in the gloom under the hills, and that might have been why standards authorities hadn't swooped in and shut it down yet. JJ made most of his money selling death-traps masquerading as automobiles, but he hired out to customers he knew wouldn't complain, and they included Darian. JJ was another useful contact to have.

In the yard behind the office, JJ and Darian sauntered among the cars. If you took a photo of the parking lot and said it was a wrecking yard all the evidence would suggest you were telling the truth. JJ's face was almost perfectly round and yellow, with a damp-looking, thin beard, like someone had cleared out a drain and slapped their findings on a turnip. He dressed in filthy blue overalls and he plainly didn't give a crap what his yard looked like. When he spoke it was with a heavy slur that suggested he was halfway into a long line of mini-strokes and was determined to bluster his way through them.

"This one will stay underneath you."

Darian looked at the dark blue Skoda Octavia, nearly a decade old. “How many miles has that got?”

“Eesh, round the world and back, hundred and fifty thousand. It goes, though, Darian boy, got a few thousand more left to run before I turn her into parts.”

It was what he was looking for, an ordinary-looking car that could trundle round the city without drawing the eye. It was also remarkably cheap, which put it right in his price range. JJ went back to the office to get him the keys. The car, when he opened the door, smelled overwhelmingly of sweat, and even JJ, used to ignoring the hellish stenches that floated around him, grimaced.

“Hold on, I’ll get you a wee doofer to put over the blowers.”

He got an air freshener from the office to clip over the heaters, but when Darian tried to switch them on, no air come out.

“Hold on, I’ll get you a forest of magic trees.”

So Darian left with four colorful trees hanging from the rearview mirror, a mixture of sweet smells that was only slightly better than the sweat. He drove north, through Earmam and Whisper Hill and out to Heilam with the windows open. He parked round the corner from Gallowglass’s house and waited for the former cop to make an appearance.

At twenty to eleven Gallowglass came out of his house and got into his car. He drove south into the city and Darian hung back, putting his tailing talents to the test. He wasn’t going to the station to watch for Darian, which meant that the spying mission had been terminated. Tracking suspects was one of the things Sholto was markedly better at than him, because practice made perfect and Darian didn’t have as much experience as he’d expected because following people didn’t happen too often in the world of pretend private detectives. He had decided at the start that he would rather lose him than risk getting too close. Turning the tables was fine so long as you didn’t smack into one of them.

It was a long drive, back down to the end of the loch and round into Cnocaid. They went through neighborhoods that were familiar

to Darian, near where he'd grown up. All the streets look the same round there, detached houses with small front gardens, close together so few have driveways and there are rarely available parking spaces out front. Some roads have trees lined beside the pavement; Treubh Road where Darian had grown up had cherry blossoms. There were none on Pagall Street, where Gallowglass's journey ended.

He stopped when Darian was too close to do the same without being spotted, so he drove past and caught a glimpse of the ex-cop, sitting in the car and watching a house across the street. Darian drove to the end of the road, circled round the block and came back to the top of Pagall Street, finding somewhere out of view to park. He took out his phone and zoomed in the camera function, just able to make out the back of Gallowglass's head, still in the car.

This was more the sort of work he was used to. Sitting in a smelly car watching nothing at all happen nearby. For all the skills that investigations require, patience is the most important. Darian recognized what Gallowglass was doing; it was the same tactic he had used on Cage Street when he stood outside the office, unpleasant and unmoving. He was watching the house that was directly opposite his parking space, which guaranteed that anyone inside would have a perfect view of him when they looked out of the window. This wasn't a man trying to spy on someone; he was trying to intimidate them.

Shortly after three in the morning another car drove past Darian's and stopped further up the street, just in front of Gallowglass. A man got out and leaned down to the window of Gallowglass's car, talking to him. It was DC Alasdair MacDuff. They shared a short conversation in which the man in the car did most of the talking and the man leaning down to the window looked somewhere between angry and embarrassed. MacDuff went back to his car and sat in the driver's seat while Gallowglass pulled away.

MacDuff did as Gallowglass had done before him, sat there and watched the house directly opposite, making no effort to look like anything other than a thinly veiled threat. At about twenty past

seven there was movement, and Darian was just able to see a man appearing at the front gate. He hadn't seen the door open—the angle he was parked at didn't give him a great view of the house—but MacDuff had. When the middle-aged man reached the gate, the young detective started his car and drove away. No need to stick around in daylight, with neighbors seeing him, now the message had been delivered.

Darian waited for a few minutes, until he was sure the householder had gone back inside. MacDuff had wanted to be seen but Darian didn't, not until he knew who the person he was stalking had been stalking. He drove the Skoda back to his flat and parked outside. He left a message on Sholto's work phone saying he would be late in because of some extra work he had done, not specifying exactly what because Sholto was still detective enough to guess, and he went to bed.

THE CHALLAID GAZETTE AND ADVERTISER

EAR UNITED 2 - 2 CHALLAID FC

SPFL PREMIER LEAGUE UNION PARK—ATT: 34,988

It began as expected, and for eighty minutes it looked like Challaid were heading for a typical derby tale in this lunchtime fixture. A comfortable lead, holding on until the end, leaving the home of their bitter rivals with three more points. But the last seven minutes of football turned a mediocre match into a classic, and reminded everyone of the power of the Union Park crowd.

The match began in an atmosphere of noise and hate, the small away crowd drowned out, but not for long. The warning signs for Ear were flashing as early as the eighth minute, when Casper Foster flapped madly at a corner and was fortunate to see the ball fall to Challaid center-half Havard Prek at the back post only for the Norwegian to blaze it high over. The young keeper, yet another product of the club's academy, has been in fine form this season, but this was not a game he'll remember fondly. The crowd got nervous and that translated to the pitch, where mistakes became abundant and good football was substituted for blood and thunder effort.

The breakthrough, when it came, was predictable. A run to the by-line from in-form winger Florent Albert who fizzed a cross in to the front post where Arthur Samba met it with a diving header to open the scoring. Questions can and will be asked about the defending, and a young keeper beaten at his near post, but none are being asked about Samba. The £2.8 million fee paid for the Englishman, top of the scoring charts with 27 in 31 league games, continues to look like the bargain of the season.

With the crowd quietening and Challaid dominating possession the second goal was no surprise when it came. This one was all about Samba, taking possession, beating two men and driving the ball low into the corner of the net from twenty yards. Two minutes before half-time and a team known for their stifling defense was two goals in front.

As the second half wore on the game became a classic example of the two teams' styles. Ear playing at a high tempo, crunching into tackles and picking up five

bookings, without creating a single meaningful chance. For all the buzz about the derby game, this was heading for typical disappointment for Ear, who have won only two of the last ten derbies against their richer rivals. Now the Challaid fans were making themselves heard, reveling in what looked like three more points in their championship charge.

In the eighty-third minute the game changed. Ear created their first clear chance of the game when Pataki Bozsik won the ball in the center circle and played a perfectly weighted ball through for the onrunning Feliks Brozek to slip it under the keeper and into the net. 2-1 and the crowd were back in the game, the momentum behind their side. Their screaming encouragement, wordless and loud, pushed the side forward in wave after wave of attack, the Challaid defense holding firm until the ninety-first minute. A long ball from keeper Foster, allowed to bounce by the defense, and a half-volley from much-maligned Costa Rican international striker Joel Cayasso had Ear level.

In truth, a point in an away derby is not a bad result for Challaid, and although it was the home fans that left the happier, staying to the end to a man, Ear needed the three points more. The draw moves them up to third in the table, a point ahead of Rangers, but Challaid move four points clear of Celtic at the top as they aim for back-to-back title wins.

38

IN THE afternoon he drove past the house on Pagall Street just in time to see a couple walk out and get into a car. They had scarves on, Challaid FC colors of red and white, and they were heading for the football. A big derby, big crowd. If anyone was going to follow them it would be across to the game at Union Park in Earmam, clearing the scene for Darian. He spent an hour or so at the office with Sholto, before leaving again in the afternoon.

As he was going Sholto said, "I get the impression you're working hard at things that aren't your work."

Darian tried to think of something to say that would defend him. "I'm working hard."

It was no defense at all, and he felt bad about letting Sholto down the way he was. He was abandoning the man who had given him a job for no reason other than he was his father's son to work alone while Darian chased a case with Maeve. He deserved better, and Darian's belief he was doing the right thing was zero consolation.

He parked the Skoda on the next street and walked round the corner. There was no cop or ex-cop watching the house on Pagall Street now, so he took the opportunity to jog along the side of the house and wait in the back garden, out of sight of the road.

It only took thirty minutes of standing around like a burglar with Alzheimer's before he heard a car pulling up in the driveway, two doors thudding shut as the couple got out. He heard the front door close as they went inside and counted to ten before he knocked on the back door. It might alarm them, someone knocking on the back

door when they knew their house was being watched, but he was working on the assumption they wouldn't be so scared that they wouldn't answer.

The same man who had been at the front gate hours before stood in front of Darian when the door was opened. He had a pale and featureless face, eyes and mouth barely noticeable, like someone had poked some holes in a lump of mashed potatoes with their finger. He looked concerned and a little angry.

"Yes? What do you want, hm?"

"My name's Darian Ross. I wanted to talk to you about the people who've been sitting outside your house recently."

The man's first reaction was one of shock, then a look of horror, as though he had been caught doing something he shouldn't. Then a different look, something that might have been a rush of relief. He said, "Come in, please, you need to speak to my wife."

The man led Darian through the house to the living room where a wary woman in her late forties was standing with her phone in her hand, the expression of a woman who'd pressed two nines and wanted to know if she needed to press a third. The man said, "This is my wife, Moira, it's about her."

She looked puzzled and annoyed with her husband, so Darian jumped in and said, "My name's Darian Ross, I'm working on a private investigation into Moses Guerra and it's led me here."

She was a short woman, short brown hair neatly styled, and she looked older than she probably was. Her large glasses showed the lines around her eyes, her veiny hand around the phone showed a cluster of diamonds on a gold band. If you saw her selling cakes at a church bake sale you wouldn't be the least bit surprised. Her face crumpled into resigned disappointment, a woman who had been expecting an unwelcome visit for some time but didn't quite know what shape it would take. There were two possible approaches for Darian to take with her. He could try to find out exactly what this woman knew with careful questioning or he could accept the scale of his ignorance and try to fix that fast.

Darian said, "I need to know why Gallowglass and MacDuff were outside your house last night, and that means I need to know your name, what connection you have to DI Corey, and why his people have been out there trying to scare you."

With a casual laugh she said, "Trying?"

Her husband said, "Moira."

She looked at Darian with the smile of a woman in charge, throwing the phone onto the couch and sitting next to it, crossing her legs. "All right, okay. You want every little detail, Mr. Ross, you can have them. My name is Moira Slight, born on 16 July 1965 in the King Robert VI Hospital..."

Her sarcasm grated and he said, "I don't think we have time for your whole life story."

"A dig at my age, how very ungallant. Fine, the bits you do care about then. I trained as an accountant and, not blowing my own horn here, I was rather good at it. My specialty was tax, which was every bit as thrilling as it sounds, but there's good money in it because a lot of people are intimidated by Mr. Taxman. He even scares the criminal class, but I don't suppose I need to tell you that. I've worked for a bunch of them over the years, helping them tidy up the jumble of numbers their work created. I knew who they were and what they were doing but I was careful and, as I told you, I was bloody good at my job, so there's no evidence to prove I did anything wrong and I'll never admit it in front of anyone that actually matters, no offense intended. Am I going too fast for you, dear, would you like to sit down?"

"Carry on."

A smug smile and she said, "One day DI Corey came to me, a cop who knew a lot and was able to pile plenty of pressure onto my shoulders. He came to me with money, told me it was clean and that he wanted me to handle the tax side of it, filter it offshore. Of course I knew what dirty money looked like, even if it was in the hands of a cop, but I didn't say a word. I made sure his money took a plane to Panama and snuck past the taxman in such a way that Corey

would never be associated with it and when it came back across the Atlantic I tucked some of it safely away, nice and tight, for him to collect when needed. Now he wants his money, but he wants a lot more than that, he wants a lot of the money from other criminals that he knows I can get my hands on. I don't know how he found out so much about the money I have in circulation right now, but he did and it's why he has his pet thugs outside. I know you're not here for me, Mr. Ross, because you mentioned Moses Guerra and that means you're here for Corey."

Darian had frowned through the monologue, hating every ounce of the confidence the swindler before him possessed. She had hidden any fear behind a wall dripping with sarcasm. He said, "Those men will only be outside your house for so long. If Corey wants something from you then it's only a matter of time before they make their way in."

"Don't I just know it. I had a phone call from Corey this very morning, telling me his men would be in the house tonight if I don't come up with the money he craves by five o'clock. I'm trying to work out whether to give him his own money and hope it'll stall him or take his dirty money and run like hell with it. One thing I will not do is steal other people's money for him because he's not the only scary bastard in Challaid that I can call a customer, I can assure you. I told him I wouldn't be able to get him more than what he'd given me, and that I was going to the derby today with my husband. He did at least tell me to enjoy the match, so he's not totally without manners."

"He said tonight?"

"And he meant it. Corey isn't mucking around. Not like him to grasp at cash like this. He has the terrors in him; a patient man turned desperate, whatever's gotten into him all of a sudden."

"I'll be here to find out. Someone will come here tonight and I think I know which of his men it'll be. Your husband can go, stay with a friend or family or in a hotel tonight, no need for any more people to be here flailing their arms at fight time than necessary.

You and I are going to stay and provide the welcoming party for your visitor."

"Oh, wonderful, you're really selling it, young man. I'd rather a night in a hotel, if one's on offer."

"I think we're past the point where you get to do the things you'd like."

"Ha, been that way for a long time now. Don't worry, I'm quite used to life's disappointments."

Mr. Slight left, albeit reluctantly, to go and stay in a nearby hotel. Darian and Moira settled in to wait.

"You can tell me a few stories about your criminally minded pals to pass the time."

Moira Slight smiled easily and said, "I'd need to be very drunk for my loose tongue to invite that sort of danger."

"No drink."

"Well, you are a lot of fun, aren't you?"

39

THEY SAT and they talked for a few hours. Moira liked to rattle through her sentences without ever giving away a word more than she wanted to; she was a woman with long experience of evasion. The only time she delved into any meaningful detail was when she was talking about Corey, having decided that on that subject some honesty would go a long way.

Darian asked, "You seem relaxed. Do you fear Corey?"

"Well, of course I do, I'm terrified of him. You're either very brave, very stupid or both if you're not afraid of him, Mr. Ross. I suppose we'll very soon find out which it is. I'll tell you, I may be more afraid of DI Corey than I am of any other criminal I've ever met, and I've had the pleasure of the company of many. You want to know why he scares me?"

"Go on."

"Because every other criminal in this city has to at least pretend to fear the law."

"So does Corey."

"Oh, come on now, if Corey had to fear his colleagues he wouldn't have earned a tenth of the money he has in the time I've known him. He really should be in a cell in The Ganntair along the corridor from a lot of the people he's locked up. Not that he'd last a fortnight inside, by the way, and if I know it then so will he. I've heard people in the criminal world talk about him; they all hate the man to his bones. Just because he's bent doesn't mean his fellow crooks like him. They know he can't be trusted and he's locked some of

them away for doing no more than mildly upsetting him in the past. People who thought they had his protection only for him to pull the rug away and send them falling into a cell because it suited him. I assume the fact he's still a more effective cop than the honest ones is the reason he keeps dodging responsibility for the mountain of slime he sits on."

"Shouldn't matter how good he is if he's crooked."

"Ah, but it does, in this city it really does. I don't know a lot about heady things like justice, but I know about gold. In business a person can be the biggest shit you ever met, a liar and a bully, corrupt to their blackened core, and all anyone will judge is whether that person makes a profit. That's the attitude this city was built on."

"Then maybe it's time this city changed, and that happens by taking action against people like Corey."

"Ha, that's good, oh, I needed that laugh. Good grief, you are young, aren't you? Let me tell you, as a woman with considerable experience of what a corrupt culture cultivated over a millennium looks like, it isn't ready to change. Challaid ten years from now isn't going to be radically different from Challaid ten years ago, or a hundred years ago. The cosmetics change, the faces are different and the buildings keep getting taller and shinier, but the spirit of the place has been unbendingly the same since day one. All the stuff that's deep down in the black heart of this place, that won't change because most people don't really want it to. They much prefer a profit maker to an honest man."

Darian didn't argue because he didn't want to go further down that badly lit road when only Moira had a map. She would have gone on for hours about the wicked ideals the city had been built on, but Darian didn't want to hear it. Talk of a conspiracy of corruption being ingrained in a city was defeatist.

Nerves were rising and Moira had sent a couple of reassuring texts to her husband. It was coming up to eleven o'clock when she said, "Of course I might be the biggest fool of the lot of us for believing your charmingly naive talk about being an honest young man. You

could be one of Corey's boys for all I know, sitting there pretending you're David looking for Goliath when really you're the chains that keep me in place, stop me running with the money. I'm sure a man like Corey could tempt an idealistic little squirt like you to his side, flash a few glimpses of his dirty power your way."

"You have nothing to be concerned about there."

"Well, I do hope not. You'd have to be a very sadistic young man to be stringing me along like this, but you don't have the shifty eye of the sadist."

Every so often Moira would get up and take a look out of the window to see if anyone was outside, but the inconvenient bushes in her front garden didn't give her much of a view of the road. They had the light on and the curtains open. At one point Darian sent Moira to the front step to make sure she would be seen.

"They could shoot me on the doorstep."

"I think, having talked up his evil genius for the last few hours, you can credit Corey with more subtlety than that."

Moira went out for a minute and came back in complaining of the cold and its effects on the joints of a woman her age. She hadn't seen anyone, and seemed relaxed. Darian could see that somewhere in the back of her mind was the faint hope she had wriggled off Corey's inescapable hook.

He said, "You can go upstairs, put on the bedroom light, make a show of looking out of the curtains, and then put the light off like you've gone to bed. Then come back down here."

Moira did as she was told without complaint, taking a few minutes to replicate her usual bedtime routine before jogging back downstairs, nervous about being alone up there. They sat together in the now dark living room as the clock passed midnight. They weren't waiting long.

40

MOIRA SAID, “What was that?”

There was a sound at the back door, like someone trying to force it open. Darian said, “Is it locked?”

“And bolted.”

Darian smiled. Corey’s man, or men, had thought that beating the lock would be enough to get them in and now they were forcing the door, not willing to waste any more time announcing what was supposed to be a low-key arrival. There was a loud thud from the back of the house as a large man shoulder-slammed the door. Darian left the living room and went into the corridor. He whispered to Moira, “Stay there, don’t get involved.”

“Don’t you worry.”

Darian moved along to the kitchen door and stopped without going in. He pressed himself back against the wall and waited. Someone was already inside the house, walking slowly in a belated attempt at stealth. It wasn’t one of Challaid’s intellectual giants in the kitchen then, tiptoeing around after battering down a door. Listening carefully, Darian worked out, to his relief, that it was a single stupid person.

The large figure stepped out of the kitchen and into the unlit corridor, a foot away from Darian and not knowing it. Darian recognized him even in the dark, they were so close. Gallowglass, on the prowl again.

Darian said, “You can stop there.”

Gallowglass paused, stood where he was, the cogs turning slowly.

Darian said, "This doesn't have to be trouble, but breaking and entering is a very serious offense for a man who isn't a cop anymore and you're going to have to talk your way out of it very carefully. You can tell me what you're up to, that would be a start."

Gallowglass turned slowly and looked at the silhouette talking to him. Seeing it was a single person, and smaller than him, was all the analysis he needed. Gallowglass bolted for the kitchen, trying to leave the way he had come in, only quicker. Darian leapt on the bigger man, locking him in a bear hug and pulling him backward. Gallowglass threw his head back, catching Darian on the cheek and sending a snap of pain through him. He let Gallowglass go and the former cop tried to run again, back into the kitchen. He was close to escape, but Darian was never a quitter. He lunged into the darkness, through the doorway and onto the floor, managing to reach out a hand and trip Gallowglass up. They were both on the kitchen floor now, a graceless tangle, Darian diving on top of the bigger man. They grunted and rolled around a bit, both throwing punches with no force because they had no room to pull their arms back and a fear of punching the floor. The former detective was bigger and stronger and he was getting the upper hand until a shadow moved behind them and swung something solid into the back of Gallowglass's head and he collapsed forward onto the floor beside Darian.

The light was switched on and Moira stood there, looking down at Darian and Gallowglass with shock, and said, "Well, thank God I hit the right one of you."

Darian got unsteadily to his feet and looked down at Gallowglass and the broken lamp that was now on the floor beside him. He said to Moira, "I told you to stay out of it."

"And miss a chance to clobber that bastard? Shame, though, I liked that lamp."

Gallowglass was conscious, but it was a thin thread supporting the weight of his awareness. Darian and Moira had to half drag him through to the living room and get him into one of the chairs there.

Moira put the light on and they both stood over him, waiting for him to regain whatever wits he'd had at the beginning of the evening.

When Gallowglass looked up at him with a frown Darian said, "I already asked you to tell me what you're up to."

"She assaulted me."

"You broke into her house and assaulted me. Last time, what are you here for?"

"Ask her."

"I already asked her. I want to see if your stories match."

"She's a criminal."

"I already know that, and it's not an answer to my question. Tell me what you and Corey are doing leaning on her, trying to rob money. You just hoovering up easy cash like a common crook now, that it?"

Gallowglass scoffed and looked sideways. He had no fear of Darian, no fear of the situation, and there was nothing Darian could say to change that, although he tried.

"You think Corey's going to protect you from this? You think he's all-powerful, capable of twisting every situation to fit his needs? You're very wrong. Things have changed, Gallowglass, Corey's on his way out, that's why he's chasing dirty money that doesn't belong to him. Surely you can see that he's finished and he's planning to leave you a long way behind when he goes. All that money will buy a lot of miles between him and Challaid, but I'll bet a finger it only buys a ticket for one. You'll be sitting in your house in Heilam wondering where he is, and if I'm on a roll with my gambling I'll say that your fingerprints will be on Corey's crimes, not his. You have very little chance of getting out of this mess, and I'm the little chance you have."

Gallowglass laughed at him. "You think a guy like you can lay a glove on a man like Folan Corey? Get your head out of your arse, kid, Corey's running rings around you and you don't even know it."

"You're living in the past and you don't have a future without my help."

Gallowglass looked past him to Moira and said, "You've blundered again, up to your armpits in shite. You should go call Corey right now, tell him you're sorry and that you'll do what he tells you."

Darian said, "Shut up, she's not calling Corey. You've broken in and committed an assault on me. Do you really want to have to sit in a police station and explain that? Even if Corey gets you out, it still neuters you, makes you useless to him. He can't have one of his little dancing monkeys on the police radar, he knows that. The only thing you'll be able to do for him then is be his patsy."

He ignored Darian again and said, "Go call Corey."

Darian turned to Moira and said, "Can you wait in the kitchen? I'll come and get you when we're done here."

Moira looked at Gallowglass and at Darian before she walked out of the room and left them to it. With that distraction removed, Darian felt he could make some progress. "You need to tell me everything. Tell me what Corey's had you doing for him."

"You don't need to lean over me, kid, I'll talk to you."

"Talk the truth, and all of it. I bet there are a bunch of cops who would love to charge you with something if I called them up right now."

"Oh please, you think I haven't heard every half-arsed threat under the sun? I'm the one who's usually delivering them, so don't try to scare me with that crap. You're just some wee kid who thinks he can be a superhero without the cape. Let me tell you, junior, you can only save people who want to be saved and that isn't me and it isn't most people in this shithole city. People won't take you seriously either, not with your father worse than Corey. You can't throw a punch at him."

"I can get other people to throw the punches for me, just like he does. He's got his little failed projects, the cops he took under his wing and didn't train properly, didn't protect."

"Ha, aye, very good. That your clever wee attempt to turn me against him, is it? Pretend that everything I did wrong was actually his fault, that you sympathize with me? Very good."

"So you're happy working as muscle for Corey?"

"It isn't like that, I don't just go round intimidating third-rate crooks like your new best pal Armstrong. I do all sorts of important things, for Corey, for Challaid."

"For Challaid? You don't really think this is your civic duty?"

"Take the piss all you want but you said to tell the truth and I'm telling it. I've stopped more crime since I left the police than I ever did when I was a cop, and that's not a word of a lie. Not all justice comes from authority. Not all good is done by the decent."

"Stopping more crime than you did as a cop is not a high bar given that you've always committed more than you prevented."

"Not true, son of a killer, not true. You said the truth so you got to stick to it, too. I did my fair share of heavy lifting when I was a copper; my record was worth pinning to the wall. But, see, since I've left, that's when I've been able to go after some really bad eggs, exercising crime prevention that's done more for this city than you'll do in your self-absorbed little life."

"So Corey has you operating as part of his own private police force. Does he pay you for your work, or is it all out of the goodness of your bloated heart?"

"I'm not doing charity work. I'm good, but I still got to eat."

"So he pays you by stealing large sums of money from people like Moira Slight because he thinks a crook like her can't complain."

"Nah, nah, that's not what this is. Corey isn't Robin Hood. The little I get paid he doesn't need to rob the rich for. This is something totally different."

"So tell me all the gory details."

"Well, if anyone's going to be telling gory details it'll be me."

A new voice from the doorway behind Darian. He spun round to see Corey standing there looking amused, MacDuff behind him looking like he'd rather be anywhere else in this world or the next. Darian looked down at Gallowglass again, at the smile that told him it was three against one and the circle Corey was running round him had just formed a noose.

THE CHALLAID GAZETTE AND ADVERTISER

23 JULY 1950

HERO WITH HIS OWN STREET

World heavyweight champion boxer Cliamain Craig was in Cnocaid on Friday morning for his final public appearance before his title fight against German challenger Lothar Eisenberg on Saturday night at Challaid Park stadium. He attended the unveiling of a new street name for a development near the waterfront in Cnocaid that will now be called Cliamain Craig Square. Mr. Craig was full of smiles and seemed relaxed as he pulled the curtain aside to reveal the street sign in his honor. Mr. Craig said, "I'm thrilled to receive such an honor from my home city. It means the world to me to be recognized in this way."

There had been speculation about the city council recognizing its most famous son since Mr. Craig won the world title in London almost eighteen months ago, although it had been expected that any honor would be in Whisper Hill, the area of the city Mr. Craig hails from. Nonetheless he was in fine mood ahead of what many are saying will be the biggest fight of his life, and the undefeated champion, with a record of forty-eight wins (thirty-eight by knockout), no draws and no defeats, was buoyant.

When asked about the sell-out crowd of over 60,000 for his fight on Saturday evening Mr. Craig was quick to praise the fans, saying, "I can't wait to fight in front of so many people, and in my home city. I want to thank all of the fans who have bought tickets and who plan to come along and cheer me on." Indeed, the fight will provide the largest crowd Mr. Craig has ever fought in front of, and the largest ever for a sporting event in the city that isn't football or camanachd. It's thought many of the fans will be traveling from the east of the city and people are reminded that trains will be extremely busy in the hours before and following the fight, which is scheduled to start at 8 p.m.

Mr. Craig's trainer, Mr. George Lyall, was in confident mood ahead of the fight, declaring that his fighter has never been in better shape. "We respect the German, he's a fine fighter, but Cliamain has been working hard to ensure

that he's in the best possible shape to defend his title in front of his home crowd. We're confident about the fight ahead." There was much cheer in the gathered crowd and among the dignitaries present as the towering figure of the world champion told the crowd he would knock out his opponent during the fight.

The street named in his honor is currently being developed by Glendan, and is a picturesque cul-de-sac with family housing and a small square at the end of it. It's expected that families will begin moving into the houses by September and all of the houses on Cliamain Craig Square will be occupied by the end of the year.

DISPUTE OVER DOCKING COSTS

Fears have been raised that an increase in the cost of docking ships at the south docks in Bank will lead to all docking in the future being carried out in Whisper Hill, and the end of centuries of tradition in Challaid. A spokesman for Murdoch Shipping, who own several warehouses on the Bank docks, said, "Docking charges have been rising steeply every year, but only at Bank. Ten percent increases every year are pushing companies north to the new docks, where prices have been frozen in each of the last four years." Fears have been rising since Duff Shipping began to dock all its ships in Whisper Hill two years ago.

It's thought there has been shipping of some sort using Bank for almost a thousand years, with some arguing the culture of the city is being irrevocably changed by the move—P12.

41

DARIAN STOOD and looked at the two detectives, but he didn't say a word, not until he had some idea of how hot a fire he had stepped into. Three to one were odds he couldn't beat, but he didn't yet know the price of losing. He needed to find out what had brought Corey there so damn quickly.

Gallowglass, sitting comfortably back in the chair now, said, "I told her to phone, and I bloody well knew she would."

Darian's face fell and Corey chuckled. The detective said, "Well, you're half-right, which is still half more than young Mr. Ross here. My dear friend Moira texted me much earlier and told me Darian was waiting for you with open arms. She called me again as we were heading here to tell me Mr. Ross was in the corridor and about to bop you on the head. I told her that, if she got the chance, she should intervene on your behalf."

Gallowglass rubbed his head and said, "Yeah, well, I don't think much of her aim."

"Ah, never mind, you were taking one for the team. You see, Moira was sitting here all evening in the company of the noble Mr. Ross and decided she didn't want him here anymore, but he wouldn't leave. That was when she asked me to send a friend round to remove him but when that friend entered the house, with her permission, he was attacked by Mr. Ross. A terrible set of events."

Gallowglass said, "Don't see why she had to clobber me in the process."

"A temptation too great to resist, I'm sure."

Darian said, "How you don't choke on the shit you're so full of I don't know."

Corey laughed. "Oh, Darian, Darian, no need for insults, we're all friends here. This isn't about me beating you, it's never about that, never. It's about the job, doing it properly, making sure the people of Challaid are protected from corruption in all its many forms, and making sure the bad guys are hobbled. You're young; you don't understand that the best way to do my job is not always the way it's portrayed on television by heroic but quirky detectives. I mean, you're not going to learn much working alongside Sholto Douglas, God love the man. I want tonight to be a valuable lesson for you, but here isn't the place to teach it, in another person's house. Come on, the four of us will go for a drive."

Corey stood in the doorway with an arm extended out into the corridor where Darian had thought he'd won this fight. Gallowglass got up from the chair and stood in place, making sure Darian was thoroughly surrounded. MacDuff, who hadn't spoken a word yet, led him out through the front door and down the path.

As they went through the gate Corey said, "We'll all go in my car, just for this wee trip."

Corey was enjoying himself, and the casual tone of his voice suggested he was well used to the pleasure of such victories. As MacDuff held the back door of the car open for him and he dropped in, Darian cursed both Corey and himself. It was humiliating to think of how that old crook viewed him, the daft kid grasping out for heroism he never had a chance of catching, sickening to realize that Corey didn't fear him at all.

Gallowglass sat on the back seat beside him and MacDuff drove, the city rushing past. Corey was in the passenger seat, looking back over his shoulder at Darian. He said, "So what part of my fair city are you from, Darian?"

"Cnocaid."

"Cnocaid, of course. You'll have grown up in a good neighborhood, not far from here, not far from the station where your old

man worked. I remember him, you know, I worked with him. A nice, middle-class family, comfortable. Your parents probably hoped you'd become a doctor or a lawyer, something like that. Mind you, I didn't know your mother. Maybe she was the artsy-fartsy type, hoped you'd be a playwright or a poet. Was that her type?"

Darian sat in silence, knowing there was no answer that mattered when Corey just wanted to hear the sound of his own voice.

"Oh, come on now, don't be like that, sitting there in a big huff and blanking me. You had a grand plan to bring me crashing down and I went and spoiled it for you so now you're pouting. Well, Mr. Ross, I'm afraid your plan was doomed to failure from the start, and it was doomed because of the simple fact that I am a far more honest cop than you have ever given me credit for."

They were driving north, still in Cnocaid, taking a route direct enough to suggest the driver was aiming for somewhere in particular.

Darian said, "You can lean on me all you like, it won't change anything. You can get your gullible gorilla here to knock me about, but you know you can't overreach. If you killed me there would be hell to pay."

"Kill you? Bloody hell, lad, you need to cut back on that sort of talk; it's making you sound awfully stupid, and you didn't sound blindingly bright to begin with. Nobody respects that sort of melodrama outside of a Greek play. I can put my hand on the holy bible and say that I have never killed another man, have never tried to kill another man and have never asked anyone else to kill another man. I know you want to think the very worst of me and the best of yourself, but you need to get it out of your head that I'm the devil in a Debenhams suit and that all the world's morality emanates from your good self."

Darian decided to revert back to silence. They were driving along Cliamain Craig Square, the square itself gone now, the area redeveloped and turned into a cul-de-sac of half-empty business units.

No one much remembers the life of the man it was named after, just his death and the aftermath. At this time of night there were no lights and no people. MacDuff pulled the car over to the side of the road and Corey got out. He opened Darian's door and nodded for him to follow.

Corey said, "We'll go for a wee walk."

He led Darian down between two buildings, along the damp grass, Gallowglass a short distance behind and MacDuff staying at the car. It wasn't quite a long walk in the woods, but it was designed to feel that way.

As they moved up a slope Corey said, "You think I was there to try to extort money out of Moira Slight, don't you? I bet that's what she told you, the old she-devil, and because you're so desperate to believe I'm the big bad wolf you accepted every word without question, even though questioning should be your instinct. I'm disappointed in you, very disappointed, but I suppose I shouldn't expect anything better when you're learning from your father the killer, your brother the thug and Sholto the coward. The reason I was there tonight is a reason you actually agree with me on."

"Is that right?"

They reached the top of the rise at the back of the buildings and stopped. The view looked down on the loch, the lights of the city around it and of the boats on it.

Corey said, "I love this area. It's worth reminding yourself now and again that there's beauty in this city, even if you have to go looking to find it. Now, I'm about to agree with you so you should savor the moment in picturesque surroundings. I don't believe that Randle Cummins killed Moses Guerra, I don't think the half of a wit he has left is strong enough for the job, so I continue to look for the person who did the deed, a person that will be easier to find when they think I've stopped the search. My investigations in that direction led me to the doorstep of my long-time acquaintance, Moira Slight."

"You thought Moira was involved?"

"I thought, indeed still think, that Moira may have a good idea of who was involved, even if she wasn't in the middle of it herself. I've known she was handling dodgy accounts for a while, it's why I always kept close to her, a hell of a potential informant for the anti-corruption unit, and she has proven useful several times. Now, Moira's been chatty enough in the past, throwing others overboard to protect her place on the gravy boat, but she wouldn't tell me a thing about her work with Guerra and she got downright evasive after a while. So I've been leaning on her to loosen her lips, give me a few details about Guerra's recent business activities, and then you came stumbling into the picture like a frightened rhino, armed with nothing but your righteous hatred of my good self. You've probably done me a favor, mind you, turning up and rattling her the way you did. She thinks she can handle me because she knows me, but you're new and new is dangerous. I have a better chance of getting the truth out of her now."

"Happy to have helped."

"Ah, degenerated to sarcasm now, Darian, a new low. My point is that you and I are chasing the same shadows on the Guerra killing but the difference is that I actually have a net in which to catch the person responsible. You, on the other hand, would be doing yourself a considerable favor if you stopped getting under my feet every day of the bloody week."

"A threat? What sort of low is that?"

"There you go with your exaggerating again. That was hardly a threat and pretending it was is the sort of childishness that gets a young man a reputation as unreliable. This is me generously trying to teach you, seeing as you've only been learning at the feet of failures so far in your life. You're very lucky I've taken an interest in your future, so I'm willing to impart all this wisdom."

"I feel lucky."

Corey chuckled and shook his head. He turned on the spot and said, "You can take a walk back to your car; I'm sure a young lad like yourself will enjoy the exercise on a fine night like tonight."

Corey walked away from him, Gallowglass ten yards behind, falling in beside his former boss, and they made their way back to MacDuff at the car. Darian gave them a few minutes before he started his walk. Letting them get clear, taking in the view and calming down.

42

AS HE went into the office the following morning, Sholto said to him, "I hope she was worth it."

"Eh?"

"Whoever left you looking as knackered as you do. If it wasn't some buxom beauty then you had a waste of a night."

Darian decided not to ask who the hell used the word buxom anymore and just said, "Good one."

"All my jokes are good ones, you just don't listen close enough to realize. I'll assume it was Maeve Campbell and I'll delay my lecture on the subject of that woman if you tell me you've made progress with the Murdoch case."

"The warehouses? Not unless you consider ongoing confirmation of their legality progress. There's nothing to see there, Sholto, and I'm not going to make stuff up."

"I don't expect you to make stuff up; I just don't accept that any shipping company that's ever worked out of this city hasn't been up to something. I've seen that industry and its ways before; I know they're all playing tricks to bring down their costs, thinking they can pull the wool over the eyes of the goofy landlubbers. You get down there and poke about some more, maybe see if you can get a low-paid and loose-lipped member of staff talking. Be proactive."

Darian did as he was told, heading back to the warehouses at the marina. He didn't try to make contact with a member of staff, just drank coffee and watched the old brick buildings to pass the time.

In the late afternoon he went back to the office and wrote another report that turned doing nothing into three hundred words before he took the Skoda round to Sgàil Drive.

Maeve opened the door and quickly said, "I'm glad you're here, I've..."

She stopped when she saw the look on his face. She held the door open and they went through to the living area. They sat opposite each other and Maeve looked hard at him, waiting for Darian to explain the angry and miserable expression.

He said, "I had a long night last night. I thought I was making progress, found someone that was connected to Moses and might have had knowledge about his killing, but it all fell apart in my hands. Corey showed up, took me for a drive, made a bundle of threats that he dressed up as valuable life lessons."

Maeve was silent for a few seconds. "You found someone who might know what happened to Moses?"

"I thought I did. An accountant that was involved in handling a lot of dirty money and might have been a link in the chain tied round Moses's money. I found her through Gallowglass, he was hassling this woman. I thought the connection might just have been to Corey, a chance to take a swing at the corrupt bastard, but it grew legs. Then it ran off a cliff. The accountant, she was working with Corey all along, I think. Made me look stupid, and I suppose that was the point. Gave Corey the chance to laugh in my face and warn me about sticking my nose into his business, lean on her at the same time. She said Corey's trying to force her to hand over all the dirty money she has, he said that was bullshit, but I don't know. He did say that he agrees Cummins didn't kill Moses, and that he's going to keep working the case to try to find the person he should have found long ago. That should be good news, I suppose, if I believed a word of it or trusted him to conduct an honest investigation. At this stage he's just looking for ways to shut down everyone else's questions and escape with the cash."

"You must have rattled him into action."

"Nah, if he is going to keep looking for the killer it's not because of anything I did."

"No, I mean, you're not the only one that had an unwelcome warning. I was going to tell you when you came in; I had a visit early this morning. It was before eight o'clock, I stumbled out of bed and answered the door and there was DC MacDuff, looking a whole flock of sheepish."

Darian remembered when he had turned up unexpectedly and Maeve had opened the door, wearing nothing but a T-shirt. He could understand the sheepishness. "What did he want?"

"He said he knew I had been asking questions about the police investigation and that it was hampering their ongoing efforts. Tried to make it sound like official police speak rather than a weak thug's threat. I told him I thought there were no ongoing efforts, that's why I was still asking questions. He didn't know how to answer that. I could tell he'd been sent here to speak someone else's words that his tongue isn't forked enough to handle and once he had to think for himself he was stumped. He said I should stop what I was doing because I was putting both myself and the investigation in danger, which I think was supposed to be his hardman act, but he sounded like he didn't believe it himself. Then he asked me to tell him everything I had found out about Moses' killing so far."

"Did you?"

"Of course not. I told him the reason I was asking questions myself was because I couldn't trust him with the answers in the first place. Then I told him to leave and he did, faster than a confident man should. He was just following orders, although you can still prosecute a man for that. He didn't scare me, but the phone call I got not long after he left was more effective. A man, local accent, telling me it was time to stop asking questions and hanging out with people that were going to get me into trouble. By which I think he meant you, incidentally."

"How long after MacDuff left?"

"Just long enough for him to tell this person I hadn't been as cooperative as they would have liked so needed to be leaned on by someone with a little more grunt."

"It must have been Gallowglass, must have been."

"I've never heard him before, I don't know. He sounded like he was a lot more comfortable playing the part of grand thug than MacDuff."

Darian looked at her and sighed. He was complicit in dragging this woman into something dangerous, even if her tendency was to walk toward the threat.

He said, "I'm worried about how aggressive they're getting. I think they know who killed Moses and I think they're involved in protecting that person. Corey is dangerous. If he's going to run with the money then he's desperate, and that makes him more dangerous than usual."

She got up and walked across to sit next to him. "Well, I knew that from the first conversation I had with the bastard. He carries his nastiness in the open with him. I'm not scared of him, but I'm scared you might stop helping me with this."

"I won't."

They were face to face, an inch apart. They kissed, Maeve put her hand up to his face, and they pulled apart. She hugged him tightly again and said, "I know I can trust you. Will you stay here tonight?"

They kissed again and Maeve led him through to the bedroom.

43

DARIAN WAS in no hurry to leave in the morning and Maeve was in no hurry to let him. They spent a couple of hours together that we don't need to describe in excruciating detail. Let's leave it at the fact that they were a young couple who had just kicked down the thin fence that had been holding them apart since they'd first met and they were, understandably, full of imaginative and exhausting ideas about what to do with each other.

Eventually he left because he was contractually obliged to get to work. Had to stop at a petrol station on the way to fill up the Skoda, which was more expensive than he had been hoping for and more than the car was worth. He drove home to change and shower and then went round to Cage Street. Sholto was there long before him, and didn't try to hide his annoyance.

"You know this job isn't optional."

Darian said, "I'm here, and I've been working long hours, late into the night."

"Is that what you were doing last night, working?"

"Sort of."

"Maeve Campbell?"

"Maybe."

"Well, if you're not sure either it wasn't much of a night or it was a hell of a night. We need to talk about that girl, I told you that already. We need to have a good, long, detailed, angry conversation about her, but before we do that we need to have an even longer one about Uisdean Kotkell."

"Go on."

"I was actually hoping you'd be able to start it because I have nothing. We need to make some sort of progress instead of running down more dead ends. It won't be long before Durell Kotkell is phoning in a huff wanting an update and I don't have half a sentence to say to the man."

"You could tell him to ask his son. We know Uisdean is holding something back, holding a lot back maybe, so point the finger in that direction."

"That's not what he wants to hear so it's not what I want to tell him."

They sat at their desks and they talked through everything they'd learned so far, a tactic Sholto swore by. In his mind it got them thinking of all the little details, got them talking to each other about things they'd noticed that they might not have mentioned before, the subtle hints they thought they'd picked up along the way. Darian was happy to talk about the Kotkell family rather than Maeve, so he kept the conversation going.

He said, "What I find strangest of all is the fact that he didn't sack us when we upset him. You saw how annoyed he was, didn't you?"

"I saw. I remember everyone who's ever complained about me. I need a good memory."

"It would have been easy enough for him to cancel the contract and go and hire Raven instead, but he didn't."

"Maybe he knows what a shower of piss that lot are."

"I hardly think that would bother him. He works with worse people than them every day of his life, not least himself. Maybe he didn't sack us because he thought we were doing the right thing, even if he didn't like it. Us questioning his son like that, upsetting him, it showed we were willing to do the dirty work. He liked that. But we weren't on the right track and he knew that, too. He's convinced it wasn't random otherwise he wouldn't be pushing us this hard, and he already knew it had nothing to do with Uisdean's private life."

"Are you implying that the father shares the son's habit of holding back information that would tell us what happened?"

"Why did he hire us, rather than Raven, in the first place? Raven handle contracts for Sutherland, don't they?"

Sholto tutted at the gaudy sums of money his rivals were making from that and said, "Yeah."

"So it would be the easiest thing in the world for him to go and hire them. He's probably met all their senior investigators before. Instead he came out of his way to get us."

"It might just be that he heard we're good at our work."

Darian didn't look at all convinced. "Might be, might not. Did he say who had recommended us?"

"I think he might have said it was a cop the first time he called, I don't really remember. He wasn't what you would call keen to give me details, just orders."

Darian got up and went out of the office, fishing his phone from his pocket. He stood on the stairs, sure that no one could hear him, and phoned DC Cathy Draper. Took a little while for her to answer, but she did. They hadn't spoken since they'd met at the record store to talk about Corey and the Moses investigation.

"Cathy, do you remember if you spoke to Durell Kotkell, his son got beaten up outside Himinn a wee while back?"

"Yeah, I spoke to him. I think it was the morning after it happened. He was looking to hire someone in and I suggested you and your boss instead of his usual people."

"Why?"

"He didn't want anyone that was connected to the bank, I don't think. When I mentioned you two he asked if you had any connections to Corey, and I said not good ones, you had stood up to him already and he didn't like you for it. I figured he wouldn't hire you because of that."

"Oh. Well, he did."

"Good, that's another favor you owe me."

"I'm really not sure it is, you've dropped a nightmare on our heads and we're struggling to wake up. Anyway, thanks, Cathy."

Darian went back into the office. "Kotkell hired us after hearing

we'd stood up to Corey. You know I've been digging around in the Corey stuff, right?"

Sholto nodded and grimaced at the same time, making him look like he'd swallowed a spider that was trying to crawl back out.

"Well, I know that Corey was connected to an accountant called Moira Slight and I know she was connected to Moses Guerra. What I don't know is what companies those two were using to filter money through. I think I might just have worked out the answer. We need to go round and see Kotkell."

44

DARIAN KNOCKED on the door of the posh house in Barton and the unseen dog started barking again. Sholto took a step back and then straightened his tie, wanting to look presentable for when the posh dog bit him. He said, "This is a bad idea."

Darian said, "This is the only idea we've got."

"I wish we were smarter."

The door opened and Leala Kotkell looked back at them, her face falling into an expression designed to let them know there would be zero effort on her part to play the polite host, the bridge to her good books had already been burned. She said, "What do you two want now?"

Darian said, "We'd like to speak to your husband or your son or both."

"They're not in."

"That so? Uisdean must be feeling a lot better if he's gone from stifling headaches after one conversation to out and about already. What we'll do then is we'll wait while you call one or both of them and tell them we're here. We can wait out on the street if you'd like."

If looks were weapons she could have held the world to ransom with the one she gave Darian, but he just smiled back in response. She didn't want them out on the street where the neighbors might see them so she reluctantly let them in, Sholto nodding apologetically as they went through to the same study they'd been in before.

Leala Kotkell stood in the doorway and said, “Stay there and don’t touch anything.”

Darian sat heavily but Sholto stayed standing, already sweating and looking around the room, glancing often at the doorway as if he was afraid the now silent dog might be planning to creep up on him. He said, “I bet she’s giving the dog our scent right now, telling it to chew us to pieces.”

“She might be telling her husband that, but I doubt she’s telling the dog. If she knew you were as scared of the dog as you are of the husband she might.”

“I’m not terrified of the whole dog, just its teeth.”

Darian thought, when they were quiet, that he could hear her voice from another room, trying to talk quietly but her volume rising in anger every few seconds and betraying her. He said, “She’s on the phone.”

“We shouldn’t have forced our way in like this, it’s just antagonizing them more.”

“It’s now or never.”

“And what if we’re wrong about this?”

“Then it’s never again.”

“Aye, well, the way my wee heart’s pumping away right now it might be never again for me anyway. When I started this business it was supposed to be police work without the pressure. No murderers or madmen to catch, just good old pilferers and runaways, simple follow the bread crumbs stuff. I could always do those. Maybe Corey was right about me, hiding from the serious stuff.”

“If he was right you wouldn’t be here.”

“Maybe he was right and I’m just too lazy to prove it.”

Leala had been silent for a couple of minutes and Sholto was still pacing when a figure emerged in the doorway. Uisdean Kotkell stood looking at them, not saying anything at first. Sholto sat down on the couch just as Darian stood up and said, “Come in, Uisdean, sit down. There’s just one question I want to ask you.”

Uisdean looked like he was considering the offer when they heard

Leala's voice from the other end of the long corridor, shouting to her son. "Uisdean, what are you doing?"

She appeared beside him in the doorway and Darian said, "Look who showed up. I really just need to ask him one question."

"He's not fit for it; he needs to be resting in his bed."

"That's a remarkable deterioration; a minute ago you said he was out and about."

Leala glared at Darian, but Uisdean said, "If it's just one question."

He walked across to the opposite couch and sat on it, his mother sitting beside him. Darian sat back down beside Sholto and said, "Uisdean, when Randulf Gallowglass beat you up, what message did he give you for your father?"

Leala turned her head to the side and Uisdean stared straight at Darian for a second before he said, "He told me to tell my father that it was time to do what he was told, and that if he didn't he'd come after me again."

"And you told your father this?"

Leala put up a hand. "My husband is on his way, he won't be more than another five minutes. You can ask him."

Sholto said, "Five minutes? Bloody hell, what road is he driving on?"

His attempt to inject a little humor was met by steely looks from the Kotkell family opposite and his smile crumpled. Leala bundled Uisdean out of the room, wanting to protect him from any more outbursts of honesty. He already knew more than he should about his father's work. It was four minutes later that a car stopped with a small squeak of tires outside and Durell Kotkell burst in.

"What's going on now?"

Darian stood up and said, "Why did you hire us when you don't have any desire to see the man who attacked your son being brought to justice? You don't want Gallowglass put away; you don't want Corey in the dock because you'd end up next to him."

Kotkell straightened and held eye contact with Darian. Huffily, he said, "Well, shit, you've got the wrong end of the right stick. Took

you long enough to get this far. I hired you because I knew it was Corey and I knew the police would never get off their backsides and do something about that man, no matter how much pressure I put on them. They close ranks. I do want Corey in the dock, but it'll never happen, not with that one, but I want him to know he doesn't get away scot-free. Attacking my son. My son. I wasn't letting that go unchecked, so I brought you in to put some pressure on him."

"Because he's been using you to clean dirty money."

Kotkell shook his head. "It's a hell of a lot more complicated than that. He hasn't been using me, but I run the department at the bank that handles Caledonian accounts, business accounts mostly, the majority in Panama. That bastard's dirty money goes into a clean company that then runs it through us, it looks like Panamanian money so those are the tax rules we apply. An accountant called Moira Slight was the link, she took money that had been picked up here and banked it through us under the names of clean companies. We put the last sheen of respectability on it, but we were just at the end, I don't know who was involved earlier in the chain. Hiding money is a lot harder than it used to be and a lot of the young banks run scared from it these days. When I found out it had been going through my department, well, shit, heads rolled, I'll tell you that."

Darian said, "But you don't want the police involved."

"Ha, that's a good one. You know what department handles this sort of crime? The anti-corruption unit."

Sholto looked at Darian and said, "So Moses was the first link, collecting it from the criminals. Him and Moira worked it through companies and banked it with Sutherland because they had people at the bank who wouldn't ask any questions about it."

"Which reinforces the link with Moses."

They stood looking unusually thoughtful for a few seconds before Kotkell broke the silence. "Corey has money tied up in accounts with our Caledonian branches, most of them controlled exclusively by Moira Slight. I've dug around and found them. He wants control of the accounts from Slight and he's been causing trouble to try

to get it. A good system when things were going well, he was too distant from them to ever be caught, but now he wants them and she doesn't want to let go. There's about half a million there, hardly enough for this sort of mayhem."

Darian and Sholto looked at him like he'd grown a second head and Darian said, "Your son's beating may tie in with other crimes, and I can't guarantee that we can keep your involvement out of the story."

Kotkell was fighting to keep the bank's reputation clean. Links to money laundering would blacken the name and cost him his job, and that was worth a good deal more than half a million pounds. "If you do, you will have a very valuable friend within the bank. We do a lot of investigations, and I could make sure some of that starts coming your way."

Sholto perked up but Darian didn't look impressed by the offer of money for silence.

Kotkell said, "He attacked my son. All I wanted was to force him to back off, leave my family alone. Picking a fight with me is business, but my family are not a part of that. The money my department handled for Slight, I knew nothing about it and when I found out I sacked everyone connected. It can never be proven that we knew where it had come from so it would be no good pointing the finger at us. We can make sure the bright lights of any investigations burn others instead of us. If you help me a little, I can help you a lot."

Darian said, "We'd better go; we have a lot still to do. We'll be in touch."

Sholto wasn't so enthusiastic about departing on these terms, but they left without committing to anything Kotkell wanted of them. They had what Darian needed—the truth about what had happened to Uisdean.

As they got into the car Sholto said, "Moses got killed and that sent Corey running to get his dirty money from Slight and Kotkell. That's what the Moses killing provoked, but it still doesn't tell us

who killed Moses. It's a good spot to take our next step from, though."

Darian was thinking about it as they went back to the office. Corey was the fraying thread that ran through all of this, him and his hired thug Gallowglass. There was a man capable of violence, perhaps murder. If Corey had decided he wanted his money before Moses was killed, then the link could be stronger than Sholto realized.

45

THE REST of that working day was spent putting together two separate reports on the Kotkell case. Sholto was writing one for Durell Kotkell to have, Darian was writing the other for their files. This wasn't rare. There had been plenty of cases where Douglas Independent Research sent a different message into the world than the one they kept back for their own records. Kotkell's report would be full of the things he wanted to read, it would reassure him. The one they kept in the office would be splattered with every unfortunate speck of truth.

Sholto went home and told Darian to do the same. He said, "You're having too many late nights. Don't care how entertaining they are, if you want to be able to do the job then you need to be at least half-interested and two-thirds awake. Off you go home."

Darian nodded, almost a commitment to do what he was told but no words to implicate him should Sholto find out he had done differently. He was planning on going to Sgàil Drive to see Maeve again. He walked down the stairs and out onto Cage Street, pausing as he realized he was hungry. He walked into The Northern Song to grab some food he could take round to Maeve's with him.

It was busy, and he had to wait twenty minutes for his order. Chatted with Mr. Yang for a while, then Mrs. Yang emerged from the back with his food and passed it to him. She had a rather sly smile on her face, like a woman who knew the food for two wasn't for Darian and Sholto because she'd seen Sholto go home already. She didn't, thank goodness, say anything about it, because Darian

wasn't ready to have a running conversation about a relationship that was still learning to walk.

She looked almost proud when she passed him the bag and his change and said, "Have a nice evening."

He was blushing when he left the restaurant. He walked down to the bottom of Cage Street and onto Dlùth Street where he'd parked the Skoda. The war between the air fresheners and the car's natural smell was being lost, but the food helped to paper over the cracks of defeat for a little longer. Darian had just started the engine when his phone rang.

No name, which made it a number that hadn't called him before. He answered and said, "Hello?"

"It's Vivienne Armstrong. You and I need to meet, right now. I have something to tell you."

She sounded harassed, like she wasn't keen to share what she had to say. Darian said, "You can tell me now."

"No, no phones, I don't know how safe yours is and I bet you don't either. You need to come to me, I'm not going to you because I don't trust anywhere you choose. You know the old multistory in Whisper Hill?"

"I know it."

"Go in the old main entrance and there's a blue door on the left that leads down steps to the underground level. Meet me there in half an hour or forget about it."

"I don't know what I'll have to forget about."

"Don't be stupid, of course you do. There's only one thing you've been pestering me about in the last week. It's starting to cause me a problem and you're going to help me solve it."

Vivienne hung up. Darian sat in the Skoda and thought about the call, the danger of it. Meeting Vivienne Armstrong anywhere came with risk; meeting her in the basement level of an abandoned multistory car park was something few with a brain would consider wise. Darian considered it, started the car and drove quickly north.

The building, if we can still call it that, is on Letta Road in

Whisper Hill, not too far from the Machaon Hospital. It had been four stories tall, with another parking level in the basement, and had been useful in an area with too few parking spaces. Then one of the floors had collapsed. About a year before Darian met Viv, the second-story floor had descended onto the first, injuring several people and wrecking a lot of cars. There had been fears the whole building was going to come down but it didn't. Engineers had managed to make it safe for the time being. It should have been pulled down, but there had been a long delay because of the investigation into what had caused it, and the suspicion that it wasn't as much of an accident as it had looked. That was why the owners hadn't received the insurance payout they thought they were entitled to, why everything was in limbo and why Darian could meet Vivienne in the basement without fear of being seen.

He parked across the road and watched the entrance. Viv had told him to go in through the main door at the front, which was flimsily boarded up and easily entered through. The building had no defenses worthy of the name and had become a haunt of bored children, inquisitive dogs and desperate drug addicts. He didn't want anyone but him and Viv to be there, and it wasn't the kids, the dogs or the addicts showing up he was worried about.

Darian sat in the darkness and watched for fifteen minutes. Nobody came out and only one person went in. Vivienne walked across the street and down toward the car park from the opposite direction to Darian. She wouldn't have been able to see him on a street whose lampposts were cheating a living. He gave it another couple of minutes, knowing he would be late but wanting to see if she was followed. Nobody showed. She wouldn't leave if she was anything like as desperate as she had sounded on the phone. Whatever problem she had with the Cummins money, she wasn't going to walk away from a potential solution because it showed up two minutes later than requested.

He got out of the car and locked it, for all the good that would

do if someone in Whisper Hill decided they wanted to break in. He walked slowly up Letta Road, on the other side from the car park, and took in the scene. There are high buildings on either side of the road and only a few windows on the upper floors had lights visible that night. The concrete car park was squeezed unnaturally into what had been a gap between old, red-brick buildings. In the middle of a densely packed part of the city, and with occupied flats and offices all around it, the car park seemed remarkably isolated. He crossed the road and went in behind the boarding, enough of a gap for a person to squeeze through. The place was dark, silent and cold, and the blue door stood to his left, exactly where Viv had said it would be.

THE SEA MY BROTHER DROWNED IN

Sorley opened his eyes slowly. He could feel her, asleep on his chest. He raised a hand and slowly tucked her hair back. He wanted to see her face. Asleep she looked peaceful, awake she never did. She frowned at the touch and the moment was gone. Vivienne scowled and opened her eyes, looked up at the man she was lying naked on top of.

Sorley smiled and said, "Good morning."

Viv said nothing. She lay where she was, looking down at his chest. There was no happiness in her expression, instead a look of regret. She seemed almost guilty.

"We've done nothing wrong," Sorley said quietly.

"That doesn't matter," she told him, and rolled to lie beside him.

They hadn't planned to be there. They were, technically, competitors. Sorley and his group worked at a much lower level than Viv and hers, but even small scavengers are considered an enemy of the big predators. The Creag gang had long been the biggest in Challaid, and they maintained that position by crushing anyone who tried to make money from criminality in their city. It could be argued that the Creags did more to stop crime in the city than the local police because they stomped on even the smallest possible rivals. It could also be argued the reason the government plans to have a national police force fell through was because the Challaid force refused to be a part of it to protect their own criminality, but that's not the story I'm telling here.

They had met a couple of years ago, Sorley a rising star in the criminal world. An awkward man, not filled with the same enthusiasm as his contemporaries. He was the son of a cop. He was smart and tough, but they said he had only got into the business to make money for his siblings. Once they were old enough to live for themselves, he was stuck in an industry that traps any it likes. He built his own little group around him, a tough lot, and

they worked small scams. Viv was going to destroy them like all the rest.

The Creag gang doesn't have any one leader. There's a group at the top and Viv was a part of it. She handled moneylending, which meant she was in control of a lot of cash. Not the biggest earner of the senior group, but it was a good number. Others were jealous, and she knew it. Other people wanted what she had. People in that senior group. People who worked for her. Viv was always on the lookout for trouble, from inside the Creags as well as outside. Sorley Ross was the challenge on the outside, and she wasn't aware of any trouble inside.

Not until she met Sorley. Viv didn't believe in going to war unless you had to. War is expensive. First she would try to scare the opposition off the battlefield. She sat in Sigurds pub and watched the young man sit opposite her. He had come alone, as instructed. Sorley smiled across the table at her.

"Nice to finally meet you," he said. He sounded casual, which she didn't like.

"You need to retire," she said. "Get out of the business, go travel, buy a boat, sink it, whatever. You need to stop working in the business and you need to stop living in Challaid."

He smiled at her. "I'm a little young and a little poor for retirement."

"There's more than one way to stop living in a place," she said, almost bored by her own threat, she had made it so many times. "On your terms or mine, you're going to stop."

Sorley smiled and reached into his pocket. Viv tensed and he smiled again, more broadly. "Just my phone," he said, and took it out of his pocket. He tapped the screen a couple of times and a recording began to play.

"She's going to come after you," a local accent said, a muffled voice. "She wants rid of you, I want rid of her. Easy-peasy, we work together. You get her in place and I'll take care of the rest. Get her to the multistory that fell over, down in the basement, that's a good spot."

Viv looked at the phone. She didn't want to speak because she didn't like being boxed into a corner.

"You know that was MacPherson," Sorley told her. "He came to me, I didn't go to him. He wants you out of the way because he thinks he can take your share, and he wants me to help him. Thing is, the offer he's put on the table for me to help is not one I like. I don't trust him. Once he's done with you I become his next target, I know that. So my question is, what's your offer?"

"Why would I need to make you an offer? You've already told me that MacPherson is working against me, what else can you do?"

"I can get him into the right position for you."

Someone stopped living in the city, but it wasn't Sorley. It was the young man who had worked under Viv and hated her and her family. The young man who had been in a fight with her brother and had been blamed for it just because his punch bag was related to someone senior. He watched her get rich from his efforts and he wanted what she had. His plan to kill her hinged on someone else being the lure, and Sorley was the man he wanted for the role. Instead Sorley lured MacPherson into place and the young man disappeared while Viv grew stronger than ever.

They had another meeting, a couple of nights later. She told him that the job had been a success and their deal would be honored. He would be allowed to continue to work, and the Creags would break the habit of a lifetime and avoid stamping on him. There were conditions. He declared his loyalty to the Creags so that he couldn't declare it to anyone else. Not that there was anyone else, but the Creags were always wary of outsiders coming in and getting help from people like Sorley. He wouldn't have to kick a cut up to her, though, and she would let them continue to operate so long as he didn't expand.

"You stay the size you are now and work the places you work now, nothing more," she told him.

"Deal."

They drank to it, and they drank some more. It was two in the morning when they left the bar and got into a taxi. Sorley's memory of it was blurred, but it was his flat they woke up in. Viv naked on top of him, him tucking her hair back to see her peaceful face.

She got out of bed and walked across the room to pick up her clothes. She started to dress, her face hard again. When she was finished she stood at the foot of the bed and looked down at him.

"Remember what I told you. No expansion. If I think you're building your own little gang, you will have violated our agreement and I will remove you from the city. Remember that."

She walked out of the flat.

46

DARIAN WENT through the blue door and down the dark concrete stairs to the basement. It was cold in there, and there wasn't much light. He opened the door at the bottom and stepped out into what had been the underground level of the car park. It was a square of bare concrete, flat and empty, no cars allowed in since the collapse. There was one light on, an industrial spotlight that looked like it had been left behind by the engineering team that made the place safe and must have been stealing its electricity from one of the buildings next door.

Viv stood in the circle the light made, dropping the cigarette she had been holding and crunching it under the heel of her boot.

She said, "I'm glad you came, Darian."

At the mention of his name there was movement. The blue door opened and shut behind him as a man stepped in, blocking his exit, leaning back against the door and crossing his arms. The ramp up to the ground floor was covered by the arrival of a young woman in shadow, something glinting in her hand. It looked like a screwdriver.

It wouldn't be a gun, possession of one carried a mandatory seven-year prison sentence so only morons, the desperate and the very professional dared carry. Being caught with a knife was a year in The Ganntair, not worth it when you could arm yourself with something else, like a workman's tool. You could walk down the street with a screwdriver in your pocket and the police would have to prove you weren't heading home for some DIY. It was a soon-to-be-closed loophole.

The two new arrivals both looked like a fight with Darian would be a small piece of cake to them. And there was Viv, standing facing him in the circle of light, her expression unchanged.

Darian said, "I'm not."

"No, I thought you might change your mind pretty quickly. You've been annoying more people than just me, it seems, and you were bloody annoying for me. Important people are angry with you, and do you know what happens when the VIPs get huffy?"

He looked right and then back over his shoulder. The threats around him, none of them with even a hint of reluctance. It was a question of how far they would go, whether killing a man provided any of them cause for moral concern. It didn't look awfully likely.

He said, almost in a whisper, "Bad things."

"Yeah, bad things. It's a shame, but it's a shame that you brought on yourself."

Viv stood and stared at Darian, a long ten seconds of silence before she finally took a step forward. Her people tensed, the one on the right stepped forward and closed the circle around Darian. He looked quickly left and right, searching for an escape to run to. His chance of getting out was slim, but it was no chance at all if he stood where he was.

There was movement behind the woman on his right, someone who had presumably just come down the ramp. Darian looked away, assuming it was another of Viv's people, looking to the left where he still thought his best chance of escape lay. There probably wasn't an exit there. Surely Viv would have had someone to cover it if there was, but turning this into a race was his best hope. Then he heard the voice.

"That's probably enough."

It was a familiar voice, and when Darian turned he saw a familiar face move into the edge of the light. Sorley stood and looked at the brutal people looking back at him. He didn't flinch, and didn't look to have a single drop of the nerves Darian was suffering from. The reason for his calm became clear when the other shadows around

him moved into the dim light by the bottom of the ramp. There were two of them, two young men, both as ready and willing to embrace violence as their savior as Viv's people were. The former wrestler TLM stood on one side of Sorley, both of them looking positively dwarfish beside Gorm MacGilling. Supposing the seven-footer had been the only person Sorley had brought for backup, he would have looked enough to even the odds. There would be no guns there either, but they would be tooled, and they had bulk on their side.

Viv looked at Sorley and said, "I remember when your gang was too small to stand in a fight like this."

Sorley said, "This isn't a fight yet, just a get-together that doesn't know how it'll end."

Viv turned to Darian and said, "I told you to remind your brother about the last thing I said to him."

"I haven't seen him since we last spoke."

Sorley, his voice bouncing across the large space, said, "It's a hell of a thing when me and my wee brother see more of you than we do of each other, isn't it, Viv? There's a solution, though. I'm going to need you to give me your word that you'll leave Darian alone."

Vivienne moved across the no man's land to stand in front of Sorley. Gorm flinched when she moved, waiting for someone else to start the defense before he joined in, the sort of hesitation that had marred his basketball career. Viv stood what would have been nose-to-nose with Sorley if she hadn't been five and a half inches shorter than him. In silhouette they would have looked like lovers, going for a kiss.

She said, "Why would I give you my word?"

"Because I did ignore the last thing you said to me."

"And why would you trust my word?"

"Because I'll always enjoy checking up on you."

She smiled at the idea he would be checking on her instead of the other way around. The smile disappeared and she turned her back on him, walked past Darian and over to the safety of her people. Darian had already taken a couple of short steps toward his brother,

and moved a little more quickly now. This could still turn nasty and he didn't want to be standing halfway between the two sides if it did.

Viv said, "What good timing you have, Sorley. And what wisdom your little brother has, to call you for backup. We'll see how well that wisdom serves you both."

She led her people through the blue door and up the stairs. They had come to beat someone up, not to fight. Viv wasn't going to let this turn into something she might not walk away pristine from, big fights needed planning this did not have. The woman with the screw-driver shot a dirty look in the direction of the ramp, empty hatred for people she wasn't sure why she despised. The door shut behind them and Gorm breathed out the hurricane he'd been holding in, TLM laughing nervously.

They waited a few minutes to be sure they didn't bump into Viv's lot on the way out. Wouldn't do to dodge battle in the basement only to collide with it at the exit. Sorley's two went up the ramp first to make sure it was clear and he and Darian walked slowly up behind them.

"You're gathering an interesting collection of enemies in a short space of time."

Darian said, "I didn't upset her that much."

"You're right, that wasn't about Viv, that was about someone else. My guess is you've upset someone who's leaned on Viv to try to scare you off. She's good at scaring people is Viv."

"Except she didn't want to scare me, did she? You turned up just in the nick of time and she tells her colleagues there that I called you for backup. I didn't, so I'm starting to think she did."

Sorley smiled and said, "Viv's a decent person, except for most of the time. Her letting you go doesn't give you a free ticket; you still have to be wary of her. It just means she didn't want to do the bidding of the dirty cop, that we'll call DI Corey for simplicity's sake, who sent her here in the first place. You be okay to get home in one piece?"

They were out on the street, Sorley's thugs eager to leave. Darian said, "I've got a car, I'll be fine. Thanks, Sorley."

"No bother, but, remember, I ain't the fourth emergency service so don't expect me to turn up on a rescue mission again."

Sorley and his gang walked up Letta Road to the corner and disappeared round it. As Darian walked down to the Skoda he heard the sound of a car and a motorbike starting up. His big brother, still looking out for him, and then he thought of Corey. This dark business had moved onto another level, more vicious than before, and while it felt like he'd stepped out of a trap he knew this had to be the endgame. Corey had made a desperation play, a last resort.

47

DARIAN FELT exhausted and decided to go home. He dumped the food from Mr. Yang's in the bin, but he didn't go to bed when he got back to the flat. Instead he sat at the living-room window and looked out at the lights of the city and the darkness of the loch, the lights of a single boat snaking through the water toward the southern docks. There was often a squat boat out dredging the loch in the darkness, keeping it clear for larger shipping than the first people to dock there had dreamed possible. It was a view that usually soothed him. His mind was racing and he was feeling frustrated, the overwhelming sense that the end of this investigation was close but wasn't in his grasp. Corey still had the power, so he could dictate events while Darian had to sit and wait for things to happen to him.

As he ran his finger over one of the many fissures in the table he closed his eyes and tried to line his thoughts up in a neat row. He had wanted to destroy Corey from the moment he met him, and he still believed he could. Going to Viv for help just showed how scared he was, how much he had to hide. All of this because of the Moses Guerra killing, and Corey's devotion to covering it up. The cop knew more about what had happened than anyone, and it was another secret he would have to be forced to spill.

It was a pathetic and selfish feeling and he shook his head when it ran through him, but he couldn't help resent the fact it wouldn't be him who got the credit for bringing Corey down. Whatever cop led the investigation into their colleague would get most of it; Sholto would be sure to gather up whatever crumbs were left, and Darian

and Maeve would be left with little but a pat on the head for their efforts.

Darian took a look at his watch and tried to work out where Corey would be right at that moment. Viv would have been in touch with him by now, would have told him she confronted Darian, but that Sorley and his gang showed up and forced them out of the building. Corey would hit the roof, accuse her of chickening out and blame her because his last resort was closing down. Viv would probably shrug it off, a smart enough woman to know that Corey had reached the end of his rope and might be out of her hair if she could play for time just a little longer. Hard to know what a man like Corey might do next.

Darian looked down at the street where Gallowglass had been sneaking around stalking him. Darian wanted to do something, to break the inactivity and quieten the voice telling him he needed to be out in Challaid making use of the dark hours before someone else did.

The heavy silence was chased from the flat by the shrill ring of his phone, lying on the table. He was guessing it would be Maeve, Sholto or Sorley, and wasn't expecting any of them to be calling with good news. He picked it up and looked at the screen. A number with no name was showing, someone who had never called before. That made him nervous, but he pressed green anyway.

"Hello?"

"This is finishing now, Ross, it's finishing now. I'm not letting him get what he wants, I'm going to get that bitch of a girlfriend of yours and you're all going to tell the truth about it, you understand me?"

The phone cut off. It had been the angry voice of a young man spitting with emotion. Young in that he was younger than Corey, but not as young as Darian was at the time. The sound quality had been poor, but he was sure it was Gallowglass, ranting into his phone as he drove. That had been the background noise, the drone of an engine moving fast and needing a gear change that a driver with

his phone in hand couldn't execute yet. A man barely in control of himself and his car.

The threat was to Maeve. Gallowglass was going there and he was going to get her, and his reasons made little sense in the few seconds he'd spent shouting them. Gallowglass was driving to Maeve's flat. He called Maeve, growling for her to answer as the phone rang through to voicemail. He tried again with the same result.

Darian sprinted out of the flat, the keys to the Skoda in his hand, pulling the front door shut behind him with a slam. He jumped down the stairs two at a time, almost falling down them, and ran out into the street. It was the one time he drove the Skoda and didn't notice the smell, pulling out into the middle of the road and racing east through Bank. There were still plenty of cars on the road—there are at every hour in this city because there's never a better alternative—and the city didn't race past nearly as fast as he wanted it to. It felt like the longest drive up the east side he'd ever made, despite the fact he almost lost control a couple of times when he clipped the curbs, calling her again on the phone and getting no answer. He turned onto Sgàil Drive and stopped with a screech on the street outside her flat, parking between the car he had seen Gallowglass drive when Maeve took him to see Gallowglass's house and the car in which Corey had taken him for his nocturnal chat after their unexpected encounter in Moira's house.

CONFIDENTIAL INVESTIGATION INTO CONDUCT OF DC RANDULF GALLOWGLASS, CONDUCTED BY DI ADOLPHO PUGA, BAKERS MOOR STATION

SUMMARY OF CONCLUSIONS—

- DC Gallowglass did attack [redacted] on Fair Road in Earmam, breaking his nose and a tooth and then refused to call for medical treatment before questioning him. There was insufficient evidence to suggest [redacted] was a suspect in reported crime.
- DC Gallowglass repeatedly pursued suspects in cases that were not assigned to him, interfering in areas of investigations and districts of the city where his work obstructed other officers, despite multiple warnings.
- DC Gallowglass, in at least one provable case, suppressed evidence against a suspect he considered a source of information, and in so doing prevented a charge and likely conviction being brought against that suspect.
- DC Gallowglass used his position to pursue vendettas against several individuals who had angered him, either by refusing to work as a source for him or by proving investigations of his to be wrong. These vendettas included threatening the individuals and harassing them by informing neighbors and employers that the individuals were under investigation by Challaid Police when they were not.
- DC Gallowglass did attack [redacted] in a corridor of Cnocaid police station. DC Gallowglass had gone to the cell in which [redacted] was being held and attempted to force her to talk to him without a lawyer present. He did become violent when she refused, dragging her out into the corridor and striking her twice about the head.

In the course of investigating the conduct of DC Gallowglass I have found evidence of seventy-one clear breaches of conduct and twelve criminal offenses of varying severity on his part. His colleagues have repeatedly stated that they no longer feel safe working with him, and his behavior toward fellow officers, witnesses and suspects has routinely fallen far below that expected of a serving officer. For the sake of the dignity of the force and the trust of the public, it is not conscionable that DC Gallowglass should remain a serving officer.

Further to the investigation into DC Gallowglass's conduct, I recommend that those working most closely with him, particularly his direct superior officers, be investigated. In light of the catalog of misdemeanors carried out by DC Gallowglass, it is improbable that none of his direct superiors could have been aware of his conduct. Several officers have informed my inquiry that they reported DC Gallowglass to his superiors and yet not only was no action taken, no record of the complaints was kept and the complainants were made to feel intimidated within the station.

Challaid Police continues to suffer low trust ratings among the public, and it is the actions of officers like DC Gallowglass that are to blame for this. He has been allowed to behave as though the laws he enforces do not apply to him, and not only must that culture end, Challaid Police must be seen to be the ones ending it before an external force does.

48

DARIAN COULDN'T remember if he locked the car or not as he ran into the flat, and an unlocked car in that area was a vulnerable beast. He sprinted into the building and up the stairs to Maeve's flat, running along the corridor and seeing her front door open. His heart sank; Gallowglass must be in the flat.

He stepped through the front door and saw a glut of people along the corridor in the living-room doorway. Corey was the first he saw, face red and angry, spit on his lip like he'd just been hissing at someone. He turned and saw Darian, his anger touching a new height, and he snarled at him.

"Oh, brilliant, fan-fucking-tastic, look who else is here to join the party. More stupidity to throw on the pile. There isn't one of you with an ounce of sense, not one of you."

He was trying to say it in a whisper but his rage twisted it into a hiss. Darian stepped along the corridor, getting close to the doorway so he could see what was happening inside. Corey was of little concern to him at the moment; it was Maeve he wanted to see.

She was in the living area, back toward the window, a large kitchen knife in her hand. She was pointing it at Gallowglass, the big ex-cop standing in the middle of the room, staring at her, a concentrating silence. This looked like a standoff that had been going on a while, Gallowglass uncertain about going for Maeve when she had the knife and Maeve unwilling to push past him to the door because she didn't want to have to get blood on the blade. All the while Corey was in the doorway, sniping at the pair of them.

"Come on, Randulf, get out of there. You've lost the plot."

Gallowglass didn't take his eyes off Maeve as he said quietly, "You're going to arrest her, gaffer, you're going to take her in and charge her. It ain't going to be me. I'm not taking the fall for this. No way. No way."

Corey looked quickly at Darian and then back into the room, talking fast and quiet as though Darian might not hear him. "I don't know where you got that into your thick ugly head but you're not taking the fall for anything. Nothing. Now get out here."

Darian could see Gallowglass shaking his head. "No, you're stitching me up. I should have known it from the start. Get rid of me. The pair of you are stitching me up. You hearing this, Ross? Your girlfriend and the cop, stitching me up from the beginning."

He was shouting the last sentence. He knew Darian was there and he wanted him to serve as a witness. That was the point of the phone call, to bring him here to bear witness to the ending. Darian couldn't affect it, couldn't change what had started without him, but he would be made to see the truth. That seemed to matter a lot to Gallowglass.

Maeve spoke for the first time. "Don't you come any closer, you're scaring me."

That prompted Darian to take a step forward and try to push his way past Corey, but the old cop grabbed him roughly and shoved him back. He went nose-to-nose with Darian and said, "You stop trying to be a bloody hero; this ain't the place for them, this is the real world."

Darian thought about forcing his way through but he stopped. It seemed Corey wanted Gallowglass out of the room, and there was nothing else Darian wanted more. Corey had a better chance of making their shared ambition happen. The cop looked at him with disgust and turned away to talk to Gallowglass before he thought of another insult and turned quickly back to Darian.

He said, "You know this is your bloody fault. You sticking your

nose in, trying to solve every injustice like a dime-store batman. All you've done is make a bad situation worse. You made this."

Maeve shouted, "Don't listen to him, Darian. This is his doing, him and Gallowglass. You were right about them both."

That provoked Gallowglass, as though it confirmed the fears that had driven him madly here. He took a step toward Maeve, Darian and Corey watching from the doorway, knowing they were too far away to stop it. Gallowglass lurched at her, grabbing out with both arms.

Corey shouted, "Don't."

The two men ran into the room but it was over, Gallowglass had jumped at her and Maeve had instinctively stuck out her hand. The knife had gone deep into his stomach, up to the handle, and Maeve had let go. She took a step back so that she was pressed against the window and watched Gallowglass. He stood still, looking down at the knife. His hands reached for it but when he touched it he grimaced and stepped back, scared of the pain he had created.

He whispered, "I knew it."

Gallowglass took another step back and stumbled, all of his strength falling out of him as he tumbled. He fell against the wall of the room opposite Maeve and slumped down into a sitting position, the handle of the knife still protruding. He held his hands around the plastic but not on it, fearing it might move. Maeve stood and watched him. Corey stepped toward Gallowglass and stopped, unsure. Darian ran to Maeve and threw his arms around her.

49

HE HELD her tight and she held him back, both afraid they might drop to the floor if they let go. The fear that had rushed through Darian when he saw Gallowglass move was a new intensity to him, but it was over now.

"Ross."

Darian turned around. The low grunt of his name had come from the man bleeding on the floor. Corey was standing over his protégé. Darian had expected to see the DI with his phone out, calling an ambulance, but instead he was standing still, looking down with disgust at a man he'd thought he'd known better. Gallowglass was ignoring him, focused on Darian.

"Ross, I'm going to tell you."

Corey said, "Shut up, Randulf. Don't listen to him, Ross, he needs help, he's raving. The man has a knife in his guts and a fever in his brain, for fuck's sake."

It was Corey's tone, the desperation of it, that had Darian walking across the floor toward Gallowglass. If this was something the DI didn't want Darian to hear then it was something he wouldn't allow himself to miss. He stood over Gallowglass, letting the man's fading eyes meet his.

Gallowglass said, "You need to know because you're the only one that cares about it. Them... They don't care. Since the night it happened they've been lying. Playing games. With you, and with me."

He grimaced and stopped, looking down at the knife but still not daring to touch the thing that was trying to take his life. He was

in pain and breathing fast, but his voice held rising strength and he seemed like he was going to make it. Darian felt comfortable letting him take the time to tell his story. Corey opened his mouth, but Darian spoke first.

He said to Gallowglass, "Go on."

"She, your girlfriend, she was supposed to be getting the gaffer, Corey…she was supposed to be getting him information about Guerra's business. Incriminate people. Find out where the money was. He was scared. Lucas, others before him…Other stations are standing up…standing up to him now. He wanted money to get out. She helped him. Then they split up, Guerra, he chucked her…found out, I don't know. She went after him. It was her. It was her that killed him. Went to his flat because there was more she had to get for Corey. He had…that night he had the papers on him. All of it. Got them from the bank. The gaffer's money, Slight, all the details. The bank tipped the gaffer and he told her…told your girlfriend. Didn't want him using them…Chased him and stabbed him. Then she got him in to clean it up for her. Him. Corey. Him and me went round. We took the body away to buy us time. He went…we went into the flat and took away all the stuff about his money. Anything dodgy. Protect the cash so Corey can get it. Then we put the body back…Back in the alley where it was before. The guy who found it, he was our guy, working for us. We controlled the whole thing. Everything. Made sure Corey was in charge of the investigation. It was all up to us, but he was so damn greedy…Wanted everything for himself."

Gallowglass paused again because his breathing was rapid-fire. Darian looked at Corey, saw the expression on his face change from curious to sickened. He looked back over his shoulder at Maeve, standing by the window. She seemed fascinated, but not scared and not ready to step in and defend herself.

Gallowglass said, "She's not right, Ross. She's dangerous. Always was. Corey covered up for her because she helped him get the papers from Guerra, that was what he wanted. It told him everything.

Everything. He knew where all the money was now...Not just his own, either. He's been scared lately, scared. His contacts are getting picked off. He's not getting away with it anymore. So he wanted to take all the money and run. Use Guerra's papers. Needed to protect your girlfriend for that. Keeping a killer on the streets. A killer. That was when I knew he'd lost it."

That was as much as Corey was willing to listen to. He shouted at Darian, "He's talking shite and you're stupid enough to listen to him. Maeve killing Moses? Give me a break. Me letting her get away with it? Not a chance, not a bloody chance. This is insane. The man's losing his wits with his blood; you can see that, you can hear it."

Darian didn't pay any attention. He turned and looked at Maeve, the person who mattered most to him in that room. She smiled. A little curl of the lips at either side, cheeks dimpling sweetly, her eyes on Darian, judging him. She wanted to know what his reaction was going to be before she provoked it, so they held eye contact for five or six seconds while Corey shouted and she didn't leap in to defend herself. Just smiled.

All the talk of wanting to get justice for Moses, and now she stood there and smiled. The confusion was dizzying. It was Gallowglass that snapped him back to clarity, talking to Corey.

"All that talk about doing the right thing, that was bullshit. You said we were going to help the city. You said I was going to still be doing police work. I was intimidating people for you to make money from them. I was covering up for a murderer. A murderer...You made a fool out of me. Well, I put a stop to it, didn't I, gaffer? I put a stop to all your lies. That's what a good cop does. Now you got to face the music. You and me together. I'll tell them every damn thing."

Corey said nothing. He stood looking down at the man he had trained and considered a worthy apprentice. This was betrayal, a failure of priorities the DI couldn't comprehend.

Darian turned fully to face Maeve. She had been dumped by Moses when he found out she was feeding info to Corey. She waited

outside the flat and she went for him, cut him. Moses ran but he was carrying the paperwork that shone a light on his work, so he tried to be careful, tried for escape without looking for help. She killed him and called Corey to cover it up. He covered up a murder because she got him into the flat to clean out the rest of the paperwork that would tell Corey where mountains of dirty money were. That trail of soiled wealth led him to Moira Slight and Durell Kotkell.

Darian looked at Maeve and said, "Why did you hire me? You could have been clear if you hadn't brought me in."

The smile spread. "I didn't want to be clear. I told you, I wanted justice for Moses. You know what really surprised me? I went to his flat and I didn't know what I was going to do, but when I did it, it was perfect. I've never felt anything like it. The excitement, Darian, there's nothing in this world like it. The power of life in your hands, running on the edge of death. You'll never experience the thrill of it, and I wanted to keep that going. It was fun. Don't pretend you didn't have fun with me, because I know you did. You loved it, and I loved it."

He didn't know when it had happened but the window behind her was wide open. It was uncharacteristically still out there, the curtain hardly moving. Maeve still smiled, looking Darian in the eye. This had always been her plan. Ride the thrill all the way to whatever ending it arrived at, and here it was.

Darian said quietly, "Don't."

She shook her head and laughed. Then she stepped backward and perched on the windowsill. She dropped back into the dark Challaid night.

50

IT TOOK two steps for Darian to reach the window and lean out. She fell through the darkness, a shape twisting in the air. Darian could only see the movement, not the person. She hit the ground hard on her back with a crack. She landed in the small circle of light thrown out by a weak lamppost and Darian thought he saw a spray of red burst out of her mouth and fall back onto her. From above she looked like a broken picture, and he wanted to run to her. He stepped back from the window, awed by the moment. It was all instinct for the next few minutes, no considered thought. He turned and ran past Corey and Gallowglass, out into the corridor of Maeve's flat. He heard someone shout after him but he couldn't stop. The front door was still open and he ran, slow and unsteady. He couldn't remember going down to her. He found a large bruise on his knee the following morning that he thought might have come from falling on the stairs, but he didn't remember it happening. One second he was looking out the window at Maeve on the ground, the next he was on the pavement beside her.

If it wasn't for the speckles of blood on her face and the pool forming under her head it would have looked as though she had walked to the lamppost and lay happily down there. Her left arm was by her side, her right arm across her stomach, her legs together. Her eyes were half-shut, and that same smile was still on her lips. She looked like a woman who had achieved what she had set out to, who was content with the ending she had chosen.

Darian dropped to his knees beside her, careful not to touch the

blood. Under the shock wasn't a sense of grief but of embarrassment. Later he would be angry with himself for feeling that way as he knelt beside the body of a person he had been close to, but you can't suppress your true feelings. He was humiliated. He had been so close to Maeve and she had fooled him absolutely. He wasn't accustomed to being made to feel stupid, and this moment was crushing. It changed how he saw himself.

He didn't know about time. He might have been on his knees beside her for ten seconds or ten minutes, he had no idea later. No cars came along Sgàil Drive, nobody approached on the pavement. He snapped back to the real world, and pulled his phone from his pocket. He dialed 999 and gave them the address, told them he needed an ambulance fast because a girl had fallen out of a window and a man had been stabbed. He gave little detail, and, even though they asked him to stay on the line, he hung up. That call served its purpose, making sure Corey couldn't so completely control the aftermath of this situation in the way he had Moses' murder.

Next he called Vinny, the first honest cop he could think of. It wasn't his patch, but Darian couldn't think of a cop in Earmam he knew and trusted like Vinny.

Vinny answered his phone and said, "Darian, mate, what color of trouble have you got for me tonight?"

"Vinny, I'm sorry, I really am, but you need to get to Sgàil Drive, under the hill in Earmam. A girl's dead. Maeve Campbell. She jumped, and Corey is here and he's involved up to his shifty eyes. He's here, and Gallowglass has been stabbed. Corey's here and he'll try to get his cops involved in this to protect him and I need people I can trust."

There was stunned silence before Vinny said, "Wait, what the hell are you talking about? Is this real?"

"Please, Vinny, I need help here. Sgàil Drive."

He hung up on his friend, because there was one more call to make. His hand was steady, he was feeling calm now, calling Sholto and expecting to have to wait for an answer. Sholto liked an early

bed, and a late-night call would be met with a grumbling, sleepy, delayed answer. Not this time. This call was answered on the second ring and Sholto was talking before Darian had the chance to open his mouth.

"Darian, good, I was about to call you. I'm at the docks, watching Murdoch Shipping. I've got them, Darian, I have. I got a hold of all the shipments they're registered to receive this week and there's an extra one being made right now. Something coming in without being registered. That alone is enough, but I bet what's being..."

Darian interrupted him, saying, "Sholto, listen to me, you have to come to Sgàil Drive in Earmam. Maeve's dead. It was her who killed Moses, and she's stabbed Gallowglass and killed herself. Corey helped her cover it up, and now he's here and he's going to try to save himself again, I know it. I need you here."

He hadn't been frantic; his voice sounded calmer than it had when he'd spoken to Vinny. Still, Sholto understood that this was no joke because he didn't pause before he said, "I'm on my way."

Darian slipped the phone back into his pocket and looked at Maeve again. Seeing her happy and peaceful, a smile on a pretty face covered in blood. It was hard to look away from her, as it always had been. He forced himself. This long night wasn't over just because Maeve had left, there was dark work lurking ahead.

51

HE RAN back upstairs, emotions packed away. All of what remained ahead involved Folan Corey, a man capable of slipping through gaps left by hotheads. Darian remembered going back up the stairs, his mind clear enough now to take in every detail. The front door of the flat still open, but no sound or sight of the neighbors. All that had gone on and nobody in the building had taken an interest, hiding until they understood the consequences.

He walked in and along the corridor to the living area and stopped in the doorway. Corey was on his knees beside Gallowglass, the reddened knife on the floor beside him. Blood was pulsing out of the wound and rolling thickly down his side, and Gallowglass was lying with his head slumped sideways, eyes shut. Darian took a step closer as Corey stood up and looked at him.

Corey said, "The knife fell out. Have you called an ambulance?"

It was only later that Darian thought how revealing it was that Corey hadn't used the last few minutes to call an ambulance himself, relying instead on a man who wasn't even in the building to do it for him. Instead, Darian was thinking about the knife, about how firmly planted in Gallowglass's stomach it had been before Darian left. It had stood upright without being touched, Gallowglass lying back against the wall and letting it rest there, settled and waiting to be removed by a medical expert. He wouldn't have pulled it out, and it couldn't have worked itself loose.

Corey seemed to read his thoughts in his expression, and said, "It was his breathing. He was breathing faster, coughed a bit, and his

stomach pushed out the knife. He's losing a lot of blood. Have you called an ambulance?"

"Yes, I called an ambulance."

Darian dropped down beside Gallowglass and put his finger to his neck, trying to feel for a pulse. There was nothing, but his own nerves could have been causing him to miss the target. He jumped up and ran to the kitchen area, coming back with a towel. Corey was still standing in the same spot. Darian dropped down and pressed the towel against the wound, trying to stop bleeding that had finished its escape, trying to keep a dead man alive.

Corey said, "It's too late, he's gone."

He was right. Darian left the towel where it was but he stopped pressing it, stopped fighting a battle that had passed by without him. Death always walks a little faster than life. He stood up and glared at Corey. "Why didn't you try to stop the bleeding? Why didn't you help him?"

"I did help him. Jesus, I've been helping him his whole working life, long past the point where he deserved it. I've carried his deadweight longer than any man should and as long as I could. I did nothing but my best for him. It was too late, Ross. It's over."

They were both silent for a few seconds, staring over the body at each other. Corey almost smiled when he said, "I take it your flying girlfriend landed hard. Is she dead?"

It was an attempt to bring mindless anger into a conversation that Corey didn't want to be mindful. Darian said, "She is."

"Probably just as well, a trial would have been embarrassing for you. An evil woman like her, getting you under her thumb and into her bed. Tricking you like that, tut tut. No, this is the best thing that could have happened for you. A truly evil woman."

Darian could see where this was going already, and he thought he knew where it had come from. "He said you were going to set him up, make him the scapegoat. He had sussed you out, Corey. He knew you were only in it for yourself. If he didn't know it before Moira Slight's house then he knew it after. That's why

you pulled the knife out. Making sure he couldn't repeat what he told me."

"The only people left who heard him are you and me. You, the son of a murderer and employee of an unregistered private detective agency who appears to have been in a seedy sexual relationship with a double killer. Murder seems to hang around your family like a noose. And me, the decorated DI, head of the anti-corruption unit whose protégé died trying to stop that evil woman. He was like a son to me."

The smile on his face as he spoke said as much as the bloody knife on the floor beside Gallowglass. Darian wanted to lash out because he knew Corey was right and knew he was going to get away with it. There might be consequences for him, but they would be no more than a single drop of the bottle of poison he deserved. It was a stark reminder of the futility of truth.

Before Darian could say something in response he heard the first distant scream of a siren in a hurry. Things began to happen more quickly now. From the still of death to the energy of life racing to confront it. It could have been an ambulance or a police car; it didn't matter to Darian which; he just wanted to be the first to meet them. He ran out of a flat that contained no one he could help, and back down the stairs. He was standing next to Maeve when an ambulance careered round the corner, the driver enthusiastic about the freedom his siren gave him.

Darian told the medics what had happened, both to Maeve and to Gallowglass. He repeated the story again thirty seconds later when a police car screeched to a halt, half on the pavement, and Vinny spilled out of it. He had PC Sutherland with him, but the young cop stayed pale and silent in the background. Darian told Vinny everything quickly, and Vinny wrote it all down.

In seconds the place was throbbing with people, cars and ambulances choking the narrow road, all the neighbors rushing out to form a gawping crowd now authority had shrilly announced its arrival. At one point Darian was sure he spotted DC Vicario talking to Vinny,

reading from his notebook on the pavement near where Maeve had fallen. She was from Whisper Hill station, this shouldn't have been her patch either, but Vinny must have called her. Then Sholto was there, a hand on Darian's shoulder, trying to comfort him.

He watched them cover Maeve and her dead smile with a blanket. He watched the police debating among themselves who should speak to who. Corey left with a detective Darian didn't recognize, but was later told was Lee Kenyon from the anti-corruption unit, and MacDuff. Sholto made sure Darian was left alone for a while by marshaling former colleagues away from him. After half an hour of empty movement and light, Sholto drove him to Earmam police station. Above them, on the crest of Dùil Hill and lit by moonlight, the Neolithic standing stones, An Coimheadaiche, looked down on human folly. It's a cruel moon that shows you all the night can hold.

52

DARIAN IS one of a rare group of people who couldn't legitimately complain about the way they were treated by Challaid Police. They questioned him politely, diligently took down all the details from the recorded interview and didn't accuse him of anything. The process was professional and respectful. It seemed as though they were eager to get as much muck on DI Folan Corey as possible, and make some of it stick. They didn't seem confident.

The same questions, over and over, followed by the same uncomfortable answers. There was no way of telling the story that didn't make him seem like a little boy, led with ease by the wily Maeve Campbell, and he had to keep repeating the tale. He blushed more than once as he told them every damned thing that had happened, but he didn't hold back a bad word of what had been said or a grim detail of what had been done. They seemed less interested in Maeve killing Moses, that had been settled and they had no punishment to give a dead woman. Their interest was Corey, and what his role had been.

Darian didn't know how long he was questioned for, but it must have been hours. He walked out into the corridor when they were done, Sholto still sitting there waiting for him, several paper cups that had contained weak coffee at his feet. They shook hands, but Darian paused before he thanked his boss, looking toward the voices that were drifting down the corridor.

At the other end, just outside another interview room, was a gaggle of people. There was some laughing and joking among the group.

It was MacDuff he noticed first, standing on the edge of the circle looking tired and annoyed, like a teenager waiting for a lift from a parent who hadn't turned up yet. The female detective who had arrested Randle Cummins, DC Lovell, was there, and DC Kenyon who had taken Corey away from Sgàil Drive, and presumably at least one lawyer, and in the middle of them all was DI Folan Corey, the star of the show, relaxed and happy.

Darian stood and stared until Corey noticed him and there was eye contact. Corey gave his slyest grin, said something to the people he was with and made his way along the corridor alone. Sholto sighed loudly, but Darian stood his ground.

Corey said, "I hope they weren't too hard on you, young master Ross, but it might be the only way you'll learn."

"No harder on me than they would have been on you."

"Me? Oh no, they've nothing to be hard on me for. I was a cop working with a former colleague to try to catch a killer. I've suffered a devastating loss. You're the one that was rolling around on top of a murderer; I would think they'll have a few questions for you about that, even if they haven't fired them at you yet. And you, Sholto, running an unregistered detective agency and working a case on behalf of a killer. Dear oh dear, that won't go down at all well. No, I worry about the pair of you, I really do. What future is there in this city for two men like you?"

He smiled and walked away down the corridor, back to the group at the other end. Darian could see that none of it was bluff. His word against Darian's and that was a duel he could win with a blindfold on.

Darian said quietly, "He's going to get away with it."

Sholto said, "He's probably not going to prison, which is where he belongs. But he won't go unpunished, there are too many people who want rid of him and will see this as their best chance. That pal of yours from Whisper Hill, Vinny, he brought a lot of colleagues with him. They want Corey's head on a stick, but they'll settle for pushing him out of the force and defanging him. Don't

underestimate them; there are still some cops with actual talent and a will to point it in the right direction in this city. He thinks he's so smart, but the problem with always being a step ahead is that it tends to leave a lot of people standing behind you. Corey's been helping criminals stay prison-free for a long time and it's been annoying them, but Ash Lucas was one of the last straws. A violent sexual offender and Corey walked him out of the station like he was a VIP. They didn't like that at all up at Dockside station. He might get away with his freedom, but he won't get away with his job."

It was a small victory for decency, as decency's victories usually are. Darian said, "He's going to come after you and me, try to shut down the office."

Sholto laughed and put his arm around Darian's shoulder as he led him toward the front door of the station. "I'm not worried about that guy. We have more friends in the police than he does, and we have some powerful backers now as well. How about that, us with influential friends. Kotkell would have made sure we had a tremendous reputation at Sutherland if this had broken his way, but as it turns out his successor will have a lot to thank us for and I'll be sure to point that out in a firm but politely worded letter that hints at what we know about the bank's business. And now that I've got the evidence for Murdoch Shipping taking illegal deliveries we'll have another hulking bodyguard in Glendan. Having some corporate bullies in our corner might not be the most noble way to keep our heads above water, but it's better than drowning."

They stepped out into the cold at half past three in the morning. It was dark and the streets were empty. They got into Sholto's car and he drove them back to the scene so Darian could pick up the Skoda. They stood together on the pavement near the lamppost that marked the spot and they were silent for almost a full minute.

Sholto said, "You sure you don't need a lift home?"

"No, I'll be fine. I'll see you at Cage Street tomorrow."

Sholto understood that he'd done his bit and Darian now wanted to be left alone. What he really wanted, as Sholto drove away, was to lie down on the pavement and go to sleep. He was tempted to go to Misgearan and find amnesia there, but even drinking was too much effort so he drove home instead.

ABOUT THE AUTHOR

MALCOLM MACKAY's novels have been nominated for the Edgar Award for Best Paperback Original, the CWA John Creasey (New Blood) Dagger, and the Theakston's Old Peculier Crime Novel of the Year. *How a Gunman Says Goodbye* won the Deanston Scottish Crime Book of the Year Award. Mackay was born in Stornoway on Scotland's Isle of Lewis, where he still lives.

FLIP THIS BOOK

for another Saviors novel.

FLIP THIS BOOK

for another Saviors novel.